Ransom to Love

Chloe Keto

With special thanks to the marvellous team of people who have encouraged and educated me while writing this book. You are all amazing! Plus, my long-suffering wife, without whom none of this would be possible – thank you for putting up with me!

Chapter One

Teri swivelled in her chair, chewing on the cord from her black Gap hoodie absentmindedly. Everything on the three computer screens in front of her was frozen in time, awaiting her input. After a moment's consideration to double check everything was ready, she grinned and entered her final command, hitting enter with a flourish. "Make it so!" she whispered with a big grin.

The command line prompt came to life as her program executed. Several other windows disappeared and a pop-up box appeared, '*Hello! I'm a friend you don't know but I found you. Send $10,000 in bitcoin to me by Friday. If not, I hope you have backups! ShadowRainbow*'.

She always tried to make her cyber ransom demands sound friendly. Many people got caught in her line of work, being rude or grasping for too much. She always set her ransoms low, chose her targets carefully and gave them a warning period. Also, she made sure everything her malware did was reversible when they paid up.

She only targeted companies who were negligent with their security and carelessly left vulnerabilities unpatched. Her targets were always also large enough to survive but small enough to keep her antics private.

Living in her neat, but basic, one bedroom studio flat in South London wasn't the glamorous life that movies portrayed for a freelance hacker, or officially, 'security researcher'. The freelance earnings from finding vulnerabilities and collecting rewards only went so far. To make ends meet, she'd turned to using ransomware. After she lost her job as a corporate security analyst, she had been really excited to turn freelance with altruistic dreams of improving the world. She hadn't given up on the dream but you could only go so far when spending on cat food exceeded your income!

A furry grey shape curled around her feet, softly caressing her ankles. She bent and scooped up Number One lovingly, placing him on her lap and stroking his silky soft, mottled fur.

"You appreciate the chase, don't you Number One?".

He looked up with feline disdain, his expression saying quite clearly that so long as Teri kept stroking him like that she could do what she liked, but don't expect him to show gratitude. "Well, a girl like me certainly should know how to please a cute pussy, shouldn't she, Number One?" She tickled under his chin.

Number One stretched his hind legs and lazily got to his feet, jumped off her lap, and stalked away. Clearly, he didn't appreciate the lesbian jokes. *Maybe he's heard them all before.*

She smiled. Number One had been her late Nan's cat – there's no way she could afford a British Shorthair. Dear old Nan, the closest family member she'd had. Indeed, Teri's only family when she sadly passed away a few years back.

Teri got up and stretched, feeling distinctly unfeline. Her short, bobbed, chestnut brown hair was neatly trimmed but that was the only indulgence she allowed herself. Faded jeans, a button up tartan shirt that was just visible under her hoodie and dark rimmed glasses completed her cheap wardrobe and anonymous lesbian hacker image.

In her line of work it didn't do to be memorable. However, she couldn't help wondering if it might not be nice to have a special person, someone who did remember her.

Momentarily she was reminded of a refined, sexy blonde she had seen at a party the month before. Black lace cat ears had capped a body that moved with almost feline grace and superiority.

4

As a rule, Teri didn't go to many parties but this one had been for a mutual friend's birthday. Maisie had threatened her with an 'accidental' broadband outage if she didn't turn up. Having cyber security people as friends could get tiresome. Ever since the party, the blonde had captured her daydreams.

She obviously needed more work to keep busy. Daydreaming about blonde, cat-eared, cute kittens wasn't how she should be spending her time. However, it sure beat worrying about bills.

On cue, the letterbox clattered and a pile of slim but threatening-looking envelopes slid onto the doormat. Teri knew they were from her friends at the electric, gas and phone companies. She sighed. *Why is just making ends meet so hard these days? It never used to be like this.* Her Nan's inheritance was almost gone, she might have enough in her rainy-day-fund to cover another few lean weeks, but she needed a payday soon.

It certainly wasn't because she spent lots. She looked around the tatty apartment. Dominated by a white Ikea desk against the blue wall, the lounge doubled as her study. The two monitors and laptop gave out a flickering artificial light that matched the artificial world she inhabited so often.

She had yet to open the curtains but, walking over to the window, her eyes were drawn to the beige carpet. "Builders special" she called it. Nondescript, like her, it was wiry and rough after years of use. It was certainly not a plush sheepskin rug in front of a roaring open fire. No, not something you could passionately make love on with a gorgeous woman. Who was she kidding? She was no suave and sophisticated lover, she'd had girlfriends but they were all short term hookups in nightclubs or dark apartments rather than anything more substantial in the bright light of day.

The rest of the lounge was an apology for a seating area. A single black leather sofa her Nan had left her and a TV pushed to one side to make room for her desk and chair. The one bright spot, her desk chair, was her pride and joy. The black leather gaming chair had

5

been purchased with her first payday and she saw it as something she'd achieved, a mark of her progress. Sadly, that progress had been short-lived but it reminded her that good things were possible and kept her hopeful.

Chapter Two

Sophie's Tuesday had started out well. Her monthly catch up had been productive and done while relaxing over her favourite warm Starbucks caramel latte. Walking back down the busy shopping street once they'd finished business in the coffee shop, she and Mike warmed their hands on the takeaway cups they bought for others on their teams.

Work talk gave way to friendly chatter as they walked. Mike still worried that Sophie was single and made several comments encouraging her to find someone. "Come on, Soph. I know Hannah hurt you, but you can't let her dictate your life."

"Mike, I'm fine. I'm not a hermit, I go out, you know. I am just enjoying a break from women, that's all. Anyway – you know how busy Cyber Security is due to this new account!"

Sophie and Mike were peers, both IT managers for Beaverson Bros, a medium sized but respected London consultancy firm. Sophie was a hands-on cyber security lead and Mike's team ran all the servers. They were large enough to have a passable IT department but not large enough to give them the resources either of them really wanted. The small office size gave them the freedom to have a meeting at Starbucks instead of a stuffy conference room.

Sophie sighed, she knew Mike meant well, but the trouble with such a small company was that everyone knew everyone else's business. She was twenty-eight, she was no spring chicken but she wasn't exactly long in the tooth either.

As soon as they got back to the office they handed the coffees to their assistants. Sophie had no sooner closed her office door than it opened again. "What now, Mike?" She turned and saw that the intruder wasn't her colleague. "Oh, hi, Dave."

"Sophie, sorry to bother you, but have you seen the code repo server?" Dave was the bearded office security administrator whose natural home was in the company data centre. He practically lived on caffeinated drinks and his best friends were the servers he worked with. His waving hands told Sophie something was terribly wrong. When Dave left the computer room it normally was for food, but he had no coffee, energy drink or snacks with him today.

"No. What's wrong with the bloody thing now, Dave? Has it gone down again?" Sophie turned to her laptop while talking and opening a window. She inhaled sharply.

Her screen showed the cause of Dave's panic: a message flashing pink and white on an orange background. *'Hello! I'm a friend you don't know but I found you. Send $10,000 in bitcoin to me by Friday. If not, I hope you have backups! ShadowRainbow.'*

"Who is ShadowRainbow? What do we know and have you contacted the response and server teams?" Sophie went into analytical mode. Her sleek blonde ponytail swished as she became more animated. Her short, but colourful, nails waved in the air. "Why do these bastards do this sort of thing to us?"

It wasn't the first cyber attack Sophie had dealt with, but she was full of caffeine and this ShadowRainbow dude had ruined a nice day for her.

"I called Zach already, he'll be here in an hour. Bit unusual to give us a few days' warning, don't you think?" Dave asked. "You remember the trick with Blaster in oh-three to set the clock back? What if we pull the plug and keep the clock on today?"

"Is anything else infected?"

"Not yet."

"OK. Pull the plug. Get on the console for that box and keep the date back until we can get everyone else in to handle it." Her mind was flying with crisis management and already forming a list of things she needed to do.

First, Sophie told Mike and the rest of the management team the bad news. She also told the developers the good news that they got to go home early.

Halfway through another phone call, Dave came bursting back in panting. He looked like he was about to cry or scream, face all bunched up and arms waving around like a 3D windmill. "Sophie, the other servers just went down. As soon as I yanked the jack from the one box, the others displayed the same message. The hacker must have a link between them. We've got less time on the others though – only until Thursday."

Sophie pulled at her ponytail and wound it round her hand while thinking. "It was a good thought anyway, Dave. Looks like we need to do a full shutdown and restore. Shall I order the pizzas? It's going to be a long night. It's only you and me for an hour until Zach arrives."

Dave pulled on his beard thoughtfully and scrunched his face, almost looking in pain. "There is always the possibility we could pay them, Sophie? I know it's not great on principle but it would be quicker!"

Sophie knew if they could eradicate this fast, there'd be no need for this to go up to the board. Big companies had to be strict about calling in the police. Medium-sized companies, like her own, often weighed their reputations against the cost. But this ShadowRainbow guy had another think coming if Beaverson would be one of his "rollover and beg" targets.

Sophie faced Dave, fire burning in her eyes, her ponytail flicking viciously from side to side as she shook her head. "Not until we're desperate. We've got forty-eight hours and I'm going to beat this bastard who has already ruined my day. Let's go around them and get everything back up."

Chapter Three

Teri was on a high. She loved to pretend to herself that she was a social justice warrior exerting revenge against her corporate enemies. In fact, she knew she was a good guy turned bad, living in a crummy flat in Vauxhall. Even so, after initiating a hit, the adrenaline was enough to allow her to maintain the illusion for a few hours.

Luckily, her friends Anna and Maisie had appeared shortly afterwards and dragged her out, so her spirits were still up (helped by a few different types of spirits). While Anna had student problems typical of any average twenty-three year old, Maisie was still in the corporate cyber security department where Teri had first met her. Teri was never quite sure how Anna and Maisie had met but they had been firm friends as long as she remembered.

However, Maisie's type of bad day needed lots of after work commiserating from Teri. She had no idea what Teri did for a living, so she still considered her to be on her side. Today had been particularly bad with a cyber attack actually hitting her company. The irony wasn't lost on Teri but she pushed it, and the guilt, to the back of her mind while focussing on Maisie.

"Those bastards seem to target us so easily. Why us? This latest is some guy called Rav-xn, I mean seriously, how do you even *say* that?" Maisie wailed as soon as they were seated in their favourite bar.

Teri's normal approach of nodding frequently avoided having to talk about her own job. However, today the tequila had loosened her tongue. "Because you haven't got any better at patching since I left. The server guys never listen. You're as easy a target now as you were then."

10

While what she said was utterly true, it didn't stop her from feeling guilty. If she was totally honest, it was that lesson on how poor some companies were at protecting themselves that gave her the knowledge for her current job. She felt guilty that she was one of those "bastards", even if not the specific one Maisie was talking about.

Teri insisted that it *did* make a difference how you went about these things. She always set the ransomware bounty as low as she could afford to live and she always gave as much notice to her victims as she thought possible. She tried to be a 'humane highwayman'. *Is there really such a thing*? she wondered.

She made a lot less than the big, organised criminal, hacker groups who spread their attacks indiscriminately with many attacks at once. So far though, she'd escaped the law and managed to still look herself in the mirror. She had a cast iron rule that she never went near anything that could hurt individuals, but this left lots of consultancies and IT companies, who should know better.

She shook herself back into the moment, realising that Maisie and Anna had moved onto moaning about their respective partners of the time. At least she could contribute without guilt to that subject. She thought both were immature and unworthy of her best friends, but then who was she to judge with her lack of relationships? Jessica, Maisie's current girlfriend, was nice but feeble in Teri's eyes. However, since she seemed to have a new girlfriend each week, Teri wasn't sure Maisie was actually still talking about the same woman. Anna was the odd one out with them, being straight. Her boyfriend Ben wasn't that bad, but Teri just didn't think he had the kind of spunk Anna needed and deserved. In all, he was a bit too nice.

Her mind drifted away again, an image popping unbidden into it – a slim, beautiful woman with thick, long blonde hair pulled back in a ponytail, head reclined, mouth open laughing, with a cute pink drink in her hand. A smile crept across her face, recognising this pleasant tequila-fuelled daydream as familiar. It was the girl from the party that Maisie had dragged her to the previous week. She felt a warmth in her chest. What was otherwise a purely cute picture was made more intriguing by the slightly vampish look of the black lace cat ears on the woman's head. If they'd been white or fluffy she'd have dismissed the girl as being a cutesy femme, but the black lace captured Teri's imagination. She wondered if it was suggestive of her underwear. Sadly, her friend didn't know the girl in question and asking had caused some drunken smirks in the taxi. She didn't know if the girl was single or even gay, however, something had pinged her drunken gaydar and the image wouldn't leave her mind.

"Earth to Teri." Maisie and Anna chanted loudly, breaking her from her pleasant reverie. Her face heated and she must have been blushing deep enough to clash with the pink cocktail Maisie had put in front of her while she was merrily living on planet sexy-kitty. "Oh sorry, just tired," she tried to recover.

"Oh yeah – whatever you say, babe." Anna smiled kindly, while immediately giving Maisie the side-eye and adding sneakily, "that smile didn't look tired to me – something else entirely!"

"Can't a girl have a momentary daydream without you pair making her out in love or something?" Teri was definitely now blushing. Her friends just laughed at her embarrassment. *Some friends!*

The evening carried on, lurching drunkenly between work bitching (mainly Maisie), men bitching (Anna), 'lack of girl' bitching (Teri), 'too many girls' bitching (Maisie), uni bitching (Anna) and occasionally flirting or sizing up other patrons (all of them). Teri didn't see any feline, blonde goddesses but she managed to take her mind off things for a few hours. That was something to be grateful for.

~#~

Teri got home before midnight and had sobered up enough to remember she had work to do. Unlocking her laptop, she checked her bitcoin account and looked for updates on this afternoon's attack, or a couple of others running in the background. She saw three more servers had been infected but no payments had been made yet.

Number One prowled out from under Teri's desk. He brushed past her leg, his form of affection, she assumed, although it may have been disdainful smirking. He left a sheen of grey hairs on her black skinny jeans. He looked up at her and Teri decided that she'd either been alone too long or had too much tequila. She was convinced she saw him wink challengingly at her. Either way, she smiled.

"Yes, I know Number One – time for phase two tomorrow. Let's let 'em stew overnight. Maybe a night of work will make them more willing to do a deal tomorrow."

~#~

The next day, Teri awoke with a splitting headache. Tequila was always a mistake. Through bleary eyes she checked her laptop and saw she still hadn't been paid from the latest attack. *Hmm, still toughing it out*. By lunchtime, she had still heard nothing. The waiting was the hardest part, no matter how many jobs she had running at once. She started to fear that this one wasn't going to pay out. However, what she could see was that someone was trying to track her down from her email and the malware she had planted.

Number One prowled across the lounge. "Think we need to ramp up the pressure, mate. Let's execute phase two." With a flourish, she kicked off her next job that would either make or break some beardy IT geek's day.

Her screen glowed. "Email Sent: Consultancy Offer Regarding Your Ransomware Attack - Support"

Chapter Four

Dave's beard was showing the signs of a long night of tugging as he tried every trick in the book to avoid having to completely rebuild things from scratch. Sophie was sitting next to him typing away at a console, twirling her ponytail absentmindedly. The background noise of the server room air conditioning fans acted as their companion and soundtrack. She had never been the type of manager to sit in her office for long and much preferred being at the coalface for an event like this. Zach's security contractor team had also arrived overnight and were working in a different part of the building. Sophie was in command though, so she might as well make herself useful as they all worked on different servers.

Dave's email pinged, but Sophie was deep in the zone and ignored the noise. While he and Sophie would usually ignore email at critical moments like this, something must have told him to read it. He let out a low whistle before shouting out. "The bloody cheek!" He jumped up off his chair and waved his arms around.

Sophie almost fell backwards in surprise but then looked up at him questioningly. "Come and look at this email. A supposedly unrelated consultancy firm has just *happened* to talk about increases in ransomware and *coincidentally*," his voice continued to raise as his fingers made air quote marks, "offered to help us for a fee. *Bloody cheek!* How dare they?"

Sophie scan-read it in his preview window over his shoulder. 'Email Received: Consultancy Offer Regarding Your Ransomware Attack - Support'. "You didn't click on anything did you Dave? That looks dodgy as hell!"

Dave looked at her with a scowl. "What do you take me for Sophie, a bloody newbie? Course not! That's on my other laptop and it's in the preview window with all scripting disabled, same as you do."

Something caught Sophie's attention. The 'consultancy fee' was half the cost of the original ransom. Compared to the company being down for a week, this was cheap. In fact, it was so cheap, she had the authority to approve it as an emergency expense. That was strange, this was the kind of cost she'd associate with a hoax rather than the level of technical sophistication currently evading her combined efforts with Dave and the team.

Something else caught her eye. *"Consultancy will be provided via video link. This offer price is only valid for the next 6 hours."*

"What do you think, Dave? It goes against the grain but that's cheaper than Zach's fee!"

"Well, you're the boss, Sophie. I hate the idea as much as you, but I do see what you mean."

"OK, let me go and talk to Zach about it. He's been around this loop more than us. Can you print it for me; it's safer than forwarding it through the network. That email is probably riddled with more viruses than a clinic for iffy diseases. Then quarantine it will you, we might need it as evidence?"

Sophie walked next door and spoke to Zach, their on-call consultant, who was hard at work on a different set of servers with his usual Paramore playing in the background. "Hmmm, I agree, Sophie, it seems unlikely to be anything worth getting excited about, but it might help me track the attacker?"

Zach did have good news, somehow the attack had missed the most sensitive data on customers and employees. He had confirmed that no valuable data had been stolen, it was just disruption to their operations, not theft. Sophie relayed this good news to Paul, her boss, so he could agree they didn't need to alert the authorities. It wouldn't help their reputation if this got out too soon.

Zach's team had already started using the network to track back to the attacker. He was pleased this email would give them another source and a Zoom call might do even more. "I agree, it's too much of a coincidence. This 'consultant' is probably the hacker but officially we can't link them."

The security pro stroked his beard, "This is an interesting tactic, Sophie, I've not seen it before. Feels like that parking fine I got last week; pay up within 5 days and get the parking fine for half price." He had a look in his eye Sophie almost took for admiration. He also said it might be a neat tool to escape the law, as they may not be able to prove in court that the two were the same person.

Their company was the perfect size for Sophie to have flexibility in how she responded. Sophie returned to Dave and replied to the email with payment details. She figured that the equivalent cost of a short business trip was worth the gamble and it would give Zach plenty of ammunition to use in his counter-sleuthing.

She left her email and went back to rebuilding the server, her adrenaline racing by the challenge of beating this guy.

An hour later Sophie was chewing her lip over a particularly difficult bit of repair when her email pinged. She flicked her eyes over while still thinking about the hard drive. The email was from her new security consultancy 'friend' and included a Zoom link to join. She forgot the hard drive build and swivelled around to join the meeting via her Zoom client, setting her PC to record the call in the background as evidence. The Zoom room opened with a person called "Security Consultancy Pro". She smiled – hardly an inventive name. The voice was a croaky voice with no discernible gender or accent. "Hello, good morning."

Sophie turned on her camera and greeted the anonymous person, probably the hacker responsible for this mess, she thought. "Hello, my name is Ms Keegan. I'm the Cyber Manager here." The camera turned on at the other end and she saw a figure silhouetted against bright daylight from a window, obscuring all the details. *Not much for Zach to go on there.* There was a pause on the other end and she wondered for a while if the line had dropped.

"Hi Ms Keegan, good morning! How are you? Normally, we use these consultancy appointments to run through diagnosing the breach and helping you solve it. However, since you're in London, I wonder, in your case, if it might be better to do so in person?"

"In person?" Sophie looked a little surprised and started to wonder if this was a ruse to get access to their building. It didn't escape her notice that she'd told the hacker nothing about the ransomware or their location. She was also sure she heard a little waver in the otherwise steady voice when it said that.

"Well, a face-to-face meeting. Somewhere neutral. Your office is in the city, right? What if we said, a meeting in the bar at Liverpool Street later today? How does two pm sound?"

Sophie was beginning to think this was some kind of elaborate fraud or hoax. Who ever heard of meeting a ransomware hacker at a train station bar?

"OK, fine!" Sophie said, rolling her eyes. "The bar, Liverpool Street station, one hour. Don't expect me to bring cash or wear a red rose."

The voice laughed. "I promise no cash or red roses will be involved."

Sophie heard the laugh and paused for a second. While it was still distorted, there was something about the sound. She wondered for the first time if this person was a woman and the laugh didn't sound that old.

They disconnected the call. "Dave, we're going for a drink to do some detective work... Zach has all this in hand anyway. Can you ring the train station bar and ask them to make sure their CCTV is working? I know they have it after that incident with the drunk guy last year."

Dave looked at Sophie as though she'd lost her mind. "You want to stop bringing back our business-critical servers and go out... for... a ... drink? What do we need CCTV for anyway?"

"Welcome to Wonderland, Alice! Let's go and meet the Mad Hatter... You're going to be my backup."

Chapter Five

Teri couldn't believe her eyes, right there on the screen had been the blonde from the party. Of all the bizarre and annoying coincidences. She couldn't decide whether to be happy or sad. The first thing it left her was feeling horny but she tried to quickly push that to the back of her mind, that wasn't what this was about.

She was trying to work out what to program the attack to do next, when Number One strolled purposefully into the room. He utterly ignored his pet human until he reached her desk. The cat looked up and appeared to consider his options for a moment before leaping up onto the desk in front of her. Having a ton of furry cat sitting on one's keyboard does tend to slow one's typing and Teri rolled her eyes.

"Seriously, mate, you choose *now* to want a stroke?"

Number One barely turned his head enough to look at her, but those piercing yellow eyes communicated quite clearly, 'Yep... don't be stupid human. I am the supreme ruler here and you will attend to my wishes. Stop typing and ply me with affection.'

Teri wondered, not for the first time, if she needed to lay off the vodka but concluded that all cat humans got this feeling of ownership from their pet... it was how cats work – right?

Being forced to stroke his soft fur took her mind off the keyboard and what she needed to type on it. Instead, she thought about her life. What was she doing? This was a mess!

'*What would Nan have said?*' she wondered.

She was pretty sure her Nan just wanted her to be happy. She'd said that she didn't care who Teri settled down with, so long as they were worthy of her, but she needed to find that one person she could give her whole self to before she'd know if they would do the same in return.

Teri was fairly sure, however, that her Nan wouldn't approve of her current job. She smiled as she recalled being the excited student who saw wonder in learning and came home buzzing with excitement.

"Nan, you'll never guess what we learnt today! This concurrent programming is so awesome. If only I could get this stupid assignment right."

Her Nan had said very little but merely smiled indulgently and listened patiently. Teri liked to think her Nan got pleasure from seeing her so excited about learning. That twinkle in her eye never dimmed, the pleasure of seeing her granddaughter growing and spreading her wings.

The twinkle was always extra bright when Teri talked about people. She'd had a few girlfriends at uni (and even one boyfriend, when she thought she should see what all the straight fuss was about. He was very short-lived and their relationship was mutually unfulfilling – though he was a lovely guy). Nan always took an interest in who they were and how Teri felt. She was never judgemental and seemed genuinely happy to see Teri gaining that contentment, even if it meant also being the one to stroke her hair comfortingly and dry her tears when the relationships inevitably ended after a short period. Nan had always been there... but now she wasn't.

Stroking Number One and feeling her eyes growing heavy, she felt her loss more acutely than she had for a long time. She buried her face in his soft fur, feeling soothed by the texture and almost reassured the way she had been when sitting with Nan.

She did have one sister who had started to speak to her again after they'd ostracised Teri. The problem with Malini, however, was that she seemed more intent on telling Teri what she was doing wrong than helping. Maybe that was the way with older sisters but, oddly, what Teri *should* be doing was always what Malini *had* done. She supposed it was better than nothing, but her sister was no good in a situation like this.

"Oh mate, what do I do?" she asked him.

His response was to shake his fur back into place. Oh, how she wished she could be this unruffled. The truth was that seeing the blonde on screen had unnerved her. The image of the woman brought what she was doing into the real world and it was too close to home. She began to think, for the first time, about the harm she was doing. All her reasoning about carefully choosing targets somehow didn't seem so solid at that moment.

It wasn't just that she liked the look of catwoman – there were lots of women she saw who she liked the *look* of. The issue was that looking at her reminded Teri of the gap inside. Doing what she was doing in order to pay the bills had taken away a part of herself and she didn't like what she saw in its place.

"Is this how you feel when you go after a mouse, Number One? Do you stop and think how the mouse feels and whether it will fill the empty space in your belly – or heart?"

Number One turned his head again and Teri swore the damn cat rolled his eyes at her. If he wasn't thinking, '*Soft git,*' she would be amazed. Mind you, this cat never caught mice, he was far too pampered for that, so he could keep his hypocritical opinions to himself.

Something grew in the pit of Teri's stomach. At first she wasn't sure what it was but the combination of remembering her Nan and the mental image of the cute blonde, with or without the cat ears, added up to a fluttery feeling. It could have been indigestion but somehow she suspected it was something different, something that she wasn't used to. Maybe it was loneliness, maybe shame.

She turned this idea around in her head for a few minutes before realising her plan had another big practical flaw. She was hacking someone she had a mutual friend with and she might well run into again in the future.

Number One mewed and purred contentedly, his paws lazily reaching out for her hands. He caught her eye and stared at her. In that moment, she felt she was looking into her Nan's eyes, her combination of steely determination but unending compassion having made so much difference to her younger self. She could hear the older woman's voice in her head. 'Do the right thing!' 'Get your life sorted out.' 'Don't be alone.' Nan was big on not being alone.

The problem was, below the bravado and confident lesbian hacker image, Teri really wasn't sure who she was or why anyone would want her. She'd had a number of partners but never anyone serious enough to fully open up to. Perhaps it was time to change that and stop looking for 'Ms. Right For The Night' and find 'Ms. Right For Her'. Why would they want her though? She'd been to a few counsellors over the years and been told she had deep seated self-esteem issues. No matter what they'd tried, her thought patterns were so set that she kept coming back to feeling like a waste of space. She craved to feel wanted and useful but that had to take a backseat compared to paying the electric bill.

That thought led to her other problem – she was broke! She knew she had a little left in the savings account from Nan. Enough to get her through the next month, maybe two, if she stretched the cat food some more, but after that – nada. She needed income and she needed it fast.

So, she had a woman she felt captivated by, who had mutual friends, a need to settle down and a need to find a job. None of that was compatible with hacking this company. Somehow she had to recover them, without getting arrested, and start to think positively. That last one was probably the most difficult for her.

Could she meet this Ms Keegan and recover her servers without admitting that she was the hacker? After all, she was just a 'consultant', right? Then she'd find every job advert she could see and apply to everything; she couldn't afford to be choosy anymore.

She stopped stroking Number One and looked at her watch, she only had twenty-five minutes to get across London to the rendezvous. He put his head down on the keyboard and ignored her, his job done and sympathy exhausted, she figured.

Five minutes later, she was boarding the tube and ten minutes after that, she was walking confidently onto Liverpool Street Station. If there was one thing Teri knew well, it was how to imitate confidence!

She found a table and got comfortable – blending in naturally. Looking around, she observed the dim bar which would come alive in the early evening for commuters to have stylish, expensive drinks. The bar was subtly lit by concealed LED lights and it all had a classy feel to it. No doubt, all to raise the drink prices.

Her breath hitched a little as she recognised Ms Keegan walking in and looking around. She seemed so confident, but Teri spotted that she was pulling on her ponytail and wondered if it was a nervous motion. Scanning the bar, the blonde somehow overlooked her, which suited Teri just fine – a few more minutes to observe this woman was good for her and for the plan. A bearded guy came in and sat down, ordering himself a drink, as she finally stood to approach Ms Keegan. He ignored both women so she paid him no attention, focussed instead on the woman who still looked beautiful to her even after what was clearly a long day and night. A flash of guilt hit her at this thought.

Focussing on the mission she felt like some half-baked, spy film villain. *I need to get her to agree to let me help her. Once I can get her onto the servers, I can give her the kill switch commands. That'll have the code delete itself. Thank goodness I added those functions to the program.*

Chapter Six

The station bar was open but quiet, the lunch trade having died away. The only people around were coming off their day shift, homeless or mad IT staff seeking weird internet contacts. She arrived and Dave followed her in separately two minutes later, sitting at the opposite end of the bar. *I may as well get a drink while I wait but need a clear head, I'm working after all.* This was mad! What on earth was she doing here? Nodding to the barman, she requested an orange juice - a jolt of vitamin C might help her face this evil genius.

Sophie sipped her drink tensely, pulling at her ponytail, when a figure rose from a table and approached the bar. "Ms Keegan?" She looked the person up and down. The girl was shorter than her, with smooth brown hair in a sharp bob. Her deep, walnut-coloured eyes peeked out from underneath the hair. Her eyes sparkled, looking cheeky and full of personality. The black t-shirt she wore did little to disguise the swell of her chest and her tight jeans hinted at a great view from the back too.

Woah – where am I going here! This is probably the hacker that's taken me down and I'm ogling her? If truth be told, Sophie was starting to feel a little warm.

She remembered the conversation she'd had with Zach before leaving the office, *Get as much info as you can on this guy then we can decide what we hand over to the cops or lawyers. Don't make them suspicious or angry, don't take any risks.* The trouble was, she hadn't anticipated that the hacker might be... well – cute!

"Hi, yes I'm Ms Keegan - you are?"

"Tami. I'm a security researcher, specialising in ransomware attacks. I used to work in the City but now operate independently."

24

Straight down to business. Sophie reminded herself. "So, what can you tell me about this attack?"

"Well," Tami's eyes flicked around the room but came to rest back on Sophie, almost eagerly, "based on the infections I've seen so far, it's a worm that exploits the buffer overflow error that Microsoft patched three months ago but is still open on a number of companies networks. Including yours apparently."

"So now we paid the hacker... I mean you." Sophie's voice showed scepticism and that she knew they were one and the same. "What happens next in your consultancy?" She pushed aside the pointed comment about the vulnerability not being patched, she'd string up Mike's team when she got back to the office.

"Well, either I could buy you a drink or we could deactivate the malware – your choice." Tami replied with a rather infectious smile.

Sophie decided there was something quite un-darkworld-like about this girl. She couldn't work out why, but she somehow felt her heart wasn't bad. However, she was still furious at her nerve and the damage she'd caused. "Well, since I'm losing money, I guess we should go for option B – what do you think?" Her reply was sarcastic and cutting.

Tami gestured to a booth where her laptop was set up and waiting. Sophie followed and pulled out her own notebook. She fired off a text to Zach on the way, letting him know about the buffer overflow vulnerability and that they should have caught it. She got a reply instantly, *Ouch, Mike's gonna flip. #Awkward*

"Do you always meet your clients in bars?" she couldn't help but ask.

"Only the beautiful ones." Tami stopped and turned bright red, laughing awkwardly. "Only the ones I think are really important and..."

Sophie looked at 'Tami' and felt a laugh bursting through her anger, shaking her head. There was no way Tami was her real name – she would be far too easy for Zach to locate. Surely it had to be an alias. But for now, she was running on anger and was determined to get the intel Zach needed.

"And...?" prompted Sophie as they sat down, going back to business mode, the hard edge re-entering her voice.

"Well, no, I don't insist on meeting all clients face to face but when I saw you on screen..." her eyes stared down at the table and her face deepened in colour to match Sophie's lipstick. "Well, I realised I recognised you."

Sophie was surprised. Where on earth did she mix with a hacker? She wracked her brains for how she knew Tami but came up blank. She was sure she'd have remembered her. "Where from? Have we met before?"

The other woman's voice returned to its confident, almost cocky tone, "You were at a party last month ... cat ears?"

Now it was Sophie's turn to blush and she subtly turned to check Dave was out of earshot.

"You remembered me from that? I don't remember us talking? Although, to be fair I don't remember much of that party. It was a bad evening for me." That was an understatement, she'd been there as part of her effort to show the world that Hannah, her ex, hadn't broken her. What Sophie couldn't decide was who she was trying to prove it to, herself, Bonnie – her best friend whose nagging never let up – or the world in general.

"You certainly stuck in my mind, yes. I'm sorry to hear it was tough for you – you certainly didn't show it from where I was."

"We aren't all what we seem on the surface." Sophie replied sadly, her thoughts distracted. Her words reminded her why they

26

were there and dragged her back to the present. "On the subject of which – what about my servers?"

Tami looked at her as though she'd asked something in a foreign language, before recognition dawned across her face. "Oh, yes, sorry. Once I saw who you were, I never actually intended to take your money anyway. I'd rather help you as a potential friend. You'll find that your purchase has been cancelled. If we can get this cleared up, any chance you'd consider meeting me for coffee in the morning. I'd like to show you I'm not really a bad person?" Sophie started to frown. "Cat ears optional!" Tami joked.

She couldn't help but laugh. "There is no rational reason on this planet I should agree to have coffee with the person to blame for me having been up all night... but I think you owe me a coffee at least."

Maybe this will help Zach track her down. It's all good evidence.

"Deal! Let's do this."

They talked as they worked for twenty minutes and she became reluctantly impressed with this earnest young woman. Tami shared the commands they needed to execute – the "kill switches" – and they saw the servers quickly coming back to life. Although Sophie was still sure *she* had attacked them, she'd done it in a way that was entirely reversible and there didn't appear to be any long-term damage. As they worked, she also noted that Tami pointed out all the flaws she saw on the servers which needed to be fixed. There were quite a few patches missing and Sophie got more and more embarrassed. She wasn't looking forward to the conversation about this when she got back to the office.

Finally, Sophie looked up at her. "So, is that it?"

"Well, apart from coffee, of course... "the other woman quipped.

Sophie looked over to where Dave was still ignoring them. "Dave, come over here."

Tami looked shocked, "Oh, I suppose it was a bit naive to expect you to meet me alone. Hi Dave, great to meet you."

"Dave, this is Tami." Turning to her, she added, "Assuming that is your real name?"

Sophie thought that Tami looked guilty at that. She continued to Dave. "She's the consultant who helped me to clean our servers."

Dave looked at Sophie like she'd sprouted a second head but she continued. "While we were doing that she found this list of areas where we're still vulnerable and need patching. Can you get the server team on this before the rest of the office comes in tomorrow, please? Also, can you get Zach to verify everything is clean?"

Dave still looked as though she was smoking something and not offering him a puff. He replied slowly, "O...K..., so we are all best pals now?"

"Course not, Dave. However, Tami had some very useful suggestions on other vulnerabilities that need sorting. Why wouldn't we want to act on those? In fact, she and I will meet tomorrow to discuss what other security vulnerabilities we need to consider. We have employed her as a consultant after all, so I want my money's worth!"

~#~

The coffee shop down from her office was bustling the next day. Sophie was taking control of the situation so had got there early, grabbed a sofa and was now sipping her latte. They'd arranged an early coffee, so this was her first of the day and she was just waking up when Tami entered, looking around uncertainly. Sophie stood and nodded to her.

Tami approached and reached out her hand, Sophie took it and shook. "Hi, are you OK? How are the servers?"

"I'm good thanks and according to Dave, they are humming away normally after the damage. Tell me about yourself though, how did you get into this scenario? You don't appear to be getting rich – with the best will in the world?"

Tami looked away before taking the seat opposite Sophie. "I'm really sorry you got attacked." She looked down at the table again, blushing a deep red, "The choice of job, I'm afraid is about money. I was made redundant last year. I used to work in a department like yours and it's been really hard to make ends meet. I do freelance bug hunting, but I still have bills to pay."

If it were possible, her blush deepened even more, or maybe it was the way her eyes flicked anywhere but to Sophie. "I knew I needed to help you as soon as I saw you. I'd been thinking about you since the party but assumed I'd never see you again."

Sophie looked around the cafe briefly, before looking back at the brunette woman, "That sounds great, but didn't you look outside cyber security for a job? I mean, even this shop is looking for staff – look." she pointed to a notice over the counter.

As she looked back up, Sophie saw guilt again in Tami's eyes. This woman was an enigma. It seemed that money was her motivation, so why hadn't she considered other options? Sophie was still pretty sure Tami was the hacker, although she hadn't actually admitted it. What Sophie couldn't understand was why someone who appeared so skilled was having to freelance on the wrong side of the tracks in the first place?

Why isn't she doing my job? Technically she's hot... And maybe other ways too. Sophie wondered before shaking her head, clearing out the last thought.

The brunette seemed to regain her composure and her blushing subsided. "Let me get a coffee and we can talk. I would like

29

to make it up to you and help you out some more. What would you like?"

"Well, I wouldn't say no to an Americano, it's only early so I need the caffeine boost, and well... that Rocky Road Cake looks good." Tami smiled as she stood and headed to the counter. Sophie knew the cake would probably give her a sugar rush but it would be worth it. At this time in the morning, after a late night, she needed all the boost to her brainpower she could get. Moments later, Tami came back with two steaming coffees, cake for Sophie and a muffin for herself.

Sophie took the rocky road and bit into it. "Mmmm, this is good," she groaned, closing her eyes, "I missed breakfast." She could somehow feel the other woman's eyes burning into her face even through her closed lids. Peeking through her lashes, she was surprised to see how hypnotised the brunette looked as she swallowed.

"You... You're welcome." Tami stuttered.

Sophie opened her eyes fully and she looked over at her. "Right - you were telling me about why you do what you do?" Sophie said, intrigued, before remembering to be angry again.

"Oh well, I mean, everyone needs to make a living. There should be much more awareness of these vulnerabilities – they've been announced for ages. Enough time that they could have been resolved and avoided."

Sophie sighed, "You sound like Dave – he's always complaining that the server teams don't patch quickly enough. I guess you're the proof."

Tami smiled, "Well if you will let me, I'd like to help you spot more vulnerabilities and protect you from other attacks. I could work with you to check your network out and see where else you have dangers. Don't worry – I don't expect you to trust me, but I'd like to try. What do you say?"

She wasn't going to let this woman access her network, she couldn't trust her as far as she could throw her, but on the other hand, she did have a point that their server patching was lacklustre.

"I don't think we need to go quite that far but I'm certainly interested in what you've seen as you've been snooping around both last night and previously?"

Tami blinked heavily. Surely she couldn't be upset that Sophie was turning her down. She'd hacked them for crying out loud.

"OK. I understand."

Sophie thought the wide, dark eyes – which she had to admit, did rather grab her attention with their different shades of gold flecking throughout, like a tunnel into the distance – took on a brighter, watery look. She pictured a scared Bambi. Her extra wide, dark irises caught the light and drew Sophie's attention to her slight frown. Maybe this woman was a good actress but somehow Sophie didn't think so. She looked genuinely scared.

"Let's work together to make that list of places that need fixing. I genuinely want to help you, you know."

"OK, so let's do that and we'll take it from there. What did you find?"

"There were several boxes that were missing these security patches."

As she spoke, she pulled a tablet out of her backpack, a cute black one with a white Hello Kitty logo. Sophie smiled a little, without Tami seeing. As much as she meant what she'd said, it was actually proving hard to stay angry on a personal level. She wasn't sure what was wrong with her, was she really feeling sorry for the hacker that had attacked them? She was clearly a soft touch.

Tami started typing and Sophie shuffled around the table so she could watch her in action. She typed out a list of fixes that were needed, her tongue slightly poked out in concentration. Flicking through some notes, she added the server names that she'd seen in her research. Sophie watched her work and was impressed with how thorough she was. She added some more details before emailing it to Sophie.

"I guess this is goodbye then?" Tami said, running her hand through her hair and chewing her bottom lip. "Again, I'm really sorry."

"For what it's worth Tami, I believe you. It doesn't change the facts though, does it?" Sophie was determined to maintain her business face.

Tami held out her hand, although her shoulders were visibly hunched and she looked deflated. Sophie, feeling sorry for her, smiled and shook it.

~#~

Sophie headed back to the office, deep in thought. She had noticed how detailed Tami was and how much she concentrated, remembering all the details that needed to be fixed. You could argue this woman might improve their security in the long term. That didn't assuage her anger at being hacked.

When she got back, she sought out Zach. He was working away checking the servers with Dave and Kelly, a woman from Mike's Server Team. It genuinely did seem that there was no long-lasting damage, nothing had been stolen and Tami had stayed away from anything that would harm people like payroll or HR data.

They headed back to her office and she told Zach about her conversation with Tami. He nodded and stroked his beard in a thoughtful manner.

"This person has done a good job of covering their tracks and the attack was technically far hotter than it seems. There's a lot of effort gone into causing as little damage as possible. I can see why you are torn."

32

Zach laughed, humourlessly. All security professionals understood that their same skills could be used on either side of the tracks and there were times when the lines blurred. "Anyway, you guys don't pay me to think, Sophie. You pay me to clean up these here boxes and ensure you are secure. In all honesty, while I didn't think anything would come of your meeting last night, I reckon you saved us a good week of work rebuilding them with whatever this person gave you. Plus, I saw your text and this is going to look really bad on Mike when it gets out how you were attacked. There is no way those vulnerabilities should have been left. There are no two ways about it, I'm sorry. It was sloppy of Mike."

Sophie nodded, she didn't want to see Mike get into trouble, but she did agree with Zach.

"In fact," Zach continued, his Michigan drawl becoming more pronounced as he was distracted by a train of thought, "it could be said that this Tami woman has done you a favour. If she genuinely has caused this little damage, then a day's downtime is cheap in exchange for the warning. If someone else had attacked you, I guarantee the ransom would have been at least three times as much. Plus, they'd have come back at you the next day using all those vulnerabilities you now are fixing."

"You're right. I'm not sure Mike or Paul will see it like that. Not that I'm sure why I care, of course. I'm still mad that she had the nerve to hit us like that in the first place."

Sophie mused on this, Paul was her and Mike's boss. He was a pretty reasonable guy but she couldn't always predict his mindset.

Zach shrugged, "As I said, I'm not paid to think, that's your department. She stayed well clear of anything that would cause you to legally have to report a data breach, she's technically very savvy. If you want me to investigate more – just say the word. However, I do have to admit, she's covered her tracks expertly and the emails, the software and the Zoom call all led us nowhere. The trail went cold pretty quickly. The only lead we have to her identity is your meeting and you should remember that, legally, you spoke to a consultant – she never actually admitted doing it did she?"

Sophie cast her mind back. "The implication was there but did she clearly admit it, actually no – she didn't. That's frustrating."

Getting up, Zach nodded, "She's clever – while she might be naive in some ways, technically she's outstanding. Just remember, whatever I know is confidential to you guys, so you decide who needs to know or do anything." He sauntered off back to the data centre to keep working.

Sophie watched him go and wished she could be as level headed and unemotional as Zach. Maybe then she wouldn't keep picturing the big, brown doe eyes that had looked up at her. Something shifted in her heart and she didn't know what was wrong with her – maybe she'd watched too many cartoons or princess movies as a kid.

Later that day, she was sitting in her office daydreaming a little when she saw Mike walk past her door.

"Hey Mike, got a minute?"

"Sure Soph, what's up?" He plonked himself down on her visitor chair with legs and arms flailing out like a relaxing starfish. Mike was an astute businessman and a great IT problem solver; he was no graceful athlete!

"I'm worried about this hack. I was chatting to Zach and I'm bothered it reflects badly on us if it gets out into the press. Did you hear how the attacker got in?"

Mike's relaxed posture tensed a little and he sat up straighter, "Yes, I did and I'm not happy. I know what you mean about looking bad Sophie, I've been wondering how this is going to pan out," he admitted. "Perhaps we should have a chat with Paul and see what he thinks. It sounded like the directors were all guns blazing for calling in the cops. Maybe he can rein in the other managers a bit."

"That might be a good idea. Speaking honestly, neither of us is going to come up smelling of roses and you know what it's like when the high-ups get a sniff of something. We'll be bogged down in writing status reports for a year and not have time to *actually* fix anything."

"You got that right. Let's talk to Paul later."

~#~

Later that evening, Sophie was sitting in her lounge with a glass of red wine and Bonnie, her best friend since school. Bonnie was also in cyber security but, contrasting with Sophie's suited, neat ponytail look, she had a boho vibe. Her long, curly, flame red hair was like a cloud of excitement that moved around her head as she gestured with her hands. A conversation with Bonnie somehow always felt like a workout but she was the most supportive friend Sophie had ever known.

"So, what's the deal with this attack then? You sorted yet?"

"Well, yes. We thought that it was going to take us days to rebuild, but we had some help from a rather unlikely source."

"Oh?"

"While we were working on the response I had an email from a consultancy firm."

"Bloody spam."

"Not so much... turned out that a very 'helpful' consultant just happened to have the kill-switch commands for the ransomware."

"As if..."

"Well, Tami turned out to be very helpful. What can I say?"

Bonnie held her wine for a second and narrowed her eyes at Sophie.

"What?"

"What aren't you telling me about this Tami?"

"Well, she's skilled, claims to be ethical," Sophie scoffed before continuing, "about five three, slim but athletic build, short dark hair, brown eyes. What more do you want to know except she's got to be the hacker. I mean, who else could deactivate it that easily?"

"Okay, there's quite a bit to unpack, so I'll start with the last thing first..." Bonnie began holding up her fingers and using them to mark her points, "Firstly, why did she deactivate it you paid up? Seriously? Secondly, brown eyes was the thing you noticed? Thirdly, you've got that tone of voice when you say her name. What's going on?"

Sophie pursed her lips, "Firstly, I tried to pay for her consultancy, I certainly wasn't paying a ransom. She actually refused the money – can you believe that? Secondly, she had brown eyes – why wouldn't I notice them? Thirdly, I have no idea what you're talking about. She's an evil, conniving, hacker that ruined my week."

Bonnie kept looking at her with those annoying narrowed eyes which seemed to give her x-ray vision or something. "You like her."

"I do not *like* her. She's made my life hell and embarrassed Mike."

"Sophie Keegan, I've known you most of your life and I know that tone of voice. You're denying it to yourself but you like her. When are you seeing her next?"

"I'm not seeing her again and I *don't* like her – did you forget the part that she's a hacker who compromised my servers?"

"I didn't say you wanted to hire her, but I know your type– strong, athletic bad girl? Mark my words – you'll see her again."

Sophie snorted in derision and took another chug of her wine. "Enough about me... let's get onto your week. What's new?"

"I'll bite… for now, but we'll be back to your brown-eyed Tami, don't you worry."

Sophie rolled her eyes and finished the glass of wine in one gulp. The worst type of person was a friend who was right, and she wasn't going to admit that Bonnie might be one of those. No way!

Chapter Seven

Teri was sitting on her sofa ruminating on her life choices, present situation and lack of job hunting success. The last few days had also shaken her faith in the idea of a 'humane highwayman'. She needed another source of income and she needed it fast.

The blonde's words in the coffee shop came back to her. Teri could do anything; she could work anywhere. She had focussed on the kind of job she had before, but when push came to shove, she needed to look wider. The notice they had spotted in the coffee shop came to mind – they needed help. Surely, she could make coffee?

Obviously, it would be a bad idea to look into coffee shops near Beaverson's; she couldn't go back to the same one they had met in but she could start closer to home. Excited to put her plan into motion she pulled up her CV and made a few tweaks. She couldn't do a lot about her gap in employment or her lack of barista training but she did what she could. Printing out copies, she grabbed her coat and headed out.

An hour later, she was despondent again. There were plenty of coffee shops near her flat but she hadn't realised how competitive the job market was. She got the knock back from one after another. The final shop had a kinder old guy who sat her down after seeing the desperate look in her eyes. He explained how the shops south of the river had a constant stream of locals looking for jobs. She'd be better off looking over the river in the City proper.

Teri figured that she had nothing to lose. A few stops on the Tube later, she sized up the independent coffee shops as she walked through the steadily more affluent and touristy parts of the City of London. She was getting some great exercise but it wasn't doing a lot for her job hunting. She'd only left three CVs in the last hour of walking.

38

Eventually, she came upon a small independent shop off Covent Garden. The sign outside was pink and dark red, traditionally signwritten as 'Marion's'. She decided this was her limit. Walking in, she prepared her pitch for the twentieth time, looking around at the warmly decorated interior and smelling the delicious coffee and baking.

Greeting an older woman behind the counter, she took a deep breath and began her spiel. "Hi, good morning. My name is Teri and I'm looking for a job in this area. I've got lots of experience with managing teams in stressful situations and I handle pressure well. I'm a great communicator and I love meeting people, so I'm hoping that would be of benefit to help your customers?" Teri inwardly cringed as she spouted her sales diatribe.

"Can you make coffee?" the sceptical but not unkind voice replied.

She was about to reply how she'd made coffee for her team many times when she stopped and looked into the woman's hazel eyes. Something about her made Teri stop. "You know what, no. I don't know how to make proper coffee, not like I can smell coming from your machine, but I am a quick learner."

The woman smiled and nodded. She gestured to a free table in the back, "How do you take it? Sit down and tell me how much of that you actually mean."

Teri wasn't sure what she meant but decided that the opportunity for a coffee and to rest her feet was worth whatever rejection this woman was going to dish out.

"I don't know what you mean, but, black please."

The woman followed her over with two mugs of steaming coffee and Teri gratefully accepted one, closing her eyes and enjoying the rich aroma.

"You like?"

"Mmmmm, I do like. This smells amazing. How do you do it?" Forgetting that she wanted a job more than anything, she was genuinely curious how they made it smell so good.

The woman smiled again before continuing, "If I hire you, I can teach you, but how much of that initial spiel do you mean? Plus, why are you looking for a job here when you never mentioned working in a coffee shop before?"

Teri sighed, there was something about this older woman that seemed to command total honesty. She knew straight away that exaggerating or lying would get her thrown out.

"I meant it all but, if I'm totally honest, the only coffee I've made is for myself and my team. I used to work in cyber security but things went wrong for me and I'm struggling." The woman remained silent, seemingly waiting for Teri to continue, "I'm sorry, what was your name, that's really rude of me - I was carried away with the smell of your coffee!"

"Marion, I'm Marion Keymis and I've owned this shop for 30 years. You look like you need more than just coffee, though."

Teri wasn't sure what she meant and frowned, waiting for Marion to carry on.

"What I mean is that when you walked in you were spouting confidence, but when you get to my age you can spot fake confidence."

Teri's eyes widened and she went to protest but stopped, maybe Marion had a point. She didn't feel confident and if she was honest, she hadn't for some time.

"Have you considered a career as a psychiatrist?"

Marion laughed a throaty guffaw. "I'm a coffee seller, they are much the same thing. What was the last dishonest thing you did?"

40

This question caught Teri off guard and she looked agape at Marion before instinctively looking down and away from her. She could feel the older woman's eyes bore into her and, in a quiet voice, she answered truthfully. "I got so desperate lately I turned to hacking some companies for money. I'm not proud of it and I want to stop."

Silence stretched for a few moments before Teri dared look up. Marion was looking at her, head tilted to one side and eyes narrowed, nodding slightly. "OK, when can you start?"

"Pardon?" Teri thought her ears were tricking her.

"4 days a week, rotating schedule, a month's probation, couple of days unpaid training until you can actually make coffee and you get all the caffeine you can drink. Now, when can you start?"

Teri couldn't help but grin and stare at Marion who must have thought she was simple by now. She wanted to cry, shout and hug the older woman but all she could say was "Thank you." Fearful she was about to become a watering pot, she quickly added, "How about now?"

Marion nodded knowingly, "You got it!" and she headed off behind the counter, throwing Teri an apron. Teri put it over her head and followed her before being introduced to Callum, the big silver coffee machine. *'Of course he has a name... this woman is nuts but I like her already!'* Her first attempt was a frothy disaster and she had to jump backwards to avoid the steam. "He's a bit temperamental!" warned Marion before leaving Teri to practice.

By the lunchtime rush, she had managed to actually make a cup fit for a customer and she got into a rhythm with Marion where she made the simple lattes and teas.

At two PM Teri realised she'd not eaten anything as they quietened down for the first time. "Phew, is it always this busy?"

"Yep, that's the city rush for you. Well done, by the way. You weren't joking when you said you were a quick learner. You won't need those couple of days training after all."

Teri felt herself blushing at the compliment. In truth, it felt good. Being 'freelance', she didn't get compliments and it had been a long time since someone had taken the time to teach her something.

She thanked Marion and headed home after arranging what time to come in the next day.

~#~

The week progressed and Teri became more confident. She served more and more customers, whizzing around the kitchen area preparing orders as she went. She felt her confidence building and didn't realise how much confidence she had lost outside of her cyber world.

Friday came and she was buzzing around enjoying the rush when a sharp voice behind stopped her, as though she'd been slapped. "You?"

She put the latte she'd been making down and turned slowly to see a familiar face - a set of frowning blue eyes surrounded by blonde hair. *Oh shit, how can she be here? She hates me.*

"Oh, hello Ms Keegan. I didn't know you came here!"

"I don't but I had a meeting over this way with Zach, our security response guy. I'm sure he'd love to meet you..." The woman paused and looked down before looking up with a grin on her face, "Teri..."

Oh shit! What have I done? Teri had forgotten she had a name badge on. *So much for anonymity – that's blown it.*

"Errr, yes, it is actually Teri. Sorry about that." She knew she was blushing furiously and it wasn't helped by the grin on the

42

blonde's face. The other woman was enjoying her embarrassment, she was sure.

"Well anyway, *Teri*, I'll have a latte and a danish to go please. As you know, I have a sweet tooth so I guess you better add a caramel shot in there to keep me sweet?"

She went to get her purse out but Teri stopped her, shaking her head. "You already know I can't take your money. It's on me!"

Five minutes later, she was gone, sipping her coffee and heading off to the tube. Teri was sure she could smell her perfume lingering in the shop but that was probably her imagination.

Chapter Eight

Sophie couldn't believe she'd found where Tami–*no, Teri*– worked. She was reflecting on her discovery the next day and she had to admit, she'd taken great amusement in the blushing face of the previously confident hacker. *That should knock her down a peg or two and put her on the back foot,* adding a *ha!* for good measure. The problem was, and she had to admit this, she wasn't vindictive and while she was mad at Teri for what she'd done, she wasn't sure that having her arrested would do any of them any good. It wouldn't bring her wasted evening back, wouldn't really help Mike and it would make the other woman's life far worse – probably meaning she had no choice but to turn fully to crime if she had a record.

But, who is to say that just because she's working in a coffee shop, she isn't still hacking people or won't just turn back to it when money gets tight?

This was an entirely reasonable argument to be having with herself, she decided. One thing was sure, Bonnie was wrong. She didn't like Teri, but it was sensible to plan carefully, right?

Anyway, there are a few good shops in Covent Garden so while I'm here for another meeting with Zach, it would be a good chance to look out some shoes Bonnie mentioned. Plus, that plan for a full security sweep isn't going to write itself! We had to do that face-to-face, didn't we?

Regardless, somehow, she wound up outside the little coffee shop. She chanced a look through the door and saw the brunette hard at work behind the counter. An older woman was clearing tables but Teri looked to be working pretty hard.

Without thinking, her feet took her into the shop and joined the queue. She used the wait to observe the hacker. She had to admit, there was nothing about her that would give away her other career. She smiled at customers and seemed popular with the regulars. Sophie wondered how long she'd been working here. She also found her eyes wandering down as Teri made someone's cappuccino, facing away. *Hmmm, nice bum.* The thought escaped before she could stop it and she mentally slapped herself. *Seriously?*

Her turn to order came and Teri turned, speaking as she looked up from the till, "How are you, what can I get …" she seemed to lose her words momentarily as their eyes met and Sophie felt a mischievous grin coming to her lips.

"I'll take a latte please, no danish, I've already eaten."

Teri seemed to struggle for words before nodding and grabbing a takeaway cup.

Sophie thought she might have a little fun. She was clearly making this woman uncomfortable so why shouldn't she torment her a bit? Even if she wasn't going to turn her in (and Zach confirmed they had no direct evidence anyway) she could still make her sweat a bit.

"Oh, I'll have it to eat in please, if you have a table."

Teri nodded and carried on making her coffee, finally turning around and passing it over on a tray. "Did you enjoy it *that* much you needed another or are you just after free coffee?" She was smiling.

"Well it was good, if I'm honest. How much?"

"It's on me, least I can do."

"Well thanks. If you have a break, you're welcome to join me and tell me more about yourself?"

The older woman appeared behind the counter and nodded to Teri, shooing her off to join Sophie. "You're due a break love, go on."

"Oh, thanks Marion."

Sophie took her drink and sat down, Teri following and sitting opposite her.

"How long have you been working here? I thought you said you didn't have a job?" Sophie started thoughtfully, sipping her coffee and enjoying the rich flavour.

"I did and I do. I've only worked here a week. It was your suggestion that set me looking for something different. Marion was kind enough to give me a chance."

Sophie was impressed, it seemed that Teri had listened to her. Maybe this earnest side of the woman she saw was actually real, she didn't seem to be a bad person — just driven to bad things by necessity. That didn't stop Sophie feeling resentful about the attack but maybe that would fade in time.

"That's great... that you've found something, I mean. Are you enjoying it?"

"You know, yes, I am! Marion is so supportive and I'm enjoying all the faces I get to see . It's certainly different to a job in cyber where I stare at a screen all day. Plus, Marion says I make a mean latte—I'm still working on the cappuccino though. That one is *hard*!"

"I'll remember that for next time," replied Sophie, feeling cheeky again for reason she couldn't explain. "I meant what I said though—your latte game is tasty."

Teri seemed to blush at this, for some reason.

They talked for a little while longer before Sophie had to head back to work and she left feeling warmer inside. *Must be the buzz from the coffee.*

~#~

That afternoon, Sophie was back in her office and talking to Mike again.

"Did you manage to talk to Paul about whether we're reporting the ransomware to the police?"

"I had a brief chat but we need to talk again. He was more concerned, rightly, about whether we'd closed all the gaps."

"Glad he's got his priorities straight. Great idea to talk to him – we could pop up this afternoon?"

"Yep – let's do that. I've got that meeting with my team now to rip them new a-holes over why we hadn't patched all these issues you found but swing by in half an hour and we'll head up together. I'm going to need a break after ripping into them."

With that, Mike rose and headed off back down the corridor in his hunt for pre-meeting coffee. Sophie was pleased to find an ally who shared her uncertainty.

While she waited for him to finish his meeting, she thought more about what she was going to say to Paul. She also mused a little on those big doe eyes again and had to admit, her initial anger was starting to take a back seat.

When she and Mike got up to the IT Exec's office, they explained their concerns. She shared both that she'd met the individual she suspected of being the attacker but also Zach's doubt they'd make any charges stick. She had also pointed out that in meeting the person, she'd been shown how the attack worked and that it had exploited open issues that really should have been closed months ago. "Hmmm, I see what you mean, this could be a bit embarrassing for us if it were published. Do you agree, Mike?" Paul pondered, his brow furrowed as he listened to Sophie.

"I do, Paul. In the most bizarre way, we could consider the attack to be good for us in the long term – we've been talking for a while about engaging someone for a security audit. This could work out an awful lot cheaper. You remember what Zach quoted – he wanted over a hundred thousand! This woman has already buried my server team in work all this week. I'm afraid to say that most of it should have been addressed a while back."

It did sound like they were all seeing this the same way. She didn't want their department to get a bad reputation. A little bit of her brain, a *tiny* bit, pointed out that maybe she also wanted to protect Teri just a little bit. She told that tiny bit to shut up. She was clearly mad, she should be exacting all the revenge she could on her, but somehow, that idea didn't make her feel better.

Paul nodded thoughtfully, "That's true, Mike. Let me talk to the rest of the board. I don't want to unfairly demonise your team though, they are a good bunch, even if they missed some stuff."

Sophie struggled to keep her face straight as Paul said that – he was edging into "old boys' network" territory but she couldn't complain about him looking after the server admin guys. She settled for a mini eyeroll. After all, he was right, they weren't bad guys – just overworked and perhaps a little complacent. Maybe this would be the kick up the arse they needed.

She headed back to her office and went back to work. As much as she was starting to think she didn't want to convict the apologetic, brown-eyed Teri, she hadn't done Sophie's workload any favours.

Chapter Nine

A week later, Teri was still having sleepless nights worrying whether a knock at the door would see her world come tumbling down now that the blonde knew her real name. She seemed to enjoy playing with Teri and teasing her. Last night she had barely gotten three hours sleep and she was feeling dead on her feet.

In the meantime, Maisie had insisted they attend some random friend's birthday party. How she knew all these women was a mystery to Teri, who really wasn't in the mood. However, Maisie rarely took 'no' for an answer so here she was, already standing quietly in a corner of someone's kitchen at nine o'clock, nursing her vodka and waiting for a sensible time to jump back in an Uber with Maisie.

After an hour, she needed the loo and headed through the hall in search of one, just as a blonde woman came out of the lounge door heading the same way. They collided, albeit gently, and she reached out instinctively to steady the woman who seemed to sway. As the blonde curls turned, Teri's breath caught and her mouth went dry. She knew this woman. In fact, not only did she know her but she hadn't left her mind much in her sleepless nights this week. It was Ms Keegan! That felt wrong, she needed to know her first name. Her mind also registered that, what she'd thought was just blonde hair actually had so many different shades, from honey to almost gold and even sections of what she was sure had been a pinky blonde.

Ms Keegan's eyes widened as she recognised Teri too and she stood upright, glaring at her. Teri sighed, *Oh great, she's going to say I've attacked her again. I should just go.* She was surprised when her gaze softened and she spoke. "Hi, Teri. How are you?"

"Hi. I'm fine, you?" *Way to go Lady Lover! Is that the best you've got for the woman you've been lusting after all week?*

"I'm fine."

"Good." *Well, this is awkward.* "Oh, actually. In the spirit of being honest. I'm not really okay. I've felt terrible about everything, all week. I'm so sorry, about everything. Really, I am." Teri glanced down at her feet in order to avoid the gaze she could feel running over her body before almost inaudibly adding, "I can't stop thinking about you and I don't even know your name"

Teri put her face in her hands and groaned. She could feel herself blushing and this was worse than 'fine', why did she have to open her big fat mouth and say stuff like this? What was wrong with her?

She felt a hand touch hers and pull it away from her face. Looking up and expecting to see anger, she saw a gentle smile instead.

"OK, I'll come clean too then. I've wondered about you too since I saw you at Marion's. I know I shouldn't but..." her voice tailed off and she looked down, seemingly realising at that moment she was still holding Teri's hand and let go quickly. "Sorry, that sounds weird. I am still really mad at what you did but after you said you'd listened to me, I was actually a bit worried for you. Despite your job, I can't help getting the feeling you're actually a good person and don't deserve the hand you've been dealt..." Her eyes flicked up and she saw Teri looking wide-eyed at her before continuing, "... and my name is Sophie."

Teri smiled, Sophie thinking of her was the best thing ever — well no, the best thing ever would be going on a date with her but even she didn't have that vivid an imagination.

"I've been worried about what was going to happen, I will admit, but you have every right to be angry with me."

Sophie sighed and pulled on her ponytail. "Teri, you're right, I was angry when we first met. I could have ripped you apart but I don't know why, I just can't see you as some evil force or some criminal mastermind. I saw the look in your eyes when you realised I'd seen the real you in the coffee shop. You hadn't planned that, had you?"

Teri blushed and her cheeks went hot. "Well no, obviously I didn't intend for you to see my actual name. Meeting you in the first place was risky, I know, but I couldn't help myself."

"I've been doing some soul searching this week thinking about what I'd do in your position and I don't think I can vilify you for earning what you can – even if what you chose was wrong and cost me a fortune in pizza for my team. I guess there are worse things you could have been driven to – I wouldn't wish those on anyone. I just wish you'd been able to find a job before you met me. I mean that in the nicest possible way, of course."

Teri shook her head, sighing and feeling a heavy weight returning to her insides, "You wouldn't believe how hard it is out there. Nobody seems to be hiring or maybe I just don't impress them." She shrugged, sadly.

"Well, my management seems to be viewing you as someone who has done us an arse-about-face favour. I mean, don't expect any security contracts from us but they seem to be erring away from calling the police."

Teri couldn't believe her ears. "Oh, thank you, Sophie. You really don't know how sorry I am. Is there anything I can do to make it up to you? Please?"

Sophie rolled her eyes and seemed to smile at her pathetic expression. "Well, I'm hating this party. I don't know why I got talked into it, so how about you tell me more about why you're in such a bad position?"

Teri almost passed out – she was getting the chance to sit down and talk to Sophie for more than a passing few pleasantries away from the coffee shop... like really form words and everything with her. Maybe she could get to know her better, the previous, heavy feeling of sadness she'd been carrying inside felt suddenly lighter.

"Totally, I'm yours for as long as you want me, only one thing though - I need to pee first... can you give me two minutes?"

Sophie wrinkled her eyes and burst into a genuine, throaty laugh. "I wouldn't deny even *you* a pee, Teri. What are you drinking and I'll meet you in the kitchen?"

After Teri had taken care of herself, they met back up and scored themselves a sofa in the corner of the room. "So tell me, what's the deal?" Sophie had started off.

"Well, my background is in corporate security. I used to run a team but things went sour and I've found whenever I apply for jobs it comes to nothing. It's a very tough market out there. I'm not in contact with any family except my sister." She rolled her eyes before continuing. "My Nan died a year ago, so everything came all at once. I'm lucky she left me a very small inheritance but that's about to run out, so yes, I am as poor and desperate as you probably think I am."

Teri wanted to be open but she didn't want to lose face with this woman so she resorted to her usual joking persona, opening her arms wide in a 'ta-da' motion, like someone demoing a prize on a game show. She forced herself to add an upbeat but deliberately sarcastic, "On the plus side, I'm gorgeous!"

"I suppose you're not wrong." Sophie continued, "Anyway, tell me about this sister of yours."

For a moment, Teri actually wondered if that comment was Sophie flirting with her, but she dismissed it as an impossibility. She rolled her eyes, "Firstly, that sounded wrong, you can't talk about gorgeous and my sister in the same sentence to me. Secondly, urghh, my big sister Malini who always knows best. We never really got on, she's five years older than me."

Teri could practically see Sophie's brain working before asking, "So how old are you then?"

"I'm twenty-six. Why? How old are you?"

"I'm twenty-eight, just gone. You look younger is all. I figured you were in your early twenties, maybe twenty-four? Anyway, sorry – your sister..."

"You look a lot younger than that," Teri felt her ears going hot again as she put her foot in it, "sorry, I shouldn't say that, I don't mean to embarrass you."

"You aren't, don't worry."

Teri played with her fingers and chewed down on her lip, she couldn't believe her luck, both that Sophie hadn't turned her in but also that she seemed to be willing to become ... something. Maybe even friends? (She didn't dare hope for more.) Maybe she should learn to open up and show herself more if this was what could come from it.

"Anyway... Malini, well she's annoying but she's the only family I have to talk to so I suppose I shouldn't complain. Sometimes I get the feeling that she calls to tell me everything I'm doing wrong. I guess that's what big sisters are for."

They chatted companionably for a while, drifting into talking about their jobs and various incidents they'd both worked on, losing track of time and getting through several refills of their drinks.

Sophie was laughing at one particular anecdote, "There's no way you recovered from a server attack by turning it around on the attacker!"

"I did! I spotted the commands he was using and replaced the drive with a local link to his remote share."

"That's not possible!" Sophie said in a loud, excited and somewhat shocked voice, "Oops, sorry, volume – I'm not used to vodka!".

Teri shrugged, "Well, whatever I did, it worked. He infected himself. The fool had the same file share vulnerabilities he was attacking me through. That was how I got into this game."

The time had flown by and Teri only noticed as Sophie looked down at her watch, "Wow – it's midnight. I'm not keeping you, am I?"

"Not at all. Knowing Maisie, she won't have even registered that it's dark until someone kicks her out of bed."

"Ha, sounds like Bonnie, perhaps they are together somewhere."

Teri considered this for a moment, who knew with Maisie? Frankly she could be in bed with any woman at this party. Not her problem though.

They chatted for another hour until finally Sophie said, "Thank you, it's been really great getting to know you better. I probably should be getting home – with or without Bonnie. Good luck finding... Maisie, was it?"

Teri nodded and chuckled. "Yes, that's her. She'll turn up at some point, she always does. Do you think you'll come by for coffee this week again? Can I tempt you with a danish?"

Sophie smiled and Teri felt the air suck from her lungs. While the smile was only a simple little upturn of her mouth, there was something about Sophie that drew her in. Shame the other woman didn't feel the same. In fact, she didn't even know if she was gay – but she was pretty sure she was on the right track.

"I might just go for that but you have to let me pay, it's not fair on you to keep buying me coffee. Not now you're getting somewhere to get things sorted." Sophie's gaze floated away a bit and

54

her voice softened to a more nervous tone, "You *are* getting sorted, aren't you? I mean, you aren't hacking anymore?"

Teri smiled, "You know what, I really *am* trying to and I think Marion would beat me around the head with a coffee cup if I was naughty. The woman thinks she's my fairy godmother or something!"

"Good, sounds like you need one to keep you on the straight and narrow."

"Narrow maybe, never straight." Teri replied cheekily and with as much flirt in her voice as several vodkas could allow.

Sophie raised an eyebrow. "Good to know. Night Teri – see you next week sometime." She winked at her. She *actually* winked. Teri felt her stomach do a backflip and it was like all her jackpot paydays had come at once.

Chapter Ten

Monday dawned and Sophie was in another meeting at Zach's office.

"You know Sophie, I don't think I've ever seen you over here as much. Is there something you're not telling me about this hack or do you just use me as an excuse to get out of your office?" the bearded security pro quizzed her good-naturedly, "I mean, you're welcome here anytime, of course."

"No idea what you mean. I've got to follow up with what you're finding haven't I?" she responded, wondering why he was making an issue of it. This was her job for crying out loud. She didn't let on that Dave had asked her the same question when she told him where she was going to be this morning. *Also, there's a dry cleaners around the corner that I want to drop this skirt into.*

Zach picked up his phone and listened for a second. "Nope... it's still working. Wondered if we had lost all other means of information exchange there..." he replied with a grin.

"Okay, yes, I suppose I do like getting out of the office," she grudgingly accepted, "plus you have these nice cookies." She bit into the delicious white chocolate cookie, enjoying the warm gooeyness of freshly baked goods. Why couldn't her office have these?

"Noted... If I want more business from you, I need more baked goods. Anything else you want to talk about?"

"Nope – we've covered the latest on the attack and planned out this month's security sweep. We're good." Sophie's mind wandered a little, *I wonder what Teri would find if she did a sweep of our network?* The reminder broke her daydream as she realised that the woman *had* been in the network and that was why she couldn't trust her.

They broke up the meeting and she headed out after a little chit chat, still musing on her thoughts about Teri. She also remembered their chat at the party, which was still on her mind. The trouble was, and she wasn't admitting this to anyone – least of all herself – she didn't need to be at Zach's office in person but there was a rather nice coffee place on the way.

With that thought, she arrived outside Marion's, the warmly coloured interior practically pulling her in. Teri spotted her walking through the door as soon as she looked up. Her face broke out into a welcoming, warm smile that seemed to radiate friendship towards Sophie. Luckily the queue was short but as soon as Sophie got to the front, a latte and danish were waiting for her on the counter.

"Your usual, madame," Teri gestured with a flourish. "If you are still stubbornly insisting on paying, then it's £1.50 for the Danish."

OK, maybe this place is drawing me just a little to Covent Garden. "What about the coffee?"

"Well, no charge for that. I insist."

A laugh came from behind Sophie and she whipped around to see the older woman shaking her head and looking directly at Teri. She turned back to see the brunette looking sheepish.

"OK... alright, as Marion is finding my generosity hilarious, I probably should, in the spirit of full disclosure, tell you that she gives me free coffee as part of my wages so *technically* it's on her. Thanks Marion for outing me with that."

"My pleasure darling... you're welcome." Laughing some more she turned to Sophie, adding, "Enjoy your coffee dear – you've got to keep your girlfriend here in line."

"My girl..." Sophie started but Marion had already scooted off, chuckling, into the backroom.

She spun back to Teri, feeling shocked and angry. "What have you told her?"

Teri had the good grace to look mortified. "Nothing, honestly. I promise."

Sophie raised an eyebrow, staring Teri down, but while she continued to blush deep red, she didn't confess to any indiscretions. "Hmmmm, well - are you going to join me for a coffee or not? However, I should tell you I've changed my mind and I want a choco-mocha-latte-tino with half almond and half albino yak milk, to serve you right." A little smile escaped her mouth at the thought. She wondered momentarily whether having Teri as a friend might not be entertaining. *Girlfriend? That woman is off her rocker.* She shook her head as she took the tray to a free table.

Ten minutes later, Marion relieved Teri and she joined Sophie with a coffee of her own. "Marion says sorry, she assumed we were together. Apparently, the way we look at each other or something."

"As if..."

"And I might have happened to let slip that you were really attractive. Sorry!"

"Ha, whatever. You know what? You could have said worse."

"Well, I've put her straight on how we know each other now."

"You told her you hacked me?" said Sophie with a sarcastic tone and a raised eyebrow.

"Yes, I did."

Sophie was taken aback; Teri had told her boss about her other job. Perhaps it really was in the past for her – for now, at least. "Wow. She must be very special to admit that."

"Marion has been amazing. I know working in a coffee shop looks like a come down from a team leader in cyber security. It's been great to have someone believe in me for a change, someone who is willing to teach me things without all the politics. Surely you must get that too?"

Sophie snorted a laugh, "Do I? Blimey, it's like the House of Commons sometimes with all the politics going on but that's just the job isn't it?

"Well, you're better than me. I couldn't do all that backstabbing. This is so refreshing to be somewhere I feel good about myself and I'm, you know, growing and being me. Does that make any sense? It's not going to pay the bills forever but I already feel more confidence in myself. Enough about me though, how are you?"

Sophie took a long sip of the last of her latte and thought about her answer. "I'm fine, apart from everyone suddenly wanting to ask what's going on between you and I. It's not just Marion, Zach is teasing me that I'm meeting him in person too. I mean people only need to know you're gay and suddenly every woman you meet is your girlfriend. It's so annoying."

She swore she saw a slight smile creep across Teri's mouth but it was gone before she was sure.

"I..." Teri started before hesitating again as Sophie spoke at the same time.

"What are..." Sophie had said before pausing and raising an eyebrow, "you first..."

Teri appeared to take a deep breath, "I'm really enjoying your company." She seemed to wipe her palms on her black jeans, looking nervous. "Do you think you'd like to meet up some time? Outside of coffee?"

Sophie was surprised by the question but even more by the vulnerability she saw before her. Before her brain had a chance to

59

object, she allowed her mouth to run away. "Yes, me too. I can't believe I'm saying this, but yes, I think I'd like that," she replied quietly.

"Oh well, it wasn't importa... Sorry? Did you say yes?" Teri looked up, wide-eyed and shocked.

Sophie laughed a little at her expression.

"Teri, I said yes. I enjoyed your company too. I'd like to meet you again. No idea why I'm saying this and how I square it with my job but – well – I actually missed you last week, which is stupid, I know. What would you like to do?"

Teri's eyes took on a shocked look and her mind clearly was racing to come up with an answer. Sophie realised that she hadn't expected her to say yes.

"How about Saturday? I'll choose something for the morning and you can pick the afternoon? Then we get to know each other a little bit more? What do you think?" Teri looked pleased but still nervous.

Sophie recognised the consideration for what it was and smiled at the way Teri was going out of her way to not push her luck. "I love that. Thank you for being so considerate, that's really sweet. I hate the awkwardness when people decide to do something then you have to pretend you like it to avoid offending them!"

"OK, so if I get to kick us off, how about a relaxing morning? Where do you live? I'll come out to you."

"Chelmsford, it's further out than this on the Liverpool Street line. I can come back in though, no problem."

"No, that sounds perfect. You know what, let me do some research – I'm good on the internet you know." Teri grinned, some of her cheekiness returning, before continuing, "If you give me your number I'll text you a suggestion, will you let me know if it's OK?

60

Don't worry if you don't like it, just say. I'd much rather you told me than do something you won't enjoy."

"You really are quite sweet, aren't you? That sounds perfect. Saturday morning then."

~#~

A few hours later, Sophie's phone beeped with a text containing instructions for their date. It was a date, wasn't it? She suddenly realised that they hadn't actually *specifically* said it was a date.

'*How does 9am in Central Park, Chelmsford sound to you? I thought we could explore and you could tell me about your town?*'

She loved this idea; Teri was so easy going. 'Sounds great! *See you Saturday! X*'

Although this meant she needed to think about the afternoon … what could she take Teri to do that would be fun but show off a bit of herself? Hmmm…

Chapter Eleven

Sophie arrived at the park early on Saturday morning. She enjoyed the peace and quiet of the mature autumn trees rustling gently in the breeze and smiled at the occasional dog walker passing through. It was cold but bright and she breathed in deeply, enjoying the fresh air. Thinking about Teri, she smiled and a chuckle escaped thinking about how the face she presented to the world could be so different from the moments of vulnerability she spied underneath.

"What are you laughing at?" a familiar voice asked from behind. Sophie turned, Teri was grinning as she approached her. The brunette put her arms around Sophie and pulled her into a momentary hug before pulling back, seemingly accidentally brushing their cheeks.

Sophie smiled, not wanting to reveal quite where her mind had gone, "Oh nothing special. I'm glad to see you again. What do you think of the park?"

"It's pretty! I thought we could hang out here first, head over to the cafe for a coffee and head into town. I've never actually seen Chelmsford so I'm interested. According to Tripadvisor the cafe here has a great Rocky Road – it's out of this world, said several experts."

Sophie appreciated that Teri had already picked up her love for sweet goodies. "Well, who am I to argue with cake experts? Now you're talking – that's definitely the way to my heart."

She was starting to wonder if her heart was in danger of getting involved. That was a bad idea. What if fun easy-going Teri was an act? What if being bad was ingrained in her given how they'd met? Sophie knew she was getting ahead of herself but it was hard not to compare this girl with Hannah, her ex. Sophie had taken their breakup hard – she'd been really invested in their relationship and, she hated to admit, she thought she was in love with Hannah until she'd cheated on her. If she was that bad a judge of character then how could she trust her own judgement now?

"Earth to Sophie… where've you gone?" Teri teased, pulling her attention back.

"Oh sorry, I was miles away."

"So long as it wasn't something I said!"

"No, of course not – just daydreaming." Sophie sensed her voice had lost its initial excited vibrancy. She saw Teri frown and study her face closely, clearly looking for something.

"We don't have to go anywhere if you'd rather not…" Teri started uncertainly, looking worried.

"Oh, no. It's not you…" replied Sophie quickly, keen to reassure her that her distraction wasn't any kind of negative reflection on her. "You're great… it's…" She paused, not really wanting to talk about Hannah but unsure how to reassure Teri. She didn't want her to think she was less interested. "It's…" she tried again but got no further.

Teri put her hand on Sophie's arm before taking her hand, still hesitantly. "If it's a worry about me then tell me – I can handle it, don't worry."

Panicking, Sophie blurted out, "Oh no, nothing about you. It's Hannah".

Teri dropped Sophie's hand like a stone. "Who's Hannah?" She asked, the barbs of her voice sharper than the rose thorns in front of them. Her face took on a hardness Sophie hadn't seen before, her eyes deepening to a darker mahogany and narrowing with the poison of suspicion.

"My ex. She cheated and it's made me question things more." Sophie's voice tailed off. "That's silly though, let's go and eat cake".

The deflection failed as Teri took Sophie's hand and held her back from walking off towards the inviting cafe.

"Oh no. I'm sorry I was harsh there, Sophie. I would never cheat; I never have and I never will. It's not my style." Her deep espresso eyes bored down into Sophie's and looked full of earnest conviction. "I can be tactless, I'm far from perfect, but I am trustworthy. I don't expect you to believe that overnight, especially given how we met, but I'd like to try and change your mind and show you that there are good people who can actually fancy the pants off you."

Sophie smiled at Teri's cute mini-speech. It actually was just what she needed to hear. How did the other girl know her so well and was she talking about Sophie when she mentioned fancying people? "I'm sorry for spoiling the mood, don't worry. I'll get over it, I just need a bit of time."

"I'm not going anywhere, Sophie," Teri said grinning, before allowing them to walk on down the path together. She didn't release Sophie's hand but held it gently and caressed her long fingers affectionately.

Sophie might have been slow to trust. Deeper feelings would take time to have confidence in but this affection felt immediately genuine. There was something deeper about Teri which appealed despite the surface disparity in their roles and how they'd met. Sophie struggled to put her finger on precisely what attracted her but whatever it was, it was doing so firmly. She caught her mind wandering inwards and looked up to see Teri gazing at her with a curious smile playing around her lips.

"Are you back with us? I wondered if you were returning." She teased affectionately, her smile flashing white teeth and her eyes crinkling in a fashion Sophie found unaccountably heartening.

Sophie chuckled, "Sorry, I was just thinking about you. You're a lot more than you appear."

64

"What do you mean?" she asked cautiously.

"Oh, nothing bad, you're like an onion – so many layers."

A splutter escaped Teri as she laughed at the comparison. "I'm an onion? Well, thank you. So long as I don't make you cry!"

Sophie smiled, "No, I somehow doubt you would. Although you clearly can make me frustrated. My Mum always says I'm as placid as a lake until someone frustrates me, then I erupt like a volcano. Takes a lot though but you'll know about it, trust me."

"I can't wait. Your Mum sounds nice. You are close?"

"Fairly close, yes. We talk most weekends one way or another. I grew up in Colchester, so not far. It's just far enough that I can visit easily but they don't drop in unannounced and find how much of a mess my house is. Mum is quite houseproud, I'm not. Life's too short."

"Oh, you live in a pigsty then?" Teri teased.

"I wouldn't go quite that far. I guess some of her has rubbed off on me. I do like it when it looks nice, but I hate vacuuming – feels like a waste of my life. What about you?"

Teri smiled and rolled her eyes, "I live in a one bed flat with a cat who does his best to reupholster everywhere in grey. Trust me, any vacuum that lasts for more than a few months is a miracle. You don't have pets then?"

"Oh no, my dad was allergic growing up so I could never have any. I always liked the idea of a cat but it never seemed to be the right time."

"Oh, he's great company when he wants to be, but he's a judgemental son of a bitch when he disagrees with me."

Sophie could see the affection as Teri smiled. "Does he argue with you often then?"

"You're laughing at me... just wait until you get a cat. You'll see. He's like a ball of pure attitude wrapped in fur."

Sophie laughed and looked over the park at the wooded area. "I don't come here enough, it's nice to be able to be here and enjoy it."

"I know, the view is good, isn't it?" Teri replied cheekily, looking firmly at Sophie rather than the trees. Sophie smiled.

They walked around the park together, chatting about everything and nothing for another hour before Sophie started to shiver a little and her tummy let out a badly timed rumble. Teri suggested they get a coffee and some breakfast to warm themselves up. "Oh yes please! I'm a caffeine shot down this morning. There used to be a lovely cafe near the swings years back, is that the one you meant? I wondered if it's still there."

"Only one way to find out," said Teri with an excitable grin, "let's warm up. I'll race you there!" She took off at somewhere between a clumsy gallop and a run. Sophie followed her, laughing at her adorably klutzy antics.

~#~

"Oh, that feels a lot better." Sophie sighed, leaning back after warming herself up and finishing a huge slice of rocky road. "So, what comes next then in our wonderful date?"

Teri kept a straight face, replying, "Oh, so it's wonderful *and* it's a date?"

Sophie's eyes widened; they *were* on a date, weren't they? Teri had not actually said the words but it was clear, wasn't it? "Calm down Soph, I'm teasing. Any time with you *is* wonderful and I certainly hope it's a date!"

Sophie felt all fuzzy at Teri's usage of her shortened name, it may not have been a big deal but somehow it felt right coming from

66

her. "Oh, stop teasing! You're horrible to me!" Sophie whined but knew she was smiling.

Teri was smiling kindly while laughing at her, "Oh but you look so cute when you're puzzled or thinking."

Sophie's ears blushed a deep pink. "Enough teasing, we won't get through the morning."

"Well, in my extensive research of exciting things to do in this town, I found reference to the park, the museum and the river. So, what do you like most?

"Oh, well I get so little free time that I almost never walk about and explore. Would you believe that I've lived here for five years since uni and only actually visited this park once? How about we head for the river and then if it gets too cold, we can warm up in the museum? I bet they have a cafe with cake too!"

Teri laughed, "You really *do* have a sweet tooth, don't you? If the lady wants cake, then cake we shall find but let me walk off this slice first!"

They spent the next hour ambling contentedly down one side of the river, ending up in the town centre, chatting non-stop the entire time, one minute talking about TV and the next discussing stuff they'd read online. They got onto politics, specifically LGBT+ issues in different countries. Sophie was thoughtful about this for a second, "Yes, we are lucky, I mean we're walking along here in daylight and nobody gives a stuff."

"Maybe they think I'm your ugly sister?" joked Teri.

Sophie laughed, "That's easy to clear up..." and reached out to hold Teri's hand, adding, "and I'll ignore the ugly comment which doesn't even deserve a response." After a pause, she continued, "Do you travel much?"

"Not lately, for obvious reasons, but back when I was working I used to enjoy citybreaks. I went to Amsterdam one time with Lisa from work. She wanted to try everything, I was a bit more timid. Can you believe that I've never actually smoked anything? Gawd, I sound like a right goody two-shoes. I'm supposed to be this badass character, aren't I?"

"Oh me neither, just the smells put me off. If I really thought you were a badass, you wouldn't be here with me. Don't get me wrong, I love the idea of the bad girl as much as anyone, but I want someone to trust." *Not like Hannah*, she added silently.

During another moment of daydreaming, admiring reflections on the river's surface, she'd thought that perhaps this was an unusual date, but she felt so happy that Teri hadn't felt the need to impress her with a flashy venue. She didn't want that — just to get to know this woman, who she shouldn't like at all but seemed to be growing on her day by day, even hour by hour. The nagging worry about whether she could trust Teri was still there but today she was determined to push it to the back of her mind and enjoy herself.

Although Sophie hadn't been to the park in years, she *did* know the town centre and it occurred to her that Teri might like an eccentric shop she was fond of. "I know this is your part of the date to direct, so we can go wherever you want, but there's a shop that I wonder if you'll like just down here."

"Hey, I've done a rubbish job at directing it so far but I'm enjoying learning more about you and having the chance to talk. I'd love to see this shop!"

Sophie led them down a side street and stopped before a narrow row of shops built recently and designed to give a cozy olde-worlde feel. Sophie always liked the atmosphere down here as something out of a storybook, expecting a wizard to be standing on the steps with some form of goblin.

68

However, the first window was full of dresses and lace underwear of varying sizes. Pushing aside the thought of how Teri would look in a particularly sexy black lace bra, she was sure that none of this was the hacker's style. Sure enough, Teri looked at her incredulously before clearly trying to remain polite with a noncommittal, "Here?"

Sophie kept a straight face for a few seconds before bursting out laughing. "No, don't worry. I was just teasing. We actually want next door but you should see the look on your face!"

Teri looked momentarily relieved before her confident face returned and she answered with a raised eyebrow that Sophie found disproportionately attractive for a simple body part. "Of course, I'm sure I'd look great in whatever you chose, but that looks more like somewhere I'd have fun shopping for you."

The clear flirtation in her tone caused Sophie to feel both warmed and apprehensive. *Are we going there yet? I'm not sure what I want from her yet, or maybe I am but I don't feel I should?*

She smiled as wolfishly as she could manage and looked Teri up and down with a raised eyebrow of her own. Two could play this game, even if she was faking her own confidence. She said nothing before brushing past Teri to move to the next shop window. She saw Teri swallow and smiled inwardly, pleased that she could give as good as she got.

The next window was full of books, games and cardboard cutouts. Xena from Warrior Princess rubbed shoulders with Wynonna Earp. Sophie was pleased to note that they'd also added a few subtly placed flags – one rainbow, the other shades of red, orange and pink. Looking at the latter, she was reminded of something but it took her a few moments to realise.

"You did NOT use the flag as the colour scheme for your ransomware dialog box!" she exclaimed loudly, "How on earth did I miss that? I thought you were some creepy dude!"

69

Teri smirked, "You mean you'd have paid up quicker if I'd said 'Hey, fellow lesbian, pay up or I delete your data.'?"

Sophie shook her head, "Of course not, but I could have reported you to the Grand High Lesbian Council for crimes against sapphics!" before muttering to herself, "How did I not twig, seriously?"

Teri held the shop door open for Sophie who watched the other woman's face come alive as she looked around. To say this place was an Aladdin's cave of sci-fi and fantasy nerdiness would be an understatement. Sophie had come regularly since it opened, enjoying the relaxed and cosy atmosphere. She wasn't massively into roleplay or cosplay but she did love the artwork and they actually had an LGBT bookshelf she liked.

She concentrated on Teri and smiled as the other woman continued to look in awe. "Wow, Sophie, this place is amazing."

The secret of this shop wasn't in its stock, there were bigger places in London, but none of them could quite capture the homegrown atmosphere of a slightly dimly lit room painted to resemble a cave, where shelves of different heights brought different ranges into view as you moved about.

Teri walked over to the t-shirt section. Sophie smiled, realising she had guessed the woman's style preferences. She enjoyed how consumed she looked flicking through the rail. She regarded each top with a carefully appraising eye and serious frown. Eventually she pulled one out, a dark t-shirt with an image of a cat with Princess Leia-like side buns. Sophie smiled, she should have guessed Teri wouldn't look at the obvious but she loved how she seemed to effortlessly combine quirky with authentic. Even the fact that the caption was in pink sparkles somehow seemed apt given the way Teri wore her femininity comfortably but without obligation.

The amusement in Teri's eyes dimmed when she subtly glanced at the price tag. The expression was fleeting but Sophie saw the disappointment, sadness and possibly even shame. How she saw all those emotions in a brief flash she had no idea but they were there and she wanted to pull Teri in, kiss her and reassure her. But that wasn't her role, nor was her conscious brain agreeing it was a role she wanted. *Remember who she is.*

Teri put the t-shirt back, turning and smiling at Sophie. "That's cute, don't you think?"

Sophie looked her up and down, "Yes, looks cute to me." The slight blush Teri's ears took on and the awkward lopsided, bashful smile told her that her flirting had hit the spot.

They window shopped some more, Sophie's mischievous side spotted something interesting. Holding up the slim, red catsuit she gestured to Teri. She coughed to get her attention before saying, "You know, they have a fitting room over there…"

Teri looked down at the catsuit dubiously. "Seven? You see me as a Seven of Nine?"

"Strong, independent, badass," she stopped before adding *fanny-flutteringly gorgeous*, thinking of both the attractive Star Trek character and Teri. "Let me think for a bit… Uh-huh duuuhhh."

"I always fancied myself more as a Janeway but, if Catwoman sees me as a rebellious badass then who am I to disagree?"

Sophie scoffed at the idea of Teri in leadership but didn't want to hurt her feelings. "Badass is definitely more your thing … go on… pleeeeease?" Sophie wasn't above a bit of puppy eye pleading to get her own way and, of course, it worked.

Teri headed into the back of the shop to try on the costume and Sophie swiftly grabbed the t-shirt she'd been admiring, handing it to the shop owner with a smile and a finger to her lips indicating she wanted to keep this quiet. He nodded, smiling at her and quickly charged the card she presented. She stashed the t-shirt in her bag just in time for Teri to emerge.

She saw a flash of uncertainty in Teri's eyes before her trademark confidence fell back into place and she posed. "What do you think? Think you'll be assimilated?"

Sophie's mind was suffering some kind of malfunction and she had to blink twice to regain her senses. So far, she'd seen Teri's personality and felt something she liked. Her confidence tinged with hidden vulnerability had drawn Sophie in. However, the sight of her in the very fitted, almost purple catsuit was not what Sophie had expected, this was a whole new Teri. This woman was hot! She turned to the owner, "How much?"

Teri laughed, "You aren't serious?"

As the owner said some number she barely registered, Sophie threw her card on the counter in haste. "We're taking it."

Teri looked surprised, and if truth be told, she was equally shocked at herself but this was a sight she wanted to see again. "Oh, I'm sorry – I should have said – do you like it?"

"Well, yes, if you think it looks OK... but..."

"OK, done – we'll take it, thanks."

Teri returned to the fitting room to take it off and Sophie smiled while paying, she wasn't sure quite what had got into her but something had shifted in the way she saw this woman. Before, she'd been looking at her in terms of how they'd met. Now she looked at her first and foremost as a woman that she felt attracted to.

Teri returned, shaking her head and passing the garment to the store owner who packed it for them. "Whoever would have guessed that under that mild mannered IT manager front lay a voracious consumer of Starfleet officers in catsuits?"

Sophie picked up the bag and threw it at her head, rolling her eyes.

72

"Whoever would have guessed that you had a thing for cat ears? I think we're even, don't you?"

While Teri was keen to still impress Sophie, they agreed on a light lunch in a cafe halfway back along the river to where she'd parked her car. Sophie didn't want them eating too much knowing what she had planned for the afternoon.

~#~

Once finished eating, they headed back to Sophie's red Mini, each licking an ice cream from the cafe Teri had insisted they get to help Sophie's sweet tooth. "My turn now," said Sophie with a smile, "I get to spoil you now. I've got an interesting time planned for us. After getting cold in the park and eating these, we're going to get cold again. You up for it?"

"Are you there?"

"Of course, silly."

"Then I'm all in – lead on."

~#~

"Sophie... this is an indoor ski slope..." Teri exclaimed when they arrived at the large building on the town outskirts.

"Well done, 10 out of 10 for observation."

"OK... So I see what it is but what are *we* doing here?" Teri asked, beginning to sound a little nervous.

"Well, I wasn't sure what your skiing level was so I booked us a sledging session to have some fun. We'll work up to skiing another time." Sophie could tell Teri was a little nervous because she let her comment about 'next time' slide without a sarcastic comeback.

They headed to the kit-room and Teri appeared wearing pink ski salopettes a size too big, blue boots, a grey bobble hat and holding a green sledge. She looked quite grumpy about it initially and then noticed Sophie looking at her in her lilac outfit, purple boots and a grey sledge. She felt her ponytail swish side to side as she stomped towards Teri and a huge grin formed on her face. She was enjoying herself already and Teri seemed unable to take her eyes off her. Teri lost the grumpy look and stared open-mouthed at Sophie. "You look...well amazing".

Sophie looked surprised, she hadn't even particularly thought about how she looked. Being a semi-regular, the staff here must have known her well enough that they gave her a smart outfit rather than looking as mismatched as the other visitors. She hadn't paid much attention but looking at the rag-tag colour scheme Teri was sporting made her smile. The pink was so not Teri's colour but she looked so adorable that Sophie felt her heart practically melting out of her chest. This was a hacker who had attacked her, she shouldn't be getting her heart involved. In fact, shouldn't she still be angry and wanting to turn her in? Somehow, she couldn't see that person in the dorky, geeky, mismatched pile of cuteness in front of her that she just wanted to hold close.

Sophie started, "You look..." and then spoiled the moment by giggling.

Teri burst into a wry smile, "Ridiculous?" She finished Sophie's sentence unhelpfully.

"Adorable," corrected Sophie firmly, but still feeling rather amused.

They picked up their sledges and walked towards the slope, focussed on the touch of holding each other hand in hand. They might as well have been walking up a mud hill for all either of them noticed

74

the crunching snow under their warm boots. They arrived at the top and saw the steep slope for the first time. Teri started fidgeting a little, she looked nervous again. Sophie squeezed her hand through the warm mittens. "Let's go down together."

Teri raised an eyebrow muttering something about going down anytime Sophie liked but took the offered hand. Sophie was pleased that she trusted her. "Lay your sledge down, sit down with feet flat in front – that's right. I'll count to three and then we'll push off with our outer hands and lift our feet together – got it?"

Teri nodded with a frown. The promise of holding Sophie's hand seemed to have helped persuade her. They sat down and held back the sledges with their feet.

"One... Two ... AND THREE!" Sophie counted, ending on an excited shout and lifting her feet. Teri quickly did the same and the two women pushed forwards. For about five or ten metres they picked up speed and headed relatively straight. Teri was heading a little left but Sophie leaned in to follow her and they sped on for a few seconds, maintaining their hand connection. Unfortunately, Teri leaned a little right and Sophie couldn't correct in time, their sledges crashing a few metres down the slope and both women rolling out and landing, together in a heap on the still fluffy snow.

"Are you OK?" Sophie quickly asked, feeling concerned.

"I think I broke my face, Babe," quipped Teri.

"Babe? Babe is a pig," snorted Sophie putting her nose in the air with mock offence.

"Oink," griped Teri before adding, "my face does actually feel bruised."

Sophie rolled her eyes but leaned in with eyes sparkling – eager for any excuse to touch this woman.

Chapter Twelve

Their lips touched gently and Teri felt the cold from the snow melt away, chased by the heat from Sophie's lips. Time stood still as their hearts connected through their mouths. Their lips said what Teri couldn't admit out loud. After a second that felt a lot longer, they broke apart, both slightly dazed. She reopened her eyes, maintaining the connection even when their lips were forced to break. Recovering quicker than Teri, Sophie pulled away and jumped back on her sledge.

"Race you to the bottom!" Shouting, she launched off – picking up speed quickly. Teri was left behind, lying on her side with her ski mitten still touching her mouth in awe.

"Oi, no fair," she shouted in return, righting herself and pushing off as Sophie had shown her. She wasn't sure how to steer this thing but figured out that it was mostly about leaning. She arrived at the bottom, wondering how to stop, and dug her heels in, toppling off and rolling into the snow. As she stood up, Sophie came over and hugged her.

"I won!" Her voice was happy and trilling in excitement. Teri smiled, watching her standing, wiggling her hips and waving her arms, her blonde ponytail swishing behind her mesmerisingly. Teri was taken with how this woman seemed to make everything fun, or maybe everything was fun when she was with Sophie. Even dancing about like an excited little girl somehow looked stylish and cute when Sophie did it. Teri stood and hugged her before running off up the side of the slope, calling back over her shoulder. "Race you back to the bottom." Her competitive instinct had kicked in now she'd got the hang of it.

The women carried on for the remainder of their hour together, sometimes competing, sometimes sliding together but whatever they did, the smile never left Teri's face. Not only was she enjoying something that looked scary at first but she had a fantastic companion to hold hands with and they managed a few more warming kisses – purely to ward off the cold, obviously.

As they handed back their kit and left the snowdome, she turned to Sophie and looked her deep in the eyes. "Thank you so much. No matter what we do next, I want you to know that I've had the most wonderful day. I feel as if I've known you all my life, but I'm pretty sure I've been waiting all my life *for* you either way."

Sophie's eyes widened, whether in shock or agreement, Teri couldn't be sure, but she hoped it was harmony. "You know I would normally be sticking my fingers down my throat and going 'eurggghhhh' when people make comments like that but you make my heart go 'awwwwww' instead."

She put her arms around Teri and whispered in her ear, "You are the most wonderful, kind and caring woman."

Not for the first time, Teri felt her feelings slipping away from her and her heart expanding in that warm, fuzzy way where it feels like it's filling your chest and pumping warm mulled wine around your veins.

"Oh Sophie, you are the sweetest. I feel exactly the same. I've loved today and it's not over yet."

Both women smiled happily, enjoying the feeling.

She leaned back forward to continue the kiss they had started, enjoying the feeling of Sophie's cold skin from the snow and how warm their breath mingling made them both feel.

Once they separated and got back to Sophie's car, she asked. "So, are you ready for dinner yet?"

Teri nodded and Sophie continued, "Are you OK with seafood? No allergies I need to know about?"

Teri smiled excitedly. "Nope, solid as a horse, me! I love seafood." She added, quietly, "I don't get it very often though."

Sophie turned to her while starting the car. "Why not?"

Teri looked down, playing with the cuffs of her hoodie without thinking. "It's expensive. I don't eat out much." She could feel herself blushing at the admission.

"Luckily, it's my date so you get to enjoy it guilt-free!"

Sophie set off driving, the two of them chatting freely. The drive was about twenty minutes and Sophie hadn't told her where they were going. However, she didn't really care so long as she was with Sophie. They pulled onto the seafront at Southend, Teri's excitement grew. "Wow, this is lovely. Are we having fish and chips, I love them?"

"Not quite," Sophie replied as she found a space and pointed to the white rectangular building halfway up the cliff-face. It looked very art-deco, as though it had been around longer than both of the women combined. Entering, they were met by a smiling waiter, "Good evening ladies, table for two?"

"Yes please. I've booked, name of Keegan?"

"Ah yes, Ms Keegan, no problem. Come right this way." With that, he swept them off to the front of the restaurant, seating them side by side at a table, both of them facing the sea, the white foam crests of the slightly rippling waves barely visible, and brought over a candle to light in front of them. The view was lovely but all that Teri could think about was the warmth from the woman seated just close enough to her left.

He handed them the menus and explained the specials before walking away.

Teri stared at the menu, chewing her bottom lip. "What's up? Can't decide?" Sophie asked her.

"Well, I've never had several of these dishes and they all sound so nice! I do have a thing for mussels, if you think they would be good?" Secretly, she'd been scanning the prices and thinking she couldn't afford any of this. She'd picked the cheapest thing on the menu.

"I'm sure they'd be excellent," Sophie replied. The quizzical look in her eyes made Teri wonder if she had guessed the real reason for the order.

"OK then."

The waiter returned to take their orders, listening before nodding, taking their menus and disappearing in a flash. Teri looked out of the window and was lost in memory for a moment.

A voice broke her reverie, "Penny for them..."

Teri snapped back to the moment, "Sorry?"

"Penny for your thoughts?"

"Oh, I was just thinking about mussels. When I was little, before I left home. We used to go on holiday to Cornwall and I remember having them fresh off a boat with my dad. He loved doing, what he said was, blokey stuff like that. I didn't know how things would turn out back then but I remember some lovely holidays." She sighed, there were some good memories, even if they were clouded with what had happened since.

"You don't get on with your parents anymore then?"

"No, not since I came out. We don't speak at all; it must be for the last ten years. I saw them at Nan's funeral." Teri knew she sounded quite desolate as she remembered her Nan but they had been so close. She noticed Sophie reach out to hold her hand. "They never spoke to me once. Nan would have been so upset."

"You were close to your Nan then? She sounds like an amazing woman."

"Oh, she was *the best*." Teri's mood brightened. "After they threw me out, she looked after me. She'd have loved you, you know. She always used to tell me I needed to find a classy girl."

"Am I classy then?" Sophie looked surprised.

"You? Hell yeah! You outclass me any day. If I'm honest, I thought you were perhaps a bit too classy, maybe even a bit snobbish, at that first party. I'm sorry, knowing you now, I couldn't have been more wrong – you're not one bit snobbish. You are classy though."

"Ah, well I may have been a bit standoffish. If I'm really honest, I didn't want to be there. I only went to make a point to Bonnie and to get her to shut up about Hannah."

Teri felt her protective anger begin to rise at the mention of the woman who seemed to have dented Sophie's confidence by cheating. "Ah, the delightful Hannah. I know we lesbians are stereotypically all about happy families with exes but from what you've said about the way she hurt you, I hope I never meet her."

"Well Hannah is certainly all about the lesbian stereotypes, that's for sure. Anyway, on a nicer note, what do you think of the view?"

The sun was setting over the estuary and the tide was in, causing a calm sea to adopt splashes of colour from the remaining blue and the incoming orange, supplemented by reflections of a few neon signs off the prom alongside them. In short, Teri thought it was spectacular.

"Oh, it's so pretty." Teri turned her head before adding, "Although, so are you."

Sophie rolled her eyes but Teri suspected she felt secretly complimented anyway.

She was enjoying talking with Sophie so she actually felt sad when their food arrived so quickly. The taste of the mussels took her back to those long-lost family holidays and made her feel a little sad. She didn't realise she'd been daydreaming until she heard Sophie put her knife and fork down and touch her cheek gently. She was wiping up something wet and Teri realised a tear had escaped. "Oh, I'm sorry Sophie, I didn't mean to go off like that, I should be concentrating on you. I don't think about my family so much these days but it still hurts, you know."

"Don't worry Teri, I know and you don't need to hide it. I'm honoured that you feel relaxed enough with me." She leaned in a touch and kissed Teri on the cheek exactly where the tear had been before continuing, "I really enjoyed today, thank you."

"No, thank *you*. I know I was the one who asked you out but you blew me away with the sledging, all I did was wander around a park with you."

"Not at all, you showed me *you* and that is the most precious gift anyone can give. Come on, I mean you hacked me so I shouldn't like you at all but the more I see of you, the more I get to know you, the less I see that original person who video called me. Is it wrong to say that I'm kind of glad you did in a weird way – you know?"

Teri felt her cheeks bunch and her eyes crinkle as a genuine smile grew. "I know, I feel the same. I couldn't be more sorry for how we met but I'm so glad that we did. I really like you, Sophie."

"Me too, although," and Sophie smirked as she went on, "this was an elaborate way to get me out on a date, you know? You could have just asked me at the party originally!"

Teri snorted. "Me? I can't imagine you accepting grungy me!" The notion that this woman would have agreed to a date with plain old her was farfetched to say the least.

"But I did, didn't I – we're here today aren't we? Actually, I'm sure I'd have found you kinda cute. OK, maybe you didn't have cat ears but I like your style. Your hair, you have beautiful eyes and, and..." Sophie blushed. She didn't get to finish the sentence as Teri reached out and put her finger on Sophie's lips. It had crumbs of bread but Sophie hardly noticed as the soft pad practically scorched her lips on contact.

"Shhh, there's one of us that has beautiful eyes for certain." Teri breathed, captivated and wondering why her voice sounded so quiet and breathy.

"Well thank you, but you know that's rubbish, of course. You don't have to flatter me, I'm a big girl." Sophie looked off somehow and Teri was puzzled what she'd said. There was something deeper hiding behind this reaction but she wasn't always good at spotting things like this.

"Why is it rubbish?" she asked, genuinely puzzled at this reaction.

"Because I'm not beautiful or pretty, I'm just an average, boring, IT manager."

"You, average? You're kidding me, right?" Teri realised that Sophie was hiding as much insecurity as she was. Well, maybe not quite as much, but far more than she gave Sophie credit for. "Sophie, you are beautiful, I love your hair, I could get lost in your eyes and don't even let me think about your mouth – I'll be here for days. But none of that matters compared to who you are, you're this beautiful person inside who gives off kindness. I mean, look at how we met, yet you've been willing to give me a chance. I had no right to expect that, but you have. You're amazing."

Sophie blushed again, resting her face on her arm on the table, looking up at her. Teri spotted that the way she'd pushed her hair back, she could see her ear was going as pink as her face and it was possibly the cutest thing ever.

She reached out and stroked the silky curls, allowing them to run through her fingers and loving the sensation but, even more, loving the look in Sophie's azure eyes whose flecks of silver reflected the wavelets out on the estuary. She leaned slightly down and kissed

Sophie again. This wasn't a kiss of strong passion or arousal, somehow, this was a kiss of appreciation. Sophie's mouth opened in acceptance but Teri didn't add her tongue, she just wanted to show her what she felt as she sucked her lip gently.

Teri wasn't sure which one of them pulled away but they both seemed to be a little glassy eyed when they did. "I don't understand how you can't see what I do – you're amazing Sophie!"

"Well, I guess it's hard when people have shown you that you're not. Anyway, let's finish up, we've not looked at the dessert menu yet!"

Teri frowned, trying to make sense of this comment and the obvious deflection. *Was this in relation to her ex cheating, did she really not believe in herself that much?* She wasn't sure what else to say so she left it at, "Well, some people are idiots," and she went back to her mussels.

When their waiter came to clear away, bringing with him the most delicious-looking list of desserts, Teri's worry about the cost came back. Something must have shown on her face, because Sophie said, "You know this is my treat, don't you? This afternoon is my date so I'm paying. You bought breakfast and lunch; I'm buying dinner."

"That's not fair, we only had pastries for breakfast! We should go dutch on this!" Teri exclaimed.

"Look, I don't want to hear any of your alpha, chest beating, nonsense. This is my date, I'm paying, we're having dessert – it's the best part of a meal! You'll have the opportunity to impress me again next time, but you need to know that money isn't the way to do it. I don't care if you have a flashy credit card, what I care about is who you are. Now, dessert – this *is* a really important decision that might change whether you get another date, after all. Are you an ice cream or a cake girl?"

Teri laughed, "Well, given free choice, clearly both!"

Sophie laughed back and made googly, puppy dog eyes at her, "Awwww, my soulmate."

Teri rolled her eyes. She could get used to this woman, she really could.

They ordered dessert and a further important test came in the form of whether Teri was willing to share hers with Sophie. The pleading big, wide blue eyes and pouting bottom lip sealed the deal. *I'd give her anything,* was the first thought that popped into Teri's mind as she watched, hypnotised by Sophie looking rapturous swallowing the rich chocolate fudge cake she'd chosen. The ripple of her throat as she swallowed caused Teri to wonder whether they'd turned on a heater in the restaurant as she flushed.

Sophie did pay the bill as promised and silenced any objection with a single raised eyebrow. Getting back to the car, Teri was only too grateful to repay her with a much stronger kiss than last time. Gone was the gentle sentiment, replaced with more of a hunger and she kissed Sophie with far more abandon, one hand up in her hair, the other gently on her cheek. As they parted, Sophie's immaculate curls looked thoroughly ruffled but neither of them seemed to care.

Sophie pulled back a little before asking in a hopeful tone, "I've got to go away to Birmingham next week – the Cyber Security Trade Show. Are you going?"

Teri pulled away and looked up with a quizzical eyebrow and a quirked mouth. "Really? Isn't that the fox visiting the hunters?"

Sophie smiled and chuckled. "*Everyone* goes, don't they?"

"Yes, you're right but I figured it wasn't so important while I'm unemployed, or perhaps I should say 'freelance self-employed' and you know how expensive train tickets are!"

"Well, I get to take a poolcar. So, if you are free, I know someone who would appreciate the company. You never know, you might make some contacts to get that job you need?"

Teri couldn't believe her luck – a trip she couldn't afford and the company would make it amazing. That's if she could tear her eyes away from Sophie long enough to concentrate.

"Oh, that sounds amazing!!! Our first trip away together!" Teri's mind decided that it had enough of thinking about jobs and focussed, instead, on the relationship potential of the trip.

"Oh no, you're taking me away somewhere far more glamorous than the N.E.C. for that. I'm thinking Paris, Milan or Athens? Maybe New York..."

"Hey – let me get a job first. If I can break back into the corporate world then you and I are on for Paris. May take me a while before I can save up for New York, Gorgeous. Although did you really just invite me to an IT conference for our second date?"

Sophie blushed. "Oh, I suppose that does sound a bit sad when you put it like that!" She giggled, looking away from Teri and her heart melted further at the sight of an embarrassed Sophie.

Teri continued, "I don't know about sad, to me it sounds utterly perfect. Anything does, so long as you're there."

Reluctantly, Sophie had dropped her off at a train station so she could head home. Teri had insisted she shouldn't drive all the way back into London. Both of them tacitly acknowledged that nothing further was going to happen yet, it was too soon. That 'yet' hung in the air like a fog.

~#~

The next few days dragged on for Teri. She sat in her lounge on Monday morning, her day off from Marion's, moping around. It felt like an eternity since she'd seen Sophie on Saturday and a lifetime until next Thursday – their trip. It was probably OK for Sophie, sitting in her fancy office surrounded by interesting people, she was sat at home with only a cat for company. At which moment, Number One prowled out from behind the sofa and jumped onto her lap. She stroked his back absentmindedly and his tail flicked back and forth encouraging his human to pay him more attention.

She grabbed her phone off the side and, before she had a chance to question herself, sent a quick text over to Sophie. '*I MISS YOU LOADS*'. Why she'd put it in capitals, she wasn't entirely sure but it just felt right. She wanted to shout from the rooftops.

Despite the fact she knew Sophie was at work, a response pinged back almost instantly, 'Miss you too. Can't wait for Thursday.'

Teri decided she better go and have a shower now, maybe a cold one, before she got herself into trouble. She had a habit of taking things too far. Others said she had no filter, she preferred to say that she got caught up in the moment.

Once she'd cleaned herself and put the vacuum over, dislodging a disgruntled Number One from his spot on the rug in the process, she felt better. She wasn't obsessed with this woman; she was merely interested. Interested in a mature, adult, caring relationship kind of way. "Oh, who am I kidding Number One? I *am* utterly in deep with her. Her eyes, her hair, I think I love everything about her."

Number One stood, stared at her with his trademark disdain and flicked his tail in annoyance.

"Yes, I know, scratch that 'L' word. Far too soon. I'm not saying I *love* her, just that I love everything *about* her. That's different, right?"

It didn't escape Teri's notice that she was seeking sanity and grounding from her pet feline, not a great state of affairs, especially as he curled himself around, rolled his eyes and coughed up a grey furball at her feet.

"Ewww, mate gross! If that's your opinion of me getting a girlfriend then you can shove off. I like her, who knows, maybe you will too. She has cat ears after all. No competition though – she's mine."

A feline eye roll later, he put his head on his paws and went to sleep, showing her the contempt and indifference that a superior being such as him owed his lowly human servant. Teri sighed, imagining Sophie curled up sleeping and had to shake herself to her senses before she needed to head off for the second shower of the day. These flights of fantasy were getting too frequent.

That resolve only lasted five minutes before her attention wandered to her text from Sophie and she found her fingers swiping a reply, *'Love you, want you, miss you, need you.'* She quickly backtracked and removed the first couple of words, where had they come from – this was ridiculous!-No more than a few moments later her phone flashed again.

'Aww you soppy thing, I can't wait to see you too. P.S. Miss you MISS YOU Miss you. (Is that enough missing?)'

Teri's face almost cracked from the smile that was plastered over her face before she tapped out one final reply. *'68 hours until I see you, Miss you loads. I'll go and do some work.'*

She got up and went to her desk, opening her CV and taking a deep breath before doing something constructive ready for the show. Maybe she needed something impressive for all the recruiters she was going to knock off their feet. *Sophie's optimism is certainly doing a number on me… still I guess thinking positive won't do any harm!*

Chapter Thirteen

Thursday morning, bright and early, was cold but dry when Sophie pulled up outside the tube station in her company car and beeped the horn to get Teri's attention. She had to admit she'd pulled a few strings but she just wanted to be comfortable... she wasn't trying to impress Teri... no way.

Teri turned by the newsstand, where she'd been waiting, looking around for Sophie. As she turned, her mouth dropped. "Sophie! You said you were getting a pool car... What's this?"

"Well, I may have batted my eyelashes a little at Les from Facilities. They typically keep this beauty for the execs but I promised to take good care of her." Sophie replied, gesturing to the sleek, grey Ford Mach-E she was enjoying driving already.

Teri jumped in the passenger seat eagerly.

"Anyway, you talk about me. What's this with you?" Sophie smiled as she indicated and pulled out into traffic. "You never told me you looked this smoking hot in a trouser suit."

She was understating it a little for modesty but as Teri had turned earlier, it had bought Sophie time to admire the rear-view of a pair of very nicely tailored black trousers that showed off Teri's body and, particularly, a very curvy but firm-looking arse. Sophie quickly got onto the dual carriageway and engaged the cruise control thinking that it could help if she were going to be this distracted.

"I don't know what you mean?" Teri was being modest. Sophie thought she sounded genuine too. "It's a trade show, I need to look the part, right? Main goal here is to find a recruiter to represent me. Is it too much?"

Teri looked genuinely worried and Sophie found it so endearing. This woman could be so confident when she wanted but at other times she had a little girl innocence that melted Sophie's heart and made her want to put her arms around her.

"Gorgeous, the main goal right now is for me to get us there without combusting… but yes, you're absolutely right. It's only that I've never seen you in anything but jeans, T shirts and trainers! Don't tell me you brought heels too?"

"Don't go too far. I've got smart flats though, these Converse are only for travelling."

Oh shame, Teri in this suit with heels would utterly slay me. Innocently, she asked, "What shoe size are you?"

"What's wrong with these shoes? They are comfy and I really like them. I mean, I'm a 6 but why does it matter?"

"Oh – same as me – great!" Sophie exclaimed. When they got there, she'd grab her heels and see if her imagination was accurate. "Oh, by the way, open the glove box, you'll never guess what I found in it."

"Why?" Teri queried, opening it up and pulling out a glass bottle, "What's this?"

"Apparently, it's perfume they are giving away to sell the car. It's a cologne that smells of … well, car. Give it a try, I think it would suit you."

"You want me to smell of *car* and you made fun of my thing for cat ears?"

Sceptically and tentatively, Teri squirted the perfume on her wrist and immediately sneezed at the strong woody aroma that filled the car.

Sophie laughed but leaned over as Teri wafted her hand around. "Mmmm, that smells goooood". She couldn't help but look up at Teri's face thinking, *Wow, this woman doesn't just look smoking hot, she smells it too!*

The journey passed quickly in the luxury of the Mach-E and the quietness of the electric motor meant their conversation was continual and the quiet flirting wasn't drowned out by the car.

Arriving at the conference centre they parked and plugged the car in for the return journey. Teri pulled Sophie in for a hug that swiftly turned into a deep kiss as their eyes caught. "Oh, I've been waiting to do that all up the M1!"

"Me too. What do you think we should do first?" Sophie's eyes raked up and down Teri's figure in the smart suit.

"Well, we could find a room but I got all dressed up for a reason so I think we should head over to the conference and get some networking in before lunch."

"Spoilsport!" Sophie pouted but didn't say anything more – just nodded and grabbed her bag.

Teri bent and retrieved a smart pair of flats from her tote but before she could slip them on, Sophie had pulled her heels out and thrown them at her. "Oh go on – I bet you look smoking."

The brunette quirked an eyebrow and slanted her mouth up to show her displeasure. However, with an encouraging "Pleeeeasse?" and some big doe eyes from Sophie she slipped on the black heels, getting out of the car as she did so.

Sophie came around the car and gestured with her finger for Teri to twirl for her. Teri complied again and Sophie's eyes darkened, her mouth went dry and she felt her pulse speed up.

"Should I borrow them?" Teri asked innocently.

"If you think you're taking them off for any reason other than us getting a hotel room, you've got another think coming. You look *hot*. The badass bitch always does it for me."

Teri smirked. "I will remember that. Come on then, let's head through. If I fall on my butt then you're catching me."

They walked through the lobby and entered the show, grabbing their passes on the way. "What do you want to do first?" Teri asked, flicking through the show guide. "You're paying for this so I'll fit in with you." She paused before continuing a little quieter, "Unless you want to meet back here later?"

"Split up?" Sophie looked horrified and she saw Teri's demeanour relax. "Don't you dare – we're doing this together. I want to help you find a recruiter. Got to get you into a job where you won't be chatting up other IT managers now you're my girlfriend. Why would we separate?"

Teri stopped dead and looked over at Sophie. They hadn't used the "g" word yet. Sophie blushed, realising she had gone too far. She had gotten carried away.

"Girlfriend?" Teri queried.

"Oh sorry, I got carried away - you know what I mean... I'm running too fast... Sorry, Teri." Sophie babbled.

"I love the idea." Teri said, grinning. "If you will have me, I'd love to be your girlfriend!"

Sophie sighed and relaxed her whole posture, her shoulders dropping again and her eyes feeling a little moist at the emotion running through her. Teri reached over and gave her a peck on the lips. Standing in the entrance to the show surrounded by guys in suits and jeans they attracted a few looks but neither woman cared.

Sophie was puzzled what had prompted Teri's question. "Why would we split up, you sounded like you thought I might want to?"

The bashful, shy Teri returned and Sophie's heart leapt and skipped a few beats at how cute this woman was one minute, and how hot the next. "Oh, I was worried you might be ashamed of me – a hacker would spoil your corporate image?"

"Spoil it? In a place like this? Look around you. I could shout that I'm going out with a hacker to the rooftops here, it would make me a queen! Anyway, it's not like anyone is going to know that's what you do so let's go – I want to talk to a few people about that idea of yours to install protective kit on our network." Sophie continued hurriedly, feeling flustered from the kiss but grinning from ear to ear.

~#~

They found the vendor she wanted a few stands down. The stall was busy and Sophie stood flicking through a brochure waiting for a rep. Teri wandered off to poke about the demo equipment. Sophie looked over and saw her bending down looking in a cabinet at some wiring. She smiled, Teri was cute when she was excited and the view from this angle wasn't bad either.

"Can I help you, Miss?" A guy with a bushy moustache, that made him look like an old film villain, had sidled up and was talking to her. She pulled her eyes off Teri and looked at him. He hadn't noticed though – he was too busy looking down at her chest. She sighed. Oh great, one of *these* guys.

"Hi, I'm curious what you're offering please?"

"Oh sure Miss, so the IDS is an Intrusion Detection System. It protects your network from attacks."

Sophie could feel her blood pressure rising. This guy was so patronising and he barely kept his eyes on her face while he was talking.

"That's nice, thank you. I was more thinking around response times, prognostic or heuristic capabilities and what sort of options I have for alerting?"

"Oh, the technical stuff then! Wow, well let me talk you through, do you need to take notes for someone?"

Sophie felt, rather than heard, the heels coming up behind her before she felt a presence over her shoulder. A familiar voice spoke. "Ms Keegan needs to be polite as she's on company time. I, on the other hand, am freelance so I don't give a toss about calling out misogynistic arseholes. Take notes? Take notes? Who is she going to take notes for – she *is* the IT Manager."

She looked to her right and saw the fire flashing from Teri's eyes, if this guy were made of wood, he'd have combusted by now. Sophie looked back to him and saw him visibly swallow, nervously, while looking at Teri. She was so impressed with this woman leaping to her defence. She didn't need it but it felt so reassuring that she was there on her side.

"Oh I'm sorry Miss, no offence intended. Obviously I can see you're a professional."

"Correct, I am well aware what an IDS is and why I'd want one. We recently suffered a cyber incident." She heard the snigger come from behind her and felt the hand brushing against her own. She smiled, despite still staring down Mr A Hole, as she had termed him. "So, I've got board level remit to consider how to update our defences and wanted to determine how companies are meeting the state of the art but if you'd rather not deal with women then obviously I'm sure our account manager at Cisco would happily talk me through their thoughts."

"Sorry, sorry – no offence intended." He backpedalled so quickly Sophie thought he was going to fall off his metaphorical bike. "Our model 3 is certainly state of the art. We've successfully combined a blockchain logging system with a no-trust system of authentication to detect anomalies."

A non techie's eyes would have glazed over at this point but Sophie was sure they both recognised the latest marketing buzzwords of the IT industry.

"Oh really, that's interesting," came the voice from beside Sophie again. Sophie smiled – from the tone of it, Teri wasn't impressed and was still boiling from the salesman's treatment of her. "So, once you've transformed your paradigm and implemented a blockchain based ecommerce stream to online support your always on protection sphere how does your system actually *work*?"

The sarcasm was so cutting that Sophie almost felt embarrassed for the guy.

"How are we doing over here, Mark?" An older woman's voice broke in.

"These ladies were just asking about the Model 3, Mary. I think they had some questions for you."

"No problem, how can I help?

The voice belonged to an older woman with short, choppy, blonde hair wearing black jeans and a black t-shirt. She looked interested, open and knowledgeable. She was quite a contrast to Mark the A-Hole. He took the opportunity to scuttle away to ogle someone else.

"Mary Rassmussen, lead developer – how can I help you?"

Sophie smiled, Mary pinged her gaydar but primarily, she was pleased to be talking to someone who treated her with respect.

Teri got into an in-depth conversation with Mary about the security features of the product. Sophie followed most of it but even she got lost when Teri got into her stride. Teri and Mary were having a really deep conversation on different ways to attack a network. At the end they'd followed each other on LinkedIn and promised to stay in touch. Sophie had plenty of good information to take back to her

94

board and put a proposal together. She would talk to Teri later about it and ask her to help.

~#~

The couple stopped by the ladies at the end of the afternoon to freshen up before finding somewhere to enjoy dinner together. They'd decided that spending time with each other was far more important than the evening networking events the conference provided. "They'll be full of bros patting each other on the back and comparing the size of their metaphorical balls." Sophie had said, eliciting an "Ewwww" from Teri.

Regardless, Teri had a great afternoon at the show, thought Sophie. She was proud of the way the woman scrubbed up when she needed to. As Sophie hung back and observed, she'd seen her meet a couple of recruiters and had got some good leads for a job. Apart from the sleazeball on the stand, it had been a good day. Sophie got a warm feeling thinking about how protective her girlfriend had been towards her. She loved the idea of that protective side.

"Sophie, I'm sorry if I came on a bit strong with that salesman. I know you're capable of dealing with guys like that on your own but he annoyed me so much." They had taken it in turns to change their outfit in the cubicle and were standing by the mirror with Sophie touching up her blusher. Sophie wished she could have done more and properly curled her hair but she'd put on a black fitted dress. She could see in Teri's eyes what effect her dress was having. She may have distracted the other woman a little as she bent over to do up her heels. Teri had a smart button-down flannel shirt and black jeans, looking every inch the hot Lesbian Hacker she was. Sophie felt a warm flush looking at Teri, those jeans made her butt look hot!

"Aww, don't worry. I know you think I'm capable, but it's so sweet that you are willing to protect me from the big bad guys." Sophie sniggered, with a mischievous glint to her eye.

"Don't say it…" Teri warned, mock frowning but ending up in an adorable pout.

"Oh come on… you might have hacked us but you're as far from a bad guy as you can get. You're a soft-hearted cutie under that exterior." She leaned in, kissing Teri with all the passion she could muster. "I like your protective side, it makes me feel safe and …" Sophie paused.

"And…?" Teri prompted

"Well … and …" Could she say this? *Should* she say this, she wondered?

"Sophie Keegan… you're blushing…" Teri teased with a grin.

"Well… and… cared for…" Sophie finished in a small voice.

Teri just burst into a big grin. "Oh, you are catwoman, you are cared for a lot." Sophie's heart soared. She hadn't been rejected or dismissed by Teri – not that she really thought her girlfriend would ever do that, but it was a big thing for her to trust enough to declare feelings. They weren't declaring love for each other but they were certainly acknowledging their feelings.

"What is it with you and cats?"

"Mmm-hmm," Teri said, nodding. "I can't help thinking about you that first night I saw you. Your lacy ears, tight skirt and strapless top certainly got my attention! Far cuter than Number One."

"I suppose I asked for that – well you're still my cute fluffybunny, even if you have claws when you need to stand up for me… which I like. Plus, who is Number One?"

Teri cringed, seriously 'cute fluffybunny'? She could see the mirth on Sophie's face as she teased her though. "He's my cat. You'd get on well with him."

Sophie laughed softly, "Sounds lovely."

96

Nevertheless, something did still worry Sophie. Her face dropped and she looked pensive for a second. Teri clearly wondered what was going on in her head and reached out to touch her face softly, cupping her cheek. "Teri", Sophie started in a little voice.

"Yes?" prompted Teri, stroking her face gently. Sophie leaned into her touch.

"Don't hurt me..." Sophie whispered and looked down and away from Teri, feeling silly.

"Sophie, look at me. I can't promise I'll never do anything wrong. You already know I'm a klutz and I'm not good at fancy words. But I promise you, I'll never set out to hurt you. I want you to feel like a princess with me. You're way too good for a goof like me!"

Sophie looked up with fire burning in her eyes and an indignant tone taking over her previously quiet voice. "Not good enough? Don't you dare run yourself down. You are clever, talented and one of the most caring and protective people I know. You're also damn sexy!" She grabbed her girlfriend's arse to prove it. "I was just being silly, but I do have feelings for you and it's a bit scary."

"Me too. Those feelings must be catching! Let's not worry about the scary bits now, how about dinner?"

~#~

They found a good-looking French restaurant, not too far from the show, and ordered. Teri started with a glass of house red wine, since Sophie was driving back. They chatted while waiting for the starters and time seemed to fly by. Teri seemed, somehow, edgy. Sophie couldn't put her finger on it until she realised that the glass of wine had disappeared as their starters arrived.

Teri looked equally surprised and turned to the waitress, ordering another.

Sophie became a little concerned. She didn't want to upset Teri, but something was off and surely she didn't normally drink this quickly?

"Teri, I don't want to nag, but," she paused to work out how to ask this, before continuing, "is there something wrong? You seem a little nervous?"

"Nervous? No - why?" Teri replied, looking surprised.

"Oh, well you seem a bit preoccupied and jittery. I wasn't sure if you normally drink this much?"

"It's not that much... I'm enjoying the company. I'm sorry."

"You don't need to be sorry. I was worried I'd done something wrong?"

"Oh my god. No, you've certainly not done anything wrong. I am loving being with you."

"So why are you nervous?" Sophie asked as calmly and encouragingly as she could, taking hold of Teri's hand across the table. "If we're moving too fast, we can sort that. If it's work, perhaps I can help?"

Teri looked startled, as though recognising she was upsetting Sophie. "I'm sorry Sophie. I told you I don't deserve you. You are so amazing and beautiful. What am I?" She took another gulp of wine. "I'm just a dykey hacker. I'm not a beautiful woman like you. The truth is I'm..."

Sophie interrupted her, "You are not *just* anything. You are an amazing woman who inspires me, looks after me and is fearless. Don't you dare run yourself down like that. I won't hear it, and wine won't help. It breaks my heart to see how you see yourself because it couldn't be further from what I see when I look at you. I see the beauty, I see the intelligence and I see the spark. I wish I was half the woman you are!"

98

A tear fell down Teri's cheek. She obviously wasn't used to hearing these kinds of words and she clearly didn't believe them.

"Teri, you aren't a one-night stand to me, I've already decided that. You're someone I want in my life and I wouldn't do that if you weren't an amazing person. What can I do to help you see you the way I do?"

Sophie loved Teri's fierce protective side that she'd seen this morning but since she'd first met her in the bar, she'd noticed flashes of this insecurity. If that was driving her to the bottle then Sophie wanted to help. She wasn't sure how but she was sure that drinking wasn't the answer.

"Now, what were you going to tell me you are, apart from gorgeous, funny, adorable and mine, of course?"

Teri looked undecided as her eyes darted up and down from Sophie to the table, as though deciding what to say. "You know what – it was nothing..." she eventually replied. However, her voice didn't sound convincing and Sophie was sure that whatever it was, it was a lot more than nothing. She'd get Teri to share it sooner or later but for now, she didn't want to push the woman, she wanted to help her.

The mains arrived and the previous atmosphere started to return – the two chatting freely. Sophie learnt about the job Teri used to do, her friends and she felt the love in the other woman's voice when she talked about Number One. She couldn't wait to meet him. There weren't many males she was keen on stroking but he sounded such a cutey. In turn, she told her about her friends. Teri obviously already knew about her jobs.

"I also have such a ragtag family but they are amazing really." started Sophie before stopping abruptly, "Oh sorry, that's a bit insensitive."

"No, you don't need to apologise. It's good to know that there *are* actually good ones out there!"

"Well, my mum's a nurse and my dad just retired. He was in IT. I guess that's where I got my passion for it from."

"And did you get your caring from your Mum?"

"Maybe. I certainly got my tolerance for bullshit from her."

"How did they take you coming out?" Teri asked

"Oh, I think they already knew. I've never been interested in boys. They are really accepting. I had a trans friend, Claire, once. They got on so well with her so I don't think it was just because I'm their daughter."

Teri smiled and her eyes seemed to light up as she nodded, Sophie assumed she was pleased to hear about good parents.

As they ate dessert and the conversation turned flirtier and more suggestive, Sophie noticed Teri becoming shakier again and she took bigger gulps of the wine. There was clearly something wrong. She started to wonder if it was the idea of taking their relationship to the next level that somehow scared her. In truth, her feelings that were developing scared her too and she wondered if they were going too fast.

She affected her best casual tone, "You know, it feels that we're moving pretty fast. We don't have to go any further than we're comfortable with. If I'm honest, it's a little bit scary."

Teri looked startled and then a brief flash of, what Sophie thought might be, relief, followed it. She suspected her guess was right, something about them being together more intimately was scaring this woman but she couldn't work out what.

"Well, of course not, whatever you want." Teri replied with a pretence of confident swagger. However, now being more in tune, Sophie saw that the smile didn't quite reach her eyes. Whatever was bothering her was deep seated. While thinking of Teri in her suit and heels from earlier made Sophie squirm in her seat as her core tingled,

100

equally this flash of vulnerability melted her heart and made her want to scoop her up and hold her tight.

She was fine to wait for more – Teri was worth it.

~#~

Sophie did continue to worry as they met up for some after work drinks on the Friday evening after they got back from their trip. The fact that they'd only just parted seemed irrelevant. They made it to an evening date in a lively sports bar near her office. Teri looked gorgeously casual, as ever, in her uniform of black jeans and Sophie was sure she'd been knocking back double vodka and Coke all night. She stayed quiet and observed Teri carefully, keeping her own drinking in check. She was beginning to suspect the girl had an issue with alcohol, not so much an addiction but more a matter of using it as a crutch when she was feeling down. What she actually wanted to know was what was getting her girlfriend down. She didn't seem upset but even though they'd only known each other a short while she could tell that something was upsetting her. She was a little over enthusiastic at some things but would suddenly pull away when things became too heated between them. She wondered if it was something she'd done or, worse, something about her.

They'd bumped into Anna and Maisie, Teri's friends, at the bar and Sophie had enjoyed getting to know more about her girlfriend from those who'd known her longer. Of course, they had to tell them a modified version of how they'd met. Sophie found it interesting to hear how Maisie talked about the professional Teri she used to know – a quite different sounding woman from the one in front of her now. Although from the stories they told about her at work, she had the same charisma and passion.

"I bet she didn't wear jeans and converse back then?" Sophie joked while Maisie teased Teri about when they first met ten years ago. Anna and Maisie exchanged a brief fleeting look. Sophie almost missed it.

"Oh, she certainly did, she's never been one to like suits, our Teri," said Anna with a smile.

Sophie grinned, looking at Teri, "Oh I don't know, I've seen her in a suit and I think she totally rocks it."

Anna and Maisie narrowed their eyes and looked confused.

"Oh come on, it's not that unusual that I dress up for a proper event! I just don't go to events that often." Teri joked.

Teri pulled Sophie to one side, asking "Do you play snooker?"

"No? Why?" She looked back at her with a puzzled expression.

"The table is free – come on, I'll show you. Maybe Maisie and Anna will join us, you can't usually keep them away!"

Teri and Maisie explained the basics about holding the cue, which balls to hit and that you get two shots for potting a ball but lose your turn if you miss anything. Sophie found their good-natured arguing over the rules and exact nature of play to be quite endearing. Teri set up the table for them then demonstrated how to hold the cue and to take a shot, gesturing Sophie to kick-off with a wink, "Ladies first".

Sophie leaned down and narrowed her eyes to take in the shot she needed to make, rocking the cue back and forth as they had shown her. She hit it but the cue ball glanced off a red and rebounded to the other side of the table. "Oops."

"Don't worry, you'll get the hang of it in a bit." Maisie smiled. She took her turn and potted a yellow. She missed on her next shot and stood back to watch Sophie. Sophie tried to line it up and realised this was going to be a bit of a challenge. She felt Teri touch her arm, "May I?" She adjusted Sophie's fingers a little.

She took the shot and potted a red. Jumping up, she grinned, "YESSS," she hissed.

102

"Well done, you get two free shots." Maise smiled at her and Sophie noticed she seemed to be flicking glances at Teri. These two clearly had some friendship communication going on and she suspected it was about her.

Sophie lined up her next shot and felt Teri come up behind to guide her again. Unfortunately, she missed. She stepped back and let Maisie take her turn. This time she missed with an "Oh man!" The ball ended up in the middle of the table. Sophie tried to reach but found it was much further out than last time. She leaned out at full stretch and was about to take a shot when a cough distracted her.

"Maisie, you utter cow!" Teri rolled her eyes and pointed at the other woman.

"I don't know what you mean, Teri." Maisie replied, looking like butter wouldn't melt as Teri wagged her finger.

"Oh yeah, like you'd miss that shot. You know that I know perfectly well what you're up to. Pack in your usual tricks and play."

Sophie looked confused, looking between the two women. Teri was still pointing at her friend. "She just had a bad shot. What's wrong?"

Teri's face turned, instantly softening "Oh Sophie, you're so adorable. You didn't see she was aiming to ogle your arse?"

Sophie turned to look at Maisie who was blushing and looking away from them. She started to laugh. She could see why Teri was friends with these women but she still loved that she was protective enough over her to call her friends out.

"No idea what you mean..." She smiled innocently and leaned out at full stretch across the table to address her shot. She heard a groan behind her coming from her girlfriend and she wiggled her behind a little, just to get comfortable on the table and hummed in concentration. She took her shot, missing, obviously, but turning back around with a big grin on her face... "Is that how I should do it?"

Maisie and Anna were looking at her wide eyed, Maisie still blushing a deep red. Sophie winked at her. That was enough for Teri's self-control to snap. She launched herself at Sophie and pushed them both against the snooker table. One hand tussled through Sophie's thick hair while the other landed at her waist, pulling her into Teri's warm and welcoming torso. Teri kissed possessively but both women pressed their lips together and Sophie returned the message of possession tenfold, deepening the kiss as though nobody else around mattered. From Sophie's perspective, the noise in the bar disappeared and all she could feel was Teri's surprisingly soft lips and firm, strong, hands holding her tight. She loved it.

Chapter Fourteen

Teri's annoyance towards Maisie quickly became a surge of passion and she felt a certain area tingle and pulse as soon as she touched Sophie. She just had to hold her, the butt wiggling had broken her self-control, not that she had much of that around Sophie anyway. As she opened her eyes a little, she remained in the blonde's personal space and blocked her view of anything except Teri. All the party were so engrossed in their own drama they didn't notice that their noise had attracted attention and a few women were looking over.

Maisie seemed to notice one in particular, a tallish, trim, butch-looking woman with short brown hair, wearing denim shorts and flannel. If she was aiming for Ms Stereotypical Lesbian of the year then she was in pole position. Teri saw Maisie wandering over to her. Maybe Maise thought discretion was a good plan. At that same moment, Sophie let out a low "Mmmmhhh" and Teri's attention snapped back to the tongue caressing her lower lip and the firm curves her right hand was grasping selfishly.

Teri continued kissing Sophie intensely and possessively against the hard sided pool table for a few minutes until her blood pressure dropped, or at least was replaced by a familiar pull between her legs and a warmth she couldn't deny. She pulled away. "I'm sorry Soph, that was a bit rude of me – I got so mad at Maisie... and..." She felt so guilty she'd let her jealousy run away with her.

Sophie put her finger to her lips, silencing her. "You don't need to apologise; I like feeling wanted – makes a change. Plus, you can kiss me like that ANY time." Her grin spread and Teri couldn't help but feel uplifted by it, she started to smile too.

She pulled her torso away so she could see Sophie clearly. She couldn't believe how amazing this woman was and looked. Her blonde hair shone in the bar's harsh spotlights and although she felt quite light headed from the alcohol, she felt even more floating on air when she looked into the deep pools of blue in Sophie's eyes. She knew it was a cliche but she did feel lost in them.

"What?" Sophie sounded slightly dazed.

"You're beautiful, you know... I just wanted to look at you, I can't keep my hands off you." Her hands squeezed at the warm, caressable hips lovingly. Sophie's hands mirrored them, gripping equally as hard and her grin grew as hungry as Teri felt, but a shimmer of worry showed across Sophie's face as she broke away and looked around the bar.

"I'm not, you're drunk and we're in a public place, Gorgeous."

"You ARE beautiful." Teri emphasised, disbelieving how modest this woman could be. "I may be drunk but I'm still right. Plus, I don't care – I'd show you right here on this pool table."

She could feel Sophie's hungry eyes burning into her face. While she normally looked away from eye contact, she just couldn't break away from Sophie – there was a magnetic force stopping her from breaking contact.

Sophie looked away while blushing a gorgeous pink. Despite the fact that Teri had her bent up against a pool table, somehow it was the compliment that had embarrassed her.

A noise behind her caused Teri to break away. She turned and realised the noise was Anna and Maisie standing behind her and mimicking them. Quite why Maisie had Anna bent over backwards and was loudly making kissing noises Teri wasn't sure. What she was sure of was that she needed new friends. She rolled her eyes, "Oh thank you... very funny. I didn't come up and interrupt you with that girl earlier, did I Maisie? The stereotype on legs? Plus, I've not forgiven you yet for ogling Sophie!"

Maisie looked straight past her and nodded to Sophie, "Nice arse love..."

106

"Thanks babe," Sophie replied cheekily, grinning at Teri before she pulled her close and planted another firm kiss on her lips. Teri's mind blanked.

Sophie pulled back, taking Teri's hand in her own and squeezing it gently. "Who was this utter babe you both noticed then, and should I be worried?"

"Some tall brunette with a thing for tartan and her claws into Maisie already," Teri replied. She almost thought she saw Sophie shiver but it was so brief that she couldn't be sure.

"Are you ready to call it a night?" Teri asked Sophie quietly.

Sophie looked at her watch and caught a yawn.

"Oh my, I never realised how time flies when you've got someone else's tongue giving you a dental check up," she joked, stifling a yawn.

"Let me take you home, you do look tired," Teri continued, still quietly. She squeezed Sophie's hand and got lost again in the bluest eyes she'd ever seen. She genuinely wanted to care for this woman.

~#~

The Uber had already dropped a loud, swaying Maisie and Anna at one of their flats. Teri didn't care which, her attention entirely focussed on Sophie and the way her honeyed golden hair seemed somehow brighter in the streetlights as they pulled up outside her house. She wasn't sure if the other woman was asleep yet, she was certainly quiet. "Cupcake," she whispered to the sweet woman. She gently pushed back the blonde hair and brushed the back of her index finger against the smooth, porcelain, cutely freckled skin. Teri felt her heart clench, this woman really was special and she was beginning to feel something inside of her that she'd not experienced in a very long time, a very very long time.

Sophie opened her eyes, looking up at Teri blearily. Teri's breath caught and she leaned in, touching their lips. The warm welcoming feeling of a sleepy Sophie captured her attention and caused a shiver to shoot down her spine. Sophie reached up and caressed Teri's face lightly, kissing her back warmly as they took turns sucking, nibbling and caressing each other's lower lips. Teri was busily exploring how full and lush a bottom lip could be, while wondering if Sophie's top lip was feeling left out, when a cough sounded from in front of them. Both women looked up, dazed and broke apart.

"Sorry darlin's and while I totally appreciate the show, I do have other fares to pickup. Sorry to rush you." The driver smiled, doing a passable impression of a kindly guy, although the glint in his eye clearly said that he was very torn between the idea of watching two women making out in the back of his cab or earning money.

"Oops – sorry mate. Come on sleepyhead, let's get you inside." Teri opened the door and helped Sophie out. She wondered why she wasn't more tired but if it meant that she could ensure Sophie was home safe then it was fine. She held her hand, opening the door with her other.

"It's OK Gorgeous, I'm not going to run off – you can give me my hand back you know," Sophie joked.

"Not taking that risk, I'm the clingy type, haven't you gathered that yet?"

Sophie looked at her, her face serious but kind. "You know, no – I hadn't. You have this hard outer shell you put up but the Teri I really feel is the woman I see through the cracks. The one who shares her vulnerability."

Teri blushed, what was she on about – she wasn't vulnerable – was she? The blonde rolled her eyes, "Don't you dare put up a flash of bravado to cover it up... you are sexy as you are, Teri. You don't have to act. I want to be with the real you. Not the hot, confident hacker image you use as a defence."

108

Teri looked down at the sleepy blonde resting her head on her shoulder and felt scared, seen and sweet, all at once. What was this woman doing to her – all her usual layers of defence and bravado meant nothing, it felt like Sophie could see into her head. That thought alone scared the shit out of Teri who was used to people seeing what she wanted them to. In fact, for years, her life and her identity relied on it. A small part of her brain couldn't help but think that maybe it was time for a change, perhaps it was time to let someone in, let someone see her for the woman she really was. The trouble was, in order to do that, they'd have to see far more than just her sensitive side. She was far from a virgin but when it came to relationships, she was a novice. That level of exposure, of someone knowing you, was scary. At the same time, it felt right whenever she looked at Sophie. She wanted today but she also wanted tomorrow with her.

"Sophie, are you busy tomorrow?" Teri blurted out, her brain escaping through her mouth.

Sophie looked up, slight surprise in a quirked eyebrow. "No, why?"

"Can we spend the day together?"

"Sure, I'd like that." Sophie smiled up at her and Teri felt instantly warm. She could feel the tension in her cheeks from the grin fixed on her face. Oh, she so wanted to work her kisses all the way down this sexy body but some small part of her held back and it was killing the rest of her, her throbbing core was slick with desire for Sophie, she could feel it under these jeans and she pressed her thighs together without thinking. Something must have shown on her face because Sophie looked quizzically at her. She brushed that same index finger across Sophie's smooth, warm, silky cheek revelling in the downy feel of tiny blonde hairs as she neared her jawline. Teri was much darker and the contrast between the two of them in that simple, insignificant detail brought her close to a tear. She choked it back, focussing on the other woman.

"Sophie," she started quietly, barely whispering, "what do you do to me? How do you do it?"

Sophie's eyes held a questioning look before replying, "I've no idea, but you do exactly the same to me," before spoiling the moment with a huge yawn.

Teri smiled then laughed. "We need to get you to bed, you look knackered," before adding quickly, "but in the sexiest way possible obviously!"

It was Sophie's turn to laugh and she led them both into the kitchen where she offered Teri a nightcap. Sophie's words from earlier about drinking came to mind and Teri declined. "We said we'd take it slow and get to know each other, I'm not going to push that. I won't get any more drunk and I'll get the last train home to feed my cat but I needed to know you were home safe."

"You're so sweet," the yawning Sophie said before Teri felt herself being led to the sofa for a cuddle anyway. It might be the hardest cuddle she'd ever had to stop turning into more, but she was determined.

A few moments later she looked down and smiled. Sophie's eyes were closed. Her heart felt a pang at how beautiful she looked sleeping there. She leaned down and touched a soft kiss to her forehead before lying her down and calling an Uber to the station.

Chapter Fifteen

Sophie had dozed off in Teri's arms on the sofa last night and she woke up on Saturday morning snuggled under a blanket, with a pillow under her head and a bottle of water by her side. The sun was starting to stream through the lounge window, suggesting that she was in for a nice day today. Sadly, there was no sign of Teri, but Sophie appreciated the effort she'd gone to to look after her.

She's even found my phone charger and made sure my phone is here. What a woman – I'm so lucky! A flash of uncertainty followed this thought, it was less than a fortnight since Teri had hacked her but the woman she had feelings for felt like a totally different person.

Her phone was flashing, so Sophie swiped and read the message. *'Hey, sorry I am not there to wake up with you. Hope you are feeling well – don't forget to drink plenty of water. I loved last night and if you're still up for hanging out today then message me when you're up – no rush. love T x'*

Sophie felt warm inside reading the text. This woman came across as devil-may-care, but she was really a warm, cute, fuzzy cuddlebug – and Sophie loved it. In fact, she knew what that fuzzy feeling meant and she knew the hurt that came to your heart when it went wrong. She buried her face in a cushion and enjoyed that it smelled of Teri – that slightly fresh but a little woody scent made her smile. She thought about her girlfriend, the passion and chemistry were there and the way they talked felt like they'd been together for years. Thinking of the positives reminded her of the reasons she shouldn't trust her but she was finding it harder to hold back.

Sexually, things were going slow for some reason, it wasn't through lack of chemistry but something was making Teri hold back when she got too close. Sophie couldn't put her finger on it but she was sure that it wasn't a lack of attraction so there had to be something else. She hoped she could believe that it wasn't alcohol.

It's not like Sophie was the sleep-on-a-first-date type, but something certainly seemed to be holding Teri back. She inconveniently remembered Hannah, her ex, with her short dark hair, her thing for looking like a walking lesbian stereotype. Her strong arms, her clever fingers – oh the things her fingers used to do. *'Stop it! Don't go there!'* her brain screamed. This was a memory lane that didn't have happy endings. While Hannah's hands were heavenly, her mind was sadly from another place. The way she'd made Sophie feel had left her broken and questioning herself.

She struggled to trust and questioned why women were interested in her—even Teri. However, she felt reassured that they were taking it slow, the warmth of reassurance helping to counteract the cold of doubt Hannah had left behind in her.

Maybe Teri would get bored of her before long but she could enjoy it while it lasted. However, everything Teri said and the way she acted gave Sophie confidence she was genuine, if only she'd share why she was so nervous. When she was with her, she felt that she could achieve anything and the old doubts that Hannah had created melted away. She felt like the most beautiful woman on the planet when those deep brown soulful eyes locked on her. In those moments nobody else existed. Her conscious mind reminded her that Hannah had created that doubt and urged her to believe Teri.

Sophie could lie here all morning going backwards and forwards or she could get up and put an end to the inner brain snarking. She should grab something to eat and clean herself up. She lifted the blanket and sniffed, oh wow, yes, she needed a shower. As much as the pillow was heaven, the blanket told a different story. No amount of self-confidence could convince her that she smelt pleasant, good job Teri wasn't here and she hoped that she smelt better when they were cuddling last night.

112

She threw off the blanket, sat up and grabbed the water Teri had thoughtfully left for her, silently thanking the other woman. She hoped that she'd looked after herself going home, she'd been drinking far more. Sophie grabbed the phone and replied to the text. *'Thanks for the water and tucking me in. Sorry I fell asleep on you. Had a great night but need a shower. How are you this AM? Can't wait to see you. What do you want to do later? xxx'*

By the time she'd gathered her pillow, her phone beeped and she smiled while swiping it. *'I'm fine, I'm used to late nights in my job ;) Wish I could join you now but I'll settle for later. Do you play tennis? I'll borrow a racquet and come out to you if you do?'*

Sophie's smile turned into a beam and she spun around like a giddy teenager. She threw off the worries about Teri's drinking – she was obviously feeling well enough. Spinning around, she caught a whiff of her own aroma but even that wasn't enough to dampen her spirits. She ran upstairs, thinking ahead to what she needed for tennis, just remembering to reply with confirmation that she used to play at school.

~#~

Following a swift shower and some breakfast, Sophie parked up at Admirals Park, a little outside the town centre but close enough to the station for Teri. She grabbed her racquet from the boot and looked around for Teri. The park wasn't too large and she could see the kid's playground on one side and the few tennis courts on the other. The other woman was coming in on the train from her flat in Vauxhall, much further away, but she suspected that she'd chosen Chelmsford as a way to be closer for Sophie. Either way, she was glad. By the time she'd showered and eaten, she was running late. She finally caught sight of Teri standing by the courts and gave her a happy wave. As she got closer, she could see Teri's face and smiled at the look of wide-eyed astonishment followed by what could only be described as a starved, hungry expression. She smirked as she saw Teri's eyes raking up and down her body and knew that her choice of

113

outfit was clearly doing something for the other woman. She'd guessed that Teri's dark side would appreciate her innocently pleated white tennis skirt, fitted white vest and hair up in a ponytail. She'd already seen the way the other woman's eyes were drawn to her hair and suspected that the whole "innocent blonde" vibe would do something fun.

Sophie sniggered to herself until her smug brain actually registered the look of the woman in front of her. If Sophie was projecting innocence then Teri was doing the exact opposite, she looked like sin personified. Skin-tight, very short black shorts and a tight black vest top showed off her powerful shoulders. Impressive, shapely legs led down to black and neon pink Nike trainers. Sophie licked her lips and as she caught sight of the tasty curve of those beautiful arse cheeks in such small shorts her mind drifted to the idea of grabbing hold of them.

As they met, Sophie leaned in and kissed Teri firmly on the lips, initially quite tamely but deciding at the last minute to tempt the other woman with a lick on her lower lip. Teri's eyes seemed dazed and she looked down again as soon as they pulled apart, hungrily taking in Sophie's body and legs and putting her arm around her, as the other held her racquet.

"Hi Teri, how are you feeling?"

"I'm fine, bit of fresh air will do me good and, boy, are you a breath of fresh air!"

Sophie chuckled. She intertwined her arm with Teri's around the other woman's back and grabbed a cheeky handful of the firm curve those shorts were showing off.

"Hmmm, same here, trust me. Which court are we on? Hang on, why did you suggest tennis?"

"Well, I don't play many sports and I was kind of hoping you'd look hot... seems I was right," she replied, as Sophie felt a hand

114

dropping a little and the tips of one finger started to slip under the hem of her skirt.

"Well how about a little bet on the outcome? Winner gets to choose dinner."

"How much have you played? I'm up for a challenge though," Teri queried suspiciously.

"That's for me to know and you to find out, don't you think?" teased a smirking Sophie, glad to have some of her own mysteries for once. In truth she'd never made any school teams or anything and there was a good chance Teri would beat her hands down but she wasn't going to admit that!

Teri headed off to the other end of the court, her backside swaying hypnotically as she walked captivating Sophie's attention. She figured that she would have to get even with the mind games.

Waiting until Teri turned back to her, Sophie 'accidentally' dropped the ball she was holding, trapped it with her racquet and spun around before, slowly and deliberately, bending at her waist rather than her knees. She knew perfectly well the view Teri would get of her toned thighs, and as she bent further, her own shapely bum teasing beneath the crisp white, innocent pleats. She was betting that it would get a reaction. She took her time gripping her fingers around the ball, 'accidentally' almost knocking it away so it rolled a little and she had to reach out, taking one step towards it and bending even further over. As she straightened and turned back, with a flourish guaranteed to flare and spin her skirt, she could see the fire in Teri's eyes. This game was going to be fun!

She stifled a smirk and concentrated on her serve. She reached high in the air going up onto her tiptoes and stretching out every athletic sinew in her arms and legs. This drew up her white top flashing some toned skin peeking over the waistband of her skirt. She swung her racquet overhead, circling down towards the ball. Just as she knew that her skirt was short, she also knew she'd worn a slightly less supportive bra. While her breasts were not the largest, they were large enough to visibly bounce. She accompanied the swing with a "Ngggg" groan for good measure – probably a little over the top but, while Sophie had always loathed amateur dramatics at school, being cast as a tree or something, there was a time and a place for letting your inner spirit free. The ball connected and flew well over the net.

Sure enough, Teri was captivated by the wrong type of bounce happening at Sophie's end and missed the ball flying over the net until it was too late. Her racquet was still hanging, forgotten, by her side but even from a court's length, Sophie could see the white-knuckle grip Teri was holding it with. She allowed herself a smile, imagining what those strong fingers were probably capable of.

Teri swung for the ball but didn't reach it in time. Sophie saw a flash of something cross her eyes, from this distance she couldn't tell if it was anger or mischief, or maybe a smidgen of both – what a delicious combination.

Throwing the ball back, Teri shouted, "15 love. Don't get too confident!"

Sophie took her next serve thinking about Teri as she did so, *'A mischievous, sexy woman with some strong emotions to work out who was... woahhh what's this?'*

Teri had reached up and was pulling her top over her head in a slow exaggerated gesture. Sophie hardly realised she was licking her lips as the sports fabric drew up like the unveiling of a bronze statue of some mythical Greek goddess. As it got higher, Sophie noticed Teri had a black Nike sports bra underneath and she was now admiring the flat stomach sandwiched between a trim, fit set of breasts and the matching, short, very short Nike booty shorts. It took a few seconds for her to consciously register that Teri was playing her at her own game and she felt her core begin a flow of molten lava which, if unchecked, was sure to ruin her white tennis kit. She pushed her thighs together relishing the momentary friction it created on her

116

swollen clit and lips. Too late, she saw that Teri had already returned her serve and the tennis ball sailed straight past her legs.

"Fifteen all," a smug but cheerful voice shouted from across the net. The fire in Teri's eyes was not only still there but growing. Her thoughts wandered downwards and she wondered if her girlfriend had black underwear and how ruined they'd be by the end of this match. She wasn't normally one for such sexual fantasies, she always found bodily fluids a little icky and the descriptions some of her friends craved in their romantic fiction typically made her feel a little queasy. What was it Bonnie had read out to her the other day in her favourite new book release? Something about glistening pink folds and strings of arousal? At the time she'd cringed but somehow now she couldn't help stealing that same description to mentally picture what was happening beneath those tantalisingly shapely shorts at the other end of the court and licking her lips without thinking.

Preparing to serve again she played another 'accidental' ball drop, trapping it under her foot. With an exaggerated wide-eyed look, a finger to her puckered mouth and a high pitched "oops", she bent at the hips again to pick up the fallen ball, wiggling her behind as she did so. "Clumsy me," she shouted over the net. As she straightened and readied for her second serve she could see that Teri was still looking intently at her and giggled.

"You're such a flirt, you know that, Sophie!"

"Me? Whatever can you mean?" giving her best approximation of a wide eyed, innocent look. She probably looked ridiculous but the smile on Teri's face was totally worth it. She took her second serve, not quite exaggerating it as much as before. She had to admit she'd reached up a bit far and could feel her arm hurting as a result. She could see the doctor's note, "Signed off work for a tennis injury caused by excessive flirting". The ball flew at speed over the net but this time Teri was ready. Sophie had misjudged a little and it was heading towards the line. "*Out*," Teri shouted, as it bounced away.

"Hey, no way. That was clearly in!" Sophie's voice rose and she frowned. Flirting was all very well but losing a point was taking it too far. That had been in, she knew it.

"Come over here and I'll show you where it bounced." Teri replied sweetly. Sophie marched off down the court, swinging her racquet strongly. She wasn't messing about. She pointed to the spot it had bounced and put her hands on her hips assertively. "It was *there*. Definitely *in*." She tapped her foot impatiently and waited for the other woman to argue.

"I know... I just wanted to get you down here so I could do this." With that, Teri leaned forward and pressed her warm, smooth, hungry lips to Sophie's, whose body responded instantly. Her anger evaporated into a superheated vapour of attraction.

Chapter Sixteen

Teri's hands came around Sophie's waist and pulled the heavenly body she couldn't get enough of in towards her, deepening the kiss and relishing the way the lips welcomed her openly. Teri felt Sophie's hands moving up from her hips and gripping her hair in a vicelike pull that was sending pleasurable twinges straight from her scalp right to her warmed and swollen core. There was no doubt she was turned on.

She was also willing to bet that beneath that innocent, pleated, white skirt, Sophie was anything but innocent if she felt for her heat. One hand dropped from Sophie's waist to clasp her bum cheek strongly. She couldn't get enough of the feel of Sophie and ruched the fabric up more with a quick flick of her fingers. She explored the delicious curves of her girlfriend's bum.

Sophie returned the squeeze. The thin sports fabric masked none of the forceful grip Sophie was applying, and Teri could feel her short nails scratching and digging into her cheeks.

Their kiss continued with tongues stroking. Teri was so turned on by now her passion was in full force, her blood pressure was rising and she wanted to show Sophie all that she felt for her. They broke away, looking dazed and out of breath. Teri ran her fingers through her short hair, gathering her thoughts and noticed Sophie was fingering her ponytail absentmindedly. It seemed neither woman had their wits about them after such a distracting kiss. Teri quickly glanced around the park but fortunately, although it was a sunny day, it was still early in the morning and nobody was around to see them apart from a lone dogwalker on the other side of the field.

"About the tennis…" Teri started.

"What tennis?" was the reply, followed by a giggle.

"Do you fancy conceding?" Teri kept her face looking serious.

Fire flashed in Sophie's eyes, "Why, you little…" she stopped as Teri grinned. Winding Sophie up was fun. Her passion was one of the things Teri found most attractive.

"Oh, is that a no then?" Teri continued, grinning.

"You bet your sweet arse it's a no. We've got tennis to play."

She admired Sophie's back and the determined set of her shoulders, almost moaning as the other woman strode off aggressively to the other end of the court. Her insides clenched a little as she could almost still feel Sophie's fingernails digging in a few moments ago.

The next few points flew by in a haze of flying balls and hard flirting. Their tactics remained dirty with both women using every advantage in their feminine arsenal to distract the other. At one point, Teri returned a serve with a remark about how great the tennis racquet would be for imprinting on someone's arse while they bent over the net.

Sophie narrowly managed to return it, albeit looking flushed. She returned the flirting by stroking her own ass and slapping it as she hitched up the right side of her skirt. This did cause Teri to miss her shot and she glared at the clearly delighted Sophie who drew level.

The next point was hotly contested and resulted in a hot and sweaty Sophie narrowly missing a drop shot at the net. "*Aaarrgghh,*" she groaned, rolling her eyes.

"Well played, Cupcake!"

The downside of the flirting is it flared a fear in Teri. The mutual attraction was obvious but the kind of feeling that was bubbling up in her heart was, quite frankly, terrifying. Sex within a fling was her norm but getting to 'relationship' and 'commitment' level was going to mean opening up.

120

She shook her head to shed the distraction but stopped when she heard music playing from the back of the court – it was her ringtone.

She apologised to Sophie but ran quickly back to her backpack and grabbed her old Samsung Galaxy 4 from it, answering with a swipe of her thumb. She didn't have a chance to see who was calling but so few people actually bothered to call her that chances are it was important.

A male voice at the end of the phone greeted her, "Hi Teri, this is Jonathan from Ace Recruitment, we met at the show last week and I've been looking for a position as we discussed. I think I've found somebody who's really keen to take on an expert with your talents and they'd like to meet you on Tuesday. Do you think you could manage an interview at that short notice?"

"Hey Jonathan, sure I can manage it, I'm pretty sure I'm free on Tuesday," replied Teri rolling her eyes – who was she kidding, she was free everyday so long as Marion would let her, "tell me a bit more about this job please. What are they looking for?"

"Well, they're a medium-sized company out in Essex. I think you said you were OK to travel out of zone two, didn't you? They are after someone with in-house security experience as well as a hint of offensive potential. From your CV it sounded like you've done a bit of both. They are quite a young company but they are growing fast. It sounds like they've got quite a fun culture. I think you'd fit really well."

"That all sounds fascinating, Jonathan. What sort of terms are they offering?" Teri was no idealist, if it sounded too good to be true, it probably was – she bet they were after someone to work for free!

"Well, they said they are offering three-fifty a day now but from the way they were talking I got the impression they'll go higher for the right candidate and might consider taking the right person on permanently. The question is do you think you could convince them on Tuesday that you are that right candidate?"

Teri could see why this guy was a good recruiter. Plus, it was a challenge and like tennis – Teri didn't like to lose a challenge.

"Sure, let's do it! Can you email me all the details please?"

"All the details are already in your inbox. The interview is at nine AM on Tuesday in Basildon. All the address details for Kaneo PLC are in the email, as well as who you should ask for on arrival."

They disconnected the call and Teri stared down in disbelief at her phone screen. This seemed too good to be true, but she was so excited, she might have a job at last! All she had to do was convince them she was good enough. She turned back to Sophie who was standing at the net looking at her nervously. She'd obviously heard enough of the conversation to have realised it was important and the way that she was staring expectantly at Teri showed she wanted to be filled in. Teri looked at her and grinned widely, "I've been offered an interview for a job next week," she shouted, somewhat higher pitched than her normal tone, showing her excitement.

"That's amazing news! You so deserve it, I'm so excited for you. What can I do to help?"

Teri was taken aback – Sophie's first question was how could she help? She felt the warmth in her heart grow and expand as she looked lovingly at the blonde. They'd gone from flirting and teasing to wanting to support each other's lives in the blink of an eye and it was getting harder for Teri to imagine doing these sorts of things without her.

"Oh thanks – I'd love your help but remember they've not offered it to me yet. Also, I've not passed an interview in years!"

"Positive thinking! Well, luckily for you, I can help with the interview. I do recruitment as part of my job so why don't we do some practice work together?"

122

Teri was shocked – Sophie was going to help her!

"Oh wow – you'd do that for me, aren't you busy at work?"

"Of course I'll help you silly. Why wouldn't I, isn't that what girlfriends do for each other?"

"Well, yes, I s'pose so. I guess I'm not really used to people being willing to help," She shrugged and her voice tailed off a little.

Sophie looked at her with a frown. "Everyone needs help at some point and anyway, I *want* to help you."

Teri saw Sophie start to lean in and she mirrored the motion in a Pavlovian response – when one of them initiated a kiss, it was inevitable that the other would respond. It was this inevitability that struck Teri right in the heart again and she deepened the kiss, her hesitant tongue stroking Sophie's but becoming stronger as the endorphins of the kiss overrode any hesitancy she felt. The blood rushed through her ears on its way to her mouth as she rode the high of the moment, all consumed in this wonderful feeling of getting closer and closer to the woman she loved.

She paused, and pulled away momentarily, a wide-eyed look of shock on her face. Love? Was that really what she'd thought? Even if it was too early for that, there was no doubt in her mind or heart that she wanted more of this woman and not only physically. She wanted to support her and keep her safe, just as much as Sophie said she wanted to do for her.

Teri resumed the kiss with extra intensity, saying the words with her actions and caressing the back of Sophie's neck lovingly. She wasn't ready to say it out loud – maybe she never would be, what if Sophie didn't feel the same way?

Then all those coherent thoughts and feelings dropped away as Sophie's arm pulled her closer, her legs opened to allow Teri to get that little bit nearer and her tongue pressed against Teri's, the two sliding over each other as though that were the act of lovemaking that the two women were surely heading towards. The sensation of the kiss was more than just endorphins, pleasure and arousal – it was coming home, it was belonging and it felt like love to Teri.

As both women broke for air, staring wide eyed and dazed at each other, Teri had only two thoughts strong enough to break through the fog that her brain had changed to.

Firstly, she loved this woman.

Secondly, she had to tell her... everything.

Chapter Seventeen

Sophie had, in excitement, conceded their tennis game and taken her for dinner to celebrate. Teri was glad she'd brought a change of clothes for travelling and threw in a few essentials on the off chance she needed to stay out because Teri never made it home that night. Luckily, she'd left Number One plenty of food, he was a good cat but she did feel bad for him. Nothing happened between Sophie and her beyond some heavy making out in front of a movie. They had cuddled together and Sophie had shyly asked if she'd come and sleep in her bed. Teri felt bad for not taking it further but there was something to tell her before she could do that. They'd spooned as they fell asleep though and it just felt natural.

After breakfast, Sophie had cleared her table and pulled out her work laptop, "OK, how rusty are you with interviews?"

"Very!" answered Teri, "I've not had a good one for years!"

"Well, in that case, let's go through a practice interview and see what you've got! Go out and come back in again."

Teri got up and went out into the hall. She knocked on the dining room door, feeling stupid and burst in shouting "GIMMAAJOB!" Sophie looked less than impressed. She said nothing but pointed to the hall. Teri bit her lip, *OMG, stern Sophie is hot as hell.* She was getting turned on just looking at the frowning woman pointing out of the room. She turned and left again, with a goofy smile on her face.

As she had her back turned, she didn't see Sophie's stern expression break but she did hear a little chuckle behind her as she closed the door again.

Right – game face, let's do this, she psyched herself up.

Knock, Knock, she firmly rapped the door. "Come in," she heard from the other side and opened it, to face Sophie who was sitting looking down at her laptop and waving her to a chair across the dining table. She sat as indicated and waited. Despite knowing this was a practice, she couldn't help the feeling of nerves and knew she was going to make a fool of herself in front of her girlfriend.

"Good morning, Ms Simlake. I'm Sophie Keegan. Welcome to L.E.S. Bank, as you know we're looking for someone with experience. I won't beat around the bush, why do you think you are that person?"

"Well Ms Keegan," Teri began earnestly, even if she was going to make a fool of herself, she'd go down trying, "I believe I'm the best fit because I've been researching your company goals and aspirations. I know you want to expand into the retail sector and I realise that's going to put you at more risk of public data attacks. My background is one of protecting such companies. I was the senior security analyst for a large retail group and had similar challenges with customer's data. We had lots of attacks against the network but I instituted a program of automatic scanning so that we knew about any holes in the firewall before they were visible to attackers. My team alerted the server ops team to those within an hour."

"Did you never get compromised then, that's a bold claim if so?"

"Oh, I'm not saying never – that would be terribly naive of me. Yes, there were minor compromises but only one incident of customer data being breached during my time there."

Sophie leaned forward, as though sensing a story, narrowing her eyes. "So, what happened on that one?"

Teri closed her eyes, this wasn't a memory she wanted to relive, much less admit to Sophie about. It wasn't her proudest hour.

She thought back to the incident that had cost her the job. She'd been happy there; she'd built up a great team and she felt a pang in her heart for the feeling of failure that it evoked. She could see that final day in her mind, the alarm being raised by a colleague and the steadily building dread through the day as it became clearer the

126

damage that had been done. Then the recriminations started. The accusations had flown, particularly at her. Not only had she dared to defend herself but she had the audacity to be a young woman and so automatically incompetent. She remembered the tense meeting with the management where her boss had stayed quietly to the side and not stood up for her but she remembered the quiet whispers in the office even more.

Back in the room with Sophie, she continued, "That was an incident my team anticipated and warned the application owners about, a number of times. We did not receive feedback from them so I escalated the response to their manager personally. That resulted in some conflict." She paused and took a deep breath. "That was when I decided to pursue other opportunities."

"So you got sacked because there was a hack?"

Teri felt her anger flash through her eyes, "No, I got sacked because the damn application team refused to do anything about something I told them several times about." She hissed through gritted teeth, closing her eyes. Talking about this hurt. It wasn't her finest hour professionally but she knew in her heart she'd done what she could. She couldn't look Sophie in the eye and fiddled with some loose cotton on the seat cushion.

"Look at me." Her girlfriend commanded firmly, "You look like you failed."

"I did,"

"Firstly, no you didn't. Secondly, and more importantly for an interview, I don't care if you did – you need to own it. Tell me how you owned the problem, tell me how you managed the fallout but most importantly, look me in the eye when you're doing it and show me you aren't ashamed."

Teri's voice was small and barely carried across the table, "But what if I am?"

"Then you're wrong... and here's why." Sophie leapt up and grabbed Teri's face with both hands, planting a huge, passionate kiss on her lips. She pulled away a little and stared intensely into Teri's eyes. All Teri could see was determination. "You're wrong and the reason I know you're wrong is because I am proud of you. I'm proud of you and I believe in you. Most of all, Teri Simlake, it's because I fucking love you."

If Teri's jaw hadn't been supported by Sophie's strong and elegant fingers it would have dropped open. As it was her eyes went wide. "You – love me?" She almost stuttered in shock.

"Of course I love you, you total numpty. I know I've struggled to tell you, but I've felt it for some time. You are amazing but why am I the only person in this room who can see it?" Sophie was sounding almost irritated with her, but she was still holding her face with, what it appeared, was love so Teri knew it was frustration more than irritation. "I want you to know, for this interview, that I totally believe in you. Now keep your head up and give me a proper answer."

Teri's face felt empty and abandoned as soon as Sophie released her grip and moved back to her seat. How her hands had scorched Teri's skin was amazing. Without thinking, she reached a finger up and touched her cheek where it had been branded by Sophie's intensity.

"You love – ME?" She repeated. "I love you too Sophie – you are amazing!"

With which, she leapt up and straddled Sophie's, now seated, legs, grabbed her face and kissed her back with total abandon. This time lasted rather longer with Teri nibbling and pulling on Sophie's lower lip in a way that caused groans to come from the other woman. Eventually, they separated for breath and Teri pulled back, shaking her head to get some sense into it.

"Now, about this interview." Sophie murmured, clearly a little dazed.

128

Teri returned to her seat and tried again to answer the question. This time, she told the story holding Sophie's gaze and trying to infuse a fraction of the confidence that the other woman's declaration had made her feel.

"You're hired!" Sophie laughed after she finished her explanation. "That's *so* much better." After a giggle she continued, "If a good interview answer gets a kiss like that as a reward, I wonder what my reward will be when I help you get the job?!" Her mouth curved up on one side, she dropped her head a little and looked up at Teri through her lashes showing she wasn't only thinking about dinner as a reward.

Teri really had no answer to that. They both grinned at each other.

"Let's go out for some fresh air and then we can come back after lunch and try again," said Sophie, standing to grab her coat.

"The kiss or the interview?" Teri smirked, wondering what deity she'd pleased to get this much luck.

~#~

"When you said fresh air, this wasn't what I thought you'd have in mind!" Teri laughed, holding up a golf club.

"No idea what you mean – you suggested tennis yesterday, I suggested golf! Perfectly reasonable." She lined up to the ball for a putt.

"I know Cupcake, totally reasonable, except my tennis court didn't have a windmill, a helicopter and a dinosaur on the playing surface," Teri laughed, feeling light-hearted. Crazy golf on the Southend seafront, a few miles from Sophie's house, had lifted her spirits. So far, she was losing by five shots. She'd been distracted and lost a ball earlier when Sophie bent over in front of her. She was damned if she'd give up without a fight, even if the view of that gorgeous cleavage was worth a few shots.

They both managed that hole in three, Teri concentrating fiercely each time she took a shot. As she took the final putt, she looked up as the ball plopped satisfyingly into the hole, and saw a laughing Sophie looking at her. "What?" She frowned. "What's so funny?"

"Oh, the look of concentration on your face – it's adorable. The way you stick your tongue out, makes me want to come over there and bite it."

Teri felt a flush of heat run through her body at the thought but she just raised one eyebrow and quirked up her mouth trying to look unimpressed. "I'm gonna spank you on the next hole."

"Hmmm - chance would be a fine thing." Sophie flirtatiously returned and sashayed off to the next hole, wiggling her shapely and squeezable behind as she went.

Teri's eyebrow tried to rise more but ran out of forehead so she merely blinked a couple of times and followed Sophie mutely. She hadn't been expecting *that*. Sophie was really getting into her stride, and it seemed her little kitten did have a wild side. Well, that could be fun!

Sophie continued her performance streak for the next couple of holes, past a volcano and a swamp until Teri pulled it back at the helicopter. From there they went onto the crashed plane where Sophie lost it a bit and ended up two shots down.

"See Cupcake, you can beat me with dinosaurs but when it comes to aircraft, who's the daddy?" Teri boasted proudly. Sophie just shook her head.

They finished the penultimate hole when Teri exclaimed, "You know? This will be the first activity we've done that we actually finished!"

Sophie looked puzzled. "What do you mean?"

130

"We got distracted at pool, we got called away for tennis – this is the final hole. Quick, let's finish it so we can break the curse! Plus, we're level and I'm gonna win!"

"Course you are sweetie," Sophie shook her head, smiling and lined up her shot. It rolled through the tunnel and Teri looked around the mountain range with fake snow covering it to see the ball shoot straight past the hole, missing it by two inches and rolling away down the slope to finish a mocking three feet further away.

"Bad luck, Cupcake." Teri grinned, her competitive side rearing its head. She admired how cute Sophie looked when she pouted her lips and frowned. She wanted to kiss and squeeze her but first, she had to win!

Sophie headed off while Teri waited at the tee. She, slightly carelessly, putted the ball back to the hole but it overshot and bounced away. Teri could see, from the set of her shoulders, that Sophie was annoyed. After she turned to face her, Teri had to laugh at the adorable way Sophie scrunched her face up. After one more careful shot, Sophie's ball was in and she turned expectantly to Teri. She could win with a hole in one. It didn't matter that it was only the Southend Crazy Golf Centre, nor that she'd never got a hole-in-one in her life, nor that she knew she was taking this too seriously. None of that mattered, this was the US Open, the Belfry, St Andrews all rolled into one.

Teri gripped the club and spread her legs, swaying to sink into the shot. She didn't care how ridiculous she looked taking a mini mountain range this seriously, her pride was at stake. She pictured what Sophie's ball had done and how she saw it skirt the side of the hole before falling away. The scientist in her said, go left, keep it gentle. So she aimed to the left-hand side of the tunnel, sending the ball off on a slightly gentler putt than her girlfriend. She narrowed her focus on that tiny, dimpled, white sphere and followed its progress into the tunnel.

She ran eagerly to the other side, ignoring Sophie laughing at her. The ball emerged from the tunnel heading perfectly for the hole and she pushed it along with her mind, willing it on, pushing it with her hopes and dreams. This ball represented her life – wildly swinging from one location to another seemingly randomly. It represented her and the hole was Sophie – the two irresistibly drawn to each other and connected by some gravitational pull called fate. The ball rolled on and on – still on course for the hole and time slowed. As it got closer and closer, Teri's eyes opened wider and wider, her mouth falling open. It teetered on the edge of the hole for a millisecond as though questioning her force of will. Finally, it conceded, falling and plopping into the hole with a resounding rattle. Teri squealed, "I won!!! Hole in One!!!"

She was ecstatic and even forgot about Sophie for a second before looking up at the grinning woman who seemed to be enjoying her excitement by proxy as her kind eyes indulged Teri's celebrations.

"I can't believe that, well done Gorgeous." Sophie said, beaming.

"Thanks sweetheart, I thought I'd lost it. What's next? Lunch?"

"Yes, every time I come to the seaside, I have to enjoy fish and chips on the seafront with ice cream. It's been a tradition since I was little, we always used to come down here in the summer for an evening." Sophie's voice tailed off as she smiled dreamily, seemingly lost in the memory.

"Fish and Chips it is then, come on. Which is your favourite?'

"No contest, the one at the end. Come on, I'll show you. It has a beautiful art deco original feel and the chips are always fresh. Also, it's cheap!" Sophie beamed.

"Cheap is good... lead on sweetheart skinflint."

132

Sophie laughed and pulled them both along the seafront. Teri smiled, leaving her hand in Sophie's as they walked along together, each turning to smile at the other as they walked briskly along.

~#~

Teri was sitting huddled up with Sophie on the sea wall, watching waves breaking on the stones ahead of them and listening to the cries of gulls overhead and excited children behind. The families were running, parent-free, along the pedestrianised prom. She had to admit that her girlfriend was right, the chip shop was cute and the food was delicious. She was feeling satisfied and loved - a great combination in her book - possibly only topped by a roaring log fire, a sheepskin rug, a glass of Pinot Grigio with her girlfriend naked cuddling up to her. Where that fantasy appeared from she wasn't sure, but she smiled, planning to remember it later.

"Penny for your thoughts?" Sophie broke in gently, "What's got you looking so faraway?"

Teri turned her face away from the breaking waves and refocussed on Sophie's beautiful, smiling face. "Oh," she felt her face flushing with heat and looking down, "well, I was thinking – about you – and me – together."

Sophie leaned in and grinned... "Mmmmm? Together?" wiggling her eyebrows suggestively.

Teri looked up, "Oi, I was being all caring and emotional... don't make it smutty."

"Sorry, but wasn't it even a *bit* smutty?"

"Well ..."

"I knew it... come on... tell me. What were we doing?"

"Well – you were on your back, lying on a rug, in front of an open fire. We both had a chilled glass of wine to keep us sweet."

133

"Mmmmm wine... clearly that's the best thing about this fantasy..." Sophie smirked, "Pinot Grigio I hope? What were we wearing for this rug-based wine drinking session?"

"Well, we were naked, of course." Teri looked up to see Sophie's pupils dilating and her smile growing. "I mean, all the best wine says to drink naked, didn't you know?"

"Hmmm, I've obviously missed that part of the label. Just so as you know, I don't have a real log fire, but I do have a rug in my lounge and you're welcome to bring around a bottle of your naked wine anytime."

Teri felt the warmth spread through her body at the thought, originating somewhere below the forgotten tray of chips sitting on her lap. As ever, something else swiftly followed the heat, something colder and she shivered, holding her hands close without thinking.

Her face must have betrayed the turn of her thoughts because Sophie looked worried. "Gorgeous, where did your mind go? Is there something I should know? You looked so happy then I saw you freeze. What scared you? Was it something I said?"

She was quick to jump in with a defence, as ever, "Oh no, it's not important and nothing you said."

Sophie reached out and touched her face gently, stroking her cheek. Teri leaned into it wanting to close her eyes and believe in the fantasy of nothing being wrong.

"It's not nothing. Something is wrong, even I can see that. If it's not me, and I really hope it's not..."

Teri interrupted her quickly and urgently, "It's not you, I promise Sophie, you're amazing and sexy and I love you."

"Awww, I love you too, and don't get me started on how sexy you are." She continued stroking Teri's cheek and Teri never wanted her to stop but she had a feeling this was heading somewhere serious.

134

"So, if it's not me, then has something happened to you? What's wrong that's bothering you?"

Teri felt the silence becoming endless. In her mind, it was like Sophie was moving away onto the other side of the Grand Canyon. She was increasingly fearful that it would become just as deep a chasm between them. "Is it... please don't hate me for saying this... Is it alcohol?"

Teri straightened and stared at Sophie? She thought she was an alcoholic? Really? "Alcohol?" She replied, stunned.

"Well, I'm struggling, Teri. You seem to freeze when we have alcohol involved and pull away from me."

"No, I wish it was just alcohol." Teri replied sadly.

"OK, now you got me worried, Teri. I love you, if there's a problem, let me help you." Sophie started to sound genuinely scared and Teri could feel the pressure of anxiety building in her stomach. Maybe she should walk away, Sophie needed someone who could be the true, loving, girlfriend she deserved.

Teri felt a tear escape her eye and she swiftly rubbed it away. "Maybe I'm not worth your love." She choked a little and her voice broke.

"Don't you dare." Sophie's voice was angry and Teri looked up sharply. "Teri, don't you dare think that rubbish. Of course you deserve my love, I don't know what I have done to deserve you, but you're amazing and sexy and I totally want you under me on a rug. Now, OUT with it. What's this problem?"

She took a deep breath and looked Sophie in the eyes. She committed the loving look that she saw deep in the blue of them to memory – she feared she'd never see it again.

"I'm trans."

Teri saw Sophie straighten and a look of shock came over her face.

Teri closed her eyes and saw the first time she'd had this conversation with someone she cared about as much as Sophie and the look of shock she'd seen there.

One summer's day in the middle of term, they were sitting in the park, during her sixth form years. She'd turned and looked at Rachel, her long, black hair freshly straightened. Her lip-gloss glinted in the sun and her natural makeup looked sheer elegance to the young Teri. Rachel was her girlfriend at school, they'd been going out for three years by that point. She knew things were serious and with university looming, their time was limited, they'd told each other that they loved one another. She felt that warm something inside. She had to tell Rachel about being trans. She blurted it out, probably not terribly elegantly, but this was hard – she'd never told anyone this important to her before. Rachel's deep green eyes went initially wide, then narrowed into a hostile slitted stare. The look was tragic, heart-breaking and ripped Teri to shreds. "How could you do this to me, you ... freak!" she had shouted before she stood up and stormed off. Teri had been left sitting in the park alone and feeling stunned and dirty. First her parents were hostile and now Rachel was no more. How could someone she loved tell her she was a freak, just for being herself? If this was what love did to you then she would never risk this feeling again, it wasn't worth it.

Except, with Sophie, she couldn't shake the feeling that it *was* worth it, but she equally knew that the heartbreak would be far greater. She had subtly tried to test the water with Sophie as time had gone on and she knew she was accepting but that's different than wanting a relationship with someone. This wasn't something you could really pave the way for.

The look of shock burnt into her brain, she pulled away to save Sophie the embarrassment. Sophie grabbed her hand. "Oh no, don't you pull away. Come back here and explain that statement." Her

136

voice was strict but not unkind. Teri could see her eyes scanning over Teri's face looking for answers. "Do you want to transition? Is that it?"

Now it was Teri's turn to look shocked. "Want to??? I did already, when I was eighteen."

Sophie's eyes widened to the size of dinner plates and then she frowned, clearly processing.

"Oh god, oops. I guess I don't know too many trans people and I assumed I'd have been able to tell... so you must have been... oh." She put her hands over her face and, in a muffled voice continued, "Sorry, I'm rambling."

Teri smiled, this woman was adorable when she was embarrassed. She took Sophie's hand away from her face and held it. "You asked why I get scared of intimacy, that's it. I'm afraid you will be disappointed in me."

Sophie gripped back at the hand they were holding together. "Teri, I'm not going to pretend it's not a surprise, nor will I pretend I know what it means. But I am absolutely sure I am not and will not be disappointed in you." She loosened her grip on Teri's hand and, using both arms pulled her in for a big warm hug.

The tray of chips hit the floor and the squawk of gulls wheeling overhead intensified with the promise of free food. Neither woman noticed for a few moments until they released each other.

Sophie smiled shyly. "So, about the trans thing, my head is sort of whirling so will you be offended if I ask you questions to better understand? I know I want to ask you stuff because I'm not sure what it means for me, or us, yet, but I want to just get my head in gear first before I blurt out stuff and offend you. Maybe we could talk more tomorrow once I figure out what to ask?"

"Of course, it is what it is and if you can't deal with it, I understand. I mean, I'll be torn apart, but I'll do everything I can because I meant it when I said I love you. You won't offend me and you can ask me anything, I trust you. I know you won't do anything to hurt me."

"I'm not going anywhere, Teri. I love you too much for who you are. Don't misunderstand me, it doesn't make any major difference to how I see us as a couple. It's simply another aspect of you I want to get to know. Although the sooner we can get you a new job the better. I don't want to risk you meeting any better-looking women you hack and running off with them."

"Not gonna happen..."

Teri leaned in and kissed Sophie tenderly. Sophie was having none of it and her tongue licked Teri's lips and pushed its way inside to stroke firmly against hers. Sophie's hands came up from where they had been resting after the hug and held the back of Teri's head, pressing their lips firmer together. This kiss was more than just affection for Teri, it was hope, it was the future and she wished on her lucky stars that this time it wouldn't mean heartbreak.

Chapter Eighteen

Sophie had spent the rest of Sunday afternoon with her girlfriend practising for her interview so she hadn't had time to herself until the evening, when Teri had gone home, to think about Teri's revelation and what it meant to her. She didn't want the other woman to think she was put off but she wanted to make sure she wasn't missing something. Ultimately, she didn't think it made any difference – but she knew some people would say it should. She loved Teri, that much was certain and while her sexy body was part of that, it wasn't the biggest part. What drew her in was the brunette's personality and who she was.

There was one part (well, potentially one very specific body part) that bothered her but she wasn't sure how to raise it without upsetting Teri, who she could see was deeply sensitive despite her protestations of not being easily offended.

~#~

She'd been daydreaming at work when, mid Monday afternoon, Dave walked in. He was munching a chocolate bar and flopped himself down heavily in her visitor chair. She looked up at the grinning bearded guy and knew she was in for some grief – he had a happy look on his face so this probably meant some banter for her. She put her pen down slowly and leaned back in her chair.

"Afternoon Dave, not seen you today so far. What's up? You upset the server guys enough for today so thought you'd come and torment me?"

Dave grinned and carried on munching. "Yep – your little friend gave them enough work to do that they were in all weekend. I took great pleasure in taking them in coffee when I arrived this morning. Makes a change from them ripping the piss out of us cyber folks – I get to point out their mistakes for a change! Anyway, talking of little friends, how's it going?"

"Good thanks – what are you getting at?"

"Well, you and that Teri seemed to get on *very* well bearing in mind what she'd done to us and you've been in a good mood since. I've not seen you that happy for a loooong time. You can tell me it's none of my business all you like, but I was happy to see it. Don't tell anyone else in the office that I said something nice or you'll spoil my reputation as the office grinch though."

Sophie made a zipping motion with her fingers across her mouth. "My lips are sealed. We'll continue to pretend you lack a heart, Dave. Only you and I will know the truth." She paused, looking at him, "and thanks... I appreciate that concern."

"Anyway, now I've finished being nice, what's she like, have you dated yet? Did you U-Haul already?"

"Woooahhhh – what do you know about U-Hauling? What have you been reading? Are you a closet lesbian or something? You'll have to lose the beard if you want in – it's a requirement to join the club."

"Oh damn – you ruined my plans for the weekend then. I'm not losing the beard... You'd be surprised what I hear from people. My fifth cousin from Dundee, Mary, is gay. She's always posting stuff on Facebook. Anyway, stop deflecting, did you?"

"Well, yes, we did meet up. She's really nice Dave. We got on so well but no, we've not U-Hauled!"

"Ah well, there's time. Sounds like she's well known locally too."

"Well known? By who?"

"Well I was out on Saturday night down at that new bar I told you about, and met this girl. I was sure she was batting for you guys from how she looked but then she started coming onto me."

Sophie rolled her eyes. There were times when Dave had his head stuck in the last century but she knew he meant well. "So how did Teri come into that?"

"Oh yes, well I said where I worked and she asked about your new girlfriend. Seems news travels fast!"

"That's very odd, nobody knows about us apart from a couple of Teri's friends. She knew *me*? That's very odd, what did you say her name was?"

Dave blushed and looked down. "Well, errr," he stalled, eventually looking at Sophie and continuing, "I sort of, kind of, didn't actually get her name. We were a bit busy!"

Sophie barked out a laugh and rolled her eyes even more forcefully, Dave was something else. "Dave, only you could manage to talk about work with a girl but not even get her name. You really take the biscuit for stereotypical guy. Shouldn't you be working anyway – did you come here for a reason other than demonstrating your knowledge of lesbian stereotypes?"

Dave got up and wandered off down the corridor, *probably to go and torment the server guys with more unfixed vulnerabilities,* thought Sophie with an inward snort of laughter. Her musing was interrupted by the ping of her phone. Picking it up she grinned to see a text from Teri.

'Hi Sweet Cupcake, *Really enjoyed yesterday. When can we meet again? Luv T x*'

Sophie's heart warmed as she thought about the other woman and a smile crept, unbidden, to her face. Merely thinking about Teri was enough to bring up that fuzzy feeling she had every time she saw her. She was turning into a romantic stereotype for a lesbian in love.

'Can't wait to see you. What are you doing tonight?'

The reply beeped before she'd even put her phone flat on the desk.

'Coming to yours once I finish at Marion's and keeping you company then! How's that?'

'You're on. I should be home by 6. I'm shattered, so how about a takeaway and movie night?'

'Gotta love having an older woman, don't worry grandma. Fab! You pick food - I'm easy! Don't want a late night either - interview tomorrow.'

'Oi... less of the grandma, you young whipper-snapper. OK, you choose the movie then? Can you pick up some popcorn on your way?'

'Sure - see you @ 6. Love you xxx'

She paused, sucking on her short thumbnail, deep in thought. She was reminded of Teri being trans and decided that if it didn't bother her, which it really didn't seem to, then whether other people might make a fuss was irrelevant. She was going to continue to treat Teri as the Super Geeky girlfriend she loved. She just hoped they'd work together physically.

'Love you too my gorgeous geek... tell me if this is too soon but if you need somewhere to stay closer to the interview, you're welcome to stay over. No pressure.'

A long pause ensued and she was sure Teri had got cold feet, when eventually another beep sounded. She swiped eagerly, opening up the messages screen. 'That sounds lovely and it would be such a help, if you don't mind?'

142

'Of course I don't mind. We already established you perform better at interviews with suitable motivation so maybe a kiss over breakfast will do the trick. I want you to get this job!'

'Thanks. You're too good for me x'

Sophie's afternoon dragged by until it was time to head home. She phoned and ordered a Chinese from her local before leaving the office. She didn't know what food Teri liked so ended up ordering way too much food, collecting it on her way from the station. She arrived home, just having time to let herself in, dump the Chinese and run upstairs to quickly freshen up before a car pulled up and the doorbell rang.

Sophie ran downstairs and opened the door with a grin, grabbing Teri's hand and pulling her inside, enveloping her with a big hug and then cupping both her cheeks for a kiss. She broke away looking up, feeling her eyes burning with the feeling of love as she drank in every detail of the beautiful woman in front of her. No matter that she was in a variation of her usual shirt and jeans, her hair was slightly ruffled from the breeze and she smelt so warm and rich.

"Hello, Gorgeous." Teri said, with a grin on her face showing she was feeling similar to Sophie.

"Hi Gorgeous, yourself. You smell hot!"

"Oh sorry, I did have a shower...", Teri tailed off as Sophie realised what she'd said and clasped her hands to her mouth, her eyes closing in embarrassment.

"No! I mean *hot!*" she quickly clarified and wiggled her eyebrows suggestively.

"*Oh, hot...* you had me worried for a minute there. Well I wouldn't want to disappoint, now would I?"

Sophie didn't think she could ever do that – even dressed for a casual night in, this woman made Sophie smile and glow inside. She took her hand back, noticing that Teri had brought a small suitcase with her. That brought even more of a smile to Sophie's face. "The Chinese is here, you do like Chinese, don't you? We can take your stuff up after we eat, don't want it getting cold," she babbled.

"Breathe, Sophie. I love Chinese and don't worry about me, I can kip whenever, wherever. I'm just grateful to avoid the central line in the morning. Plus – that offer for encouragement before the interview is what sealed the deal," she winked cheekily.

Sophie leaned in, pressing their lips together warmly and showing just how much she wanted to encourage Teri's interview performance. "My gorgeous geek, don't you worry about that. I've no intention of only encouraging you tomorrow morning." With that, she pulled her girlfriend into the kitchen diner and set her to work unpacking the Chinese while she got out plates, cutlery and dug around in the bottom of a drawer for chopsticks.

"Who else is joining us?" Teri asked, sounding a little surprised and disappointed.

"Nobody, why?" Sophie replied puzzled but still hunting around at the back of her cutlery drawer and fighting with an errant potato masher to fully open the drawer.

"All this food?"

Sophie turned to see Teri with a puzzled look on her face and boxes of Chinese in each hand.

"Ah well, I might have gotten a little carried away as I didn't know what you liked!" Sophie blushed a little at her indecision, seeing the six boxes of takeaway lined up on the table. She walked over, setting down plates in front of each of them. "Dig in!"

Sophie watched Teri pick up her chopsticks, playing nervously with them in her fingers. "I'm not great with these things." She fiddled some more. Sophie was about to hand her a fork when she got a large chicken ball in her grip and started to lift it. Unfortunately, she

144

fumbled and the squeezing action forced the slippery sweet and sour covered ball away from Teri and out in Sophie's direction. Much to her surprise, Sophie was slapped in the face by it. She giggled. "Oh Soph, I'm so sorry!" Teri looked embarrassed but couldn't help a little laugh. Luckily, Sophie saw the funny side and was giggling.

"Well, it's not every day I get slapped by balls – does that affect my lesbian club membership card though?"

They both laughed for a while and Teri picked up a fork.

As they ate, Sophie grew pensive and also picked up a fork so she could swap to eating with her right and rest her face on her left, looking over at the brunette. "When did you find out?" she asked, out of the blue. Both of them knew what she was referring to and Teri acknowledged the change in direction with a slight nod.

"I was probably five, my parents threw me a birthday party with some friends, all girls obviously. "

"Obviously, you lesbian sex symbol."

Teri smiled, "I had to blow out the candles and make a wish. My wish was for My Little Pony," she paused before continuing quietly, "and to be a girl."

Sophie looked serious for a moment, "I cannot imagine you as anything else."

"Well yes, it took a few years but I transitioned eventually. Went through the obligatory pink and frilly phase too."

A guffaw broke out of Sophie's chest. The idea of this sexy, strong woman in pink frilly dresses was more patently ridiculous than the idea she could have ever been a boy. "Oh, I'm sure pink suits you, we'll try some time."

Teri snorted and shook her head, biting a prawn cracker while muttering, "I never did get the My Little Pony, just stupid Transformers."

Sophie mindlessly chewed her rice, trying to work out how to phrase her real question so as not to offend her lover.

"Out with it... what's going on in that pretty head?" Teri chuckled.

"Well – I'm wondering how it," she nodded down towards Teri's crotch, "well, how it works?"

"Works?" Teri had a painfully puzzled expression on her face and Sophie knew she needed to do better.

"Well I don't have any experience with... well... anything other than errr... being... well... lesbian and all." Sophie closed her eyes, presumably embarrassed at not getting the words she wanted to come out of her mouth.

"Lesbian? What's that got to do..." Teri tailed off before finishing her question as realisation crept over her features. "You do realise I had lower surgery when I was 23, don't you?"

"Lower surgery?" It was Sophie's turn to be confused. "You mean you don't have a dick...?"

Teri started laughing, she clutched at her stomach, as her eyes watered and she began to cough. After a while, through the laughs and coughs she was able to form words. "Sophie, lower surgery, or G-R-S means I have a vagina, vulva and clit. Mine looks, I hope, pretty much like yours!"

Sophie realised how stupid she was being and buried her head in her hands, curling her body forward to hide. "Oh my god, I'm so sorry Teri, how stupid am I? Have I offended you?"

She heard shuffling from across the table and a chair scraping. Opening her eyes, she saw Teri was kneeling at her side, reaching for her hands. Teri's eyes were watery and she looked almost pained. Sophie wasn't sure if that was from laughing or because she'd offended her. "Oh, I'm sorry. Are you OK?"

The other woman kneeled next to her, holding her hands and leaning forward to kiss them. She snuffled, "You didn't upset me, Sophie, you complete me. Don't ever feel bad for asking questions. I'm almost crying because I can't believe how lucky I am to have you. You thought I had a dick and you *still* invited me to stay over?"

"Well yes, I love you. I figured that if I love you then I need to love all of you. I've been really worried how I'd react though. I didn't want to offend you or make you feel less of a woman."

Teri's eyes shone and her smile widened dramatically, "Oh, Sophie, you're bloody amazing. You're a solid full-on lesbian and you were willing to consider being with me even if I didn't have a vagina?"

Sophie stared at Teri as though she was losing her mind. "Of *course* I would. I love you as a person first and foremost!"

Teri closed her eyes and flopped her head forward into Sophie's lap. Her strong arms hugged and squeezed Sophie, who was puzzled what she'd done to deserve such affection, but rubbed her back and played with her rich, brown locks. When she eventually lifted her head to look up, Teri had a beaming smile covering her face. Sophie's heart gave way in sympathy as she realised just how fearful Teri had been that she'd reject her.

"I love you, Sophie." Teri stood, capturing her girlfriend's face in her hands and pressing a firm, warm loving kiss to her relieved lips. Sophie opened her mouth to deepen the kiss and she felt Teri's tongue licking her lips before stroking her own tongue.

Sophie stood without breaking the kiss and started to slowly walk Teri backwards, the Chinese was forgotten and abandoned on the table. She took her lover's hand and broke away to look her in her eyes. A question shone out of hers and Teri nodded and smiled.

This was more than enough for Sophie who led them both to her bedroom, hoping in the back of her mind that she hadn't left any dirty underwear lying about.

She turned and cupped Teri's face again, brushing her cheek with a finger and loving how soft her skin was and how flushed it seemed. She leaned in and to the side, kissing the top of her neck before moving down, pushing her shirt to the side and kissing a track down to the exposed collar bone. She nuzzled in and inhaled Teri's scent, a mix of woody, cologne musk and her. Sophie pulled back and restarted the kiss on her lover's lips. Her scent was enough that she wanted to taste this woman, starting with her mouth and finding other intimate places. Teri's eyes were closed and her head tipped back and to the side. Sophie matched the angle of her head and pressed her lips against the full, soft, warm and welcoming home they sought. Teri opened for her and she lost herself momentarily in their coming together, her hands pulling at Teri's shorter hair to gain all the purchase her mouth needed.

As they broke apart, she pushed Teri's shirt back and off her arms, reaching straight for the black crew neck top she had underneath, drawing it up over her head before leaning in for another, comparatively, chaste kiss – such was her desire for this woman that she couldn't wait any longer. She wanted her naked on the bed and they walked back together until the back of Teri's knees hit Sophie's bed.

Her top half showed off a black, lace trimmed push up bra framing the curve of her small but firm breasts. Sophie couldn't resist tracing the lace with a finger and leaning down to kiss the exposed curve before reaching behind to undo the bra clasp with one hand. The stupid thing caught and she had to reach back with her other hand to help, pausing to look into Teri's now open eyes before pulling it away from the glassy eyed, plump lipped woman who was now looking thoroughly kissed.

Sophie looked down and appreciated the small, round dusky salmon areolas that her girlfriend's bra revealed. She leaned down to run her tongue around the outside, worshipping the circle of raised dots framing the beautiful pink centre. Two small dark red spots marred the otherwise perfect symmetry, making them feel more real

148

and more tempting. Her tongue spiralled slowly in, triggering an intake of breath. As her tongue reached the small nipple, she flicked sharply and her girlfriend jerked with surprise, reaching for Sophie's long hair. Sophie drew the nipple in with a gentle suck, a groan that echoed through her own whole body and settled firmly between her legs triggering a throb of her own. She drew her hands up and stroked both breasts while continuing to lick and suck Teri's right, before switching to repeat the same swirling lick, flick and suck on her left. Each time she sucked, the moaning, groaning noises Teri made went straight to Sophie's core. She could feel herself getting wetter.

Sophie leaned back and pressed a hand flat to Teri's chest, pushing her firmly so she landed on her back on the bed, bouncing a little as her dazed eyes opened and she smiled. Sophie dropped to her knees, pulling at Teri's trainers and discarding them behind her. She heard them clatter to the floor somewhere unseen – she'd find them later. She reached up and undid the button and zip on Teri's jeans before looking up and deep into her eyes. The hunger she saw reflected her own and with a quirk of her eyebrow she asked the all-important question again, receiving a slight nod yes, Teri was ready. She pulled from the bottom of Teri's jeans, before again discarding them to the side on her floor. She stood, marvelling at the vision spread out below her. Teri was spread on the bed; her breasts bare and nipples pink and erect. Her lips looked red, swollen and utterly enticing. The only clothing she had left were a pair of black, fitted, boxers. Sophie knew they wouldn't last long but also realised she was still fully clothed.

Luckily, she'd discarded her jacket before the Chinese so she began by gripping the hem of her top with both hands and pulling it up and over her head in one smooth movement. The hunger she saw grow in Teri's face was enough to know her knickers would be wet. "I want to be able to lie properly with you, Gorgeous, can you shuffle yourself back for me please?" She spoke the first words since they'd come upstairs and started kissing.

Teri nodded and pulled back up the bed while answering, "OK, errr, do you have lube? One thing that's a bit different for me is that I don't lubricate naturally so I do need a little help."

Sophie nodded and reached for a bedside drawer, feeling proud that Teri was comfortable sharing what she needed and eager to do everything to make this fabulous for them both. "Thanks for telling me, anything else I need to know?"

Teri shook her head, "Not apart from the fact that I want to feel you so badly."

"Me too. I'm really looking forward to learning all sorts of little things about you."

"Oh Sophie, I love the way you see these things as small. Some people see them as big deals."

Sophie paused, looked quizzically at Teri, her head on one side. "All women are different so why should you be the same as anyone else? You just have to help me know what works for you and what doesn't. Anyway – enough talking... Lie down," Her smile spread, like her hunger.

Teri turned and returned onto her back, looking up at Sophie who realised she'd been given the lead and it made her heart beat harder knowing that she could direct how their first encounter went. The trust that shone from Teri, and the hint of vulnerability she showed in lying there on her back was the most potent aphrodisiac for Sophie, who kneeled up on the bed and quickly, unclasped, and unzipped her own fitted work trousers before allowing them to fall to her knees.

Teri's eyes dropped instantly to Sophie's purple lace, high leg knickers. She was glad she'd chosen her favourite pair, the sheer mesh over most of the surface showed off her curves and tempted with the view of her skin while the lace concealed and teased what was under it.

Teri reached out with both hands, cupping Sophie's mesh covered bum cheeks and pulling them towards her. Sophie took the opportunity to roll and lie down beside her girlfriend – wearing only her matching purple lace underwear. Teri's squeeze turned to a stroke and caress that Sophie sighed and melted into. Meanwhile, she continued her exploration of her girlfriend's body, resuming the stroking of her perfect breasts and running the pad of her fingers over the erect nipple on each side. She ran her hand down Teri's side, enjoying the smooth feeling of her skin and traced the line of the boxer briefs around the top, tickling her bare belly a little so Teri squirmed. She couldn't resist any further, and gently tickled the inner thigh on each side, encouraging Teri to spread her legs and invite her closer. Sophie's middle finger very lightly swiped down the middle of her briefs, enjoying the groan it elicited and gently circling where she knew the other woman's clit was hidden. Teri pushed her legs wider apart and her hips closer into Sophie, wanting more, but Sophie wasn't ready to go there yet. She enjoyed the warm sensation spreading as she circled Teri's core.

Teri clearly decided she couldn't wait any longer because, at this, her hand caressed Sophie's side and made its way to stroke her inner thigh. Her impatient mood continued as she ran her fingers over Sophie's sodden knickers. "Wow, you're wet." She said, then moaned softly in appreciation.

Sophie didn't want Teri to miss out and whispered in her ear, "I know, and it's all for you."

"Oh Sophie," moaned a transfixed Teri, "I want to feel all of you."

Sophie decided that was enough conversation and fingered Teri's briefs to one side and caressed her middle finger along the length of her girlfriend's velvety, wet folds. "Feels good to me."

She then pulled her hand up and took a deep sniff of her finger, the musky tangy essence of Teri becoming her new favourite smell. "Smells good to me."

She waited to see that Teri's eyes were open before she finished by popping her finger into her own mouth, closing her eyes, and sucking strongly and dramatically on it. "Mmmmm, tastes *great* to me."

A subtle sweet taste, contrasting with the tangy aroma, coated her taste buds and she moaned. She opened her eyes to see Teri looking at her utterly open mouthed and wide eyed. Sophie reached for and grabbed Teri's hand, bringing it up and seeing her own glistening essence across her girlfriend's middle finger. Before Teri had a chance to work out what was happening, she swiftly popped that in her mouth too and sucked hard, genuinely enjoying the idea of their essences mixing. Her own, more acidic taste, was much stronger and her mouth watered at the idea of exploring this sensory journey more. More importantly, the sight and feel of her sucking on Teri's finger obviously did something to her girlfriend whose pupils widened and she urged Sophie closer with her other hand.

Both women were now lying side by side and Sophie decided she wanted to see more. "Can we remove these?" She asked, crooking her finger over the top of Teri's briefs. Teri nodded enthusiastically and reached for Sophie's own, nudging them down with her fingertips.

Sophie took a deep breath before looking down. She wasn't sure what she was expecting to see, but somehow, after all the uncertainty, she was almost disappointed to see a perfectly proportioned, beautiful, vulva. Almost – but not quite – disappointed, obviously. She licked her lips admiring the smooth looking, pink puffy folds that glistened with the arousal she'd already tasted. Teri was smooth and shaved apart from a cute triangle above the apex, pointing its way down to heaven as far as Sophie was concerned.

She didn't realise she was staring until a shy sounding Teri asked her, "Is everything – OK?"

152

"OK? Bloody tasty is what it is. No idea why you told me anything, that's the cutest vulva I've seen in a long time. You better not look at mine if you're worried about yours."

Teri laughed, "Looks good enough to eat from where I'm lying."

Both women giggled and, keeping eye contact, Sophie let her fingers explore. She led the way, firstly trailing her short fingernails around the three sides of the cute triangle, loving the slight scratch from the short hair. She detected a couple of little scars on either side that changed the texture, but other than those it was short, sleek and enticingly scratchy.

Then she resumed trailing a fingertip down each thigh in turn, coming back up the inside. She could tell Teri was getting eager as each time her finger came back up, the other woman pressed her pelvis into her.

After pulling her knee back to give her space between Teri's legs, she allowed her exploring hand to continue lazily. She remembered what Teri had said about lube and satisfied herself with stroking her girlfriend's velvety folds with a finger, remembering the healthy pink she found so appealing, although her own body obscured her actual view. She circled Teri's clit lightly at first, then pressed a little more insistently when the other woman pushed her hips closer for better contact. She decided to forego a finger going deeper for now though because she had other plans.

Sophie pushed up onto her left elbow before pushing Teri backwards to lie flat on her back. Realising she still had her bra on, she reached behind and allowed her breasts to drop, brushing against Teri's nipples as she reached down to restart a kiss, the tickling sensation causing her own nipples to harden in anticipation. She adjusted her position to allow herself to slide down Teri's body, kissing as she went. Swirling around the creamy left breast and flicking the nipple with her tongue, kissing her way down her tummy and

153

finally reaching the cute triangle at the apex of her legs, nudging Teri's legs further apart.

Sophie was delighted when her nose nudged through the cropped, dark triangle and the flat surface of her tongue was able to stroke the length of Teri's folds, first down one side, then the other. She inhaled deeply, enjoying the scent of her girlfriend and looked up. Teri looked at her wide eyed and Sophie imagined she could hear both their hearts beating in time. She resumed her flat tonguing of the puffy pink folds and, using two fingers, opened them to see her girlfriend's core for the first time.

Teri was right, it wasn't as lubricated as hers felt, and most of it was centred around her clit but Sophie wasn't bothered because she had plans to solve that. Curling her tongue, she circled the smooth nub of skin at the top and the resulting jolt of Teri's hips encouraged her to continue, stroking down the inside of her folds. She revelled in the fact that Teri's right fold was larger than the left much like her own but in reverse. That fact alone gave her a warm feeling of connection, as silly as it sounded. Circling that smooth nub again caused Teri to press her hips into Sophie's face and groan mildly. Sophie moved her tongue further down and circled the entrance to Teri's passage, excited to get this level of intimacy. Stiffening her tongue, she pushed inside, curling upwards and swirling around, feeling the mix of Teri's fluid and her own saliva giving a warm, seductive feeling that aroused herself more. She did notice that Teri seemed to respond better to attention on her clit and so, bringing her right hand in to scratch the cute thatch, she circled her thumb around the tender nub. The resulting groan was unmistakable this time.

"Don't stop... ohhhhhhhhh," a very distracted Teri groaned, arching her back.

Sophie used her free hand to caress her girlfriend's hip and butt, gently using her for leverage to pull her face closer, enjoying their combined wetness. She pressed harder with her thumb and picked up speed, switching from a circle to a flicking motion. This did the trick as Teri practically panted, her breath coming short, "Oh don't stop, please Sophie."

Sophie had no intention of stopping – she could feel her girlfriend getting close and with a loud groaning, "Urghh", she felt Teri's whole body tense, her back arching, forcing the beautiful pink vulva folds apart and Sophie's face further in. Sophie felt her nose getting wetter and she pulled her tongue out to lick along the glorious folds, loving the creamier texture she found. While her girlfriend wasn't a big squirter she found the taste and the strongly feminine scent addictive. Lessening her rubbing to soft, gentle strokes, she concentrated on helping Teri down from her high by licking gently until she felt her relax and sigh out loud.

"Oh my god – you are amazing!" Teri exclaimed wearily and vacantly, clearly not quite with it yet.

Sophie first kissed her beautiful vulva and then crawled up to kiss her other lips lovingly. Her face was smeared with her girlfriend's come but other than not wasting any, she couldn't care less.

Teri looked like she was struggling to keep her eyes open and Sophie just held her gently. She enjoyed the closeness and relished each stronger form of intimacy their bond presented.

She went quiet and Sophie thought she'd nodded off. "Just wait until I really show you what I can do," she whispered.

A few minutes later, Teri opened her eyes and Sophie was still looking down at her, stroking her hair as she did. "Oh Cupcake, I'm sorry, that was a bit rude of me!"

"There was nothing rude, so long as you enjoyed it?"

"Enjoyed it? O-M-G woman, you totally rocked my world."

"Oh good, glad to hear it, although I'll warn you that was me going easy on you for our first time," Sophie chuckled.

"Well, I've got something to live up to then, don't I? I think I should make it up to you – what do you think?" With that, Teri, who seemed to have gained a burst of energy, leaned up on her arm and began to shuffle down the bed...

Chapter Nineteen

Teri had reciprocated everything Sophie had given her and more, to the point that Sophie was the one drifting off to sleep in her arms. They actually slept most of the night like that, curled up in Sophie's bed resting in each other's embrace. Teri woke early in the morning, feeling immediately reassured that the warm body next to her was not a mirage. She took a moment to look around the room, liking Sophie's house. While bigger than her flat, it felt homely – the benefit of being out of London she supposed. She remembered the tastefully decorated, warm, red living room that was ideal for cuddling. Sophie had pulled her upstairs too quickly last night to remember whether there was a rug, or a fire, but somehow she suspected Sophie had created a warm little nest perfect for autumnal cuddling, whether with a hot drink or a hot girlfriend. She couldn't imagine anything better than having both.

She looked around the bedroom, which had been an unfocussed blur to her last night. She had been so super focussed on the woman in front of–or rather, below–her. It was an almost autumnal theme in itself, with oranges and reds – a combination that even Teri knew needed some skill to combine lest you end up looking like a garish 1970s restaurant. Sophie, of course, had managed it effortlessly. The red feature wall, with its accents of burnt orange, gave the room warmth but the remaining cream kept it from being overpowering. She was sure the satin pillowcases could look tacky if she bought them but in Sophie's hands, they just added class. She had to admit they felt like pure luxury.

She was waking up with a pleasant ache in her hip and leg muscles, not to mention her jaw. Both had been exercised last night. She looked over at the bedside alarm clock, the digits glowing in the dark, silent morning – 06:30. That was the other thing that caught her attention, the absence of sound. It was never this quiet in her flat, whether it was noise from elsewhere in the block or out on the street.

It would be time to get up soon though. She didn't know what time Sophie normally got up, but she'd considerately set the alarm for six forty-five today to make sure Teri was ready for her interview. She didn't want to risk waking the sleeping beauty next to her sooner than needed, she was enjoying the peaceful closeness.

Teri smiled, listening to the adorable snuffling noises Sophie made and the occasional murmur. Her blonde hair was spread messily over the pillow and her red tartan pyjama top made her look homely, as well as sexy. Teri didn't remember what she had on her bottom half but she hoped they were some sexy matching shorts. Her arm was stretched out in Teri's direction, as though reaching out to her, so Teri gave in to her urge and touched the pads of her fingers lightly against Sophie's. Sophie's hand closed onto Teri's fingers, holding her in a gentle but firm grip. Teri loved this feeling of connection; this was so much better than waking up alone with Number One's tail swishing in her face. As much as she loved her cat dearly, and couldn't be without him, she found the idea of stroking Sophie's hair far more rewarding than his fur. Even on his less disdainful days when he lowered himself to permit some affection, he didn't set her heart, body and mind aflame like this hot kitten did.

Sophie's eyes finally opened and she smiled at Teri. "Hello, sexy." She squeezed Teri's hand tightly, closing her eyes and stretching her body out. The duvet slid and the swell of her chest pushed forward appealingly, tightening her pyjamas.

Teri leaned in, "Hello sexy, yourself." She went to press her lips to Sophie's for a morning wake up kiss but mindful of her likely breath, settled for kissing her cheek and nibbling her earlobe. This really was a great way to start the day. Her leg had, somehow, ended up between Sophie's and now she was rubbing slightly on it. Teri wasn't sure if Sophie even realised she was doing it, but she liked it either way. She also suddenly registered that she could feel warm, wet skin rather than pyjama shorts. She was momentarily reminded of Number One rubbing on her leg and smiled as she, once again,

158

compared her gorgeous kitten to a feline goddess, picturing her in just her pyjama top.

Teri pressed her leg forwards a little and Sophie's eyes widened, the azure pools becoming huge, round discs. She felt Sophie rub more forcefully and next thing she knew, she was leaning forward and lifting Teri's top to kiss her breasts. Teri pressed closer into the sexy blonde, enjoying the sensation on her chest. She caressed one breast that fell to her hand, squeezing the nipple between her fingers a little. Lowering her hand, she reached down, searching for Sophie's curvy and squeezable arse to hold. Sophie groaned and Teri's nipple hardened as she felt it. Sophie's thighs tightened and her core pressed down. Teri felt her body stiffen and with a satisfying "Mmmnnph" moan she knew the other woman had found her release.

Teri looked at Sophie, who was blushing. "Wow, what a way to say Good Morning! Do you always wake up this frisky? If so, I need to be here more!"

"Good morning to you, and yes, you do need to be here more, but no, I don't usually wake up like this. I can't remember the last time I woke up this needy. I'm not used to having someone so sexy in bed with me so it's your own fault. I was having the nicest dream and just woke up in the middle..."

"Oh yes, are you going to tell me more about this dream or should I guess? You, me and a cramped network cabinet, right?"

"Not quite, but not far off actually. I was thinking about you in a car, that pool car from the other day actually." Sophie blushed redder and Teri could see the flush went down her chest too.

"Oooh, I like the sound of that, we need to explore that more. Perhaps you can borrow it again sometime?" she wiggled her eyebrows suggestively, making Sophie laugh.

"Are you all set for today?" Sophie asked, looking a little more concerned.

159

"As ready as I can be. We will see what they think of me, but I think I need a shower first." she sniffed under the duvet, smiling as the aroma reminded her of last night. "I smell of sex. Not that I'm complaining, you understand."

She wiped one finger down her upper thigh which was still wet with Sophie's juices, bringing it up to her lips, while staring into her girlfriend's eyes. With a devilish grin she popped it inside and sucked, allowing her eyes to close and a breathy moan of pleasure to escape her as she did so.

Sophie blinked twice, but the desire was obvious in her eyes, "I cannot believe you just did that!"

"Not letting a taste of you go to waste, Cupcake!" she replied, grinning widely like a devilish Cheshire Cat.

~#~

After some more cuddling and not a small amount of teasing, mostly on Teri's part, she did get up and shower. While allowing the warm water to refresh her tired body, she heard Sophie pop in and swirl her mouthwash around. She sensed the other woman pause and watch her in the shower but she couldn't be sure as it was steamy in the en-suite. She came back out to see a naked Sophie lying on her side, propped up on one arm and smiling.

"I've got to be in Basildon at nine and you have to be at work!" she chided her insatiable girlfriend.

"Don't know what you're talking about, I'm just looking..." Sophie replied in a teasingly sexy voice. She brought her index finger up to her lips and licked it before swiftly pushing it between her own legs. Teri's eyes popped out on stalks as she saw it start to circle a little then push gently in between those velvety folds that she was missing out on. Sophie had closed her eyes but then opened them, keeping eye contact as she brought the finger back to her lips. Teri couldn't believe what she was watching, but she was frozen to the spot, time standing still and her body rigid with tension. Her glistening
160

pink lips parted and the finger slid in, to be sucked and Sophie let out a groan of pure pleasure. Teri wasn't sure if she was drooling but thought it was a distinct possibility, especially as Sophie kept eye contact through the entire performance. She also didn't realise how ragged her breath had become until it hitched and she had to remind herself that oxygen was a good thing.

"Just thought you might need some added incentive for your interview, Gorgeous." Sophie purred, "After all, we know how well you did with a kiss, so I'm expecting great things with this taste on your tongue. Talking of which - come here for me."

She beckoned to Teri, who may as well have been a sailor lured into the clutches of this irresistible siren for all the willpower she had to refuse. She came to the side of the bed, facing Sophie, and bent down, leaning on her hands. Sophie swiftly dipped her finger back between her legs, returning a moment later with it glistening again. This time, she bypassed her own lips and pressed the pad of her finger to Teri's mouth—which involuntarily opened and she sucked it clean. Tasting her girlfriend was certainly going to give her some form of motivation – whether it would help with the interview, that had entirely disappeared from her mind, remained to be seen.

Sophie rolled away, standing up on the other side of the double bed and sashaying into the ensuite, where moments later Teri heard water running again in the shower. The thought of a naked Sophie didn't exactly help her to speed up getting dressed but she managed it, even adding a little eyeshadow and lippy to smarten up. Sophie emerged, rubbing a towel in her hair vigorously. She stopped suddenly in the ensuite doorway. "Oh—my—god—the—suit."

She clutched at her chest, placing both hands over her heart theatrically, tilting her head back and fluttering her eyelashes.

Teri raised an eyebrow and looked down her nose at the theatrical antics in the doorway. "Really? Keep on acting like the fluttering femme and I'll show you what happens. I'll have you know, damsels in distress are one of my favourite weaknesses," she smirked.

161

Sophie dropped to her knees, losing the towel on the way, but maintaining the grip on her heart with one hand and adding the other to her brow while still theatrical fluttering. "Oh, be still my beating heart, forsooth I am lost in the depths of thine eyes," she broke her theatrical pose before a devilish glint appeared in her eye and a smirk came over her own face, "and the depths of thine fanny too." She ruined the effect by breaking down in giggles.

Teri marched across the room, doing her best to look menacing before bending and whispering in a low, husky voice into Sophie's ear, "While I'm quite taken with you on your knees, I'd quite happily see you on all fours on the bed to return your teasing from the golf hole." She hadn't forgotten Sophie's comment about giving her a spanking at golf and thought she'd have some fun of her own.

Sophie wiggled a bit, looking uncomfortable as though certain parts of her were getting restless, and perhaps (Teri hoped) heated. She didn't reply, though Teri couldn't help but admire how gorgeous this woman was, even with her blonde hair dark and wet from the shower, her curves strokably pink from the heat of the water. "What would you like for breakfast, Cupcake?" asked Teri, her desire morphing, in an instant, to the warm glow of love.

Sophie got up, smiling at Teri and pulled a towel around her. Downstairs, they settled on scrambled eggs on toast, it being quick and light, as Teri needed to get out for her interview promptly. After eating, Sophie kissed Teri good luck and told her to call her as soon as the interview was over to tell her all about it.

~#~

Teri's Uber pulled up outside the office — a tall, red brick, office block in the town centre. She thanked her driver, got out and looked up at the building. Taking a deep breath, she thought how much this job could change her life and reminded herself of Sophie's encouragement. She walked up to the glass entry doors stencilled with the company logo. The receptionist, whose name tag announced her as Emily, was an attractive young blonde with a sleek high

162

ponytail. As she looked up and smiled a wide, welcoming smile, Teri's gaydar pinged at the way her eyes flicked up and down. Maybe there was something in Sophie's comments about her suit. She smiled back. "Teri Simlake here for an interview, I was told to ask for Roger Frederick?"

"No problem Ms Simlake, take a seat and I'll call him for you."

She turned and sat nervously in the stylish but comfortable waiting area. She spotted the receptionist looking up and checking her out a couple of times, smiling politely back but was careful not to appear to encourage the attention, if that's what it was. She pulled her phone out of the black bag she'd slung over her arm and texted Sophie. *'Arrived at office, receptionist appears to be checking me out - perhaps you were right about this suit.'*

Shame the interviewer is a guy, she thought.

Her phone beeped after about 15 seconds, it was Sophie. *'Told you. What's this about a receptionist? Hands off or there will be a catfight from this kitten.'*

Sophie's possessiveness made a warmth creep up Teri's chest, thinking back to cereal adverts when she was a kid – the warm glow from inside. She realised they'd not talked about exclusivity yet but it seemed they were both assuming it, which suited her just fine. She texted back to reassure Sophie that there was no need to unsheath her claws for Emily.

After about five minutes, a short, stocky guy appeared. His hair was longer than Teri's and was dressed casually in jeans and a T shirt from an 80s punk band. He walked up to Teri, who stood to meet him. "Ms Simlake?"

"Yes, you must be Mr Frederick? Great to meet you." She took his outstretched hand and gave it a firm shake.

"Roger, please. As you can see, we don't believe in formality here. Well not down in the bowels of IT anyway – we leave that for

163

the suits upstairs." He grinned cheekily at Teri, who took an instant liking to his down to earth personality.

"It's Teri then, please, and I will confess, though I know I shouldn't in an interview, I don't normally dress like this either."

She saw his smile creep up and he nodded. "Good, I was wondering if you'd come for the wrong job." Teasing her in a friendly way, he winked. "Let's head up - I've got us a posh conference room as I have to impress you, but we'll take a walk down to where the real action happens afterwards, if you're interested, and you can meet the team? I get the impression you'll fit right in."

"I'd like that, thanks. I'll pretend to be impressed with the posh conference room, if that helps?"

"Oh good, thanks – helps with my performance review, you know." He winked again. Teri was feeling more and more comfortable with Roger already. He was her type of guy and clearly didn't take either himself or the company pomp and circumstance too seriously. She'd be interested to see how seriously they took their security – that would be the real test for her.

They rode up in the lift a few floors and he guided her left and right down a few corridors then up a set of stairs to a door marked 'Penthouse' which caused Teri to stifle a sarcastic comment about where he was taking her. He made smalltalk about her journey and where she'd come from most of the way. She said she was usually in London so the train wasn't a problem, with the station being next door, but she was staying with her girlfriend nearby. She was pleased when the mention of a female partner yielded no reaction from Roger, just a nod and agreement that the trains were a *'right bugger this time of day'*.

They sat in the conference room and Roger pushed a glass and bottle of water over to Teri while she got comfortable. "So, I should start by welcoming you and saying I'm glad you could join us

164

today – it's great to meet you. Although, I think I already said that in the lift? Just for the record, welcome."

Teri smiled, "I consider myself formally welcomed." She bowed her head sarcastically, smiling irreverently.

Roger broke out into a grin. "I like your sense of humour. So, why don't you tell me a bit about your career and experiences?"

"Well, I started in IT straight from uni, my degree was Computer Science so I started as a developer, found what I enjoyed and quickly moved into cyber. I found that I was better on the offensive than the defensive so progressed within a few different red teams. In my last position I was leading, well forming actually, our in-house red team. We handled everything from hunting to testing new systems. They were a good team."

"Sounds good." Roger nodded. He continued with a few questions about how she handled difficult work situations before smiling as he asked. "So, can you tell me why you left your last role?"

Teri sighed, Roger had left this till last, he must already know the story. She heard Sophie's words in the back of her mind, *I'm proud of you and I believe in you. Most of all, Teri Simlake, it's because I fucking love you.* She looked Roger in the eye and started. "So, I had built the team, who were amazing by the way – great bunch of guys and we had a program of looking for issues. One day, one of the guys alerted us that a few servers didn't have a key patch and so were vulnerable. We flagged it to the server owners to fix but we didn't know they had ignored us. They heard us, they closed the ticket, they just didn't see it as important. The company suffered a breach as a result and the press got hold of it. There was conflict as a result of this which I wasn't able to resolve." Teri thought for a second, deciding that she should go further. "Let me level with you Roger, we had a really heated argument where my team was called incompetent and I wasn't having that – my job as a Team Lead was to stand up for them, so I did. The senior management didn't believe, despite evidence I provided, that we'd detected the flaw before the breach happened."

165

She couldn't help the bitterness creeping into her voice when she said this. Roger was nodding and looking at her carefully.

"So I heard," he said, continuing to nod, "but you won't have that problem here. We have a very good relationship with the senior management. I like your passion and willingness to defend your team, that's important. I also like your honesty."

Teri couldn't believe it; he didn't seem to be bothered by her past. "Well yes, I protect what's mine – you have to, right, that's what being a team means?" For some reason, the mental image of a curvy, cute, blonde girl lying naked in her bed popped into her head as she thought about things she wanted to be hers and to protect.

"I think you'll fit well into the team, Teri, I'd like to offer you the role. Would you like to come and meet the team, then you can let me know if you are interested?"

Teri heard the words but her eyes widened while her brain processed them. *Was he really offering her this job?* Eventually, her mouth caught up with her brain, replying, "I'd love to meet the team, but regardless, yes, I'm very interested."

Roger reached over and grabbed a handful of mints, emptying the bowl in front of them, winking at her, "We don't have these downstairs, so it's a team tradition that we bring back mints. Glad the conference room impressed you, let's head down to the lair!"

Teri followed him back to the lift where they stood as he punched a worn button for the third floor with a stubby, free finger, the rest of the hand holding his bounty of mints.

The doors opened and they headed to the back corner of the building, through a couple of secure doors that Roger opened with the pass on his belt.

"You know, rather than introducing me, I could conduct a test to see how far I can get into the building undetected?"

166

"Wouldn't work," Roger replied with a grin.

"Why? Think you're too Fort Knox for me?" Teri replied cheekily, quirking an eyebrow and trying to avoid sounding defensive. Did he think she couldn't get in undetected? Was he doubting her?

Roger widened his grin, "Oh, not because you can't do it. I know you can. It's because all my team already googled you. We knew you were good before you came in today. That's why I interviewed you. They are dying to meet you, you're famous, you know!"

Teri stopped in her tracks, "I'm *what*?"

Roger took a few seconds to notice that she wasn't still with him and turned, his face looking like he was mentally rewinding a video tape to see what she was asking. "You're famous, everyone knows about that hack and you know how word spreads through this industry. It's well known that you stood up for your team. In fact, you might recognise a few faces here."

He smiled a secretive smile, as though about to pull a surprise and gestured to a door on the right. Teri was still reeling from the revelation about being famous (or was it infamous)? She thought she'd lost her cool and stormed out years ago, only to be forgotten, but it seemed that others had heard and remembered.

Stepping through the door, she entered a dimly lit room scattered with a mix of about twenty low and high desks, all with at least three monitors glowing in the dim light and most with two laptops humming away. Some had one person sitting or standing, a few had people hunched over solving problems together. There was a mix of men and women and the women weren't the ones with the longest hair. The two extremes of buzz cuts and long rocker styles jarred against each other but also meshed as seamlessly as she knew their skillsets would do in a crisis. This was definitely the cyber lair!

It was noticeably hotter than in the corridor from all the electrical kit and the room had that tell-tale buzz that a Cyber Operations Centre always has as people bounce off each other. The scent Teri inhaled was that of a fight brewing in the air as they detected and fought back the bad guys. She was imagining this because what she actually inhaled was the fresh air from the aircon but her mind filled in the gaps with the scent she knew so well – a mix of coffee, coke, sweat from late nights and cold pizza. While sounding, on paper, to be revolting, this was her world – this was what she lived for.

She was even more surprised, as she looked around the room and people started to turn to her, to realise that she knew at least a quarter of the people in the room. Several of them had worked for her before. As she stood there, a huge cheer erupted from a few people on the far side and the group nearest her started clapping. Teri's adrenaline surged and she knew this was where she belonged – this felt like home and a tear formed in her eye, unnoticed.

~#~

Teri made her way around the room, the people who knew her came up to shake her hand, pat her on the back or, in one case of a particularly large, bearded guy with more tattoos than skin, envelop her in a huge bear hug. She chatted with them about what they'd been up to and what sort of jobs they got into here. As they talked, she caught the infectious vibe of a close-knit team and she could picture sitting here. Roger came up behind her, putting his arm around her shoulder, "Let me show you your desk, if you didn't get put off by this bunch of toerags."

Teri laughed as they walked over to an almost empty desk. Teri hadn't noticed it before, but it had her name on a plate on the cube wall. It also had a plastic plant and a pink and black mousemat waiting for her. She turned and stared at Roger, who was grinning at her. "You got all my stuff from the last job?"

"Yep – you can thank Lucy for that." Teri looked over and a blonde girl with a buzzcut, busy talking on her headset waved at her. Lucy had been her second in command before. They were inseparable since Teri started to explore her 'out' identity as a baby dyke – not

168

least of which because Lucy was also into women and had taken the fledgling Teri under her wing. She was so butch she made Teri (and half the guys in the room, if Teri was honest) look feminine. They used to get on fantastically but had hardly spoken since she stormed out of the office and went underground.

For the first time, Teri wondered if maybe her decision to go and hide herself away wasn't actually the right one. How could she regret it though when it had brought her Sophie?

"You got yourself a deal Roger – I'm in!"

She grinned and shook his hand.

~#~

Leaving the building and waving goodbye to Emily, who looked after her with a smile, Teri grabbed her phone and called Sophie, she couldn't wait to tell her!

"Hi Gorgeous, how did it go?" Sophie answered the call quickly but cautiously.

Teri couldn't contain her excitement, "*I got it!* It was amazing, I love it and they knew me even before I got there. They've got Lucy and a load of my old team there already – it's going to be amazing!"

There was some rustling at the other end, Sophie was clearly at work in the middle of something, "I'm so happy for you, that's great news!" Sophie sounded genuinely excited over the phone, but then calmed a little as she asked, "But who is Lucy?"

Teri rolled her eyes, she could see Sophie's green-eyed monster even without the benefit of a video call, and she was secretly quite thrilled by it. "Lucy, oh she's the most stunning girl you could imagine, blonde hair, great personality."

The silence on the other end was deafening and Teri had to stifle her laughter. "Really? You like her?" Sophie actually sounded worried.

"Calm down Cupcake, I was only teasing, you've got nothing to worry about. Lucy is the biggest butch you can imagine, I'm *sooo* not her type. You on the other hand... I may need to keep an eye on you!"

"Oh good, I mean, I wasn't worried or anything. I'm really happy for you – that is such great news!" Sophie quickly blustered to cover up her reaction. Teri could imagine how much her face was blushing and she knew first-hand exactly how far down Sophie's creamy chest that blush would travel.

"I mean it Sophie, don't worry about Lucy and me – we're mates going way back. She will utterly crush on you though, sexy cute femmes are so her type. She is good people – they all are. I can't wait to get stuck in."

"Did they say when you start?"

"Roger said I can start as soon as I want so I'm going to aim for next Monday, once I break it to Marion that she's losing her star barista! Isn't that great?"

"It's fantastic, plus it's good for my coffee intake, but tell me more about these sexy, cute, femmes that this Lucy leads you astray with?"

"Well, I know this one, she's the most gorgeous woman ever but when you get her naked, she becomes a total goddess. Long honey blonde hair with caramel highlights running through, beautiful dark pink nipples and creamy, bite-able, to die for, breasts."

An older woman on the train platform clearly overheard Teri and looked over at her with a look of outrage. Teri couldn't care less; Sophie was her total focus.

"Oh, really? When are you seeing this paragon next, do you think?"

170

"Don't know, when are you free? I'd come over now if I get to cuddle up to you!"

"Hmmm, nice as that sounds, I do have work to catch up on, after all, someone generated a load of work for our server team and now we still have to verify they fixed it all. How about tomorrow night?"

"Tomorrow it is, I'll cook for you, how about that?"

"Can you cook?" Sophie teased, sounding semi-serious in her question.

Teri let out a harumph of disgust. "Can *I* cook? Can *I* cook?" Then with a laugh she had to admit, "Of course not, but I'll try my best for you." They both giggled at each other. "I'll come to yours after work, is about six OK? "

"Let's make it six thirty, you never know what the central line is like and I get caught at Stratford loads."

"No worries, now you better get back to work!"

Exchanging goodbyes and kisses down the phone, they hung up and Teri continued her journey.

Heading home after the interview felt strange to Teri. She sat alone on the train then walked down her street, entering her flat by herself. The flat was silent apart from the mewing of Number One asking how dare she leave him alone without attention for all of twenty-four hours? It had been less than two days but somehow Sophie's house already felt like home. This empty place didn't have the same warmth – it didn't have the welcoming feeling. It didn't have Sophie.

She poured a celebratory glass of wine anyway and plumped down on the sofa, switching on the TV for a few minutes rest after the stressful morning. Number One came and curled up on her lap and she drifted off with a smile on her face, dreaming about cooking for her beautiful girlfriend.

Chapter Twenty

Teri realised she'd nodded off on the sofa sometime in the middle of the night and saw a message from Sophie, replying 'Sorry, dozed off. Love you too x' before hauling herself into her lonely old bed, regretting but not resenting how busy her girlfriend was. She woke on Wednesday morning, interrupting a lovely dream about Sophie lying naked on a flying rug, both of them drinking wine together. She was wondering whether John Lewis sold flying rugs when it occurred that what had woken her up was a knocking on her door. Not quite awake yet, she blearily got up and grabbed her dressing gown. Nobody knew where she lived so it was probably Maisie staggering back after a drunken night out and realising she'd lost her house keys again.

She threw open the door with a frown and greeted Maisie with a stern, "Where've you been now, you dirty stopout?" As her bleary eyes focussed, she saw that it wasn't Maisie standing there though, it was two people. Two quite official looking people who were staring at her, standing there in her dressing gown and giving them abuse as though she was unhinged, drunk or both.

Teri woke up fully with a start and rubbed her eyes, taking in the people properly for the first time. They were both taller than her, possibly six feet but one was a guy, clearly muscular with brown, short, tidy hair and a stern expression on his bearded face. The other was a woman but her equally stern expression precluded Teri continuing her appraisal of her further than noticing that she had a neat auburn bun and pale skin. Unfortunately, she had a somewhat large nose that gave her a sense of looking down at you along a beak.

The muscley guy spoke first, "Ms Simlake?"

"Yes, how can I help you?" Teri confirmed, wondering if she had unpaid bills due. A few were due but she normally managed to catch them before it was too late – maybe she missed the electric this month.

"I'm DS Sayne and this is DC Poynter." They held out their warrant cards and Teri looked at them as she always saw people in cop shows do. However, she had no idea what she was looking for– they just looked official and scary. Teri's heart, stomach and a few other organs plummeted through her feet. For a criminal, she was hopelessly ill prepared for this eventuality. The idea that they'd catch her was something she'd considered but not actually planned for. The flame haired but beaky DS continued, "We would like to talk to you please, may we come in?"

Teri figured she didn't have a lot of choice so stood to one side and allowed them in. She gestured them to the sofa, shooing Number One off it while thinking that at the end of whatever this was, she might at least have the satisfaction of seeing grey hair all over their black trousers.

"Ms Simlake, DC Poynter and I are from the National Crime Agency's Cyber Crime Unit, we understand that an attack took place last week at a consultancy in London? We would like your help as we believe you contacted a Miss Keegan afterwards to help clean up the attack."

The silence hung in the air; did they actually ask a question there? Teri began to wonder and started to panic, what should she say?

As she was about to start talking, DS Sayne continued. "Can you tell us what you know about the attack, please?"

Teri tried to school her features carefully, she didn't want to look too confident – fat chance of that, she was bricking it! "Well, I'm not sure I know all that much that can help, Miss Keegan contracted my services for advice, I've studied this type of attack from different companies so I offered my knowledge to help her combat the ransomware. I then followed that up by reviewing more of their network for issues and giving some recommendations. That's part of what I do as a security researcher, although obviously what I find is confidential to the company."

DC Poynter nodded but narrowed her eyes, looking Teri up and down as if she didn't believe her. "How did you know that they had been attacked?"

"Good question, I've followed this attack across quite a few companies and I try to guess where it might strike next. I'm afraid it's mostly guesswork, sometimes I get lucky and can find someone who I can help."

The two detectives still looked unconvinced, their heads were tilted to one side and mouths slanted in a mask of doubt, each taking notes in their own notebook. Teri swallowed but reminded herself to act normal.

"What do you know about who the attacker is?" The DS asked for his next question, not giving Teri chance to breathe. He emphasised the 'you' as though making a different point. Teri decided not to bite on this implication and just answer the question as it was asked, as a researcher – which she reminded herself, she was!

"Well," she leaned forward, aiming to forget what she *actually* knew about the attacker. "It's hard to track these things, an attack could come from any number of sources, disgruntled employees, individuals, hacking groups or even countries. The attack isn't terribly sophisticated really, it encrypts important files on the computers but Miss Keegan managed to bypass it."

The detectives again looked at her with scepticism. The fact that they were not saying anything stronger about her involvement suggested to Teri that they didn't have any evidence.

"So Ms Simlake, you're saying that we have local companies being attacked by a nation state? Isn't it rather more likely to be a local hacker somewhere in the UK, possibly a single individual living in a small flat somewhere, desperate for money?"

Teri forced a smile, her stomach was clenching itself in knots and her heart was running at the speed of a racehorse, she was sure the two detectives could hear it beating, the boom seemed that loud in her ears. "Well, detective, I can't tell you what's more or less likely I'm afraid, I'm just a techie, not a politician. Attacks are done by all sorts of people though, you are right. Can I ask who reported this attack? A lot of companies don't report it, so I'm interested, why did this one?"

"I'm afraid we're not at liberty to disclose our sources. From our perspective, far more crimes should be reported but we can only investigate the ones we're tipped off about. Anyway, we should leave you to begin your day. You've been very helpful." He looked her up and down subtly and that caused Teri to remember that she was still in her dressing gown. She pulled it tighter, feeling embarrassed at her state of undress. "If you think of anything that would help us identify the group," he paused, "or individual, involved, then please give me a call?" He handed over a business card and stood. She took the offered card and shook his hand as calmly as possible. "We'll be in touch."

Teri tried to avoid reading an ominous quality into that short sentence but she found it difficult to dismiss. She showed them out, but as soon as the front door closed behind them, the facade she'd managed to hold onto so far crumbled. Her hands began to shake, her mouth drooped and her vision started to blur as she felt the familiar tension in her eyes that preceded tears. Sure enough, as she slid down against the door, landing on the mat with a bump that barely even registered, the tracks of salty tears running down her face. She heaved big, body wracking sobs and curled down, her head in her hands in despair. Everything had been going so well, but no, her life couldn't just give her a break, could it? If she were under suspicion then she knew her new employer would drop her like a stone, and what about Sophie, she wouldn't hang about would she? She was doomed to keep screwing up her hopeless life. She probably didn't deserve anything better but wasn't it possible she could catch a break this once?

176

Time ceased to mean anything to Teri who could have been sobbing for five minutes or an hour but eventually her despairing emotions gave way to more coherent thoughts. Unfortunately, the thoughts were no more helpful to Teri. Her subconscious had been nagging her with a question since the detectives had arrived and it finally broke through the thick layer of doubt that was circulating in her mind. *Who told them?* repeated in her head. It formed a vocal harmony duo with her conviction that she was a horrible, worthless individual and wasn't worthy of, not just Sophie, but anyone. Her eyes opened and she looked around in shock. Someone must have reported her to the police – someone had caused this.

Her mind delved for who else knew about her hacking activities but the only people that had met her were Sophie and her colleague, Dave. She'd never before felt the need to reveal her identity and she'd never before taken the level of risk she had for Sophie. She had been convinced that this risk was worth it to see the beautiful woman who had appeared on the video call that night. The beautiful woman Teri was convinced, a mere hour ago, could be someone she'd spend her future with. Her future, that was now in tatters.

The more her mind swirled with questions inside her own head, the more her self loathing and sense of despair clouded her thinking without realising. Her automatic thoughts took over and her rational brain retreated in panic. Her fight or flight reflex robbed her of the logical brain she desperately needed.

The thought dawned,
Could Sophie have been the one to report the tip off?
Surely not?
Surely, she wouldn't do something like that! Could she have said something to the wrong person?
She had been joking about shouting about having a hacker girlfriend at the trade show.
The only name they mentioned was Sophie... what did that mean?
If someone else had reported it then they'd know of them too.

What if she didn't love me or I did something to put her off?
What if I was too needy or not good enough in bed?
Oh no – surely not.

This spiral of thought embedded itself in her brain like setting concrete, filling every alcove before it solidified into the immovable mass of dread. She saw more and more clearly in her mind that not only was her life over but so was her relationship – before it had even had a chance to start. At this moment, her mind couldn't allow room for any believable alternative. The cycle of self-hate and despair was too firm for that.

Her head spinning, Teri managed to get up and stagger across the lounge area to the kitchen, where she grabbed a large open bottle of vodka from a cupboard. She couldn't remember the last time she'd actually drunk it but she didn't care – she needed relief and oblivion sounded tempting. Normally she would only drink with coke on a night out but she needed something to numb the pain - the pain of discovery, the pain of confirming she was a horrible person and the pain of feeling that the person she loved had betrayed her.

She took one long, theoretically soothing, swig but all it did was make her thirstier. The physical stabbing pain in her chest remained as it was wracked again with deep, gut-wrenching sobs. She took another deep draw from the bottle, seeking the oblivion from the pain that it promised, as she shuffled back into the lounge area and slumped back onto the sofa again. Grabbing her phone, she went to message Sophie but the words just wouldn't come, replaced in her mouth by sawdust and her heart by concrete. She hurled the useless phone handset across the room in frustration. Frustration with herself and with the world. It bounced off a cushion and landed by the door. As it slapped down onto the floor the battery fell out but at this moment an old handset really seemed the least of Teri's worries.

Teri didn't notice time passing, she had no idea how long she had slumped or how many times she swigged from the bottle.

~#~

When she woke up, even before she opened her eyes, she could feel the sticky, salty tracks of tears staining her face, the pounding headache throbbing in her skull and the empty glass bottle lodged under her back. As she opened her eyes and extracted the bottle, she saw disappointedly how empty it was. As empty as her love prospects, she feared.

With that reminder, the reason that her head was throbbing came back in full technicolour. She was in trouble and she didn't know who had caused it. Her train of thought from yesterday also came back to her – could Sophie have been involved? Through her headache, her rational mind couldn't believe it.

She closed her eyes; the room was too bright – just like the glare of hurt she felt. She didn't know what had happened or even if Sophie had been involved but whoever had been responsible, it didn't change the concrete weight of self-doubt. Teri's stomach felt like it had a base of lead, the vodka hadn't helped that but she knew it was mostly down to the feeling of dread that had lodged there.

As she opened her eyes again, she registered that the curtains were still open but outside was dark as night. She must have slept through the whole day. Why did it matter, what did she have to get up for? What possible reason could there be to distinguish between night and day when she felt that she'd hit a permanent night.

At some level, she knew she was being dramatic. She knew that this didn't make sense, and her heart couldn't believe Sophie could be capable but Rachel's words came back and taunted her – perhaps she was a freak and nobody would want her? Maybe she'd been wrong about Sophie *and* the job.

As a moment of rational thought, she decided to go to bed. It was late and she needed to sleep off this alcohol if she was to think straight. The police would be back, she was convinced, and she needed to get herself sorted, before whoever was out to get her could do it first.

Chapter Twenty-One

Sophie hung up the phone with Teri – so excited that her girlfriend had got the job. She was still in the middle of her interminable Tuesday workday. Teri had just completed the interview. She was so pleased for her and remembered the excited voice with a smile. She loved hearing that vibrancy in her voice, her excitement gave it a rich, melodious quality that sometimes was missing. She much preferred hearing this excited, passionate Teri. Although, she loved the honesty she saw in Teri's vulnerable side and felt privileged to be one of the few people she trusted enough to show her full self.

Something had obviously happened in the past with this ex-girlfriend around her being trans and it had affected Teri deeply. Sophie felt that it made very little difference to her, so she struggled to see why others would have been so critical. Well, it didn't make much difference once she got over her embarrassing misunderstanding on genitals, anyway. She felt such a div for that. Thinking back to the previous night, she smiled to herself. Teri had forgiven her quickly and the memory of her girlfriend writhing as Sophie got to taste her for the first time caused her to press her thighs together under her desk as her core heated.

It was a shame that Teri couldn't come over that evening but Sophie did need to work late and after all, she did have her flat and cat to look after. *'Perhaps she'd consider moving in with me now she has a job locally and can be out of London? … Where did that thought come from? … It's way too soon to be moving in together, surely?'*

Sophie resolved to bring up the topic at some point anyway, even if it was for the future, she wanted Teri to feel as welcome at hers as she could and, frankly, the idea of the woman living with her longer term had a pleasant feel to it. She could picture them snuggling down with a movie and just pottering about through the weekend.

Later, she texted Teri, 'Congratulations again, so happy for you. Hope you're enjoying yourself. See you tomorrow!'

~#~

The next day, Sophie saw she'd had a reply from Teri and smiled that she'd obviously been celebrating. Well, she deserved it! Throughout the morning she was surprised not to hear from her but she guessed if she'd had a few drinks the previous night then she was probably sleeping them off. Throughout Wednesday, she sent her a few texts letting Teri know she was thinking of her but no reply came.

By the time she finished work at five pm she was starting to get concerned but also running late. Calling her girlfriend went straight to voicemail. She hoped that meant she was on the tube heading out of London.

She had to get showered and ready for Teri coming over shortly to cook. She grinned excitedly as she bounded up her stairs, two at a time. Entering her bedroom, she quickly stripped, chucking her clothes carelessly in the direction of the laundry as she strode into the shower, pulling off her bra and knickers at the last minute. The hot, steamy water refreshed her and she leaned back, allowing it to soak her hair and cascade down her body. She soaped up with her favourite shower gel, a musky hibiscus scent she kept for special occasions. The bottle of bubbly she'd bought on her way home and was chilling in the fridge said it was certainly a special occasion. They were celebrating. Rinsing the suds off her body and washing her hair, she emerged from the shower energetically, feeling ready for the exciting evening she knew was coming.

She flicked through her wardrobe; they'd not agreed to smarten up so she wanted to maintain a level of casualness but still look her best. Smirking, she grabbed her best skinny black jeans, knowing that they fitted her curvy figure like a glove. She picked another red top, lower cut and fitted this time, throwing it onto the bed, landing in a puddle of vibrantly coloured satin. Lingerie next and there was no choice here – she was going all out and picked the

181

matching lace bra and thong set she'd treated herself to for Christmas. She'd not had a chance to wear it but she knew from seeing it in the shop mirror that it suited her and would hopefully drive Teri wild. She dressed quickly, sparing a glance in the mirror and thinking that she looked more fierce than casual but she didn't care, it meant more to her to impress Teri than to be comfortable. Looking at the time, she could afford to do her hair, she had a little while before Teri was due.

Half an hour later, she was hovering in the kitchen nervously, waiting for a knock on the door. When nothing came after an hour, a feeling of dread crept up her chest. Had something happened to Teri, had she got cold feet? She could taste the sour tang of fear in her mouth and the heavy weight in her stomach as she feared the worst. *Please be OK Teri, please just be having some nerves. I need to know you are safe.*

She picked up her mobile, noting that she'd already called Teri three times today but not caring. Such was the measure of her worry that she didn't care if she annoyed her girlfriend, she just needed to know she was safe. She alternated between pulling on her hair and clutching her necklace in one hand, unconsciously seeking any form of reassurance she could find. Her heart leaped as she heard her girlfriend's voice, she went to ask what had happened to her but the voice continued, "I can't come to the phone right now ..."

Her chest tightened with a feeling of panic. Increasingly sure that something bad must have happened, she wondered how she could contact Teri when she didn't know where she lived. She could hardly call the police, could she?

Suddenly a slight rustle at the front door caught her attention, her hope rising. When the bell rang, she flew through the downstairs, throwing open the front door, ready to grab her with both hands and pull her close. It wasn't Teri though, it was two people, a bearded man and a red-haired woman with an unfortunately large nose. Sophie caught them looking her up and down, unsure whether it was the

182

crazed way she opened the door or her outfit that had them wary of her.

"Good afternoon Miss, sorry to bother you, but can we come in please? My name is DS Sayne and this is DC Poynter. We are from the NCA Cyber Crime Unit and are investigating a tip off about your company and wanted to speak to you please?". The initial fear, having been replaced by a warmth of elation, was now subsumed by a creeping cold spreading through her body. She froze. After a few seconds she regained enough presence of mind to reply, albeit with a shake in her voice, "OK, sure, not sure how I can help but please come in."

As they sat down, she continued, "I can't disclose anything about my employer without legal's approval, I'm afraid." Her mind raced ahead, *who had tipped off the police? Was it Mike or Paul? Had they gone back on their discussion? Could it be someone else, surely not Dave or Zach – she trusted them both and they weren't supposed to report stuff externally?*

The taller officer, DS Sayne, started. "We understand that your employer was subject to a ransomware attack last week. We've already spoken to one person involved who has been helping us with our enquiries."

Sophie's brain tuned out and the frozen feeling running through her veins intensified. *When they said that on TV cop dramas it meant they'd got a suspect didn't it? Did that mean they'd arrested Teri?*

Sophie shook her head to regain some semblance of what the bearded guy was saying.

"So, given that, we're looking to understand your recollections of the event and if you can supply any more insight that would help us track down the culprit, please?"

Sophie had missed half of what he said, but it sounded like she caught the major question. *What did she know?* That was a bit difficult – she knew a hell of a lot, but she couldn't share any of it.

"Can I ask why you're visiting me at home?" She bit her lip thoughtfully, it suddenly struck her as odd, why weren't they visiting her in the office tomorrow?

"Well, good question, Miss." His colleague seemed to fidget a little, but he pressed on. "The trouble is that the incident hasn't been officially reported by the company, our tip comes from an outside source. Do you know why that might be?"

"I'm afraid, as I said, there's little I can say without our legal department clearing me. I don't know if the company feels that any incident was big enough to warrant bothering the police."

The redhaired woman looked at her with a slightly pained expression, as though she was unsure what to ask but felt it was her turn. Sophie wondered if this counted as 'Good cop', 'Bad cop'. She eventually asked, "Our informant suggested the impact could have been quite large?"

Sophie was puzzled – *who would have said that? Dave and Zach both knew how quickly they'd recovered so that ruled them out surely.*

"Really? Large? I wouldn't say that," she said before she could think better of it. The company had only lost just over a day of work. In reality they had longer outages from power failures. She didn't think Paul or Mike would have described it as a large impact – not unless they were trying to exaggerate a point, but that seemed counter to the conversation she'd had with them. She narrowed her eyes as her puzzlement grew into suspicion. She tilted her head to appear confused rather than hostile, answering them. "Given that nobody I'm aware of from the company has reported any incident, I'm puzzled who your informant is officers? How reliable is their information exactly?"

184

DS Sayne cleared his throat and ran his fingers through his beard. "Well Miss, we can't disclose our sources, of course, but we have reason to believe it's accurate."

Sophie decided that there wasn't much more she could say and it might be best to get rid of them before she said something to implicate Teri, or herself. She lightened her voice and opened her eyes wide to appear as open and innocent as possible. "Ah well, in that case, I don't know how much more help I can be, I'm afraid. My director takes confidentiality seriously and, I'm afraid, so do Legal. I don't want to get into trouble by talking about anything I'm not supposed to."

Sophie was quite pleased with her tone of voice, conveying how much she was but a pawn in corporate games – rather than being the girlfriend of the person they were after. She'd not lied to them, just perhaps omitted who her girlfriend was.

Both detectives stood and shook her hand, they thanked her for her time and politely left, looking a little embarrassed to have bothered her in the evening.

She wasn't sure whether they'd contact Paul, or visit her again, but her mind turned back to Teri. She grabbed her phone and checked for new messages, nothing. She tried Teri's number and got the same voicemail as before. The feeling of dread started to grow again. It didn't sound like the police had anything on Teri since they'd not mentioned her but what if they'd visited her? Was she the person helping their enquiries – could that be why she was out of contact – or had something happened to her?

As worried as she was, Sophie couldn't think of much else she could do right now. She'd tried Teri's mobile and she didn't know where she lived, beyond it being a flat in Vauxhall. *'Yeah, great, that narrows it down to no more than a few thousand properties.'* She briefly considered driving out to London and walking around looking for Teri but decided that really was a silly idea.

Teri was now two hours overdue and, while it was possible a train was to blame; Sophie's bad feeling had been magnified by the police visit. She decided to get an early night, keeping her phone by her side. With luck, she'd get woken up during the night by a phone call from Teri apologising for being late or explaining how she'd got stuck into some riveting software code and lost track of time. Frankly, she'd rather hear she'd gone out on a bender with Maisie and had slept through, than hear she was hurt.

Sophie trudged up to her empty double bed, changing into pyjamas. She realised she'd changed the sheet but not the pillows since the other night. She pulled the other pillow over, inhaling deeply and finding the reassuring musky scent of Teri still on it. She cuddled the pillow and tried to sleep, tossing and turning for some time before sleep finally claimed her.

~#~

She woke several times during the night, checking her phone for messages and fitfully going back to sleep. When she finally woke up at five AM, she decided enough was enough and she might as well get up. She tried calling again but Teri was still going to voicemail. Sophie could go into work early and wait for Teri's call there. She might also be able to find out if anyone at work knew anything about the police interest.

Dressing quickly, with the minimum of interest in what she looked like, she managed to get to work an hour later, just as security were opening the front door. Barry, the guard, greeted her warmly but his surprise showed. Sophie couldn't blame him, she'd never been in the office this early. She'd normally take conference calls from home if she must meet someone from Australia or wherever was still awake at this godforsaken hour.

She made her way up to her office and logged in, ploughing unenthusiastically through yesterday's email that she'd abandoned in her haste to get out of the office and to her girlfriend. She had no appetite for petty IT problems and she was sure her email replies were sharper than normal, but she was in no mood to care until she knew whether her girlfriend was safe, in trouble and / or going off her. After a while, (she had lost track of time), a bearded head popped around her door.

"I come in peace... don't shoot..." Dave groused as he poked his head around the doorframe, holding up both his hands in a theatrical surrender motion. Sophie was in no mood to deal with his childish antics though and she looked up at him with a scowl.

"What are you on about Dave, you childish prat?" She exhaled with frustration. She was letting her anxiety overrule her professionalism, she knew.

"Oooh, I was right. Something's got you upset. What's up Sophie?" He lowered his arms and came in, sprawling himself on her visitor chair casually. Sophie looked at him and dropped her frown. She could see he was concerned for her beneath his sarcasm.

"Why do you say something is up?" she poked, wondering what he'd heard, or maybe *said*.

"Well, firstly, the fact that you just called me a prat... that's not happened since last year when I accidentally leaned on the computer room CO_2 release. I still maintain the cover was jammed open and I couldn't see where I was going with those boxes. Secondly though, because you fired out a ton of emails and virtually beheaded everyone who had asked you a question. So talk..." He sat back expectantly.

"OK... OK... I'm tired. I didn't get much sleep."

"Oooooh," Dave butted in, wiggling his eyebrows suggestively and leaning forward.

Sophie's frown returned. "You really are a prat Dave... No... nothing like that. I had a visit from the police last night." Dave sat up straight and looked at her expectantly. "They were asking me about the ransomware."

Dave frowned and looked askance at Sophie, "Last night? Why did they visit you at night?"

"I'm not quite sure, but it seems that Paul hasn't reported it so they didn't want to come into the office. Felt a bit suspicious but I'm worried about Teri. I've not heard from her." Sophie's voice broke a little as she finished the sentence and the reason she was in the office this early came back to her mind.

"You like her, don't you?" Dave's face was softer as he asked and he looked Sophie straight in the eyes.

"I don't know why I'm telling you this – you're still a muppet." She started to reply, but continued softly, "I more than like her, Dave... I think I love her."

"Wow, I've never seen you like this before. Well, for what it's worth, ignoring her initial actions, she's been bang on with all her recommendations and she came up with stuff I actually had to look up the meaning of. But if you tell anyone that I'll deny it," he finished with a frown.

Sophie smiled, despite Dave being her employee, she felt better having his support and if Teri had even won him over then perhaps there was hope. But where was she and why hadn't she called? "Beyond where she is and why I can't contact her, the other big dilemma is who told the police about the hack? Only you, me, Paul, Mike and Zach know all the details and only you and I have met Teri."

"Well, it wasn't me, even before you told me what you just did, you soppy woman, I had resolved to stay out of it all. After the way that woman talked, I thought that I don't want the hassle."

Sophie reacted with a spark of energy and alarm bells rang in her mind. "What woman? Did you tell someone something?"

Dave shook his head, "That woman I mentioned who chatted me up at that bar. The bi one who taught me about U-Hauling... Nah ... she wasn't interested in IT, she was just after a hookup."

"Well, she's the best lead we've got – what exactly did you tell her?"

"Well, nothing really. We were just chatting – she asked what I did, I said IT Cyber... she asked if I had any funny stories and I mentioned we'd had an incident. She went off on one about how crazy cyber women could be... I mean I know that, after all I work with you!"

Sophie reached for something to throw at Dave, grabbing some paper off her desk and screwing it into a ball before aiming it squarely at his head. He ducked and laughed at her.

"She wasn't my usual type, but she was cool in her own way. That short, dark hair and tartan – she was oddly hot."

The alarm going off notched up a level in Sophie's mind with that description. "Hang on, what did you say her name was?"

"Well, I never got it, if I'm honest." Dave admitted, looking sheepish.

"What did she look like? Come on – this could be important!" Sophie urged, leaning forward and encouraging Dave.

"Oh, I dunno, tallish – five eight, quite fit, obviously works out. Short brown hair, lots of denim, lovely muscular bum and black tight top with a tartan shirt over the top."

"Dave, you just described any one of a million butch lesbians. Come on – you must know something about her!"

"Soph – I really don't. But she obviously wasn't a lesbian. Not from the way she kissed."

"I'll have you know, lesbians know how to kiss, Dave."

"Really?" Dave looked incredulously at Sophie, gesturing down at himself. "I mean Sophie... if she's lesbian aren't I kind of outside the target market?"

"Oh... you have a point there, I suppose. That notwithstanding, she sounds like a stereotypical butch woman. Did she tell you anything about herself? Was she local?"

"Well, she said she lived on this side of London, that doesn't help much though, does it? Her favourite colour was purple, she was drinking WKD and she had a good tongue game."

Sophie's mouth dropped open, "Seriously Dave, do you have to?" Through her haze of her shock, alarm bells continued to pierce the fog and she picked up her phone, scrolling back through her gallery. It took a lot of scrolling before she came to a photo of a tall butch woman with short dark brown hair. She held up her phone and turned it around to show Dave.

"That's her! How do you know her? Don't tell me I did turn a lesbian? Who is she?"

Sophie's mouth dropped and she felt her stomach plummet. "My ex, Hannah."

Chapter Twenty-Two

Teri woke up with a mouth that felt like a sawmill caretaker's wheelie bin and a headache that was pulsing like a traffic light. It reminded her of the previous day when she came around with a hangover but this time she was, at least, sober. The smell of stale alcohol almost made her retch and it was the realisation that this was emanating from her that, unfortunately, brought all the memories back. The police visit, the suspicion, the conclusion that her life was over. She scrunched her eyes up ... pain from the hangover contended with pain from the heart.

Her brain had regained some rationality and began grasping for a sliver of hope that things weren't as bad as she thought yesterday. Whoever was to blame, (and Teri knew that the only person really to blame was herself) pretty much the worst-case scenario was unfolding around her and she felt powerless to stop it. Who had told the police and what did they know about her? She couldn't and wouldn't lose her faith in Sophie and felt ashamed for doubting her. She couldn't avoid a worry that she might have accidentally said something, because if not, surely the only other person who had met her was Dave. Maybe he had.

Other questions swarmed around in her brain like a menagerie of hungry wasps all vying for her attention and competing to sting her consciousness with yet more uncertainty, anxiety and guilt. The big problem was that Teri wasn't so much afraid, as feeling utterly defeated. Her heart and chest felt heavy, her heartbeat gained in speed and strength and her chest felt like it was made of lead. Looking around, she saw her mobile phone lying broken in the doorway.

Shattering the peace of her flat, suddenly, her landline phone rang, the ringtone sounding sharp and insensitively loud to her delicate hungover ears. She reached across to answer it, her eyes too bleary to read the name on the screen – only a few people had this number. "Hello?" she croakily wheezed.

"Hi Ter, how are you? Why aren't you answering your phone? What are you up to today?" a voice cheerily spoke at the other end. It was Maisie.

Teri groaned, her life was flushing down the toilet and she had to explain it to gossip-guts, who was probably calling to talk about her latest squeeze. "Oh it's great Maisie, I'm lying in bed with a hangover because I've drunk, what feels like, my weight in vodka, my life is basically over and I'm about to be arrested."

Maisie barely paused before continuing, "That's nice... well I was out last n..." she stopped. "What did you say? What on earth is going on? I'm on my way..." and the line went dead.

Part of her wanted to be grateful for her friend's impending company but a similarly large part of her also wanted to be left alone to wallow. She knew she'd been tempting some higher power with everything going right for once. How that cruel bitch, Fate, must have loved to see her flying so high in a false Icarus-like move. Flying so close to the beauty she saw in Sophie – her golden sunlike hair, her warming caring words. She was probably back to square one being unemployed as well, would even Marion keep her?

How dare she even call herself a woman, she heard fate mocking her – she wasn't a real female, no periods, no uterus. She only had to go on social media to be reminded of that with the hate campaigns always waging against people like her. Even now, in the depths of her despair, she knew that transitioning had been the best move she'd ever made and she couldn't ever forgive the people who had (and still did) call her a man. She certainly wasn't male, but a real woman, whatever those people imagined one of those was, would be able to treat Sophie as an equal.

Her spiral of self-destructive thoughts was, fortunately, arrested by a ring of the doorbell. She got up off her bed, noticing for

192

the first time that she was still wearing yesterday's jeans and t-shirt, now crumpled and smelling slightly of that alcohol that had permeated her pores.

She walked through her lounge, noting that she hadn't fed Number One yet and he was sitting on the sofa again looking distinctly upset with her, in his superior feline manner. He stopped cleaning himself and watched Teri as she opened the door. Her attention was on the cat and she expected Maisie to bowl in. "Hi Maisie, come in."

She turned her head in surprise at a distinctly masculine cough and came face to face again with DC Sayne. DS Poynter was at his side again, the two of them filling the narrow apartment hallway. Teri shook her head in shock and tried to return her eyes to a more normal state rather than the wide discs of surprise she realised she was currently looking at them through. "Oh detectives, I'm sorry, my friend just called me and was on her way over. I thought you were her. Come in, how can I help you?"

Stop rambling Teri... you sound guilty, they don't need your life story.

"Thank you, Ms Simlake." The male detective led the way and they passed Teri so she could shut the front door behind them. They all stood around in the lounge with Teri feeling awkward. "We won't bother you for long. We were just passing and wanted to see whether you'd remembered anything else about the attack that might help us? Ms Keegan has been extremely helpful but obviously you have a certain perspective that will be very helpful too."

Teri's stomach dropped – so Sophie *had* been talking to them. "Well, detective, I'm afraid there's not a lot more I can add. Miss Keegan is the manager responsible so I'm sure whatever she's told you would be accurate." They seemed to be discreetly looking her up and down again and she saw the woman detective's large nose wrinkle a bit. She figured she needed to explain her state. "If I'm honest, I'm afraid I may have had rather a lot to drink last night so hadn't thought too much about it – I am sorry about that."

"Ahh OK, I see, well that's quite understandable Ms Simlake. Nobody expects you to stop your life I'm sure. Poor Miss Keegan's company didn't fare so well with the attack, I think a lot stopped for them, so if you do think of anything then please let us know?"

"Of course! I still have your card on my desk, if anything comes to mind then I'll give you a call."

At this moment, the doorbell rang again. Teri hadn't moved too far from it so reached across, taking a deep breath before opening it, knowing this time it would be Maisie. Sure enough, she was right as a breathless bundle of energy pushed through the door and grabbed her tightly from both sides for a strong hug. "What's..." Maisie started but her words tailed off when she saw the two imposing detectives standing there. "Oh I'm sorry, I didn't know you had company Teri, I thought you said you were ill?"

Teri was grateful that her friend had caught on and was quick thinking enough not to give anything away about their phone call. "This is DC Sayne and DS Poynter," turning to them she added, "did I get that right? Apologies, I'm terrible with names."

The two detectives nodded and the bearded guy reached out to shake Maisie's hand. "Good morning, Ms Andrews. Nice to see you again."

"Oh, you know each other?" Teri looked at Maisie for an explanation.

"Ah yes, we worked together on a case last year. Do you remember me telling you about that attack on our app that turned out to be the insider guy from finance who was upset he'd been accused of misconduct?"

"Oh yes, I remember you saying something." Teri did quite clearly remember, as it happened. She also remembered how Maisie had moaned bitterly over drinks that week about the utter arsehole the police had sent to investigate it. She clearly didn't like him.

194

"Well," started DS Sayne, before continuing, "we will leave you in peace, but if there's any information you think of then please don't hesitate to call us."

"OK, thanks for the reminder and I'll certainly rack my brains today for anything else. Most of what I work with is guesswork but if I remember anything solid about the ransomware then I'll give you a call."

With this, the two detectives headed out and Teri closed the door gratefully behind them. She turned and Maisie was standing with her hands on her hips looking curiously at Teri, a question clearly going through her mind.

Teri put her head in her hands and closed her eyes, taking a deep breath and rubbing her eyelids. If only this was a dream and she could wake up. She looked up and, sadly, it wasn't and she didn't. Maisie was still there, looking like she was expecting an explanation.

"You don't need to look at me like that. I know... I stink and I look like shit."

"Forget that, you know as well as I do that I've seen you looking worse during and after a night out. The more important question is, what's all this about your life falling apart and why were the police here? What's going on Teri?" Maisie looked properly concerned. Teri could only hope she stayed that concerned for her once she told her what was going on.

"Well, I think we should sit down. I guess I need to start from the beginning." They turned and she shooed a sleeping Number One off his comfortable position on the sofa. Teri sat, curling up in the corner of the sofa and avoiding eye contact with Maisie. She pulled at her top and chewed her finger nervously through the fabric. "I've been really stupid, Maisie." Teri haltingly managed to say, in a quiet voice, continuing to chew nervously and sighing. The feeling of despair started to rise once again as she prepared to tell her friend about her mistakes. "I think Sophie is going to hate me and someone has shopped me to the police."

Maisie sat next to her, "OK, back up, Teri. Start at the beginning." She put her hand on Teri's shoulder. "I've never seen you like this before."

Teri explained, starting from the redundancy and how she'd got into hacking as a way to pay the bills. She explained how she'd really met Sophie – not the story they'd told everyone about meeting online.

Maisie's jaw had dropped long ago, Teri couldn't look at her as she sat in silence.

"Say something... are you going to disown me too?"

That seemed to wake Maisie, "Course I'm not disowning you – you're my best friend you daft cow. I can't say I'm not shocked and we'll talk about what you've done later. For now, I'm more worried about you. Why didn't you ask for help? I thought you were doing OK in freelance; I didn't realise ... Anyway, what I don't understand is how Sophie fits into this, she knew who you were and what you did before you got together, so why have you split up?"

"Well, I can't work out who could have told the police and she's not going to want to be with me when it comes out, is she?"

"Did they say who had tipped them off?"

"No, they weren't allowed to tell me – it is confidential apparently. But only two people met me so surely it's either them or someone they've told. Who could it be?"

"I don't know but I think you should find out. I can't believe it could be Sophie. Seeing the two of you together, she'd have to be the biggest hard-hearted bitch I've ever seen to pull this. Surely, it's more likely it's someone else."

"I do not feel like doing anything today. I can't face it, it's all an absolute shower of shit." With that, she sighed and partly closed her eyes, feeling weary. "Either way, I doubt I'll be worth it for her now."

Maisie quirked up an eyebrow. "OK, now I'm going to have to kick both your arses. You can stop with that sentimental bullcrap. You know perfectly well I've known you for years, and you are easily worth anyone's time. Well, maybe not mine – I'm super important, you know." Her joke fell flat and Teri just felt blank. She could see Maisie was trying to encourage her but it wasn't working.

"She deserves a real woman," she croaked in a quiet voice, thick with emotion.

"What pile of utter horseshit are you on about now? Who's not a real woman?" Maisie looked genuinely confused.

"Me... I'm not though, am I?"

Teri saw the light dawn in Maisie's eyes. She then saw the flash of fire reignite. "Right, listen up, you. I didn't realise I needed to tell you this but I'm going to... I've known you since before you transitioned. That is what some of this is about isn't it? Being Trans?" She paused, awaiting confirmation. Teri shrugged before Maisie continued forcefully. "Right, so I knew you before and I know you now. You made a shit boy because you were always a woman. What even is a 'real' woman? If such a thing exists, you're nothing but a real woman and any lesbian worth her salt is lucky to have you. You didn't come all this way just to give in to some crap on Twitter that you're not a real woman because you don't have periods."

Teri looked up and got the feeling Maisie was debating whether to encourage her or slap her round the head. She seemed to be going for the verbal hybrid of the two. "But why can't I catch a break? Why does it feel like whatever I touch turns to shit? I'm nothing special, everyone would be better off without me draining their time." Her voice tailed off and she shrank even further back into the corner of the sofa, knowing tears were probably not far away.

"You are special, Teri." Maisie started quietly before firmly continuing, "Look at me... You... Are... Worth... It. You made a bad choice and maybe something is going to happen, maybe not. Doesn't sound to me that you know quite where the hacking thing," Maisie paused, rolling her eyes, "is leading. I mean seriously Teri – you hacked someone and all you did was a bit of ransomware? I mean come on – you and I both know that you're better than that. Both morally, you shouldn't have done it but also technically, you could have done so much more cool stuff. That's script kiddy work!"

Teri sniffed, looking at Maisie before having to break eye contact. "Yeah, I'm not even a good Cyber Geek. But... I didn't actually want to hurt anyone so I chose an attack where I could stay in control of what got deleted and what got retrieved. That seemed the safest way."

"My point, exactly..." Maisie said triumphantly.

Teri looked up at this, surprised. "What? I don't follow, what's your point exactly?"

"You could have done *so* much more sophisticated stuff, you could have taken those companies down completely and caused lots of damage but you didn't, did you?"

"But I still hacked them."

"Yes, you did and you're an utter salad for it. I mean seriously... but if you're going to attack someone, I can't think of a less damaging way to do it. Maybe apart from setting all their ringtones to 'Barbie Girl'."

Teri sniffed and smiled weakly. Maisie was referring to a trick she'd played on her years ago. Maisie had annoyed Teri on a night out so the next week, she'd forced her phone to play 'Barbie Girl' at full volume as a ringtone. Maisie was really not happy with her that time.

"So," Maisie continued, her voice becoming more strident and her hand gestures exaggerating, showing her emphasis, "The question is... other than moping around here for being a total salad, what are we going to do to help you? I can't believe Sophie would have been a part of it though. I hope I'm not wrong, I did check out her arse in the bar after all and you know my taste in women is legendary."

Any levity Maisie's brief attempt at humour had caused subsided quickly and she wrung her hands together, looking down and sighing deeply. "It doesn't matter who it was, the important thing is I can't put Sophie through the pain of being with me. I can't face talking to her." She looked up and Maisie was still waving her hands around like an excited windmill.

"Even if you won't, I can. I want to know who's upsetting my best friend. Only I'm allowed to do that and get away with it... maybe plus Anna ... but that's it. What's her address?" Maisie's eyes bore into Teri.

"You can't just go around there and interrogate her!"

"Can't I? Why not? If something she's let slip has brought this on you then I want words with her and whoever has reported you. You might have been an arse, but you're my arse." Teri was sure there was a compliment in there somewhere but she was blowed if she could find it. Plus, she could tell Maisie was getting more and more upset. Her language got more sweary the more animated she became. Being promoted from salad to arse was probably not a good sign but she still seemed to be fighting on Teri's side.

Maisie stared at Teri with one eyebrow quirked upwards. "You know as well as I do that if I need to find her, I can. If I don't have to spend hours tracking her down online, it'll mean I'm calmer and nicer when I do get there."

Teri knew she was going to lose this battle and really – why did it matter? She relented and gave Maisie the address. Within five minutes, Maisie was gone and she was alone with her thoughts. *'What happens if the police come back, what if they find something?'*

Teri sat on her sofa, put her head in her hands and let the feeling of despair wash over her. Maisie's visit, and her obvious support, had been a boost but it didn't change the reality – she was alone, possibly about to be arrested and screwed! A lonely tear escaped and ran down her cheek. Focussing all her attention on its wet tracks, she imagined it could wash away all the stuff she'd done wrong, but no amount of crying was going to solve this problem.

Dimly in the back of her mind, she thought maybe it would be a good idea to clear her flat of evidence. Maybe that was something she could do later... but for now, she couldn't face touching a keyboard – the feeling of shame was too intense. At that moment she realised that what she was feeling most wasn't fear (which would be sensible), it was shame. Shame that she'd let Sophie down. Who was she kidding? Sophie could have been the one to report her and she would still be in love with her – how screwed up was that?

Chapter Twenty-Three

Sophie had rushed home, upset, after learning of Hannah's involvement. She couldn't bear to be at work and needed to be somewhere Teri could reach her. It had been two days since she'd called about the interview and all she had heard was the brief text exchange since. She was worried for her safety after the police visit – she knew Teri was more vulnerable than she let on and couldn't imagine how that would have affected her. She'd texted several times but without an answer.

Her worried reverie was interrupted by the sounds of a car outside, its engine gunned and the brakes sounded harsh on the road as it stopped near her driveway. Hurried, loud footsteps preceded the sound of her doorbell.

Opening the door, she was surprised to see Maisie but worried when she recognised the glare of anger in her eyes. "Hi Maisie, have you heard from Teri?"

"Heard from her? I just left hers. What has happened? Have you said something to someone?" She was gesturing towards Sophie with a finger.

Sophie was taken aback by the anger directed at her but as the words sunk in she had a moment of relief – Teri must be OK. "Is she OK? Where is she?" The moment of relief was short lived and swiftly replaced by renewed concern. Something *had* happened. "Hang on, I don't know what you're talking about but I have a bad feeling I can guess. Come in and tell me what's happened."

She ushered Maisie into the living room and they sat on the sofa, Maisie perching on the edge and leaning forwards as though ready to launch at Sophie at any moment. She radiated hostility but was clearly trying to control herself as she shook her head briefly, wiped her hands down her jeans and breathed in deeply.

"What's happened – is she OK?" Sophie started.

"The police are investigating her. Someone has tipped them off but only you and this Dave guy knew who she was?"

Sophie was so shocked she felt her mouth open and no words would come out. Surely her girlfriend couldn't think she was involved? "You don't think I had anything to do with it?" she managed to squeak eventually.

"It is your job, isn't it? Plus, nobody else knew of her but your Dave guy. Now she's got DC Numbnuts and his sidekick sniffing around. I don't want to believe you'd have done it deliberately, mind you, but is there anyone you talked to?"

Sophie couldn't decide whether to be angry or devastated that somehow Maisie was attacking her. Surely Teri trusted her to have her back? She closed her eyes, rubbing them with the heels of her palms, wishing this would all go away... 'and it was all a dream...' isn't that what they said in books?

She opened her eyes and Maisie was still glaring at her. "Not a dream," she whispered but continued, "Firstly, it wasn't me that tipped off the police, but I suspect I know who did. Secondly, I've been putting my ass on the line at work to try and make sure Teri doesn't get in trouble. I stand to lose my job if this goes wrong. Why would I do that for her?" Talking about this ignited the fire inside her again and she glared at the visibility shrinking Maisie.

"OK," Maisie looked visibly embarrassed, "so, who do *you* think it is?"

"Hannah – my ex. I think she's got hold of the info through someone at work but I can't work out how she knows about Teri and I." She reached for her phone and called up the same photo she'd shown Dave. Maisie's face went pale and she brought her hands to her mouth in shock. "You know her?"

Maisie looked up at Sophie with wide, scared eyes. "Know her? I made out with her that night at the bar while you were at the pool table!"

"You did *what*?" Sophie screeched, her surprise taking her voice up at least a few octaves of shrillness. What was it with everyone around her suddenly getting the hots for Hannah? Suddenly her stomach dropped and a feeling of dread made her go cold. She pulled her hoodie around herself and, without realising it, looked rapidly around the room. "Is she following me?"

"Sophie, I don't know but I'm really sorry for thinking of you for even a second. We need to tell Teri this straightaway." Maisie pulled out her phone. "On second thoughts, I think you should go around there in person. She didn't want to believe it was you, but she's so low. Sophie, I'm worried, I've never seen her like this before. Not since..." she stopped and looked down.

"I know Maisie – I know she's trans. You were going to say about her first girlfriend, weren't you?"

Maisie's head jerked up like she'd been electrocuted. "She told you that? Bloody hell, she really does love you." Sophie felt a warm feeling flowing through her chest, Maisie was right – they did love each other and they would be OK – wouldn't they? They had to be.

Maisie continued while standing up and heading for the door. "Right, I'll text her but I don't know if she's using her phone. You get over there as I have to get back to work."

Sophie stood and was about to follow her when she stopped. "I can't... I don't know where she lives."

"You've not been to her place? Call yourself lesbians? How are you going to get married tomorrow and have three cats if you don't know where she lives? Here...", she grabbed a sticky note and pen, scribbling an address. "Come on, you need to go."

Sophie grabbed her keys, phone and shut the door behind her, jumping in her car as Maisie screeched off down the road. Sophie only had one mission to worry about – get to Teri as quickly as possible. Sadly the London traffic had other ideas and it was an hour before she pulled up outside the address. Lady luck was smiling at her and she found a space on the street just up from Teri's block. She took a deep breath and got out of the car, striding down the street. Luckily a pizza delivery guy was leaving and she used the open door to slip in, checking the signs for number 43c. It turned out to be on the third floor of the slightly shabby old building. Paint was peeling in the stairwell but otherwise it was clean. She stood before the door, took a deep breath and knocked. She heard a scuffle from inside, probably the cat, but nothing else. Knocking louder, she shouted, "Teri, it's me."

She heard more shuffling, something larger than a cat this time and eventually the door swung open. She wasn't prepared for what she saw. Teri looked a mess – but that simple word wasn't anywhere near adequate. Her hair was tangled and matted, she looked sleepy but with bags under her eyes that suggested she hadn't slept properly. Her clothes looked like they had been slept in. In short, she looked like a disaster. Sophie couldn't take it and burst into tears. Tears of joy that Teri was OK but tears of sadness that her baby was clearly so not OK. She launched forward and grabbed Teri, putting her arms around her. "I'm so glad to see you. I was really worried." She managed to whisper between sobs.

Teri just stood there looking groggy and not reacting. Sophie went to kiss her but that seemed to finally wake her from her comatose state and she held her at arm's length.

Sophie looked into her eyes, the beautiful brown eyes that seemed dimmed and were looking at her with a question in them. She couldn't bear to hear Teri ask the question though, she knew it would devastate her. "It wasn't me, baby, I promise. I'd never do that to you."

At this, Teri's eyes widened and Sophie saw a tear start to form before her shoulders were released and Teri dropped her head into her hands. She dropped to the floor before Sophie could catch her and began sobbing. They were big, ugly heart-breaking sobs that Sophie never wanted to see coming from another human – let alone her beautiful, vulnerable girlfriend. Teri's chest heaved. Sophie dropped to her knees in front of her, the only thing that mattered at that moment being her ability to put her arms around Teri and comfort her. She had to make this right. No matter what Teri had done to her company, there was no way Sophie was going to let her be this devastated.

This gorgeous woman needed her. Sophie held her firmly, but lovingly, as Teri allowed all her emotion to flow. Even in this moment she felt her heart contract as she looked down and kissed the thick brown hair, as tears sobbed onto her chest. Her vulnerability was childlike in its simplicity and the picture of her wonderful Teri as a wide eyed, brown haired, beautiful little girl stuck in her mind. Her conscious mind knew she had never been that person back then but, in her vulnerability, now she could see the girl still there needing to be loved, reassured and to feel, above all, wanted.

A croaky, whispered voice rasped in Sophie's ear. "I'm so, so, sorry, Sophie. I should... I should never have thought of you – not for a second but I understand I've messed things up," and then she resumed sobbing, Sophie pulling the struggling woman closer into her and just letting her cry it out while rubbing her back.

How long they sat on the living room floor, Sophie wasn't sure, but eventually, Teri stilled and lifted her head. "But who?" her voice barely reached above a whisper. The hurt still in her eyes speared Sophie right in the chest but she knew it was no longer directed at her.

"I think it was Hannah," Teri's eyes widened at this news, "she, apparently, was at the bar that night. Maisie got together with her. We think she saw us and recognised me."

A look of recognition crossed Teri's eyes. "The lesbian woman!" Her voice sounded a little stronger and she was clearly seeing a picture in her mind. Sophie pulled out her phone and, again, showed the photo of Hannah. "That's her!" Teri exclaimed, the most vigour in her voice since Sophie had arrived. "But how did she know about me? I don't get it. I don't know her!"

"Ah well, that is where it gets really scary. She, apparently, sought out Dave and seduced him!"

"Err, Dave?" Teri looked lost and scrunched her face up. "But Dave's a guy... he's got a beard! You said she was lesbian, didn't you?"

"Yep – she always was. So either she's had a miraculous coming out as bi, pan or something else and coincidentally ran into the one guy who could give her info on you... "

"Or, she's been following you and wanted to get to me to split us up?" Teri suddenly looked scared again.

"Baby, nothing bad is going to happen to you. I've been talking to Paul and Mike. They are both with me that we don't want media attention on the company, they aren't going to involve the police. Plus, it's going to take a lot more than some interfering ex who treated me like shit to split us up."

Teri relaxed her body and looked at Sophie again. "Oh Sophie, I love you so much. I am so sorry I doubted you. Do you mean you really are going to stay with me?"

"We're here for each other, Teri. I love you too. I never want to hurt you. You don't need to feel bad, I get that you weren't quite yourself." Her eyes dropped to Teri's lips, which looked dry from tears and emotion. Sophie felt the desire to fix them and leaned forward, gently, oh so gently, touching Teri's lips with her own. She would nurse her back to health with kisses if that were possible and she conveyed that to the other woman with the most loving, passionate kiss she dared in Teri's fragile stage.

206

As she pulled away, Teri had a slightly glazed, faraway look in her eyes. Sophie held her sides in a strong embrace before pulling the other woman to her feet, "Let's get you cleaned up and figure out what to do about this mess."

As they entered the bathroom, Teri's eyes still looked a little faraway. She whispered, seemingly to herself, "I thought I'd lost you. That was the scariest part of it all to me. My brain tells me such bad things and I can't help but believe them."

"You've not lost me Teri, and you aren't going to." Sophie reassured the fragile-looking woman, tears forming in her own eyes as she saw the upset on her delicate face. She caressed her cheek softly and Teri leaned her head into the touch, like a wounded animal seeking comfort. This was not the woman Sophie had met at first. Where had all that confidence and life gone? She realised that what she was seeing was the true Teri, under all the bravado – a woman with a constant fear of not being good enough. This was the deep belief that had triggered the drinking she saw before. While she hated that she had to see it, she felt so privileged that she got to see the real person, the fact that sometimes this sexy, strong, clever woman looked as scared and lost as this. Right there and then Sophie vowed she never wanted to see her struck so low ever again.

Supporting Teri, she gently asked, "Can I help you clean up, or would you rather sort yourself?"

Teri looked into her eyes, a slight widening of them showing an unspoken hope, her deep walnut brown, watery eyes seeming to Sophie like pools of deep, pure love. "I'll be fine, but please, don't leave."

"OK, I'll be right here, I'm not going anywhere, so you have a refreshing shower and you'll feel more like yourself."

At this Teri's eyes closed and Sophie saw her face shutter, "Maybe this is the real me. I'm not as confident as I seem."

She grabbed Teri's hand and firmly held it. "No, you're not this person I see here. You're the sexy, funny, slightly annoying and cheeky woman that I've fallen in love with. We all have down patches and what you're going through is more than enough to explain that, but it will get better."

She slowly lifted Teri's hoodie top and t-shirt off her body, the other woman offering no resistance. Sophie tried not to look at the outline of those beautiful breasts under a sports bra that was revealed. Now wasn't the time.

Teri spotted her looking and a slight smile quirked up. "See something you like?" she teased lightly but nothing like her normal tone.

Sophie reached over and swatted her arm, while her cheeks blushed hot at being caught peeking. "Oi, pack it in and let's get you in that shower. With the most kindness possible, you smell of stale booze."

She reached over and started the shower running, checking the temperature while Teri pulled her bra off and slipped down her bottoms, stepping into the shower as Sophie moved away.

Sophie took one backward glance and the steamy glass shower door obscured most of the details but she could make out a pale, curvy body and her mind joined forces with her core to fill in the gaps she couldn't quite make out. She let out a breath and swiftly turned, heading back into the bedroom.

A few minutes later, as Teri dressed, Sophie noticed she paused and seemed a little distant. "What's up, Gorgeous?"

Teri looked up and her eyes focussed back on Sophie. She was biting her bottom lip and she quickly looked down again. "I... I'm kind of scared. I don't feel as safe here now on my own."

Sophie rushed around the bed and held Teri by the arms before pulling her into a hug.

Releasing her she answered, "Would it help if you came to mine?"

Teri's eyes widened, "Really? You'd let me?"

"Let you? What are you on about you daft woman? Of course I'd let you. I love you and I *want* you with me as much as possible. If you'd feel safer at mine then let's get you a bag packed and get over there. You've got a new job starting Monday and you'll be closer to it anyway."

Teri looked even more surprised, "Do you think they'll still want me?"

"Teri, you've not even been accused of anything and if I have my way, you won't be. I can't promise you it won't happen but I will do everything I can for you."

"What did I do to deserve you?" With that, she placed a gentle, warm kiss onto Sophie's lips.

Chapter Twenty-Four

It took a little while to pack Teri's things because Number One chose that moment to reappear from wherever he'd been hiding. "He clearly doesn't like the police any more than me." Teri joked. Both women sat down on the floor in the lounge and made a fuss of him. He seemed to like Sophie, sitting on her outstretched legs and licking each paw in turn.

"Your pussy seems to like me," Sophie smirked.

"Certainly does..." Teri smirked back, feeling a little more like her normal self now she had Sophie with her again. Neither of them looked at Number One while saying this and he scornfully ignored their attempts at rude humour as beneath his notice.

"Do you think he'll be OK at mine?" Sophie asked, stroking his back and ruffling his neck fur, her attention fully on the cat rather than Teri.

Teri looked up, surprised, "At yours? What do you mean?"

"Well, I thought he might be lonely here all on his own. I assumed you'd want to bring him with you?"

Teri felt like the worst pet owner imaginable. She'd assumed Number One would be OK if left to his own devices for a day or so, he had plenty of food and water. Here was her girlfriend including him in her invite, knowing how much he meant to her. "Oh, it never occurred that you'd want him tagging along. Would you really be OK with it?"

"Of course I would, he's gorgeous. He won't go off and get lost, will he, I wouldn't want anything to happen to him?"

"Oh no, he's used to staying in the flat most of the time unless I leave a window open. He never goes very far but he's certainly taken to you. We could all lie on that rug in your lounge together." Teri's overactive imagination pictured the scene and while Number One wasn't actually the focus of her mental image, she was genuine in saying she was sure he would like that.

As her eyes refocussed into the room, she noticed Sophie's cheeks had gone quite a fetching pink. *Hmmm, she's thinking the same as me...* That amused Teri and she felt her mouth widening into a smile.

"That's settled, the pussy comes too." A slightly flustered Sophie said before obviously realising she'd made things worse and putting her face in her hands. Teri simply raised an eyebrow and stifled her immature giggle. Number One didn't giggle, he just looked between both women and Teri could swear she saw him roll his eyes. She ruffled his fur in solidarity anyway, so he wouldn't feel left out.

"If you sit there with him, I'll grab his travelling cage. He's not too fond of it so if you keep stroking him then we can get him in... then I'll grab his litter box, some food and other stuff for him. I guess I need a bag of clothes too!"

"Don't forget clothes for work." Sophie called after her as she flew into the bedroom and fished the box out from under her bed.

She came back and Number One's eyes were closed, Sophie's stroking clearly having a relaxing effect. "He does like you... mind you, I'd like lying on your legs with you stroking me like that too," said Teri as Sophie turned her head.

"I can make that happen – just say the word."

With a little fuss and the odd hiss, Number One was in the crate and Sophie carried him down to her waiting car. Teri did a couple of runs to bring everything else down while Sophie soothed the annoyed animal. She wasn't sure whether he objected more to the crate or to losing his comfortable bed on Sophie's legs. She knew which would bother her more. On her second run she grabbed her bag, laptop and locked the door behind her. She wouldn't mind seeing the back of this place for a couple of days. Maybe when she came back things would have calmed down. *'Perhaps I won't need to come back? Where did that thought come from? Sophie hasn't asked me to move in, that really would be U-Haul speed!'*

The idea scared her, strangely, and she was pensive as they set off through the London traffic. Luckily Teri didn't think Sophie had noticed her mood changing since the traffic was bad so she had to concentrate.

By the time they arrived back in Chelmsford, Teri had snapped out of it. They unloaded everything, including Number One. He'd decided that being annoyed was a waste of his precious feline energy and he may as well allow his human servants to serve him ... and gone to sleep. Teri suspected he was planning a masterplan to attack them in their sleep.

Settling down and letting Number One stalk around familiarising himself with Sophie's downstairs, they cuddled up on the sofa. Sophie was stroking Teri's hair gently. "Does this feel better?"

"Mmmm yes." Teri lazily drawled, her head lying back on Sophie's collar bone and her eyes closed. This was heaven. She could lie here all day. Suddenly something dawned on her. "Sophie?"

"Hmmm?"

"Shouldn't you be at work?"

"I called in an emergency and took the morning off. When Maisie came around, I knew I was going to be out for a while and I wanted to be there for you. You were obviously going through something bad."

Teri was surprised, she knew she shouldn't be, but every time someone did something like this it caught her unawares. She wasn't used to having someone love her.

"You can stay here as long as you need, you know, if you feel safer. I do need to work this afternoon but then we can spend the weekend together. Number One seems to have settled in already."

Teri turned to follow Sophie's gaze over her shoulder and spotted Number One curling up and enjoying a catnap on the other armchair. He seemed to have quite happily staked out his territory over there.

"I think that sounds heavenly. We could play more crazy golf!" Teri smiled, teasing.

"You and your golf – just because you won, suddenly you're an expert!" Sophie chuckled, "So what would you like to do today?"

Teri considered for a bit, with the intensity of emotions the last forty-eight hours had heaped on her, she needed to slow down and relax. "Well, you'll think I'm lazy but I would dearly love to chill in a bubble bath. I brought my Kindle and I'd like to get lost in some easy-going romance. Would that be OK with you?"

"OK?" Sophie sounded surprised; her brow furrowed. "Of course it's OK but rewind a minute – what's this about romance? Have I discovered another hidden secret to Ms Simlake? Are you all soft and gooey in the middle?"

"Cupcake, you know exactly what I feel like in the middle!" chuckled an amused Teri, wiggling her eyebrows suggestively, "but yes, I do have a thing for romance, especially a nice, hot romance in a steaming bath."

"Ohhhhh? Right, well I've got a challenge for you then, Ms Sexy Romance Lover... you can have your bubble bath but you're not allowed to come... until I finish work."

Teri was shocked, her kitten did have claws, "*Whaaat*? You filthy vixen Sophie, I thought you were a cute kitten, I see you've got a bad side! I hadn't even considered doing anything like that, so you're on."

Sophie looked like she was enjoying this conversation and she developed an evil-looking grin before adding, "Actually, I'll make it even more interesting. I'll bet you can't hold off coming until I tell you to."

"Easy-peasy. I'm just going to relax anyway."

"Oh, you think so?"

There was something in Sophie's tone, a note of teasing, and alarm bells started to ring, Sophie was up to something but this sounded like a challenge that would be fun to lose.

"Yep..." replied Teri, with a slight hint of trepidation.

~#~

Sophie made them lunch and they ate it curled up on the sofa together. She said she needed to get ready for work and headed upstairs. Teri nodded, picking up her kindle and setting out to lose herself. After a little while, Sophie came back down. "OK Gorgeous, I've got some bubble bath out for you and started running a bath." She was wearing a fitted grey suit skirt and black blouse that made the piercing blue of her eyes really pop. Her hair bounced around her face in golden curls, lending her an aura of simultaneous innocence and sexuality that Teri found irresistible. The skirt was fitted to her curves perfectly and Teri had to swallow a couple of times before she could think straight.

"Thanks Soph, are you heading out now?"

"I'll get to work shortly. Go and run upstairs and check that the bath doesn't overflow, won't you dear?"

That was it, Sophie was definitely up to something. She didn't come down looking that sexy without reason and she never called her dear. She narrowed her eyes but Sophie ignored her and went through into the hall to get her laptop bag.

Teri followed, pulling her into a kiss goodbye. She couldn't resist letting her hand wander downwards and stroke the sensual curve of her bum in this skirt. Oh, how she'd love to be able to rip it

214

off her right now. Suddenly, the penny dropped. "You're trying to tempt me and get me all frustrated aren't you, you Vixen?"

"Me? Little old me?" Sophie squeaked in what Teri supposed was supposed to be an innocent tone. Teri pinched her bum, groaning at the feel.

"Yes, you. I see your game. Right, to work with you. I'll go and sort that bath." With that she swatted Sophie on the bum, the sharp crack echoing through the hall. Sophie didn't drop the smile from her lips though, just quirked an eyebrow.

Teri turned and ran up the stairs, she didn't want to flood Sophie's lovely house. That would not be a good start to the weekend. She quickly turned the taps off, dipping a hand in the warm, inviting water. Shedding her clothes, she lay back, enjoying the caress of the warmness against her tired skin. It felt like a cuddle after a hard day and she knew who she imagined was doing the cuddling. She pictured her girlfriend in this bath with her, and squirmed a little as she felt a warm tension between her legs that wasn't related to the water temperature. The woman had put the idea in her head – she'd not even *thought* about feeling frisky with everything that had happened. Somehow, Sophie seemed to know exactly what to say to help Teri's mind stay occupied and away from her problems.

Opening her Kindle, she found the place she'd left her latest romance book. The heroine was attending a family wedding and had just met the love of her life on a tropical island. Teri knew it was going to go south soon, these books always did, but she knew there'd be some fun first. Relaxing in the hot water she wasn't disappointed as Lani, the girlfriend, dropped to her knees in front of Ariel. Teri's imagination ran away with her, picturing her and Sophie in the same position. While Ariel was a redhead, her own blonde goddess could make her just as weak at the knees. Without any thought, her free right hand reached down and lightly stroked up her own thigh, the tickling motion making her exhale deeply and close her eyes for a second. She absentmindedly played with her left breast, stroking around it as, in the book, Lani leaned in and pleasured Ariel with her mouth. The descriptions were vivid, there was a reason she loved this author, and soon she was feeling some of the same sensations as Ariel. Without thinking further, she dropped her hand again down below her waist and scratched at the triangle there. She lightly stroked the outside of her folds with forked fingers, the light caress complementing the way she could almost taste the fictional Ariel's come on Lani's tongue, the way it was described.

She was so distracted she didn't hear or see the bathroom door slowly open. She came to her senses with a start and almost dropped her Kindle in the water when she looked up and saw a smirking Sophie standing there with her hands on her hips. *Her strong hands, on her sexy hips...* She was still wearing that sex goddess pencil skirt and Teri couldn't help but stare.

"Enjoying yourself, are you, Gorgeous?"

"Yes thanks, but why are you still here, I thought you were at work?"

"Oh, I'm *working*, yes, but I decided it would be much more fun to work from home this afternoon. I've got a break between meetings so figured I'd check up on how you were. I see I didn't need to worry."

Teri blushed. She was proud of her body, after all she'd been through, and she owned her sexuality proudly. However, she felt guilty she had been caught taking some pleasure that should have belonged to her radiant goddess here. However, she swiftly got over that reservation when Sophie's eyes flashed with fire and raked up and down her exposed body. Her tongue darted out and she licked her lower lip. That caused a renewal of the tension between Teri's legs. Man, this woman was gorgeous.

"Hmmm, I've got a while before my next meeting. How about I help you a bit?"

216

"What did you have in mi—" The word died on Teri's lips as Sophie reached behind and unzipped her skirt, shimmying it down. Teri licked her lips at the sight of her black lace thong. Sophie gripped the hem of her blouse, crossing arms, and swiftly lifted it up and over her head, shaking her hair out and allowing her blonde curls to flutter around her head. Standing there in her black bra and thong with electric blue detail across the sheer mesh, she looked so utterly sexy, confident and all powerful that Teri's insides melted. There was no resisting this woman, nor could she think of a single reason she'd ever try.

Teri came to her senses as Sophie reached behind and unhooked her bra, before allowing it to fall, then crooked a thumb inside the thong and pulled that down too. She toed it off on top of the bra and produced a bath pouffe Teri had failed to notice.

"I thought I'd help..." and with that, she stepped into the bath, facing Teri who almost passed out with the heat that suddenly engulfed her. Had someone instantly superheated the water or was her body just in overdrive at the sight of the beautiful naked woman opposite her?

Oh ... my... she's kneeling, was as far as her brain got before Sophie reached for her shower gel and the lemon fragrance filled Teri's nostrils.

Adding a generous dollop of shower gel, Teri felt it gently caress her skin. It rubbed small, loving circles and she felt the stress ease from her tight muscles. Teri rested her arms on Sophie's shoulders. The scent of lemon was refreshing and the steam was cleansing. It was certainly working, Teri's eyes closed and her head tipped back. She opened one eye a fraction and noticed an intent look of concentration on Sophie's beautiful face. The gentle caress of the pouffe slowly worked its way down Teri's neck, over her previously tense shoulders and spent rather more time than probably necessary caressing her breasts. Another peek revealed Sophie was licking her lips a little as she tickled the pouffe over Teri's small, rosy nipples which were budding strongly and starting to throb a little at the touch. Teri's breath hitched and her melting insides reached a temperature somewhere between molten lava and the core of a flaming sun. She stayed still though, lying back and not wanting to break the spell that Sophie was casting.

Playing the dutiful carer, Sophie carried on down, soaping up Teri's flat tummy before she got to the small triangle of curls between her legs that Teri had been thinking about when she walked in. Peeking again, Teri saw Sophie close her eyes and draw in a breath.

Sophie shook her head and continued lavishing her care upon Teri, moving down Teri's legs in small circles with the pouffe. She had shuffled back in the bath to make it easier in the cramped space. Massaging Teri's toes made her giggle and she wriggled at the touch.

"Oh, we're ticklish, are we? I'll remember that!" said Sophie with a wicked grin.

Teri felt the heat spread up her spine and she hoped Sophie could see the passion in her eyes because her mouth couldn't quite compose words beyond "ahhhh" and "mmmmm".

Sophie leaned forward, taking Teri's face in her hands. Teri felt her lips press firmly onto her own in a searing kiss that was so intense she felt her most innermost thoughts flow out of her body. The throbbing in her clit intensified and she pressed her hips forward, hoping to make contact with Sophie, who moved her hips backwards by the smallest, most frustrating, amount.

Sophie broke the kiss, grinning at the obviously frustrated Teri and backing away before standing. Teri was speechless looking at the lithe figure glistening with water, bubbles clinging to her breasts and between her thighs as though the soap found her as irresistible as her girlfriend.

"Now, you relax there for a bit and meet me in the bedroom when you get out, Gorgeous," Sophie said, blowing her a kiss as she stepped out of the bath.

Teri groaned in frustration and pressed her thighs together. The ache this woman created was something else entirely.

Minutes later, Sophie had obviously dried off when Teri entered the bedroom, rubbing her hair dry with a towel. Sophie had put her black bra and thong back on and the effect was just as electric as before. The vivid blue of a peacock feather pattern embroidered over the sheer black mesh gave her an exotic feel. Somehow that was even more sexy than seeing her naked in the bath. Teri gulped. She saw a glint in Sophie's eye and suspected she was still up to something. Sophie bent at the waist, ruffling through a drawer and pulling out something white which she threw to the side of the bed. She looked over her shoulder with a smile and Teri went hot and, she suspected, red at being caught looking at the firm, tempting arse in front of her.

"What are you doing over there? Come over here and kiss me."

Teri's feet obeyed eagerly and without question. She put her arms around Sophie, revelling in the silky-smooth feel of her, now dry and moisturised, skin. She kissed her passionately, feeling her clit pulse and before she realised, Sophie had pushed her leg between Teri's. She pushed down on it, desperate for friction on her engorged and sensitive pleasure bud.

Sophie turned them both around so Teri's back was to the bed before pulling away slightly. She looked thoroughly kissed, her red lips were swollen and her hair was gorgeously mussed. Teri loved seeing her like this, she looked like passion incarnate and the feeling of her being so close in front while the bed pressed against the backs of her knees made it feel that Sophie was asserting her dominance, and Teri loved it. Once her eyes focussed back on Teri, the hungry look appeared back on her face and she pressed a hand to Teri's chest, lightly shoving her so she fell back onto the bed.

"Shuffle back, I want you on your back. Remember, no coming until I say."

Teri dutifully shuffled backwards, smirking.

The grin seemed to fire Sophie up even more, as she ran a hand up her naked thigh and Teri jumped, electrocuted by the connection between them. Sophie's pupils were wide with desire, the crystal-clear blue flashing. She was smiling hungrily as Teri lay on her back, her legs slightly apart. Teri swiftly felt like the prey of a very hungry, very sexy, wolf. Sophie knelt on the bed beside Teri and leaned forward, touching their lips together and letting loose a spark. Teri wondered if the room had a loose circuit, or if it was just her mind blowing a fuse.

Sophie lifted one leg and straddled Teri's thigh. Teri was utterly distracted by the heat she felt burning down onto her own skin. It wasn't only Sophie's eyes that told her she wanted to devour her. In her distraction she didn't notice Sophie had picked up a large, white, cordless wand vibrator she'd thrown over earlier and was smirking at her girlfriend. "You look so tasty, lying there waiting for me. Part of me wants to make you wait some more, but luckily for you, another part of me," she leaned forward, her barely contained breasts leaning heavily on Teri's chest, "has other ideas." The black bra was thin enough to allow Teri to see the perfect outline of her erect nipples. She brought her mouth right down to Teri's ear before continuing in a husky whisper, "I can't wait to see you come utterly undone. I want to see you experience what I feel when you pleasure me and we're going to take it nice and slow until you do."

A shiver of electricity shot down Teri's spine from the hot breath on her ear. She felt Sophie's tongue quickly whorl round the outer shell of her earlobe and closed her eyes, breathing deeply. "Now, open wide like a good girl."

Teri turned her head and quirked an eyebrow at Sophie. A teasing response was about to come from her lips but was quickly silenced by another scorching hot kiss. Her eyes closed and she relaxed into it, reaching out for Sophie and holding her side with one hand and going to the back of her head with the other. As the kiss relaxed, Sophie kissed down Teri's jaw and she tilted her head back to allow this entrancing woman all the access she wished. She lavished kisses all down Teri's jaw and to her throat, before working her way back up to the ear she'd started with. "Be mine Teri, let me show you how it feels." Her husky whisper thrummed through Teri as her thighs were gently pushed apart.

She'd forgotten about the white toy momentarily but was quickly reminded as Sophie shifted her weight. A loud, deep buzzing sound drew her attention. The kissing didn't relent though and she felt her ear being nibbled. Even remembering her own name was an impossibility, let alone remembering how to open her eyes or talk. She leaned into the hot breath. The buzzing came closer and she felt it touch, and circle, her right breast. Circling inwards, she felt it ghost her swollen nipple and move off to the left side where it repeated its pleasurable torment.

Sophie kissed back across her jaw to Teri's mouth, who felt her lips being caressed and nibbled. Opening her mouth she welcomed the attention bestowed on her. If Sophie was trying to find a way to say 'you *are* worthy' she was doing a great job but Teri didn't have the brainpower to psychoanalyse this situation, she was simply consumed by sensation.

The warm mouth released her lip and the kissing continued down the other side of her jaw before alighting again at her ear. Without even being encouraged, she tilted her head to the other side and nuzzled closer into the attention. Now wasn't the time to worry about being needy – now was a time to feel, and boy, did it feel!

The sensation of those marvellous breasts feeling heavy on her own again, as Sophie leaned across, was fabulous but she was, again, distracted as the wand slipped between them and headed down her belly. Its pressure was strong against her, weighed down by the body leaning above it.

It continued to slide down until reaching the apex of her thighs. A consumed Teri had long since given up on trying to control the situation and was blissfully surrendering to the sensations. Sophie's knees pushed her own further apart. As the wand buzzed inextricably downwards, it reached her mound and lightly circled it, the tingling vibrations already starting to run through her body to her core. It pressed lower and Teri felt it caressing her thigh and folds on one side before the velvety smooth head moved and similarly caressed the other side. While it hadn't yet touched her clit, she was utterly aware of the vibrations reaching every part of her lower body. Her legs pushed as wide as her hips allowed. She opened up her very centre to the woman showing her all this pleasure. The vibrating head performed one ghosting pass up her slit, edging closer painfully slowly to her clit. Its vibrations weren't just your common or garden buzz, this was a full-strength hammer drill of a vibrator and the deep waves of sensation it created passed through and consumed every part of her lower body from her clit to stomach.

One coherent thought occurred to the depths of her oxytocin addled brain, Sophie had considered her enough to lube the toy for her from the way it was gliding, not scratching her. That act alone released a complementary set of happy hormones as she acknowledged how in tune with her body this woman was already.

That was her last coherent thought as the deep, bass vibrations reached her clit. They penetrated not just that bud of pleasure which begged for attention but through it, her spine, her ultra-sensitive back passage and upwards through her entire body. She pressed her hips forward seeking firmer contact, she didn't care how brazen she was being in this moment – Sophie wanted her, she knew that, and she wanted this feeling of Sophie closer – as close as it was possible to be. The vibrating head circled her clit and she felt her breathing hitch. She heard soft whimpers coming with the breaths and realised it was her making those noises. She kept her eyes closed, the image of Sophie on top of her would be too much in reality, but her mind's eye could see it and visualise everything the other woman was doing. The vibrations grew stronger after a click and continued to circle her clit in a smooth rhythm. There was no stopping now, she

222

could feel the tension rising for her and she pushed her thighs as wide as they would go, cursing that she couldn't turn inside out and simply absorb both Sophie and the toy. Her breaths were short and jerky now as the tension, it wasn't pain and it wasn't pure pleasure, built somewhere within her pelvis. She couldn't pinpoint exactly where it built – her body was just a mass of sensation and tension. The kissing and nibbling from Sophie and circling of the velvety vibrating head conspired to overwhelm her senses. "Ahhahaha," she whimpered, not even recognising the sounds coming out of her throat, more noisy breaths than attempts to speak.

"Come for me Teri, let yourself go," a voice whispered, the seductively husky tone finding its way into her inner brain, as the vibrator pushed harder against her. Sophie held it over Teri's clit and she jerked her hips in sudden overwhelming sensation. The extreme hit of pleasure was almost painful. Sophie caressed the head again up and down Teri's slit before again pressing firmly, moving around this time in very tiny circles on her clit. The tension was becoming too much, the arching of her back to get more contact feeling like she was going to snap in two. The pain, from forcing her legs open as wide as possible, was eclipsed by the waves of tension and she felt herself slipping. She opened her entirely unfocussed eyes, registering nothing except colours, but her mouth opened with a strangled "Ahhhghhhh". That was her body's final rise up the crescendo peak and she felt the sensation utterly overwhelm her for a second. The feeling of pure bliss, pure abandon and total ecstasy was exhausting and she collapsed back, grateful she had the soft bed to catch her. Her lips were dry, her hands shaking and her muscles weak. She barely had the strength to close her legs, allowing them instead to lie limply to either side. Sophie kept, very gently, stroking her folds up and down with the vibrations until Teri's panting had returned to something approaching a normal breathing rate.

Turning off, and throwing the wand to the side, she kissed Teri firmly on the lips. Teri felt the warmth from her girlfriend's lips and, through it, gained the energy to refocus her eyes. Speaking was a

223

long off dream, as was moving, but she felt total relief as Sophie lay down on top of her, her leg between Teri's, her arms sliding under her. She felt the squeeze of the cuddle and knew it wasn't just a caress of her upper body but also Sophie holding and caring for her heart. She relaxed back into it for a few seconds, allowing her girlfriend to kiss, stroke and hold her while she came down from the moment of explosive tension release.

~#~

As Teri regained the use of conscious thought, Sophie was looking down at her from her position to the side, propped up on one elbow. "You know, you are so beautiful when you're consumed. I love you."

Teri grinned and felt a different warmth flow through her. After the electricity of a climax, this was a soothing, reassuring warmth. "Didn't we have a bet? What happened?"

Sophie's shoulders hunched a little and her lip quirked, she was amused. "Well... firstly, I couldn't resist the faces you were making and secondly, I never intended to win – I just wanted to make you work for it a bit!" She broke into a giggle as Teri stared at her and rolled her eyes. "Anyway," she continued, "don't you think it's your turn?" and she wiggled her eyebrows for emphasis.

Teri didn't need asking twice and suddenly her languid body decided it was no longer sated. She pushed onto her side quickly, feeling the fire behind her eyes as she looked down her sexy girlfriend's body and tried to decide where to start. Her sex-mussed hair splayed out to the side on the pillow, her flushed face shone, but her breasts needed to be freed from that erotic but way too bothersome lingerie immediately. Teri leaned in for a kiss and used her free arm to reach around and undo the bra clasp keeping her from kissing those beautiful breasts.

Chapter Twenty-Five

Sophie felt her bra being undone while Teri kissed her. "Oh, I see. One-handed eh? I always knew you had covert talents."

Teri smirked, "Don't you just know it, my little kitten, now where else can I put my talented fingers to use?"

Sophie looked up at her smirking, sexy brunette and a surge of lust mixed with love flowed through her body. With her short, umber hair on the pillow and her breasts that seemed perfectly sized for Sophie's hands, this woman set her pulse racing and liquified her core. Hearing Teri groaning earlier, not to mention seeing her with bubble-bath on her breasts, had caused Sophie to heat.

Teri's fingers started caressing her breasts. Sophie could feel them tickling while the woman kept eye contact with her, her deep chocolate eyes losing the tiredness from earlier and glowing with flecks of gold and an intensity that rooted Sophie to the spot. She could feel the energy and wanted to let it consume her. Suddenly, those clever fingers reached her erect nipple and flicked it. The tweak caused another erect bud of hers to tweak within her underwear and she moaned and arched her back forward into the touch. The flick turned into more of a pinch and the momentary pain joined with the feeling radiating from between her legs to warm every part of her body. "Oh yeeees," she realised she'd whispered and closed her eyes, opening them again with difficulty. Teri flicked and tweaked her other nipple, sending a jolt of something – Sophie could neither understand nor care what – straight to her clit.

"Please, Teri," she huskily breathed. It wasn't even a whisper, just a breath, and the rational side of her brain couldn't believe she was behaving like a character out of a romance novel. What was going to happen next? The heroine saying "Oh you're mine now," and biting her?

"Oh, you're mine now, my favourite kitten," a voice whispered in her ear and if she hadn't been thoroughly occupied, Sophie would have laughed out loud. She couldn't think for much longer before Teri moved in and pressed their lips together, turning her head slightly and caressing her lower lip, before sucking and biting gently. Sophie just wanted more; more kissing, more biting, more Teri!

Next thing she knew, another persistent hand was making its way, teasingly, up her inside leg and thigh. Teri seemed to know this was a touch that undid the normally professional Sophie, it was so intimate and suggestive. One finger slightly ghosted over the black mesh of her knickers, sliding between her legs. She was sure it was obvious how soaking wet she was and pressed her hips against the other woman more. Her breath hitched at the contact.

"Hmmmm?" Teri purred with a quirked eyebrow.

"Please," let out Sophie, in a husky whisper.

Teri's thumbs reached the sides of the black panties and quickly pulled them down, Sophie felt them sensually tickling down along her legs before her girlfriend flicked them over her ankles and off the side of the bed. Teri leaned in for another kiss, Sophie reaching for her in blind grabbing motions as her eyes closed at the pleasure of these warm lips touching and branding her own. Then Teri was gone. Sophie opened her eyes and saw the other woman leaning over the bed, retrieving something. When she leaned back up, the muscles in her torso tensed and Sophie licked her lips. Then she saw what Teri was holding and licked her own lips – the wand massager she'd forgotten moments earlier was back. She hoped she'd remembered to fully charge it; she'd never live it down otherwise and she wasn't sure her throbbing clit would ever forgive her.

Teri shuffled across and lay flat on top of her, she could feel the warmth of her body all along her torso and she ground her hips against the leg that appeared between hers. Teri supported her weight on her arms and quickly popped the wand between them, in

226

the midst of their pelvises. Sophie felt her press the button and the deep buzzing started. It took Teri a few seconds to adjust both her hips and the wand but she got it firmly sandwiched between them both. Teri's weight pressed down just above Sophie's clit. The vibrations were on the lowest setting but the bass was reverbing through her mound and causing her clit to pulse. She widened her legs, wanting to expose more to this woman and invite her in. This gave Teri the opportunity to caress Sophie's sensitive folds. The sensation, that would normally be a light tickling, was magnified by the aroused state of her whole body and she rocked her pelvis, arching into the touch. Next thing she knew, those same fingers were circling her core. "Wow, you're wet!" came a breathless voice from in front of her face.

Sophie couldn't decide whether to respond with 'No shit sherlock, now get those fingers inside me' or a simple 'Don't stop' but she was silenced with another scorching kiss that divided her attention between her mouth and her core, leaving nothing left for coherent thought. Teri pulled back a touch and Sophie felt dazed from the reduced sensation. She opened her eyes to see where she was going and saw her nod slightly, almost imperceptibly but such was their connection that she heard the unspoken question loud and clear. As she nodded enthusiastically, her heart warmed at the respect of this woman who, even in the midst of such an all-consuming act, would check to see she was OK and that she wanted this. Hannah never did, she plunged in regardless – not that Sophie hadn't wanted her to at the time, but maybe it was better to be asked. All thought of her ex was instantly wiped from her brain as two fingers pushed gently inside her, that first inch being, in some ways the most thrilling as it represented the feeling of pleasure to come, the feeling of caring, loving and even, in this case, the feeling of utterly and totally giving her most intimate self to this woman.

"Oh yes... deeper," she heard a breathy voice exhale before realising it was her own. As Teri deepened her thrust, Sophie felt her beckon her fingers up, stretching and filling her, stroking every part of

227

her inner walls until she touched that special, extra sensitive patch. Sophie's hips bucked at that moment and that forced the wand closer to her clit which gave an extra jolt. She pressed into the sensation, only dimly aware that Teri was both pressing back and groaning her own pleasure into Sophie's ear. "I ... love ... it ... when ... you ... squeeze ... me," a breathless Teri whispered in her ear. Sophie's core muscles involuntarily clenched and she both heard and felt another breathy "Mmmmm" in her ear.

The clear pleasure emanating from her girlfriend's breaths on her ear, the vibrations in her clit and the filling, stroking inside her passage combined as sensations to pull her own orgasm closer. She was already close after seeing Teri explode, but she was soaring higher and higher now. That familiar tension and pressure built in her core. "Harder, baby," she groaned.

With that, Teri kissed her. A kiss so carnal and possessive that Sophie felt thoroughly owned and in this woman's control, and she loved it. The release got closer but not as close as when Teri began pumping her two fingers out and up harder, still managing to hit that lovely sensitive patch Sophie knew that caused her to clench more than any other. The combination of the three sensations overwhelmed her and she felt the pressure build before breaking deep inside her, passing through her body like waves crashing hard onto a beach after a storm.

It took her a moment to regain thought and realise how close Teri was. Despite her own sensitivity she couldn't help but reach down to adjust the wand's position until she saw Teri's eyes widen with shock and her legs spread further. Sophie felt more weight on top of her as her girlfriend's arm gave way, shaking. Pushing her own hips closer too caused that same tension which hadn't fully dissipated to quickly build again for a second time and the loud cries of "Oh...oh...ohh..." from Teri pushed her over the edge. Both their climaxes hit and the waves crashed around them together as she grabbed Teri's lips with her own, kissing her with a craving as they came down together from the high.

228

Sophie pulled the wand out and put her arms around her languid, slightly shaking girlfriend. She had no energy herself but this couldn't have been more perfect as a moment.

Oh... or could it? and with a mischievous movement she pushed her hand between them and swiped it along her partner's velvety folds, feeling the wetness there before bringing it up and, while looking deep into Teri's eyes, sucking on the finger with a loud, "Mmmmmm."

Sophie had no idea where she'd got so bold but she loved it and the wide-eyed groan from Teri told her she was quite happy too.

~#~

Neither woman wanted to move from bed so Sophie reached over and grabbed Teri's Kindle. They lay in each other's arms sharing the experience of reading the same book together. Teri had pulled up a shorter novella by the same author as her earlier book so Sophie wasn't left behind. She was quite a quick reader so sometimes she was ahead and would giggle a few seconds before Sophie, but it didn't matter to her. She found it adorable how engaged her girlfriend became. Whatever the characters in her choice of lesfic were doing, so long as there was love involved, she and Teri could totally relate to it. That there were some seriously steamy scenes was just the icing on the cake. She stroked her girlfriend's naturally silky, straight hair while watching her intently reading a particularly gripping (and no doubt filthy) passage. She still couldn't believe Teri was a romantic fiction fan but it made her all the more endearing – another facet to her complex personality that Sophie was enjoying getting to unwrap. "I love you," she said happily, the words only partly expressing the warmth she was feeling.

Teri broke away from the book, turning her head to look into Sophie's eyes. "And I love you too, more than you can imagine," topping off her words with a chaste but still warm kiss before her attention was pulled back to the Kindle.

Sophie chuckled a little, "You really get into these stories, don't you?"

Teri put the Kindle down, looking back at Sophie with concern in her beautiful deep eyes, the flecks of gold shining out. "I'm sorry, I'm ignoring you. I do love you. I get a little bit consumed; I think it's part of my personality." She shrugged and looked down. "Sorry."

Sophie shook her head quickly. "No, don't you ever feel sorry for being you. That wasn't what I meant at all! I think it's adorable the way you get consumed and I know it has no bearing on your feelings for me."

Teri smiled, "Oh good, because I love you far more than any book. I was really enjoying lying here with you and sharing this, is that OK?"

"It's more than OK, darling, it's fantastic." Sophie lifted her hand again to stroke Teri's hair before leaning in for a slightly less chaste kiss.

"Oh good," replied Teri, after pulling back a touch, with a cheeky grin appearing, "I was dying to find out what the deal is with this kiwi!"

Sophie burst into a laugh. Teri had introduced her to this author. One of the things she had explained, with a glint in her eye, was how this particular author was just one big, terrible tease who kept taunting her readers with mentions of one particularly elusive but intimate scene. Teri sounded quite frustrated when explaining this and it was her conviction that had made Sophie smile – another insight into the wonderful world of Teri!

Teri continued, "Have you really not read any romance like this before? I thought you were a romantic at heart?"

Sophie laughed again, looking at Teri's curious face, "I am, but I don't think I can hold a candle to your romantic spirit. I do read some, but not as much as you, apparently." She named a couple of books she had found enjoyable and Teri sniggered. "What?" Sophie knew she'd put her foot in it somehow, from the way Teri was grinning at her.

"Those are pretty famous... I didn't know you were kinky?"

Sophie suddenly remembered that the two books she'd named were rather, how could she describe it, 'spicy' – lots of kneeling and begging? She felt a blush right down her throat and chest. She had been a bit surprised since she happened upon them by accident, but enjoyed them nevertheless and found some of the 'activities' the sexy couple had got up to had caused her core to inflame with molten lava.

Teri came close to her ear and nibbled her earlobe, pulling on it a little before whispering, "Now, I see where the idea for the kitten ears came from, I knew there was something exotic about them when I saw you the first time. You warmed every part of me, from my heart downwards..."

A shiver shot down Sophie's spine and her core pulsed at the sheer erotic suggestion in Teri's tone and words. Suddenly, some mental pictures from the book she'd read entered her head and she looked at Teri through her lashes, her body flushed and her breathing heavy.

A pleasant ache between her legs reminded Sophie of what they'd been doing until a little while before and why they were relaxing and taking it easy. She took a deep breath to get her errant libido under control.

Teri reclined on her back, leaning once again onto Sophie's arm and looking unaffected by the whispered conversation, except for an amused smirk. She picked the Kindle back up, "Where were we?"

Sophie decided two could play at that game and lay back, attempting to carry on reading together. She luxuriated in the feel of Teri's hair in her fingers, when an idea reoccurred to her from earlier.

Over the next few minutes it grew until she felt like it was going to pop out of her mouth whether she chose to or not.

"Teri?"

"Mmmhuh"

"You know how all these cute romance books have a grand gesture, before the happy ever after?"

"Oh I know, the whole formula thing… Yeah, why?"

"Well, what would you say to a grand gesture of me asking you to move in here?"

Teri dropped the Kindle in surprise, her attention fully grabbed by the question. Her eyes went wide and she looked shocked. Sophie wasn't sure whether to be hopeful or not, she was obviously surprised, at least.

"Me? Here? Now?"

"Well, I'd quite like Lani and Ariel to join us too but they seemed a bit busy so I figured we could start with you. You don't have to if you don't want to – it was only an idea."

Teri's initial look of shock morphed into something approaching discomfort as she kept looking away from Sophie. "Wow, that's out of the blue… and … kind of amazing. I'm not sure how to react. Would you be offended if I said I want to think about it?" Sophie felt her heart sink and her lava-hot core cool instantly but she did her best to keep her face neutral. She didn't want to ruin this relationship by diving in too early but she loved this woman. Teri continued quickly, "It's not you – I love you and I'd love to live with you. It's just … living with someone, that's quite big and adulty you know? It's a scary thought, I'm used to having my own space and I'm not the easiest to live with – you might get bored of me quickly."

Even in her disappointment Sophie heard the vulnerability creep back into Teri's voice. She realised it was too early, it was half-baked, probably prompted by lust and she had only dreamt it up five minutes before. What was she going to do next – propose?

Looking softly at Teri and taking her hand, she decided to try and understand what was behind this reticence, "You're right, either of us could find things we don't like and maybe I'm being hasty but there's more to this than the moving isn't there? Are you still worried about us?" She quickly added, "It's fine if you are, it's natural."

Teri chewed her lip and fidgeted for a few seconds, clearly uncomfortable. "I love you, Sophie, there's no doubt in my mind but I still worry you'll realise I'm not all that."

Sophie narrowed her eyes, looking through them and trying to see into Teri's sense of self. "Is that really what you think of yourself?"

Teri frowned and looked puzzled at the question as though she was asking if the sky was blue, "Well, yeah, I'm pretty average – right?" she shrugged.

Sophie cocked her head, still looking through narrowed eyes. She decided to take a different tack, "Average? How can you be average with what you've overcome?"

"Oh, it's not just being trans, I mean that's a part of it, sure, but I feel... well ... average compared to you!"

Sophie felt she was missing something, it didn't make sense, "If you think you're so average, how come you flashed so much flesh at tennis?"

"Oh, it took years to get to this confidence in my body. I'm proud of how I look on the outside most of the time. It's the inside that isn't so great."

"Why do you always think you're not worth loving? I don't get it."

Teri looked shocked, her eyebrows rising instantly, "I didn't say that, did I?"

"Not directly, no, but am I wrong?" challenged Sophie.

"Well, no, you're probably not wrong. I know I'm insecure, needy and probably don't make sense a lot of the time. I mean, sorry, I'm all a bit fucked up and annoying, aren't I?"

"Don't apologise but what I want to understand is, why?"

Teri stopped again and seemed to think for a while. "Well, I suppose it's a variety of things. Maybe I was just born an anxious person or maybe starting out knowing I was a girl but being treated as a boy meant I've always questioned who I am. It's a mix of feelings, thoughts and experiences, I guess, not just one thing. It never, somehow... I never, somehow... seem enough."

"Enough for who?" Sophie probed gently.

"Anyone?" came the quiet reply.

Sophie took a deep breath, this might make things better or worse, she wasn't sure. However, what Teri had shared was really brave and made her want to protect her even more. "So, what I want you to do is to trust me, Teri. Trust me to know what I need. You don't need to worry who is worthy of whom. Let me worry about whether I'm making a mistake. I will promise you that if I'm having doubts – I'll tell you and we'll talk about it, OK? If I do, and I don't think I will, I'm as sure as I possibly can be – it'll just be because of normal boring reasons some couples don't work. It won't be because you're not worthy of being loved or that I'm better than you."

She paused, waiting for Teri to give her a slight smile and an almost imperceptible nod before continuing. "Of course, you should think carefully about moving in and until you decide, well – whatever you decide – you and Number One are staying here with me anyway."

Teri seemed to rally and smiled, shouting out "NUMBER ONE, we're being imprisoned in this crazy, sexy woman's chamber of ecstasy and horniness mate. Find yourself a comfy cushion, we'll be a while!"

234

Sophie smiled. She could see Teri putting on her usual self-deprecating humour but she was glad to better understand how her girlfriend's mind worked regardless.

"Come on, let's carry on with the book. I want to know all about this kiwi..." smiled Sophie, wishing that she was a character in a book and Happy Ever Afters were assured. She wasn't sure where her own personal story was heading and whether a Happy Ever After was waiting for her.

Chapter Twenty-Six

After the eventful previous day with her second visit from the police and her exhausting reunion with Sophie, Teri was glad to spend the Friday chilling. She liked her girlfriend's house; it was cosy and it felt like home already. Sophie had gone to work earlier and left Teri curled up, reading in the warm lounge, while Number One dozed on her lap. She found his purring soothing and stroking his fur calmed her. It helped her forget the turmoil swirling around her mind. She knew that nothing had actually changed, but lying here on the comfortable cream sofa, cocooned in a nest of red, velvety throw cushions it felt like Sophie was here, cuddling her. Being held by her girlfriend made Teri feel safe. Like her house, Sophie felt like home.

She must have dozed off part way through the morning, soothed by Number One's rhythmic purring. When she woke, she noticed it was nearly lunchtime – she'd napped through most of the morning. Though to be fair, she had woken up early with Sophie and they'd made the most of waking up together, so she was shattered. Her little kitten sure did have claws and Teri wriggled her back, remembering the blonde's nails scratching down it and the electric feeling it brought to her. She'd have to check in the mirror for scratches later; if there were any, she'd wear them proudly! Her fidgeting woke a grumpy Number One who gave her his disdainful stare and stalked off in search of somewhere to nap that wouldn't wriggle while thinking sexy thoughts.

Teri got up and went through to the kitchen, thinking she should sort some food. She admired the kitchen – she'd never had a posh kitchen before, her parents had lived in a rented flat that was tatty throughout. She daydreamed for a moment and imagined cooking here, admiring the black shiny granite worktops and white cupboards. Feeling a little guilty at poking through Sophie's fridge she found a jar of strawberry jam and made some toast. If she was still here next week, after she started her job, then she'd go shopping for Sophie and repay her kindness by refilling the fridge.

While standing at the counter and absentmindedly munching her toast, she cast her eye about and figured she should make herself useful. Sophie had invited Bonnie over and Teri couldn't wait to meet her. She was desperate to make a good impression and remembered Sophie saying she disliked vacuuming. She put her toast down before hunting down the cleaner and putting it over the lounge. She plumped up the fluffy red cushions and tidied the coffee table. She actually really could picture herself living here and, looking at the fire with its tasteful red and black rug in front, she had a vision of Sophie on her back screaming her name in ecstasy right there. She shook her head; these weren't helpful thoughts to be having while cleaning. She remembered Sophie's offer to move in the previous day and felt sad that she had disappointed her. She wanted to hug and kiss her, screaming 'YES' at the top of her voice. 'What ifs' crowded her brain though. What if Sophie got bored of her? What if she upset this wonderful woman?

All of these what-ifs crowded for attention and she could feel herself slipping down the familiar spiral of low confidence. "No, I'm not going there," she said out loud, wondering if this classed her as crazy, "game face on. Let's get this place ready for Bonnie."

With that, she continued vacuuming as Number One poked his grey, furry head around the door, clearly wondering who his human was talking to. She laughed as he shook his head and prowled off, clearly deciding his meal ticket wasn't about to be eaten by mice or anything similar he would care about.

"Thanks bud, you're a great help!" She shouted after him, his retreating grey tail up in the air as he rounded the corner of the lounge door, contemptuously ignoring his loopy human staff.

Over the sound of the vacuum she missed the noise of the front door and was shocked a minute later when she turned and saw Sophie leaning against the doorframe, watching her, a smile playing

237

over her lips. She leaned to the side on a bent forearm and had one shapely, elegant leg crossed over the other showing off her hips in the grey pencil skirt.

Teri looked further up and appreciated the fitted black top, the scoop neck showing an expanse of creamy white skin before those shapely breasts filled it out. Shapely breasts that she could almost feel in her hands.

Her reverie admiring this gorgeous vision was brought to a premature end by a gentle cough and laugh. "My eyes are up here," Sophie chuckled, "what are you up to?"

"Well, I'm taming lions and servicing a car," she replied sarcastically, gesturing to the vacuum and finally remembering it was still running and switching it off.

"You don't need to do the housework, you know, you should rest!"

"Sophie, I'm not going to take advantage of you, I will do my share. Well, I suppose I might take advantage of certain aspects of you," she finished with a wiggle of her eyebrows and a cheeky grin. The pink flush running down Sophie's throat and spreading over that expanse of chest was addictive and she would do everything she could to tease this woman if it brought forth such an adorable image again!

"You aren't taking advantage," replied Sophie, conspicuously ignoring the double-entendre, "I didn't invite you here because I felt sorry for you or because I wanted you to clean up after me. I want you to be here because I love you and I want to wake up with you, cook with you, eat with you, put the bins out with you. Anyway, we'll talk about this later, I can see in your face there's a quagmire of negative thoughts going on in that pretty but stubborn head of yours. Right now though, I need to get changed. I have somewhere to be."

With that cryptic message, she ducked out of the room and bounded up the stairs. She must have encountered Number One on his way down as Teri heard a "Sorry, cat!" shouted as the noise of feet running upstairs continued apace. It suddenly dawned on Teri that it was only midday and Sophie wasn't due home for hours, so this was a little odd. Plus, she hadn't mentioned who she was meeting. Curiosity got the better of her and she dragged the vacuum back into the hallway before galloping upstairs, two at a time.

Knocking cautiously, before receiving a distracted, "Hmmmm?" she tentatively pushed the bedroom door open and was greeted by a naked back, blonde hair cascading over one shoulder, hunched over, pulling on a pair of tight black jeans over what looked to be a very barely there black thong. The sight of Sophie's firm but deliciously curvy peach cheeks caused her to launch forward with a growl and pull her into a big upright cuddle. Unfortunately, Sophie overbalanced as she was on one leg and fell back onto Teri, who landed in a heap on the bed, side by side with the half-naked Sophie, flailing to regain her feet. "What was that for?" Sophie asked, Teri's hands not caring about the tumble and finding their way to cuddle her bare arse-cheeks while she leaned up and kissed her strongly.

When she broke away, both of them looking flushed and wide eyed, Teri replied, "Oh, sorry, I couldn't resist, you look so bloody edible right now." The thought of sinking her teeth into the peach she'd been admiring took root in her mind and she'd have flipped Sophie over and onto the bed if she hadn't interrupted.

"Well, as complimented as I am that you can't keep your hands off me, I am running late so I need to pull these jeans up." She swivelled and sat on Teri's lap, who immediately putting her arms around her waist to hold on tight, while kissing her neck.

Sophie reached down and finished pulling up her jeans, wriggling her bum in order to do so and sending aftershocks through Teri's lower body at the feeling. "Who are you meeting? We're still on for Bonnie arriving about six, yes?"

"Oh, just someone from years ago and yes, I'll be back long before Bonnie gets here. Could you open a bottle of red wine about five for us please, Gorgeous?"

Teri allowed the evasive answer to pass without comment. She wasn't Sophie's keeper but she did wonder.

Sophie stood and turned, grasping her cheeks with both hands and kissing her firmly. "Thank you for letting it go, I promise I'll tell you all about it later. I can see in your eyes you're dying to quiz me, but I don't want to say too much, yet. Do I look OK?"

Figuring it was a business thing and still tasting the kiss on her lips, Teri let it go and looked her up and down. She let out a low breath, "Phew Cupcake, you look bloody magnificent. I love those jeans. Very badass – hope you're going to kick some butt." Spotting her pulling a pair of heeled ankle boots out of the wardrobe she couldn't help adding, "Wow, *very* badass indeed."

Sophie turned with a smile, "Why, thank you, that's the plan."

"Well, whoever you're meeting won't know what's hit them!"

"That's also the plan, wish me luck!"

Teri detected a slight quiver and tremble of nervousness in her voice and stood to wrap Sophie in a big hug before kissing her neck and nibbling her ear and whispering, "You look amazing and I know you'll give whoever it is hell, go get 'em! I love you!"

Sophie smiled, "Thanks, I love you too," before she kissed Teri back and turned to go, striding down the stairs with purpose, her heels clicking on the hall laminate floor and the front door slamming.

Number One padded into the bedroom, looking up at Teri and giving out a little meow. "I've no idea mate. I don't know what she's up to but she is absolutely stunning isn't she? I really do love that woman. Do you think you'd like to live here with her as your other Mama?" She picked him up and stroked his soft fur while he purred contentedly, seemingly having no objections. "If only, my stupid brain could accept the idea as easily as you seem to, Number One."

He turned at this and stared at her with piercing yellow eyes. She was convinced she saw him narrow and roll them at her in exasperation. "It's alright for you mate, everyone loves stroking you, you don't have to feel that you have be worthy of that attention."

He mewed back at her. She wasn't sure if it was a rebuke, but she did need to get out more if she was feeling chastised by the cat.

Chapter Twenty-Seven

Sophie felt guilty at keeping anything from Teri, but she didn't want to upset her. As she walked into the bar, she rubbed the back of her neck, bit down on her bottom lip and pulled on her ponytail, nerves kicking in again. Looking around the bar she saw the person she had arranged to meet was sitting at a table by the window. She took a deep breath, straightened her back and walked over confidently, standing at the table and looking down, projecting her strongest vibes. The woman sitting there turned her head and looked up from her bottle of WKD, an expression of surprise on her face as she took in Sophie's appearance. The woman's dark brown hair was cropped short and she was wearing black jeans the same as Sophie with a flannel shirt over her red vest top. Hannah, her ex, the cheat. This was the first time she'd seen her since the day she'd walked out, slamming the door on a stunned couple in her bed.

Sophie looked at her and felt none of the feeling she used to. What she once thought was love, she now realised was merely lust and a bit of wishful thinking. She schooled her face into a firm mask. She'd dressed like this for a reason, she was no longer the naive hopeful romantic she'd been with Hannah. She was a confident woman taking care of the person she loved and she needed Hannah to see that she wasn't going to be messed around. However, she needed to tread carefully since Teri *was* actually guilty and Hannah could make her life very difficult if Sophie upset her.

She sat down in the booth, hands on the table and looked across at the woman who had devastated her life for too long. She really wasn't as scary as she'd made her out to be. After all, she was just that – a woman. Not a dragon or a mythical evil being. She was a sad individual who couldn't keep her fingers out of other people's pants.

"I'm sorry Soph," Hannah started in a small voice.

That surprised Sophie. She was expecting a reaction to her wardrobe choice or some sarcastic comment, not a quiet apology. Thinking that she needed to see what the game was before launching in, she followed Hannah's conversational lead. "So am I, Hannah. I don't know why I wasn't enough for you but I've spent ages agonising over that. I can't do it anymore. Your choices were your own, not mine."

"I know, I made a mistake. I'm sorry. If we could try again, I know it would be different." She looked across at Sophie with her eyes showing the very last thing she'd expected to see… hope. It stunned Sophie and threw her game plan off. Her emotions cycled through a full spectrum. Shock first, this wasn't the Hannah she knew or expected to see. The old Hannah had been so confident, it was the characteristic that had attracted Sophie to her throughout their relationship. She'd never seen her like this before.

The shock morphed into annoyance, why couldn't Hannah have been contrite back when she still wanted her to be? Why now? What had changed – had something gone wrong for Hannah? Sophie became suspicious. Finally though, her emotions settled on something she didn't want to feel. Something terribly unattractive… pity. She realised she actually felt sorry for Hannah.

"Hannah, what you did…"

"Which, I'm really sorry for."

This wasn't where Sophie wanted the conversation to go but treading carefully was the order of the day and even beyond that, she'd never truly got closure. Maybe it was time. "What you did… absolutely devastated me. I thought I was in love with you and it felt like you threw that back in my face. I don't know who she was or what she meant to you, nor do I want to. That's unfortunate, but I'm afraid that through the pain, I've moved on. I've settled, I've healed and I've found someone who appreciates me for who I am."

"This hacker?" Sophie saw a flash of the old Hannah run across her face as she almost spat the words. Her pity transformed again, back into suspicion. Was this a big show, surely Hannah couldn't actually expect her to take her back?

"Who is not the problem here, is she Hannah? You've hurt her and me – that's why I needed to talk to you. Look, I don't think either of us really loved each other. Sure we had very strong feelings and despite what you did to me... to us... I still don't wish you ill. But I'm not the same person and neither can you be anymore. We've changed, I know now I wasn't in love with you because I'm in love with Teri."

"She's not good enough for you, I saw her." Sophie could see anger building in Hannah's eyes.

"So, you were at the bar... and Dave?"

"Dave?" Hannah queried, frowning.

"Dave... my colleague from work. Bearded guy you chatted up. You've not come out as bi, pan or something else, have you? Was that just to get to me?" Hannah looked down and Sophie could almost believe she felt ashamed at what she'd done, but she wasn't going to be swayed that easily. Teri needed her to stay strong. That's what this meeting was about, her future, not her past.

"Yes, OK, I didn't like the idea that you'd moved on. I'm sorry Soph, if you'd give me another chance, I know it would work. We were so good together." Hannah stared into Sophie's eyes and she expected to hate it. However, what Sophie felt was ... nothing but the small dose of pity. There was no love for this woman, not even hate. There was none of the compassion she felt when Teri was upset, just – nothing. Hannah reached across the table for Sophie's hand but she moved gently to avoid her.

"Hannah, we should have talked before. You hurt me badly by cheating but I should have put that on the table some time ago, got closure you could say. I'm here now though and I do need to ask you

244

for something. I need you to stop hurting Teri because through doing that you're killing me."

She paused, seeing if this request sunk in but not waiting for any objections before continuing, "I don't know, maybe in time I'll be able to forgive you for what you did but do you really expect that we'd be able to pick up the pieces and carry on from where we left off? Really?"

She opened her hands in emphasis, "What would you do, carry on as if nothing had happened or would you constantly be begging me for forgiveness, always on edge? You and I both know that isn't your style. I know, for sure, I'd always be wondering, always waiting for you to cheat again. Always apprehensive when I opened the house door... who I'd find there with you."

She stopped again, looked away out of the window and sighed. "I expected I'd hate you for what you did to me, to us... but you know what? I don't. The problem is that I can't like you because of it either.

"I used to think I loved you, I pictured our future. I know now that I was wrong. I don't think I ever did love you and, be honest, I don't think you ever loved me either – otherwise why would you have sought someone else?" She stopped and paused, turning back to Hannah and waiting to see if her words had sunk in.

They did, Hannah's face contorted into a mask of grief. Her whispered words penetrated Sophie's heart, "Maybe I don't know what love is then because I really believed that it was what we had. I'm so sorry Sophie – I never wanted to hurt you. I just..." Sophie wondered if this usually confident and arrogant woman opposite her was going to cry but she sniffed and straightened up, obviously with a concerted effort, running her fingers through her short, dark quiff distractedly and looking down at the table. "I just... didn't think, I guess."

She looked up at Sophie with sudden understanding, mixed with sadness in her eyes. "So you have found love then?"

Sophie took a deep breath, "Yes – yes I have. I've fallen so totally in love with Teri, she's amazing." Sophie struggled to avoid beaming as she thought of her girlfriend but remembered that the goal here was to help her, not rub her ex's nose in it.

"That's why what you've done hurts so much, you've attacked her and me. I don't want to lose her. So I'm asking you Hannah, please, if what we had meant anything to you – please let me be happy and please leave her alone."

Sophie watched as Hannah's striking face fell even further and a single tear appeared in her right eye. She nodded slowly. "I get it Soph. I'm sorry for what I've done to you both, both then and now. Can I do anything for you, beyond leaving you alone? I really do, did, have strong feelings for you and maybe, one day, we could be friends again."

Sophie stifled a scoff. *Be kind, be the bigger person.* She reminded herself. "Thank you Hannah, I know you're not a bad person, you just seem to have made bad choices where I've been concerned. That's what tells me you didn't love me deep down. I do hope you can find someone that you feel that for though. When you do, you'll know what I mean.

"As for helping, Teri is now afraid of the police getting closer. It's probably best left alone." She sighed, even if she could get Hannah to back off, that wouldn't be the end of it.

Hannah stared at her for a moment, deep in thought. Heaven knows where her thoughts were because Sophie could see her brown eyes flicking slightly side-to-side. They used to do that when she was thinking. For a microsecond, Sophie remembered some of the good times. This woman hadn't always been the enemy and she was, for all her faults, both good looking and pretty clever. Suddenly a smile started to creep over Hannah's thin, slightly chapped lips. It reached

246

her eyes as Sophie reacted with surprise, "What on earth Hannah, what is there to be happy about in this situation?"

"Well, you've found happiness for one, but I may have had an idea... We're going to need some help but I think it could work if you want to get your girlfriend off the hook with the fuzz?"

Sophie rolled her eyes, "Seriously Hannah, you're not in a cockney gangster movie here. This is serious!"

Hannah grinned even wider, "So am I... you know how I love a challenge and maybe this will show you I really am sorry."

With that, she told Sophie her idea.

~#~

"Hey, Cupcake," shouted Teri's voice from the kitchen as Sophie entered through the front door, "I was just getting the wine, Bonnie should be here in a sec. What would you like?"

"Hi Sweetie," responded Sophie coming into the kitchen, aware she was possibly overdoing the luvvie-duvveyness and feeling guilty, "I'll have wine too but before that, I need to talk to you."

"Okay, that sounds serious?" Teri looked concerned. "Are you OK?"

"I'm fine, but I've got a visitor with me, the person I went to meet. I need to check that you're OK to meet her before she comes in."

Teri looked into her eyes, puzzled until a sudden change came over her. "Hang on, it's not who I think it is?" Teri looked immediately concerned. Sophie felt awful.

"Yes, it's Hannah but wait, hear me out. She is here to help you. Please don't jump to any conclusions yet until we've had a chance to talk. Let me take my coat off. Will you meet her, please – for me? I'm worried about you and will try anything if it helps."

"I'm not sure how this is going to help but if you're sure it will, then I trust you. I don't have to like her, do I?"

Sophie smiled, "You don't have to like her. Just listen. If you don't like what she's got to say then she has promised to go again. I really think you will want to hear her out though."

Teri nodded, "Okay then."

Sophie smiled and leaned in to kiss the woman who was clearly shaken and scared. "Thank you for trusting me. I love you."

"I love you too. Go on then, bring her in."

Sophie turned, opened the front door and waved outside to someone. Teri watched warily as she entered.

Hannah was, rightly, looking more sheepish than Sophie had ever seen before. Sophie smiled a little, these two women would be a force to be reckoned with if they were on the same side, she was sure. "Hannah, please meet my girlfriend, Teri. Teri, Hannah – my ex."

She took the wine glasses off Teri, who took a deep breath and held her hand out. Hannah looked surprised but reached forward to take it and shake. "Teri," she started before closing her eyes and taking a deep breath, "I'm really sorry. I didn't know you and I poked my nose in where it wasn't needed. I want to try and make things better."

Teri's eyebrows rose up her forehead and she audibly scoffed. Sophie jumped in, "She is Teri, I actually believe her. She has an idea to help you – well us."

Teri turned her gaze to look at Sophie, her disbelief palpable. "I thought you weren't happy with her?"

Sophie went to speak but Hannah got in first, "Teri, please don't be angry at Sophie. She reached out to me to put me straight and tell me to get back in my box. I, rather stupidly," she rolled her eyes, "didn't realise how much I'd hurt her. I didn't know you and I acted without thinking. I don't expect either of you to be fans but I asked Sophie to give me a chance to help you and make up for a little of the damage I've caused her – and you."

Sophie saw Teri look between them both, still clearly wary. Maybe it had been a bad idea to bring this woman here, to somewhere Teri felt safe. She had offered to help though and, for all the hurt she'd caused, for some reason Sophie believed she was sincere. She gestured with the wine, "Let's go in, sit down and Hannah can explain. If you don't like her idea then she'll leave us alone from now on – isn't that right Hannah?" she turned her head, her eyebrow raised in inquiry.

"That's right, I can't apologise enough to Sophie for what I did to her and I'm really sorry to have hit out at you in the process so if it helps to make up for that, even a little bit, then I'll do whatever I can."

At that moment, another knock at the door signalled Bonnie's arrival. "Oh great," murmured Sophie, "this should be fun."

She opened the door and went to hug Bonnie, who responded but froze partway into the embrace, looking over Sophie's shoulder in Hannah's direction.

"Oh, look what the cat dragged in. I'm surprised you have the nerve Hannah. What on earth are you doing here?"

Sophie handed the wine to Bonnie and held up her hand. "Bonnie, leave it. Hannah and I have been over it and if you want to tear her to shreds then I'll leave the two of you to sort that out later. For now, we have more important things to discuss." Bonnie had long, curly, bouncy naturally auburn hair and a personality to match the stereotypical hot-headed redhead. It contrasted with her pale skin and freckles to give her a striking appearance, but with her curvy build, she gave off the aura of casually glam... until someone upset her of course. Sophie was glad that they'd always been friends because you didn't want to be on the wrong side of Bonnie. She raised a thin, immaculate eyebrow in disbelief but they'd been friends long enough to know when each other were serious and Sophie was glad to see she took the hint in her voice to rein her neck in.

"This is Teri, by the way, Teri – this is Bonnie."

The four women moved into the lounge, where Sophie directed Bonnie to sit on the sofa.

Sophie gestured for Teri to sit down in the free space next to Bonnie. She sat on the sofa arm next to her, taking Teri's hand. This was partly to give her support but also partly selfishly to pull her back in case anything kicked off between Teri and Hannah.

Her ex sat down in the armchair across the room, stroking the arm absentmindedly. Sophie took a few moments to remember what they'd done in that very chair and blushed hot and red. She coughed and Hannah's attention snapped back to her. She looked flustered and Sophie could see in her eyes she was having similar thoughts but this time, contrary to her expectations, she didn't gloat or grin, she withdrew and looked contrite, almost sad.

"So, to catch up Bonnie, this is Teri – my girlfriend. You know this but what you don't know is that we met when she hacked work. She caused Dave and I a very sleepless night but she's made it up to me since then. Unfortunately, someone," she looked pointedly across the room to a woman who was avoiding her eye contact assiduously, "reported her to the police for doing so, who are now paying an uncomfortable amount of interest in the case. That goes for both Teri and for me, since I neither want her implicated, nor do I want the hassle at work of this being blown out of proportion." She looked at Bonnie to check she was following. The redhead nodded, waiting for her to get to the juicy bits.

"So, today I met with Hannah to put some old ghosts to rest and ensure things didn't get out of hand. We've reached an understanding…" Both Bonnie and Teri went to interrupt her but she held up a hand, "that we'll focus on helping Teri."

All three women looked over at Hannah who blanched a little under the glare of their looks but nodded agreement. "I've apologised to Sophie for the way I treated her and I say the same to you, Teri. I know that's not enough but I'm going to try and help sort out the mess I've created – if you'll let me?"

Sophie nodded, she had to admit, Hannah was being true to her word and she acknowledged that maybe what she'd said about loving her was true. "So, here's the plan... The problem we have is that the police, for some silly reason – want to look at Teri for the hacking. That would be fine if it weren't for the small detail that she actually did do it." Sophie giggled a little and gave her girlfriend a squeeze.

"I've apologised to you though and helped fix it," pouted Teri, looking up at Sophie.

"I know," she replied kindly, squeezing her hand to show she was teasing.

Looking over at Hannah, she continued, "Do you want to explain, since it's your idea?" she added in a friendly tone.

"Well, the police have no evidence of who the hacker is because they just have an anonymous, vaguely worded, tip. So, if some evidence were found on Sophie's servers that traced back to the individual or group who really did the hack then they would go and look at them, wouldn't they?"

"Errr, excuse me, I thought this was a plan to help me, not hang me?" Teri started with a tone of irritation. Sophie could feel her body was tense.

"Now why would it do that, if the evidence clearly points to someone else?" Hannah properly smiled for the first time since she got there, "And we can be sure it will, because I'm going to put it there!"

Even Sophie was surprised by this last addition. They hadn't discussed this – she'd assumed Hannah would give her something to plant and she'd have to do it. "You?"

"Yes, me. Perfect solution, they don't know me. You both are too close. I'll plant a code fragment from an attack I saw last year, it came from one of those large groups overseas. Then the server admin team can find it and share with our friends at the plod. Genius, if I do say so myself!" She held her hands out at shoulder height in a 'ta-da' gesture. *Typical Hannah*, thought Sophie, but she couldn't bring herself to care.

"You'll show us this code and Sophie can check it?" asked Teri, her body relaxing a little but still clearly uncomfortable. Sophie squeezed her hand gently.

"Of course, Sophie is in control every step of the way but the only person who gets their hands dirty is me."

Sophie looked down at Teri who was deep in thought, stroking her lip while looking off into space. Sophie caressed her soft cheek, wanting to soothe her. She smiled up at Sophie. "It could work, I suppose. I don't want you to get into trouble, Soph."

"I think we've got a good chance and hopefully actions will show you both I'm really sorry. For what it's worth, I can already see you make a better couple than we ever did so I'm not expecting an invite to the wedding but maybe we can be neutral with each other?"

Teri nodded and gave a half smile to Hannah. "Thank you," her voice held sincerity but also uncertainty and worry.

"So when do we put this plan into action?" Sophie asked hopefully.

"What about now?" Hannah cheerfully replied, "Give me thirty seconds to grab my laptop, you get yours and we can ensure there's something for our mate Dave to find. She chuckled a little

252

before looking bashfully up at Sophie, biting her lip. "Do I owe him an apology too?"

Sophie punched her ex in the arm playfully. "I think that's one mistake you won't need to apologise for. He's been boasting about turning the dyke to anyone who will listen."

Hannah didn't look amused and said, in a low voice clearly meant for Sophie's ears only, "I was actually kinda surprised, I quite liked him. Kissing him wasn't as bad as I thought."

Sophie rolled her eyes and turned to grab her laptop bag.

Moments later she was perched on the arm of the chair watching Hannah extract the code they needed. They were deep in the zone and didn't notice Bonnie and Teri exchange looks and walk towards the kitchen.

Sophie pointed at the screen, "So if we pull this binary, that's pretty distinctive, it should be –" a cough interrupted her from behind.

"Why don't you both move onto the sofa? We'll head into the kitchen and leave you to it." Teri smiled nervously.

"Thanks!" Sophie shouted at her retreating back and Bonnie lifted her glass overhead in a salute.

Chapter Twenty-Eight

"Do you think I should be worried about how well they are getting on? I thought she hated Hannah?" Teri whispered to Bonnie once they got into the kitchen together, feeling quite concerned.

"No, Sophie is the softest, most forgiving person I know but even Hannah is some way off forgiveness."

"I don't want you to think I'm the jealous type or anything, I guess I'm just a bit uncomfortable with Hannah, knowing how she treated Sophie and what she's done to me."

"Don't be daft, that's natural. I only look more comfortable because I want to wring her bloody neck. Soph is putting her issues aside for you – she loves you, you know?"

Teri let out a big happy sigh, "I know, and I love her too – she's amazing. I don't deserve her and I'll forever be trying to make it up to her for how we met but I can't get enough of her you know. Every time I see her, it feels like everyone else evaporates and it just gets warmer. I know, that's stupid."

"No, it's not." Bonnie replied kindly, her face glowing with a smile Teri took to be friendship. "That's what love feels like and I could see it clearly from the way you two were sitting together. I was watching, I've never seen her that tactile with anyone before. Even though she was concentrating, she was playing with your hair and stroking your arm. I've never seen her do that before and I don't think she even realised she was doing it. She really cares for you."

Teri couldn't contain the massive grin on her face and she felt so happy that something would burst. She swallowed the lump forming in her throat. "I love her – what more can I say?"

"Yep." Then Bonnie's face turned serious and her voice dropped lower, "So if you hurt her, I will come after you and make you wish you'd never been born, you got that? She's my best friend."

Teri nodded. She wouldn't need Bonnie, if she hurt Sophie she knew she'd lose a part of herself and never be able to forgive her actions. "More wine?" She said to lighten the mood and picked up the bottle, topping off both glasses.

"It's a shame Hannah came up with that solution to your problem," mused Bonnie after a few moments of comfortable silence.

"Mmmm, why?" enquired Teri thinking that she was quite glad of a solution to her problems.

"Well, I was going to suggest something simpler. That we get together, kidnap Hannah and lock her in the garage. I've been wanting to get that woman back for all she did to Sophie – you should have seen her, she was ruined. It was heart-breaking." Bonnie shook her head; Teri could see the emotion.

"You're a good friend to her, Bonnie, I can see that. She needs good friends."

Bonnie looked at Teri and put her hand on her arm. "She's got a new good friend. I wasn't joking when I said to look after her but I know I don't have to say it. Just looking at you, I can see how you feel about our Sophie. You two are made for each other."

Teri shrugged and laughed, "Yeah right – you sure you don't mean punching above?"

Bonnie shook her head and kept her grip on Teri's arm. "No Teri, I've only met you for a couple of hours but already I can see you're made for each other. You're both kind as anything under your exteriors – you might put up a façade but it drops when you look at Sophie and you're both in that bubble. That's what I want for her as a friend and I'm so pleased she's found it."

Bonnie straightened and lifted her arm, punching Teri lightly on the arm, "Anyway what's this I hear about you being a romantic fiction fan?" Her tone was far more cheerful, signalling to Teri that they'd had their heart to heart and were on a more jokey footing again. Teri was glad of that. She liked Bonnie and she seemed someone she'd get on with well as a friend.

"Shhhh, don't let anyone else hear you saying that! I've spread this big rumour about being a hacker to cover up my guilty secret," she replied with a conspiratorial grin, looking over her shoulder in pretence.

Both women were laughing to each other, spilling wine over the granite countertop when the door opened and Hannah walked in, followed by Sophie. Sophie looked between them and her worktop, one eyebrow raised in mock concern. Teri knew it was fake because she could see how she was struggling to hold back a laugh.

"What's going on here – care to share the joke with the class?" she began.

"No, nothing to see here," Teri nonchalantly replied, trying desperately to keep a straight face and suddenly realising too late that the reason she was struggling was due to the alcohol.

"Well," began Bonnie, "your girlfriend here was telling me about her other guilty little secret." She spilt more of the rich, red wine as she sniggered and her hands shook.

"Hey, no fair!" slurred Teri.

She looked at Sophie, who was standing with her hands on her hips, looking between her girlfriend and her best friend, shaking her head. "Pissheads, the pair of you!" she muttered before turning to Hannah, "Can I drive you to the station?"

"No, don't worry Sophie, I called an Uber, Joao will be here in his Prius in three minutes." She turned to the other two giggling women, "Teri, it's been great meeting you and I am sorry again for all the trouble. Bonnie, lovely to meet you again."

"Nice to meet you too Hannah," smiled Teri, pleased that she'd managed such a civil response.

"See ya Hannah, don't get locked in the garage on your way out," sniggered a clearly more inebriated Bonnie, which set Teri off in another fit of giggles.

Sophie shook her head again and guided Hannah out towards the door. Teri could hear them talking and then the sound of the front door closing.

Sophie came back in, grabbing a glass and filling it with wine. "Well, at least I can join you now. What on earth are you two up to here? You sound like you're cackling away behind the bikesheds!"

Bonnie looked at her, raising both eyebrows, "Excuse me Ms Keegan, I seem to remember that it wasn't just me who was behind the bikesheds and there wasn't much cackling going on."

Sophie's face flushed and she glared at Bonnie, looking away and towards Teri quickly. "You two? No way! Just throw all your exes at me tonight why don't you?" exclaimed Teri, wondering what other skeletons she had yet to find.

Bonnie filled in the gaps while an embarrassed, bright red-eared Sophie put her head in her hands. "Once," Bonnie started, holding up one finger to emphasise it, "but never again. It was like snogging your sister... just wrong on one level but so much fun on another. Oh hang on, I didn't mean I've snogged your sister Sophie, or even my sister come to think of it."

Sophie shook her head and Teri found her embarrassment so endearing, she was like a little pink pig burying its face out of the way. Oh, hang on, no – not a pig, that was bad. A flamingo with her beautiful head in the water. She gave up trying to draw a comparison in her head, the wine made her even less prosaic than normal but she knew what she meant... Sophie was beautiful and she loved her. She pulled her close and kissed her ears, first left, then right. "I love you Cupcake, ignore the horrible drunk lady, I got you."

Sophie looked up at her with a knowing smile, "Oh, I love you too Teri, even when you're pissed as a fart."

Giggling away, all three women headed back into the lounge and flopped down together on the sofa. Sophie told them all about what Hannah had done. As much as Teri didn't want to give her credit, she did seem to have done a fair job of redirecting people somewhere else. All that they had to do was wait for someone to come across the evidence. The plan, Sophie explained, was to wait for someone else to find it and tell Sophie, who would act surprised and let DC Payne know about this new 'evidence'. Teri spotted Sophie yawning and looked at her watch. Bonnie noticed too and got up to leave.

"Oh, I think it's time I left you two to enjoy yourselves in private." She wiggled her eyebrows in what should have been a comical gesture but just ended up looking drunkenly unsteady. She pulled out her phone and, Teri assumed, called another Uber. "Four minutes, sorted."

~#~

An hour later, after they'd both cuddled on the couch and made their way up to bed, Teri was lying on her side, looking over at a sleeping Sophie. She couldn't get enough of watching this woman. She shuffled a fraction closer, inching her hand closer to touch her fingers. She didn't want to wake the peaceful woman but the mere chance for that physical contact was too important to miss, like some addict seeking their lifeblood. As their fingertips touched, Teri sensed Sophie's fingers close a little and it felt like her girlfriend was squeezing and supporting, not only her hand, but also her heart, even in sleep. A feeling of calm came over Teri – a sense of contentment that she rarely felt. Perhaps it was a feeling of love or maybe it was a feeling of safety. Either way, she knew this was where she belonged. The two of them belonging to each other felt like home to her. Just

258

being able to touch this beautiful person and call her 'mine' filled not only her heart but everything she was.

She must have nodded off because she woke feeling hot and with a weight on her legs and hips. Opening her eyes, she saw that Sophie had shifted in the night and her leg was thrown over Teri's hips, the other woman's crotch pressing comfortably into her thigh. Teri tried, unsuccessfully, to avoid thinking about how warm that centre felt on her skin and how much warmer it would feel if she turned slightly so their centres were closer. She let out a small moan at the feeling of exquisite torture and concentrated on her girlfriend's breathing. She became entranced by the beautiful face and the quiet inhale but the slight rhythmic hitch in the breathy "Huuhhhharhhhh" Sophie made when she exhaled softly. Sophie made a little "Ahhhh" whimper and Teri noticed that her hips seemed to wiggle a little. She wondered what her girlfriend was dreaming about and hoped it was fun. The rhythmic breathing must have acted like a sweet lullaby because the next thing she knew was waking again, much later. This time Sophie was the one up on one elbow looking at her with a sweet smile across her face. "I love you, Teri."

"Awww thanks, I love you too." She replied groggily before receiving the most delicious 'welcome awake' kiss she'd ever experienced. Her mind emptied and she found that not only did she not know what day of the week it was, but she didn't care either!

Only once Sophie had finally had enough of her lips did she pull away, still holding Teri's neck with one hand and looking into her eyes. "You're beautiful." Teri rolled her eyes but Sophie's hand stayed firm, "No, you're not going anywhere, you're beautiful, I love you and you deserve both the compliment and the love. I know it makes you uncomfortable because you don't believe me but if I have to tell you a million times, I *will* make you believe me eventually."

Sophie flicked her eyes left and right, clearly studying Teri's face. Once she seemed satisfied with what she saw in there, she released her neck and pulled back. Teri felt the lack of closeness instantly and reached out her hand to touch Sophie — she didn't care what part of Sophie, she just needed the contact.

~#~

"What's on for today then, my little sweet geek?" Sophie asked in a teasing voice that Teri found seductive. Everything about this woman was seductive to her. They had moved down into the kitchen for breakfast and were leaning on the counter together.

"What day is it again? You kind of rebooted my mind a moment ago and it's taking a while to start up."

Sophie laughed and at that moment, her tinkly feminine chuckle was the best music ever to Teri's ears. "It's Saturday, we've got the whole weekend together. I want to forget about everything going on and just be us."

That sounded the best plan Teri had ever heard. 'Us' was her new favourite thing, a special thing she'd never had before but always yearned for. "Well, I would love to see the real Sophie – what do you normally do on a weekend to enjoy yourself?"

"Oh, I don't know. Nothing much, read a little, bum around the house, clean, shop. The usual."

Teri grinned, "Then, my lady, I shall be your honorary bum around the house this weekend while you clean. What kind of shopping?"

"Anything I need really, you know what it's like working full time," Sophie winced at the tactless comment but Teri knew it wasn't meant hurtfully and smiled as she continued, "Food, stuff, whatever."

"Well, while we're bumming together, I may get a phone call from my sister, she usually calls to bore me with how her cisnormative hetero two-point-four family is doing. That and..." Teri stopped, realising too late what she was about to say.

260

"Ha, I cannot wait to meet this sister of yours! But what else — what's the *and*?"

Teri sighed, she didn't want a fuss but she'd dropped herself in it. "I have no intention of forcing my sister on you anytime soon. She only rings me occasionally and always the weekend before my birthday."

Sophie's eyes widened and she shot upright, "Your birthday?" she screeched. "Why am I only now hearing about this?"

"It's no big deal. I have them every year and it's all a bit busy at the moment. I'm really distracted."

She was quickly shut down by a fussing Sophie, "Of course it's a big deal. We must do something together, unless you have other plans. Which day?" Her voice kept rising in excitement and it was beginning to hurt Teri's ears.

"Monday." Teri squeaked in a small voice, knowing Sophie was going to explode with excitement, "but could you drop your voice an octave, Cupcake, there's a dog down the street that is trying to eavesdrop and you're going too high for his hearing."

Sophie swatted Teri before going back to her excited voice, her blonde bed hair flying everywhere as she excitedly shook her head, "Monday? That's only two days away! I don't have anything for you. Right — that's it, shopping today then."

"No, really, I mean it, you don't have to buy me anything. You've made all my dreams come true already just by being you."

"Well maybe I'll jump out of a cake in a bunny girl outfit then," she replied in a sarcastic and sulky tone.

Teri's eyes widened, she felt her pupils dilate and her jaw drop. She also felt a sudden increase in warmth and throbbing between her legs.

"Oh, I see. We found one of your dreams then! No wonder you spotted me at the party, do you have a thing for rabbits *and* cats?" smirked Sophie, drawn out of her sarcasm by what must have been lust written all over Teri's face. Teri looked away, feeling her cheeks flush with heat. "So that aside, what do you want to do for your birthday and first day at work to celebrate? Do you want to go out or stay in?"

Teri looked back up and thought for a moment. "I don't want any fuss. To be honest, all I want is time with you. I don't care about presents or fancy meals, I'd be happy with beans on toast in front of the TV so long as it's sitting next to, or even better, on you!"

Sophie's face lit up and she held up one finger in an 'I got it!' gesture. "So, you want me in a cake, covered in beans with bunny ears? Gotcha."

"Oh, stop picking on me you horrible woman." Teri laughed, almost snorting and shaking her head. "This is why I don't tell people about my birthday."

"I'm not *people* and you need to get that through your thick skull. I want you to feel special, it makes me happy when I see that smile and I don't get to see it nearly enough. So we need a special treat for a special person but just the two of us. I'm sure we can do that." Sophie's voice tailed off as she clearly descended deep into thought, planning who knows what. "Are you taking cakes in on Monday?"

"Cakes? What, for lunch?"

"No, for your colleagues, silly. Because it's your birthday..."

"Oh, I got you. I think that might be a bit much on day one, don't you? Maybe Tuesday if they do that sort of thing? So, are you my Mum, sorting me out, and will you pack my lunch for me on Monday?"

"If I was your Mum, would I do this?" Teri's mind went blank as a pair of hot lips consumed hers and two hands strongly caressed the underside of her breasts while the thumbs circled her nipples through her pyjama top. Luckily for her, the top reduced the sensation a little or she may have melted into a puddle on the spot.

Sophie pulled away from the dazed Teri who swayed a little before focussing on the big grin in front of her. Sophie plumped her blonde hair with her head cocked to the side and smiling seductively. "I suppose if you want to talk about cake we could do that or we could forget about Monday until tomorrow?"

"Oh, I think we should talk cake…" A raised eyebrow from Sophie told Teri that was the wrong answer. "Or…?"

Teri felt the answer come in the form of one warm, soft fingertip pressed under her chin and Sophie simply smiling at her before starting to walk towards the stairs, pulling an entranced Teri with her. She wasn't physically capable of breaking the connection with that fingertip, even if she wanted to. She allowed Sophie to lead her through the house and followed her upstairs, led purely by a seductive force pulling her through the single finger. She felt like she was on a metaphorical leash and knew she'd follow this woman anywhere. They both read hot romantic fiction and she could read what was going through Sophie's mind. Her whole posture had changed, she stood straighter and her face was harder. She wasn't just asking Teri, she was genuinely leading her, and Teri couldn't get enough of it. Her mind focussed entirely on the woman in front of her, to the exclusion of all other senses. She could see the blonde hair tossing in front of her, she felt the single finger, she heard her own breathing – heavy, slow, focussed.

As they entered the bedroom, Sophie turned to face Teri and their eyes met. After a split second, Sophie leaned forward and their lips met again. While her brain was engaged with the sensory overload of the smooth lips chewing, sucking and pressing into her own, it took a few seconds for it to catch up that a pair of hands was pulling down her shorts and a cool breeze was blowing across her arse.

The lips released her and the fog began to clear from her brain, just in time to hear a loud crack and a millisecond later, a sharp pain on her arse cheek. Sophie's mouth moved around to her ear and, in a husky whisper, full of promise, said, "Get your arse on the bed so I can sit on your face. Time for breakfast!"

Teri's eyes shot open and she looked around to see a quirked eyebrow staring back at her and a grin full of erotic predatory promise. Looking down, Sophie dropped her own shorts, allowing them to fall around her ankles into a pile on the floor. Teri eagerly lay on the bed as Sophie jumped up and straddled her chest.

Teri's hands gripped Sophie's bum, guiding her closer and into the perfect position. The smooth hips bucked as Teri's tongue slid along the length of her folds, tasting the arousal already coating them and murmuring a groan of appreciation. Sophie clearly felt this as she wiggled excitedly. As she reached the apex, she circled the swelling nub and Sophie took a sharp intake of breath, arching her back in the process. The view of her beautiful tits pushing forwards under the top, as Teri's eyes looked past the mound blocking most of her vision, was heavenly and the sound of the other woman's pleasure as her breathing quickened felt like the best noise Teri had ever heard.

Sophie started moaning and whispering, "Yes, oh yes, there..." Teri concluded this was going to be over quickly unless she pulled back. She stopped her flat licking rather than going deeper as she'd planned to and pressed a kiss to Sophie's thigh, deepening that into a slight bite, her teeth gripping Sophie's flesh enough for her to feel but not enough to leave a mark. Sophie wiggled to move right and push Teri back towards her centre. When she refused to budge, Sophie leaned forward and made eye contact, her frown showing displeasure. "Did I tell you to stop?"

She tickled Teri's chin with a finger, making Teri feel trapped, commanded and valued all at once. Sophie's hand slid down and lifted

264

Teri's T-shirt, and pinched her right nipple. "Then get moving... or I'll have to make you."

With that, she pinched the erect nipple harder, rolling it between her fingers and Teri wanted to cry out but her mouth was blocked by the beautiful pink folds that manoeuvred themselves to block her vision once more and she gave in trying to prolong Sophie's orgasm, licking then sucking on the beautiful lips, enjoying the sweetness before parting them and lapping at Sophie's centre where the sweetness mixed with the fresh tang coming directly from her heart. "Good girl... there!" groaned Sophie, the last syllable stretched into infinity as the feeling became more important than the sound.

Teri swirled her, now firmly held, tongue, before returning up to circle, swirl and, eventually, flick Sophie's clit. Sophie began panting and Teri picked up the pace, settling into a rapid flicking motion with as much force as she could muster. Bringing her right hand under Sophie, she entered her slowly with two fingers and pressed her hardest, loving the feeling of her girlfriend's centre filling with her come then clenching around her fingers.

It didn't take long before Sophie reached the peak of her climax and fell over the edge with a high-pitched scream. Teri could feel her clenching every muscle in her body as it hit, her face squeezed and her fingers practically cut off at the knuckle. She slowed her fingers, holding them in place and switched to stroking the apex of the folds back to her fingers with her tongue, helping Sophie down from the screaming heights she so clearly achieved.

After a few seconds, Sophie shuffled a little and Teri withdrew her fingers and kissed the folds she had been nursing. A tired-looking but flushed face looked down at her. "O... M... G..." and with that, she fell sideways onto the bed, her knees narrowly missing Teri's chin. Teri took that as a positive. Sophie lay motionless for about thirty seconds before she opened her eyes, turned her head to the left and looked directly at Teri. "Your turn, mount up... "

Chapter Twenty-Nine

onday morning dawned far too quickly for Sophie, who had seen Teri getting progressively more nervous throughout the weekend. Her bubbly, cheeky personality retreated throughout Sunday and she looked withdrawn and slightly anxious by the evening. Sophie had pulled her into the bathroom and they'd taken a relaxing bath together, Sophie soaping and washing down her girlfriend, kneading her shoulders to try and help her relax. Then they made it to bed where they made slow, leisurely love together. Unlike the raw, hot sex on Friday night, and Saturday morning, this was all about a slow, intimate connection.

However, all too soon the morning came and Teri was up. Sophie followed her into the bathroom, cleaning her teeth while Teri showered. She'd already laid out the suit for her on the bed and made sure that she had a clean blouse to go with it. They'd discussed it and concluded a suit was a good idea for today but she'd return to her normal jeans and top tomorrow. You never knew who you'd meet on day one and she didn't want to blow her chances before she even started – no matter what Roger had said.

Teri was standing in front of her full-length mirror turning one way and another. "Do I look OK?"

"Mmmm, gorgeous. You know that suit does things to me."

Sophie looked up above her butt for the first time and saw some uncertainty on Teri's face. "What's wrong?"

"Well, it's just wearing a suit like this. It's a big deal for me. It's taken me years to feel comfortable wearing trousers. There's always a nagging voice wondering if I look a bit... well... male, still."

Sophie was stunned. "Pardon? Male? How the fuck, woman? You're bloody stunning and no, the only hint of male here is Number

One. No bloke has an arse like that." She wiggled her eyebrows and grabbed a handful to make her point.

Teri turned, smiling and hummed her appreciation while kissing Sophie.

It was a good job she'd cleared room in her wardrobe, allowing Teri's clothes to hang smartly. At the time a few days ago, Teri had objected and said it wasn't necessary but she was glad the brunette felt comfortable enough to make herself at home now. It meant she looked extra sharp when she left the house two hours later. Seeing her off at the door, Sophie gave her a lingering kiss goodbye and handed over her lunch bag that she'd made for her.

"Thanks Mum," cheeked Teri, smiling at Sophie, but the tone of her voice was a little hollow and Sophie could see through it to the nerves beneath.

"You will be awesome – just remember that. I love you," said Sophie, squeezing her arm.

Teri gave her a small, nervous smile, avoiding eye contact but replied, "I love you too. Thanks Sophie, you know I wouldn't have this job if it weren't for you. You've changed everything."

The grey Prius Uber pulled up at the kerb and Teri gave Sophie another small peck on the lips before jumping in. Sophie had offered to drive her, it wasn't that far out of her way, but Teri had said she could use the cab ride to clear her head.

As the car pulled away, Sophie waved her off, her own anxiety settling in the pit of her stomach for the first time now she had time to think. She loved this woman with her cute face, strong but caring arms, perfect breasts, firm arse to die for and confident cheeky personality. She also loved the vulnerable woman she knew existed under that front, the scared young woman who still thought of herself in terms of her past – the ugly duckling, the one who was never good enough and the one who wasn't wanted. The last thought made Sophie angry, how could anyone not want Teri, she was such a kind

267

person. She also had a seriously skilled tongue and fingers, the thought of which, from last night, brought a flush to Sophie's cheeks as she hurried back inside to start her day.

After all, she had a birthday to prepare for. They'd agreed low key at home, but that didn't mean she couldn't show Teri how special she was. She decorated the lounge with pink 'Birthday Princess' banners that she'd picked up when Teri was distracted. She knew her girlfriend would cringe. However, she was fairly sure that secretly she'd actually love it. She also blew up quite a few pink and white balloons, throwing them on the sofa.

Going upstairs quickly, she retrieved a black plastic box from under her bed, containing a small pile of gold wrapped presents. Teri had been rubbish at giving her ideas so she had to use her imagination and order some express deliveries over the weekend. Taking them downstairs, she spread them on the edge of the rug and dropped a few red throw cushions down onto the other side. She had every intention of making the most of that rug tonight. First, though, she needed to get to work.

~#~

Arriving at work, she called Dave into her office for an update. Her first job was to work out if Hannah's bait had been taken. "Morning Dave, how was your weekend?"

Dave hovered inside her doorway, swapping weight from one foot to the other in his usual excited fashion. This guy had two modes and they were both extreme ends of the nervous energy scale! "Mornin' Sophie, you sound a bit more cheerful than last time I saw you. Looks like your day off on Friday and weekend were good?"

"It wasn't a day off Dave, I worked from home on Friday. Didn't you see my emails?" She replied testily.

He waved her defence away with a flick of the hand akin to swatting some bothersome fly of inconvenient truth that was irrelevant to his worldview. "Yeah, yeah, whatever. Working-from-home, spending time at-home-with-girlfriend ... you say po-tah-to, I say..." He paused, looking up and tapping his lip with a finger, "well I say po-tah-to too but you know what I mean."

Sophie shook her head and rolled her eyes, hoping it covered up the blushing she knew she was doing at the reminder of their Friday afternoon.

"Anyway, when you've quite finished bringing my personal life into everything unnecessarily, Mr Po-tay-to-Po-tah-to. I wanted an update on how those servers are doing, how the admin teams have progressed with the rebuild and anything they've found." She wondered too late whether the last comment was a bit too leading. Of course *she* knew there was something to find but she wasn't supposed to and needed to act as though she didn't.

"Oh, I was talking to Kelly in the server lab. Rebuilds are good, we're back up and running fully and they are 67.8% through the rebuilds. You know how precise that woman can be." He shook his head, a smile on his face. Sophie suspected her bearded, gruff employee had a soft spot for the cute elfin faced, button-nosed Kelly. He stopped, and narrowed his eyes at her momentarily, as though processing a particularly hard piece of code. "She did say something funny though. I'm guessing you're going to want to hear this."

His wry tone and sceptical facial expression told Sophie he knew something funny was going on but didn't want to ask. "That woman has a nose like a bloodhound when she gets into code. She said that she was checking over the one box. There was a binary that seemed odd so she looked closer and it appears to be part of the malware. It looks like your little friend's cleanup missed a bit – luckily." He coughed but kept any further thoughts to himself before continuing, "When Kel dug into it, she found traces of code there that she was able to google. They appear to be signatures for a particular anonymous hacking group based overseas."

Sophie did her best to feign surprise, "Oh, should we be concerned? Could it hurt us?"

269

Dave shook his head, "No, it was an isolated fragment. It's weird that it's only on that one box and we missed it before."

Sophie shrugged, "Well you can't spot everything can you? Sometimes something will slip through the net, that's why we've had them verifying everything is clean now. It's pretty interesting, presumably it's good news for tracking down who attacked us?"

"Oh yeah, definitely," he replied lazily before adding, "It's such a good job they didn't spot that Teri was helping us to recover though, isn't it? I mean, we got away lightly as we didn't pay the ransom, just the consult fee."

"Your point is?" she queried, both eyebrows raised. He was clearly making a point and she had a feeling that he was pointing out the flaw in their plan but hopefully nobody else would notice it – if someone else had set the ransomware, why did they let Teri defuse it so easily?

"No point, no. Anyway," Dave swiftly moved on, "so Kelly has the suspect code but wants to know what to do with it. What is Paul having us do about the incident now?"

"I don't know yet, I need to see him in a bit.

Dave sauntered off as she checked Paul's calendar online. Seeing he had a gap she headed upstairs. Knocking on his door she was pleased when he waved her to sit with a smile.

"How are things Sophie? Heard anymore about the attack?" He leaned back in his chair, his thumb stroking his chin where, until recently he had a beard.

"Well, as it happens Paul, yes, I have. So I had the police at my home the other day. I told them that I couldn't talk without company approval, of course, but I think they are fishing for info. However, Kelly and Dave brought something to me this morning. Apparently, they found some code on one of the servers while tidying up today, it has the hallmarks of a foreign group. While I still think we should keep this out of the public eye, I wondered whether there's a way we could share this intel with the cops to point them in that direction and keep them off our backs – show willing, you know? What do you think?"

Paul was quiet for a moment but continued stroking his chin, thoughtfully. Sophie absentmindedly pulled at her ponytail again and she had to dismiss the thought that she'd prefer a certain someone to be doing it for her, harder.

"I see what you mean. Yes, I agree we want to keep this somewhat private, but there could be benefit of having the info with the police if it did get out later – we can say we shared intel with them quickly." Sophie nodded before her boss continued, "Yes, get Legal up here and we can talk it through."

Sophie got up and went down the corridor to the Legal office. Soon she was returning with the lead lawyer, a tall older brunette woman called Brenda who typically made a glacier look fast and dynamic. Sitting down again at Paul's desk, Sophie talked Brenda through their findings and the police visits. The lawyer took some convincing but eventually Sophie left with her blessing to speak to the police.

She returned to her office and dug out DC Sayne's card from the bottom of her bag. She held it up, taking a deep breath before dialling the number.

After a couple of rings, a deep voice answered, "DC Sayne, how can I help you?"

"Hi Detective, this is Sophie Keegan, you visited me last week. Is this a convenient time to talk?"

"Sure Ms Keegan, how are you? Did you have some more information for us?"

"I'm good, thank you. I have spoken to my director. He is still not keen for the company to be involved but he cleared me to share some info we have found. I'm hoping it'll help your investigation." She stopped, waiting to see what his reaction would be.

She didn't have to wait long, he bit straight away. "That sounds very interesting, what can you tell me?"

"Well, our server admin was doing some cleanup to make sure we weren't still exposed and she found some code which could have been left over from the attack. When she and one of my team examined it, it seemed to match the code used by a foreign group, according to her sources. I thought you might be able to verify whether that is true since you guys are more experienced than us?" A little flattery never hurt, she figured.

"Thank you, Ms Keegan. Sure, that sounds incredibly helpful. Do you know if your director would be prepared to share it as evidence for us?"

"I don't know, we can certainly share it informally and off the record to help your investigation. We cannot confirm at this stage that the servers have been held forensically safe for evidence, I'm afraid." She quoted the words Brenda had agreed with her carefully, treading the tightrope between admitting anything and appearing unhelpful.

"Well, that would be most helpful in any case. We can certainly verify the origin and I'd be happy to let you know informally what we find."

"Thank you, Detective, I'll have it sent over to you." She rang off without prolonging the call. Talking to the police made her nervous but it was worth it if it got them off Teri's back. The reminder of this being her first day made Sophie reach for her phone and text her girlfriend, who must have been a couple of hours in by now. 'How's day one, Gorgeous?' she sent.

Almost immediately a reply came back, 'Awesome, loving it. The gorgeous blonde says hi, BTW."

Sophie decided not to rise to the bait and sent back a 'That's nice, tell her I said hi too.' before putting her phone down. She had a dinner to organise so she needed to get through her pile of work. She worked through lunch, grabbing a bagel from the sandwich bar downstairs and eating at her desk. By the time four PM came around, she'd finished up most of what she needed to when her phone rang. The number was hidden but she answered to the sound of the deep voice from earlier. "Hello, Ms Keegan? This is DC Payne."

"Oh hi, Detective. What can I do for you?" Sophie crossed her fingers, toes and legs. Anything to maximise the chance for Teri.

"I am calling to update you. We got the code you sent across earlier and our team matched it to some attacks earlier this year from Russia. This is very useful, thank you. It contributes to a different live investigation. It seems your company was caught up in much larger activity."

"No problem, glad I could be of help." Sophie thought carefully how to ask her next question, it needed to be subtle, but she needed to know if Teri was off the hook. "How does that fit with your original thoughts then?"

"Well, the original tip off suggested a name but that wouldn't fit with what you've found so we are starting to believe that may have been a misunderstanding or a hoax of some sort. It's strange because the tipper did seem to know about the alleged attack and, as you said, your employer has been quite close lipped about it. Informally, I wonder whether one of your colleagues could have said something but obviously, I can't say that officially."

At that moment, Dave poked his head around Sophie's office door looking at her with a query on his face. Sophie wondered if he knew who was on the phone.

"Thank you, Detective, yes I will certainly look around the office for a troublemaker." She said down the phone, maintaining eye contact with Dave, who shrugged.

Offering to stay in touch if he heard any more, DC Payne hung up and Sophie sagged in her seat with a happy sigh and closed her eyes. Hopefully Teri was safe now, she couldn't wait to tell her.

Remembering Dave was standing there she looked over at him waiting patiently. For all he could be tactless, he actually was a good guy and she flashed back to the comments about Kelly thinking that the woman could do worse than him. Certainly a better pairing than him with Hannah. She smiled at the thought of him thinking he'd scored with the ultimate lesbian. She began to wonder if perhaps, given her recent support, the woman wasn't quite the evil witch she'd made her out to be – providing you hadn't trusted your heart with her. "What can I do for you Dave? Learnt some more good lesbian lingo?"

Dave had the good grace to look quite embarrassed. "Sorry Sophie, you know I didn't realise who she was. Just wondered if that was an update?"

"You got my phone bugged now? Don't worry, I'm only teasing. You had no way to know and she's nothing if not resourceful when she wants something, that I can confirm. Still, we might not have kissed and made up but we are on speaking terms again so you've probably done me a favour in the long run. Anyway, yes, that was the police. They've confirmed we were attacked by a foreign group from Russia according to that file your Kelly found."

He ignored her subtle taunt of 'your', "I take it that's good news for your girlfriend? I guess we sure were wrong about her involvement. Just a lucky break that she came to us about the consultancy."

"Exactly." Sophie emphasised her point, verbally drawing a line under Teri's involvement. "She was a good samaritan in our hour of need. Anyway, it's her birthday today so I'm off shortly. I have dinner to prepare."

"Ooooh, I didn't know you could cook?!" His face registered surprise but Sophie was sure it was at least fifty percent fake to tease her.

"Why does everyone say that? I mean, OK, I'm not one of those sultry TV chefs but I can manage to cook dinner!"

"Mmmm, that sexy brunette one can cook for me any day." Dave crooned and Sophie sat with a raised eyebrow waiting for him to get his overactive male hormones under control, not caring to admit that the sultry voiced, beautifully long, dark-haired chef he was clearly imagining was one of her celebrity older-woman crushes too. "OK, so I'll go and leave you to it. Glad things seem to be looking up. Give Teri my best for her new job."

"How on earth do you know about that? Don't tell me you've been kissing one of her new colleagues?" Sophie rolled her eyes.

"I'm liking this new impression that I'm acquiring of being a stud... but no, I was at uni with one of the team over there and they were all excited about her when we had a drink over the weekend. I wasn't aware that she's *that* Teri. I'd heard about her at her previous company but she dropped off the scene for ages. She has a good reputation. I think you're in safe hands. Although, tell her from me that she better not mess with you or she'll have us to answer to."

"Us?" an amused Sophie queried.

"Yeah – me and Kel. You have a lot of respect around here Soph, don't forget that. People have your back." He switched back to his cheeky persona in an instant, "Anyway boss, if you're skiving off then I'm going to slope off for a fag break and start my evening early!"

Sophie knew he was teasing her. As he started to walk off, she made him pause. "Dave?" He turned and looked over his shoulder at her. "Thanks," she added sincerely. He nodded, winked and walked off, heading to who knows where.

~#~

275

Sophie left within the next half hour, stopping off at a supermarket on the way home to pick up the ingredients she needed. The teasing was actually more accurate than she would admit and anything beyond a steak was probably pushing it. She bought the best steaks she could see, some potatoes, sweetcorn and a couple of sauces. Finally, she hit the bakery and picked up both a couple of trays of cupcakes for Teri tomorrow and finally sought out the birthday cake aisle. She was standing weighing up a pink unicorn cake with rainbow icing or a game console shaped one when an old lady shuffled past smiling. "How old is the birthday girl?" she enquired kindly.

"Twenty-six," Sophie smiled with a laugh.

"Oh, they do grow up quickly. Definitely the unicorn then. Happy Birthday to her from me." With that, she picked the bread she wanted and shuffled off.

Back home, she prepared skin-on wedges before readying the steak. She had a flashback to the last time she'd been expecting a meal with Teri in this kitchen and waiting anxiously for her. She had to shake the cold feeling running through her veins at the thought of the two days of silence and the state of her girlfriend when she finally found her. She never wanted to see her that depressed ever again, and if she had a hand in it then she never would.

She headed upstairs and jumped in the shower, wanting to be her best self for Teri, so she cleaned every nook, cranny and shaved most of them too. She idly wondered whether straight women had this level of maintenance and shuddered at the thought of missing out on the touches of a loving, skilled woman even if it meant a bit less attention to detail some of the time.

She dried, perfumed and added just a touch of subtle eyeshadow and lippy. She picked her most seductive black lace lingerie with purple trim, thinking it'd look great on her purple bed later. *It'll probably look even better on the cream carpet.*

276

A fitted black mini dress topped it and she moved to dry and curl her hair. She took extra care because she knew it was one of the features Teri appreciated about her. She added the finishing touch, a black hair accessory and reaching around, pinned something else to her lower back before heading back downstairs.

She came downstairs and started the dinner, getting it mostly ready for Teri but pausing just before finishing it as she didn't know exactly when her girlfriend would arrive.

She grabbed two glasses of prosecco, put them on a small silver circular tray (she knew all this kitchen crap her Mum had given her would come in for something) and headed out to the hall to wait for her girlfriend. Luckily for her, she didn't need to wait long.

Chapter Thirty

Teri rang the doorbell then looked behind her to see the Uber pulling away from the front of Sophie's terraced house. She waited less than ten seconds before hearing the door open. Opening her mouth to take the mickey out of Sophie for waiting there to open it, the words dried on her tongue and wouldn't come out. Her eyes felt like they'd fallen out on stalks – like something from a cartoon – when she saw how Sophie was dressed, smiling sweetly at her, wishing her a 'Happy Birthday'. 'Dressed' didn't really quite cover it and her eyes worked their way back up from her black stilettos, those amazing legs, the very fitted black bodycon dress with a scoop neckline that showed the delicious-looking curves to utter perfection. Her blonde hair was voluminous, curled and topped with the most seductive thing ever, a pair of black lace cat ears. The same ones which had entranced Teri the very first time she saw Sophie.

Balanced on one hand like an upscale waitress in a sophisticated cocktail bar, was a silver tray with two glasses of bubbly. Sophie held them out and Teri somehow managed to reach out and take one. As Teri's eyes started to return to their normal position in their sockets and she felt her jaw starting to function again, Sophie turned to lead back into the lounge and Teri's face lost all function again. Topping off that beautifully shapely bum was a long, fluffy black cat tail wiggling in a sexy exaggerated fashion as Sophie walked.

Teri followed her, captivated by some otherworldly power, shutting the door and dropping her laptop bag in the hall. Somehow it wasn't the outfit that utterly entranced her quite as much as the whole aura Sophie was projecting – the sexy, sultry, sex kitten. This, combined with the fact that she'd worked Teri out so well, was mind-blowing. Entering the lounge, she registered a small pile of presents on the rug and the fact that Sophie had picked up how keen she was to spend time cuddling in front of the fire sent her over the emotional edge.

278

A few deep breaths later she had regained her equilibrium. "I can't believe how you look! I mean, you look like a goddess in that dress, I don't even have words for it."

"You like it? I know you said you wanted quiet but I figured you can't go wrong with cat ears!"

"Can't go wrong? No way, I'm astonished, flattered, stunned and, quite frankly, so turned on that I'm losing my mind looking at you!" Teri finished with a throaty chuckle.

Sophie smiled. "In that case, come with me." She took her hand and led them both into the kitchen, pointing at a stool by the counter. "Perch here, while I finish off."

Teri sat sipping her prosecco and watching Sophie getting the steaks to sizzle, enjoying the occasional wiggle and swish of the tail. Her mouth began to water as the smell of succulent steaks rose and met her nostrils. She smiled as she watched the other woman clearly enjoying herself as she flitted around the small kitchen, finishing off the steaks, pulling out the potatoes and getting the sauces ready. After a short while, Sophie turned to her, "All ready, do you need a top up?" Gesturing over to the table, Sophie brought over two plates and they sat down opposite each other.

As they made themselves comfortable, Sophie said to her, "Happy Birthday Gorgeous, I love you so much. How was your first day?"

Teri practically gushed with excitement, her words tumbling over each other while falling out of her mouth like water over a waterfall, "Oh thanks, I can't believe you did all this for me. The job is fantastic, I'm loving being with the team again. They showed me their operation, it's amazing – so sophisticated! I wish you'd been there to see it; I'd love to show you."

"Hopefully I can meet the team once you get settled! Now breathe and tell me what you think about this steak?"

They both started on the steak, each making appreciative noises. For a few moments, all Teri could hear was the sound of them both chewing comfortably.

"You know," Teri smiled, "you aren't half bad at this cooking lark. This is delicious. I'll let you cook for me again, especially if I get catwoman as a waitress."

Sophie smiled a knowing smile, putting down her fork, before letting out a purring sound and pawing the air with her free hand. "She will just have to see how much she can get her claws into you, won't she?" She picked the fork back up and carried on eating. Teri watched discreetly from under her lashes while eating her own. She was entranced by the hypnotic vision of Sophie's pale throat as she swallowed for some reason, even the smallest things were so sexy with this woman.

At that moment Sophie broke the spell and seemed to jump a little in her seat. Excitedly she exclaimed, "Oh, I clean forgot – I had some excitement today too. Firstly, Kelly found some code leftover from the attack."

"Oh really?" Teri answered sarcastically. "What a surprise!"

"Spoilsport... then after he checked it out, I got a phone call today from our friend DC Sayne. I don't think you'll be hearing from him again."

Teri felt the warm glow of joy growing in her stomach and spreading up towards her face, forcing its way out through her mouth, which formed into a wide grin of pleasure. "Really? You mean he bought it?"

Sophie nodded, the smile on her own face warming Teri from the outside in.

Teri felt the grin intensifying and she jumped up, running around the table to grab Sophie's face and kissing her hard. She pulled away, looking Sophie in her eyes and wanting to jump up and down, twirl her around and hug her till she squeaked. "Oh, thank you, Sophie, this is all down to you." She felt her eyes watering but she held it together with a huge grin of relief. Sophie's finger came up and touched her cheek softly, then her lips kissed it.

"I love you Teri, but I only just found you. I can't have you being arrested yet, can I?" Sophie whispered softly.

"Technically, I actually found you..." grinned Teri. Sophie rolled her eyes at her but Teri couldn't help teasing, when this woman rolled her eyes it was so hot. She loved the attitude she projected and the prospect that Sophie could keep her slightly unruly, chaotic side under control.

Sophie smiled again before saying, "Well, I think it's time for some dessert, what do you think?"

"I think, whatever you say is great with me."

"OK, well you sit here," Sophie started as she stood, "while I go and bring it in." With that she swayed off into the kitchen. Teri sat waiting for a few moments, her back to the door, until the lights went out. She turned in surprise and saw Sophie walking in from the door carrying a cake with candles lit on it. She might have been shocked before, but suddenly Sophie started to sing 'Happy Birthday'. Teri wasn't sure if the surprise was more due to the song or due to the singing itself. Sophie was gorgeous, kind and wonderful but Teri realised she couldn't sing for toffee! If she hadn't been able to see her, Teri would have been convinced Number One was hurt!

As she put the rainbow unicorn cake down in front of them, Sophie said, "Make a wish, Princess...".

Teri closed her eyes tight, vividly picturing a cute little brunette girl at her birthday party, twirling around in front of all her friends to show off her party dress. She was smiling and loving simply being herself, before blowing out her candles. Her wish would just be the normal thing five year old girls hoped for, because she'd never need the kind of effort Teri had.

She felt warm and happy, loved even. Even through her closed eyes, tears started to form as the emotion grew and overflowed. She had to concentrate – this wishing was a serious business. She focussed on the vision of that happy five year old girl, putting behind her the actual memory of what that party had really looked like. *I wish for the woman in front of me, this amazing person who seems to care for me through thick and thin. I wish for her now and forever. I wish that we can grow old together. Is that too much to ask for?*

She squeezed her eyes shut more until she was sure the wish was properly made and then opened them, blowing firmly on the cake. Her five year old self told her it was crucial to get all the candles out or the wish might not come true. Teri was taking no chances if she had to get six engines from blue watch in with fire retardant foam – those suckers were going down.

Sophie reacted quickly, she must have seen the tears. She came over and held Teri close, the warmth from her breasts pressing into Teri's own and acting like a direct connection to her heart. As she tenderly wiped a tear off Teri's cheek with her finger she whispered, "Are you OK? Should I not have done it?"

"Oh Sophie, no. I'm so happy, you have no idea. I love it that you did this for me and I love you more than anything in this world or any other place." She paused and took a breath, as a few more tears escaped, muttering to herself, "Bloody oestrogen," before continuing in a shaky voice. "When I was five, I made a birthday wish that now has come true. I know the power of wishes. Thank you so much for being here, for giving me a new birthday wish and I promise that I'll do everything in my power to make this one come true too."

She leaned forward a fraction, grabbed both her hands and pressed their lips together tenderly. She couldn't tell Sophie what the wish was but she sure could show her. She kissed with the love, hope and conviction that her life depended on it because, right at that moment, she was quite positive that it did. She needed to somehow turn her heart inside out and show this magnificent woman everything inside, it or she was going to burst.

One of them deepened the kiss, Teri wasn't sure which and their tongues touched, sliding gently over their bottom lips before Sophie intensified it, holding Teri's face firmly but gently and tilting her head. Eventually, Sophie pulled back, sucking Teri's lower lip with her. "I love you too and whatever your dreams and wishes are, we'll make them come true together."

A thought occurred to Teri, "Err, you know you mentioned something the other day... about moving in?"

Sophie's eyes widened a fraction, "Yes?" she sounded cautious but excited, as though she was holding back a hope.

"Well, is there any chance you'd still consider it?" Teri swiftly continued, "I mean, it's totally fine if you've changed your mind, you can be honest."

Sophie just rolled her eyes at Teri and raised an eyebrow. Teri found this look so hot that she stopped thinking entirely, consumed with those oceans of blue, flecked with silver surf.

Sophie whispered, "Of course I'd do more than consider it, when can we get your stuff?"

There was only one answer to that and Teri kissed her again, harder and more insistently.

~#~

Meal finished, the two women retired to the lounge and Sophie directed Teri towards the rug before turning on the gas fire. The orange and blue flames left her feeling homely, happy and warm inside. Sophie sat down next to her and pulled a throw over them both before leaning over, caressing her face and pressing her warm, soft, smooth lips onto Teri's. Teri welcomed the kiss and fell onto her back on the waiting cushions, Sophie followed and landed on top of her, their breasts pressing together.

Sophie was the first to pull back, licking her lips, and she passed Teri a present. After the rush of heat the kiss gave her she grinned with pleasure at the small gift and ripped into the paper eagerly. A long jewellery box looked back at her and she looked up in surprise from the gift. Sophie nodded at the box and Teri opened it eagerly. It contained a gold chain with a sparkling pendant shaped as an 'at' sign. She laughed out loud in excitement. How apt for her and it was beautiful. She grinned at Sophie. "It's beautiful, thanks Cupcake, I love it. Will you put it on for me please?"

Turning around she felt Sophie's hands run up her neck, lifting her hair and the cold of the necklace settled around the hollow of her throat. Turning back, Sophie passed her another present that she unwrapped eagerly. This one felt soft and as the paper fell away she saw two t-shirts, one was bright pink. Shaking it out, she laughed as she saw the front, a grey cat face with glittery silver ears. It was captioned, "Cat Mama". She sat up and pulled her top over her head before replacing it with the t-shirt. It fit her well and she loved the cat. At that moment, Number One padded over and looked up at Teri. She smiled at him and ruffled his fur. She was sure he was smirking at her but he rubbed against her thigh and settled down on the rug between them anyway. Picking up the other t-shirt, she shook it out and realised she had seen it before – it was a black top with a picture of a cat with princess Leia hair buns. "You bought it?" she asked in excited surprise.

"Yep, while you were busy being Seven, which reminds me – we need to make sure you pack that catsuit when you move in!" Sophie raised an eyebrow suggestively.

Teri laughed but looked at the t-shirt again in wonder. It wasn't the t-shirt itself; it was the fact that Sophie had bought it on their first actual date!

284

The final present Sophie handed her was slightly harder and clearly a funny shape beneath the paper. The blonde looked almost nervous as she handed it over. This piqued Teri's imagination, thinking of all kind of sex toys that might embarrass Sophie to give her. Teri was hyper-curious and opened it quickly again, gasping in surprise as she saw the lilac plastic emerge from the paper, an ice cream logo visible and finally, a blonde mane and horse's head. It was a lilac My Little Pony with a vibrant mane. She couldn't believe that Sophie had remembered her offhand comment and she looked up at her, feeling her delight and her love warring to make their way out of her eyes. "Oh… my… god… Sophie, you remembered! I love it."

"Of course I remembered and I'm glad. I didn't have a lot of time to get you anything practical so they are only little things but I couldn't let you go by without at least a token present."

"Little? This is the most sentimental, appropriate, wonderful, magical thing anyone has ever given me! It's even better than my first vibrator that Maisie bought me!"

"She didn't!" It was Sophie's turn to look shocked. "Actually, why am I surprised, of course Maisie would do that."

They both laughed at this but Teri kept turning the pony over in her hands and looking at it lovingly. For such a simple, silly gift, it meant a ridiculous amount to her. It was that little brunette girl's hopes and dreams, it was validation of who she was and, most of all, it showed the understanding the woman she loved had of her. That was the best present she could ever hope for and she realised she had tears in her eyes again.

Sophie leaned, reaching over Number One, who was snoozing quietly, and kissed her firmly, her lips insistent and possessive but also soft and reassuring. As much as Teri found it hard to believe the words, she really couldn't doubt the act of love this represented.

Lying back while being kissed, Teri felt Sophie lying on top of her, until a sudden rush of grey fur flew across the room. Both women pulled back and turned to look, only remembering at the last minute the cat who had been between them.

"Sorry Gorgeous," started Sophie, "I nearly squashed your pussy," she sniggered.

Teri's only conceivable response was, "Kitten, come here and squash it all you want."

With that, she pulled Sophie towards her and they both fell back onto the soft, fluffy rug. Sophie started pulling at Teri's top and it was quickly lifted over her head. Sophie pulled at the button on her trousers and with a little help of Teri lifting her hips, they were swiftly down around her ankles. Teri felt exposed lying on her back in her underwear but the look Sophie gave her heated her from the inside out. Sophie stood slowly and went to reach behind for her zip.

Looking up at her, Teri held up a hand, wanting to commit the vision in front of her to memory and enjoying the warmth it was causing inside her, not least between her legs. Sophie's amazing curvy figure was shown off by the bodycon black dress, her striking legs shown off below it and above her cascading blonde curls were the sexy black lace cat ears that had originally attracted Teri's attention. Teri's eyes must have signalled her interest because Sophie smirked and turned with feline grace, running her black furry tail through her hand suggestively. The clear flirtation inflamed Teri's blood and she reached up to grab Sophie, who ducked out of her reach with a suggestive flutter of her eyelashes and a coy smile. She reached behind and unzipped her dress, dropping it down, pooling on the floor in one smooth movement. Looking back over her shoulder coyly, she tipped one hip to the side and Teri's world focussed in on her girlfriend instantly. Set against the lace ears, she had black lace briefs and a matching bra, the purple accents perfectly showing off her porcelain skin. "Oh my god Kitten, you look... you look... just... I wanna eat you."

Her voice was low, her skin heated and she could feel that her gaze was devouring this absolute goddess. Sophie's smile showed that

286

she'd noticed Teri's enthusiasm and she turned slowly, running a hand down from her throat, over her full breast and down her side to rest on her hip. Teri's eyes followed its motion hungrily and Sophie slowly dropped first to her knees and then to her side, moving her hand to mirror its motion down Teri's body from her neck, over her breast, setting her chest aflame, down her side and resting eventually on her hip.

Teri felt warm lips pressing at her throat, the hot breath tickling her bare skin, and moving upward in small motions, kissing again with each movement, heading, not for her lips, but further back. She attempted to shift her head to encourage the sinful lips closer to her own mouth but they kept moving on their inexorable path until they reached the fleshy pad of her earlobe. Here, she felt teeth nibble gently, a light bite threatening enough to cause her a strong intake of breath. A breathy, soft but ominously predatory whisper sounded in her ear, "So?".

Teri's mind was so blank already from simply the kisses that she had no idea what this single syllable referred to. After an eternity, her brain eventually shifted up into a gear capable of thinking, remembering her last comment. It sent a plume of flame through her body and, without thinking, she grasped the other woman's shoulders, leaning all her weight into them. Sophie quickly flipped over Teri and landed, on her back, on the soft and welcoming rug. Teri looked into the blonde's eyes and saw the fire she felt returned tenfold.

She moved to kiss her on the lips but Sophie wiggled at the last moment and she ended up touching her ear instead. Sophie tapped her own cheek with one short, immaculate, fingernail, in a gesture of instruction. Teri responded with a chaste kiss at the same spot. This teasing would drive her mad tonight. The next tap came at her throat and Teri dutifully responded in turn, kissing and, this time, sucking the skin enough to cause Sophie to inhale and slightly lift her hips. Smiling inwardly, she vowed she'd make her goddess beg for what she wanted.

The finger moved slowly down and two kisses later was tapping the left breast. Teri was only too happy to oblige, pulling down the lace bra, causing the creamy flesh to press pleasingly towards her. She kissed the nipple chastely again before sticking out her tongue and licking it in a deliberately long motion. Sophie's hips betrayed her arousal as her lower back arched, pushing these gorgeous nipples right into Teri's path. She bared her teeth and after sucking, she gently bit the fleshy breast, flicking the nipple with her tongue as her teeth slightly grazed the smooth skin... The intake of breath wasn't one of pain and she smirked to herself before moving over to lavish similar attention onto the other side, this time affecting a perfect love bite to the side.

Looking down, she saw that Sophie was pushing down her own knickers, before putting a guiding hand onto Teri's head, in a visibly desperate attempt to sate the need Teri assumed was building between her legs. The message was clear, but Teri wasn't going that easily and pressed kisses first down her flat stomach before running her fingertips through the inviting runway of blonde curls. The groan that emanated from Sophie's chest told her everything possible about what the woman wanted and how much she needed it but rather than pre-empt, she stroked one fingertip gently along the velvety slit, enjoying the feel of slippery essence she found along the silky surface. The groan turned into almost a purr of pleasure and she looked up to see the most beautiful sight of her life. Sophie's blonde curls were spread on the rug showing off her kitten's black lace ears, her eyes were closed and her mouth was open in a perfect 'o'. Her brows furrowed in an expression of such need that Teri couldn't resist reaching up and touching the pad of her finger to those beautiful red lips. The lips puckered before a tongue slipped out quickly and licked her finger, rewarding her with another deep groan that shook her to her own superheated core.

The hand again touched the crown of Teri's head, this time, slightly gripping her hair and insisting firmly that she heed the unspoken command. Her resistance was met by a delightful pull in her hair that further inflamed her already throbbing clitoris. Sophie's eyes opened, looking deep before those lips, now glossy with her own juices, parted and a single word escaped – almost breathed rather than spoken. "Please."

Sophie obviously rightly sensed the effect this expression of need would have on her. The feeling of control was heady but paper-thin. It snapped quickly as she dove her head down, her tongue eagerly caressing the slit and folds in a flat motion first, before gently diving between them. Finding Sophie as wet as ever and enjoying scooping up as much of the watery arousal as possible pleased her even more so she pressed further, curling her tongue to circle and press incrementally deeper inside to the entrance of the other woman's hot, sweet core. Teri found herself lost in her senses. The smell of warm musk combined with the taste of sweet but tangy nectar. Circling the entrance some more yielded several groans and another breathy "Yes, please."

Twirling her tongue again, she pushed inside Sophie and the sounds of involuntary joy confirmed she was doing her job and sure of a solid appraisal. She cursed that human tongues couldn't reach further but she didn't let that dent her enthusiasm. A character, Krissy, from her favourite lesfic romance series popped into her mind and she smiled at the author's description of her giraffe-like tongue. Making up for her lack of superhuman appendage, she doubled down on her movements with the conviction of a woman starved, lapping up every ounce of bewitching arousal that Sophie produced.

Her initial lapping and swirling caused her nose to nudge a swollen bud and she licked back up to pay it better attention, licking around firstly but quickly taking hold with her teeth and sucking harder upon it. The resulting lioness-like roar could no longer be described as a purr, her kitten was in full pleasure mode. Holding with her teeth she flicked with her tongue and hummed a deep vibration. Her own vibrations caused Sophie's body to shake and the roar to turn to a scream of pleasure as she clearly rode out a crescendo Teri had caused.

Switching her role from tormentor to willing servant, she decided one climax was clearly not enough for her queen and shifted down, lapping again at the thicker contents of her girlfriend's hot core. She reached as deep as her tongue would allow, causing contractions which pushed more of the slightly sweeter nectar right into her grateful path. Sophie panted, her breaths coming quickly again before another long, drawn out groan racked her chest, her body going rigid.

Teri lapped gently as Sophie writhed beneath her, clearly unseeing and consumed by the sensation of her strong orgasm.

As it subsided, Teri rose and took Sophie's face in both her hands, pressing a loving kiss to her lips, her reward for her passionate attention being the eagerness with which Sophie's tongue ran over her own, obviously spurred on by the taste of herself mixed with the bitter taste of adrenaline that Teri could sense in her own mouth.

She released the kiss, looking at Sophie and feeling the love burn her eyes as it escaped in her look. "I love you Sophie and while I know we met with me holding you to ransom, I hope you know that you hold my heart in your safekeeping now. I want to carry on loving you like this for a long time to come."

The response that came back was a purr of satisfaction, a hand pressed down cupping her own sex and a husky exclamation, "Well Ms Rainbow, you're a friend I certainly *do* know now and I expect a much better reward than a few thousand dollars so I hope you've got more where that came from."

There was only one answer to that, and it wasn't expressed in words. Teri lustily continued her response late into the evening, much to a hungry Number One's chagrin when the two women finally rose from the rug and retreated upstairs.

Epilogue

Three months on from that birthday and Teri was hauling a pile of boxes through Sophie's front door. The sun was shining brightly in that deceptive way it did in December. However, despite the crisp, cold day she regretted keeping on her hoodie – the exertion was making her sweat.

Sophie appeared at the lounge door, "Is that the last of it?"

"Yep, the van is empty now. I need a rest before we take it back though!"

They'd hired a small van to transport Teri's meagre possessions out of London when the combination of a job and a girlfriend in Essex meant she was hardly ever back in London these days.

Number One prowled down the stairs, looking up at Teri's sweaty face and curled his tail in disdain for the perspiring human. "It's alright for you mate, you've been curled up on the rug all day. You've never been back to London since you moved in," she shouted after his retreating tail, shaking her head good-naturedly.

It was true, after her birthday, she'd spent less and less time in London and Number One had never gone back. He seemed to like it here with Sophie too much and Teri couldn't really disagree. She had lent her flat to a friend-in-need at work. Some people had said it was too quick, even Teri wondered once, but all she had to do was look into Sophie's bright, shining blue eyes to know that it wasn't. She didn't care how many U-Haul jokes Maisie threw at her.

Looking up from the retreating furry tail, she looked up Sophie's body – her black leggings giving way to a fitted red longline top that was warm without disguising any of the curves Teri loved so much. Reaching her face, she saw a look she recognised. Sophie's pupils were wide and she was flushed.

"I think you should take those boxes upstairs. You look knackered." Sophie's voice was husky and she had a sneaky, lopsided smirk. Teri knew precisely where her mind was, and it wasn't on the boxes. Over the last few weeks, they'd played sport together and seeing her physically exerting herself always seemed to get Sophie heated up. She said she just loved the look Teri had when she was sweaty and flushed.

"As the good lady commands..." Teri replied with her own smirk. She had a good idea where this was going if she played her cards right – or frankly, even wrong.

As she headed up the stairs, she felt two hands grabbing her butt from behind and heard a snigger. Two could play this game.

"Hmmmm, since I'm so sweaty, I think I need a shower to cool down."

A quiet groan came from behind, followed by, "Hmmm, what a great idea."

Dropping the boxes in the spare room, she headed for the bedroom and pulled off her hoodie and top. Standing there in a sports bra, Sophie came in and took her face in her hands, kissing her passionately. "I'm so glad you're here properly Teri. Number One says it's lonely here without you, you know."

"Does he? So nobody else misses me then?"

Sophie plastered on her best coy look. "No, just the cat, I'm sure."

Teri shook her head. Coy, teasing Sophie was her favourite.

"Now, didn't you say something about a shower?" Sophie continued in a stern voice, "Get yourself in there, missy."

292

Scratch that, bossy, commanding Sophie is my favourite.

Teri pulled down her jeans, enjoying how Sophie's stern look morphed into a heated gaze. She pulled her black bra over her head and, stepping out of her boxers, entered the shower, turning the water on as she went.

Enjoying the sensation of the hot water running through her hair and washing away the muscle tiredness, she faced into it, closing her eyes and opening her mouth. Arching her back, she allowed the water to cascade down.

A gasp from behind got her attention, even more so when she heard, "Alexa, play Rihanna".

The strong but sexy beats of Rihanna's 'S&M' beat out of the ceiling mounted speakers and Teri felt a surge of energy infuse her otherwise tired body. She ran her fingers through her hair and tilted her hips to the side, then the other and finally rotated them in a seductive circle, following the rhythm of the electrifying beats. She placed one hand on her hip and reached for the shower gel quickly with the other, the scent was an energising lemon. Everything seemed to give her more energy these days. Her gel-covered hand caressed her left breast and she exaggerated her hip swirls.

Her seductive routine under the water must have impressed someone since she heard the shower door open and felt a warm, naked body press against her back as it closed again.

Turning, she saw that Sophie had undressed and jumped at the chance of joining her. She reached for her with a wink but one hand pushed her back under the water stream and the extended fingers travelled down her chest between her breasts. Sophie leaned forward, under the waterstream too but a hair's breadth away from Teri's face. Feeling her breath on her lips, Teri looked down before Sophie, with hooded eyes whispered huskily, "On your knees…"

Teri didn't need to be asked (or ordered) twice. Commanding Sophie was breathtaking and she knelt quickly on the wet shower tray, eyes level with the other woman's inviting pussy. Introducing her to different lesfic authors had really given Sophie ideas, and Teri loved it!

Sophie lifted her left foot, hooking her knee over Teri's shoulder and opening up one of the kneeling woman's favourite places. She felt the beats of music fade into the background but continue to pump her full of energy as she leaned forward, careful to support Sophie's weight on her shoulder. She took hold of the other woman's hips, which were flexing their own rhythm to the music and moved one hand to stroke her outer lips, now wet and glistening partly from the shower but also with a more seductive glaze.

She brought her mouth down to where her hands were stroking gently and supplemented the strokes with a kiss which swiftly became a suck. A groan from Sophie told her that her queen was impressed with her initiative and she continued, sucking on the other folds, enjoying their velvety texture and sweet taste. Her tongue delved further, the water cascading over her face unnoticed as she lapped up Sophie's arousal, the shower failing to dilute it. Her tongue circled the other woman's entrance, noting the treat leaking from it to reward her attentions. She firmly caressed the delicious inner labia and brought forward a finger to circle and lightly ghost her clit, the resulting press of hips more firmly into her face providing the confirmation she sought. Thinking that Sophie wasn't ready yet, she moved the hand around to hold her butt firm as she pushed her tongue deeper. Continuing the swirling motion she rocked her neck slightly to give her a better angle and probed deeper with each circle.

Heavy breathing and a groaned "Urgghhh" from Sophie continued to encourage her. The groans combined with Rihanna's sexy vocals to provide the soundtrack while her heart and clit came together to form the fast, rhythmic beat.

Sensing Sophie was ready for slightly more, she brought her palm to cup the curls of her lover's mons while her thumb came to ghost her clit again, before circling faintly at first, but more definitely after a few revolutions.

Her tongue kept its rhythm with the punchy music and she felt her neck strain but didn't care.

"Oh yes, yes, fuckdontyoufuckingstop," came the groaning exaltation from above.

Teri had no intention of fuckingstopping, she was enjoying herself way too much and after all, this was 'Commanding Sophie' – who got what she ordered.

She lapped harder with her tongue. By focussing on the front wall she could caress deeper and alternated with circling at her entrance, hungrily enjoying the continuing flows of pleasure her lover produced.

Pressing harder and feeling the swell of the, hopefully, throbbing clit she was running on sensation alone, her eyes closed but the other senses made up for it in spades. The scent of Sophie's arousal combined with the taste on Teri's tongue and she gripped harder with her other hand, her nails scratching the soft skin of Sophie's butt and keeping her in place.

With, what in other circumstances, might be called a pained scream, Sophie reached her peak and Teri's tongue was inundated with a warm rush of thick arousal that she greedily enjoyed. She kept her rhythm while the other woman pressed her hips into her, riding out the waves of her own pleasure.

Worried that Sophie's legs wouldn't hold her, Teri came to stand and supported her, kissing her firmly. Sophie slightly sagged against her before opening her bright, shining eyes. She returned Teri's kiss greedily.

Sophie reached up and grabbed the showerhead, Teri looked at her in puzzlement for a second until she swapped the jets to a continuous force. Smirking and raising an eyebrow she pushed the other woman back against the wall and dropped to her own knees, pushing her thighs open with a hand in one fluid, graceful motion.

Teri was already aroused and throbbing but the image of the wet blonde head from above was almost enough to finish her off. However, when the shower jet hit her core, her legs nearly buckled.

Sophie allowed the jets to play over Teri's labia before glancing her clitoris and returning to her core. The brief blast of water left her clit pulsing for more and feeling eternally empty from its absence. The sight of Sophie looking up and making eye contact just intensified this feeling of need. She didn't need to wait long because Sophie quickly obliged by circling her clit again with the powerful jet before bringing a finger to circle it as the jet again returned to her entrance.

As intense as the water was, the finger cranked up the tension as it circled, maintaining the rhythm to a slower Rihanna song. Teri could feel the pad of Sophie's finger brush her aching nub as she circled.

She keened needily, wanting more. She looked down at the kneeling woman, "Pleeease Soph". The response was an evil grin and a shouted command, "Alexa, previous track". To the heavy and far faster beat of the earlier 'S&M', Sophie's thumb picked up the pace and her other hand slid further back, clearly having dropped the showerhead, unheeded by Teri. Two fingers entered her gently before picking up the same rhythm quickly and taking no quarter. Being fucked with such force was too much for Teri, whose climax rose and rose, the intense sensations from the clitoral flicks combining with the sensation of full and forceful penetration and lyrics that matched the action.

"Come for me, darling," crooned Sophie, "show me what you feel."

No sooner had she said this than Teri felt her grip on the outside world shatter and she welcomed the intense wave of tension

296

and pleasure spread from her clitoris through her lower body. Coherent thoughts vacated her mind as she let out a cry. Somewhere between her lover's name and a wild scream, it was a shout of passion and all her poor brain could manage in the way of communication.

The next thing she knew, she was sitting sideways in Sophie's lap on the shower tray, the other woman kissing her and stroking her hair.

"Wow!" was all the exhausted Teri could manage.

Sophie replied simply with a grin and a raised eyebrow.

Laughing, she added, "As much as I love sitting here, I think we may have used all the hot water. Come on, lets dry off, I'll put the fire on and we can cuddle up together."

~#~

After drying each other off, with more than a little kissing and giggling, they curled up before the burning open flames. The room was also lit by the twinkling white lights of the christmas tree they had decorated together. Number One prowled in and settled himself down on Sophie's lap. Looking down, Sophie laughed. "Someone is jealous, he thinks you've had your quota of cuddles today, I think."

"Cat, you and I need words if you think there's a quota of cuddles from Mama here."

Number One looked unconcerned, licked a paw and settled down to strokes from both women.

Sophie looked quizzically at Teri, "Mama?"

Teri blushed, "Well, I told him a while ago I thought you'd be a great second Mama for him and maybe one day we'd all live together."

The surprise on Sophie's face gave way to a delighted smile and eyes that brightened immeasurably. "You thought I'd be a Mama for him? I thought you only got comfortable recently?"

Teri shook her head, "No Cupcake, I've known you're the woman for me for ages. You've never ceased to show me kindness even when I know I've been utterly frustrating to be with. Even though I couldn't get my head around why you'd want me, I never once doubted that I wanted you."

Sophie's felt the emotion building in her body and Teri leaned over the snoozing cat to kiss her gently before continuing, "I love you, Sophie, I've genuinely never felt like this about anyone before. You make everything real and make me feel both safe *and* excited for the future. Somehow you even work the magic of making *me* believe in *me*. That's something I've always thought was impossible, but you inspire me to believe – in us.

"Somehow, I've always held something back before, always felt that I needed to defend myself in case things went sour and people couldn't handle me or my background. That's never been even an option with you. I can't help trusting you and opening myself up fully. I may have been the one to initiate our meeting but it's you who penetrated my defences and took over my heart."

Her voice broke a little and they leaned into a gentle, passionate kiss, their lips echoing the words.

"Oh Teri, you don't get that you have the same effect on me. I feel so protected when I'm with you – I know you'd battle slimeball salesmen by the dozen for me."

Teri smiled and looked down at the sleeping Number One. His purrs were soothing and she admitted, "When I was little, I made that wish to be me, I had to work so hard to make that come true but somehow I think there will always be a part of me that fears it won't stick – that I'll wake up and it'll all be a dream. You've made it feel safe to believe that it's not going anywhere and that I am the woman

298

I've always dreamed of. I think you also made my other birthday wish come true too.

Sophie looked puzzled, "You never told me what you wished for - was it the job?"

Teri laughed, "Blimey no, far more important than that. I wished to settle down with the women I was utterly in love with. There is nothing I want more and you've made that come true for the three of us."

"Well, I'm not sure I had much of a hand in it for him – he just moved in and made himself comfortable, but I've certainly had to work to persuade you that you deserve it. I love you Teri and we will make that wish come true together, one day at a time."

Teri warmed as the utter contentment she felt in Sophie's arms beamed out of her smile. She leaned in for a tender kiss. Nothing could beat this feeling of looking forward to the future, less of a shadow over her and more of a rainbow shining in her personal sky.

THE END

About the Author

Chloe Keto is a new author but a long-time passionate fan of the romantic WLW genre.

She lives at home in the South of England with her wife and two nearly teenage football loving children. She believes that all stories can be improved with a good dose of romantic magic!

She is, sadly, allergic to cats so Number One remains a fiction in her house but that won't stop him and his friends becoming stars of her stories!

Connect with Chloe

If you enjoyed this book then please tell me! I would love to hear what you enjoyed.

Independent writers thrive off reviews which publicise our work so please consider leaving me a review wherever you purchased this eBook and / or in your favourite literary community, such as Goodreads.

@ChloeKetoWLW

ChloeKetoBooks

Printed in Great Britain
by Amazon

19117031R00173